Wild West Exodus
The Jessie James Archives

Honor Among Outlaws

Craig Gallant

Zmok Books

Zmok Books is an imprint of Winged Hussar Publishing, LLC
1525 Hulse Road Unit 1
Point Pleasant, NJ 08742

www.WingedHussarPublishing.com
Twitter: WingHusPubLLC

www.Wildwestexodus.com

Cover by Michael Nigro

ISBN: 978-0-9889532-7-7
EPCN: 2013947516

Acknowledgements

Well, you only get to do your first Acknowledgments page once, so please bear with me as I wrestle with this happiest of challenges.

Personal:

I must first thank the boys of LOJOG, the League of Just Ordinary Gentlemen, Joe, John, and Pete. Never have there been friends more tested or true. My boss and another of my best friends, Brad, has never wavered in his faith and support . . . which is eerie, given his usually sardonic personality. And of course, my family: my parents Gerry and Judy have always supported me in all I do, my sister, Melissa, if for no other reason than in partial apology for the years of torture when we were younger, and my first ever co-author, my grandmother Ethel. Grandma, it might be time to dust off THE HAPPY LITTLE RAIN CLOUD! And, of course, my amazing son Rhys and my loving wife Karen, who told me three years ago that I had helped her achieve her life's dream, and that she intended, from that point on, to help me achieve mine.

Professional:

This part is more of a segue, actually, between personal and professional. Because, as is so true of so much in life, there are many locks with the statement "If not this, then no further" inscribed upon them, and the first of these is a little, Not Too Horrible general gaming podcast called the D6 Generation. Quite honestly, without my good friends Russ and Raef, who conned me into joining them way back in 2008, and then Russ, for keeping the endeavor together when Raef moved on to greener pastures, and for his constant and genuine interest and excitement for me throughout this process, everything that followed could never have come to pass. And of course it would be downright churlish of me not to thank the thousands of listeners who joined us over the years with their support and assistance (don't you guys have anything better to do?).

I have to thank Neil Fawcett, for having faith and giving me my first chance. And immediately after, I have to thank Tim Huckelbery and all the nice folks at FFG for continuing to give me chances. Thanks to Ross Watson for all the advice and support, and to Gena Robinson for all the help, support, and ideas throughout the process. And thanks again to Pete Joe for being my two extra pairs of eyes . . . look guys, you made it in twice!

And finally, I have to thank Romeo Filip and everyone at Outlaw Miniatures, and Vincent Rospond and everyone from Winged Hussar/Zmok Publishing for all of their faith, support, and assistance. In the absolute most literal sense, this could NOT have happened without their faith and assistance.

To be quite honest, none of the great things that have led to this book you hold right now would have happened without all of these people, doing exactly what they do every day, when I needed them the most. So, if it's less than Not Too Horrible . . . we can all blame them.

And of course, thank YOU, for taking the chance and buying this book. I hope you enjoy the ride we've prepared, and the world that we've created. See you on the other side, pardner!

~Craig Gallant

New Hampshire

July 23, 2013

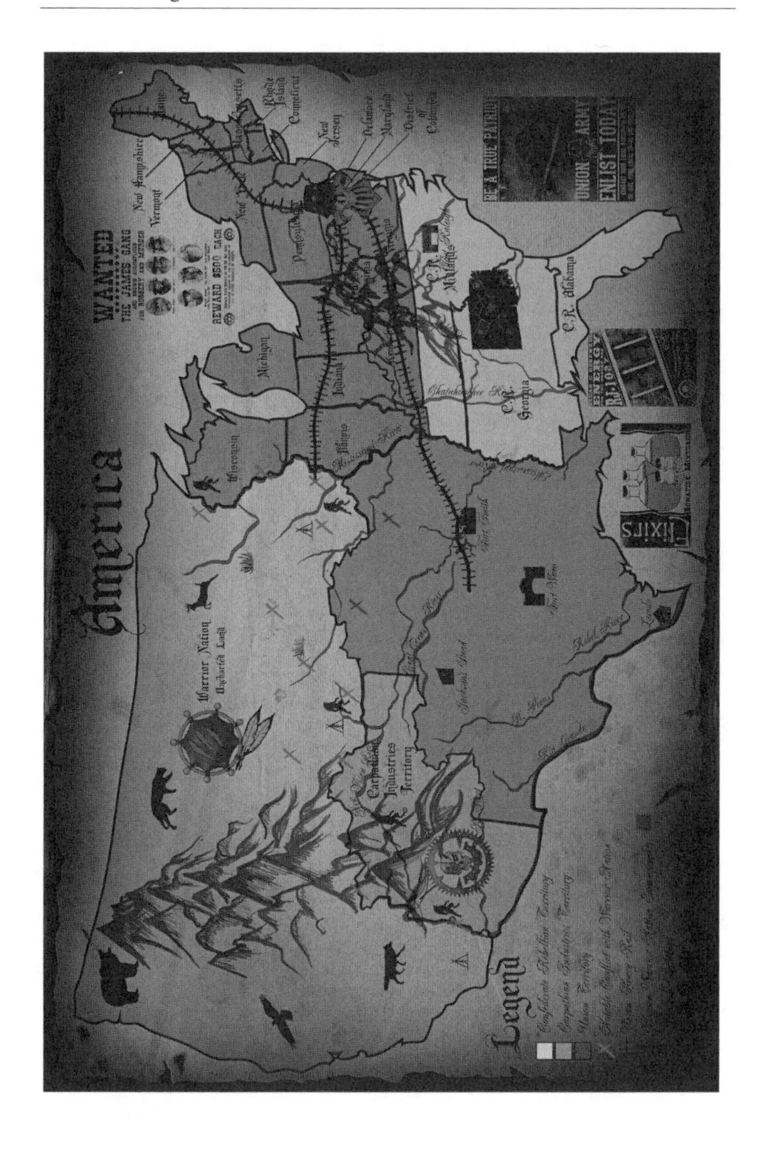
America
WANTED
THE JAMES GANG
REWARD $500 EACH
Warrior Nation
Uncharted Land
Carpathian Industries Territory
New Hampshire
Vermont
Maine
New York
Rhode Island
Connecticut
New Jersey
Delaware
Maryland
District of Columbia
Pennsylvania
Michigan
Wisconsin
Illinois
Indiana
C.R. Georgia
C.R. Alabama
BE A TRUE PATRIOT
UNION ARMY
ENLIST TODAY
Fixits
Legend

Something Wicked is Coming

Blood drenches the sands of the Wild West as the promise of a new age dies, screaming its last breathe into an uncaring night. An ancient evil has arisen in the western territories, calling countless people with a siren song of technology and promises of power and glory the likes of which the world has never known. Forces move into the deserts, some answering the call, others desperate to destroy the evil before it can end all life on Earth.

Legions of reanimated dead rise to serve the greatest scientific minds of the age, while the native tribes of the plains, now united in desperate self-defense, conjure the powers of the Great Spirit to twist their very flesh into ferocious combat forms to match the terrible new technologies. The armies of the victorious Union rumble into these territories heedless of the destruction they may cause in pursuit of their own purposes, while the legendary outlaws of the old west, now armed with stolen weapons and equipment of their own, seek to carve their names into the tortured flesh of the age.Amidst all this conflict, the long-suffering Lawmen, outgunned and undermanned, stand alone, fighting to protect the innocent men and women caught in the middle . . . or so it appears.

Within these pages you will find information on wild skirmishes and desperate battles in this alternative Wild West world, now ravaged with futuristic weapons and technology. Choose the methodical Enlightened, the savage Warrior Nation, the brutal Union, the deceitful Outlaws, or the enigmatic Lawmen, and lead them into the Wild West to earn your glory.

As you struggle across the deserts and mountains, through the forests and cities of the wildest frontier in history, a hidden power will whisper in your ear at every move. Will your spirit be strong enough to prevail, or will the insidious forces of the Dark Council eventually bend you to their will? Be prepared, for truly, something wicked is coming!

Learn more about the world of the Jessie James Chronicles at:

www.wildwestexodus.com

Prologue

The shadows of the tall pines lurched and danced to the silent music of the camp fires, giving the scene a strange, dreamlike atmosphere. Around each fire relaxed the members of a Warrior Nation scout party, speaking quietly and laughing behind raised hands. They were young men and women, the best the tribes of the Nation could spare from the ongoing battles in the east, and White Tree smiled at the sense of calm confidence they projected.

It had been many seasons since White Tree had taken to the trails with a war party. Apart from the great migration itself, when Sitting Bull and the assembled chiefs had led the united Warrior Nation into the west, he had not stirred from the comfort of a camp or long hall since before most of these warriors were born. Far more than his arm, his mind had been his weapon of choice in defense of the tribe.

However, the new age dawning over the lands of the People was drenched in crimson, and every man, woman, and child was called upon to serve in any way they could. When the existence of the ancient relics first came to the attention of the council of chiefs, there was a great deal of skepticism. The Nation was flush with the powers of the Great Spirit, resurgent after an age of dormancy, but in a succession of horrors erupting out of the east, the dreaded European and his nightmare legions had established strongholds across the plains and deserts. The soldiers pursuing the mad Doctor Carpathian cared nothing for the land or the People in the prosecution of their war, and braves were taxed beyond exhaustion trying to defend their newly-taken land. The elder council knew that behind the European, behind his implacable enemies from the north and even the chaotic lawless men of the west, stalked the ruby-eyed minions of an ancient enemy far greater than any other.

White Tree glanced back into the shadows; the scouts crouching out in the darkness should be relieved, but young Chatan was a good war leader despite his age, and White Tree knew the boy would be replacing his sentries soon. The white-haired elder looked back into the leaping flames, his mind once more wandering along dark, familiar paths.

Each generation of medicine men, for ages beyond counting, had lived with the knowledge of the ancient foe. Each had lived in the hope that the next great battle would not take place in his lifetime. White Tree sighed, for that hope, in his case, had proven fruitless. The red-eyed demons, twisting the hearts and lives of men to suit their dark purposes, were moving across the earth once more, and the elders of the Warrior Nation knew the only hope of combating them was to reclaim the ancient relics of the elder days, secreted throughout this western region in the times before living memory. Faith in the old stories was all they had; that these tales were correct, and that the relics, once united, could destroy a rising darkness that had stalked the Earth since the dawning of memory.

White Tree pulled his blanket more tightly across his stooped shoulders as a chill swept down his back. Sitting Bull and the other chiefs had pried open the Nation's eyes, and there was no denying the truth any longer. They were living in the final days of this age, with the ancient enemy rising up around them, and they were alone.

"Chatan, do you not think it time to relieve the scouts?" White Tree cursed himself even as he spoke, remembering the resentment of youth. The boy was doing fine and did not need the meddling of stodgy old men. The medicine man knew he was letting the shadows in his mind color his judgment.

Chatan looked up from the largest, central circle, the fire throwing harsh shadows across his proud face. A flash of annoyance flared in his eyes, but he mastered it quickly enough and nodded. Further proof of his strength and maturity, the elder thought.

The young war leader stood and gestured for the braves around one of the outlying fires. "Enapay, Gray Horse, gather your warriors. It is your turn to watch the forest."

The young warriors stood without question and moved off among the towering pines. Each disappeared into the shadows in a different direction. When they were gone, Chatan cocked an eyebrow at White Tree and then sank back to the ground, a shared laugh rippling quietly around the central fire.

White Tree smiled and shook his head, bending back to his own flame and the dark thoughts that haunted him. Chatan was a good man; he had listened well. The chiefs could have made a far worse choice to lead the party searching for the lost valley of Teetonka.

The first cry, tearing out of the shadows, brought White Tree's head jerking up. Around him the warriors were rising, reaching for weapons and calling out into the darkness. Chatan gestured for two groups to move into the forest while he drew two long knives already glowing with a faint blue warmth. Fat sparks of spirit energy snapped off the blades and onto the damp earth while a similar gleam erupted deep within the young warrior's eyes as he squinted out into the darkness.

"Enapay! Gray Horse! Red Leaf! What is wrong?" His voice was strong and steady, carrying none of the self-doubt of youth. Around the fires, the weapons of the war party were all glowing a deep turquoise, dripping liquid fire. White Tree had been too old to master the new ways of the spirit warriors when the Great Spirit had reemerged among the People. He was still in awe at this physical proof of the Spirit's power.

The only answer from the darkness was a heavy silence.

"Chatan," White Tree moved slowly towards the boy, eyes ceaselessly roving through the shadows. "If the scouts have been taken, perhaps more than just your blades will be called for . . . "

The young warrior looked quickly at the elder, a momentary fear in his glowing eyes, before he nodded sharply.

"Namid," another warrior sidled near, her eyes fixed on the forest around them. "Keep the clearing secure and defend the elder at all costs."

The other young warrior looked concerned for a moment before nodding. "You will take to the woods?"

Chatan was already placing his weapons beside the fire, his eyes shining like miniature stars. "The Great Spirit will guide and protect me. You protect the elder."

Even watching for the moment, White Tree was startled by how quickly Chatan disappeared into the darkness.

Namid began to deploy the remaining warriors around the outskirts of the clearing while White Tree moved to pick up one of Chatan's fighting knives. The blade was hard and sharp, obsidian polished to a deep shine, but there was no mystical fire in it now. The elder gripped the handle tightly and moved to stand beside the young woman assigned to guard the clearing. Together, they stared into the darkness.

"You boys got any room 'round yer fires? It's pretty cold up here 'n the mountains!" The voice was harsh, seeming to emerge from the shadows all around. It spoke in the English of the invaders rather than any of the languages of the People, and it sent a cold chill racing down White Tree's back. How had they defeated the sentries without a sound?

"Now, boys, you know you ain't in a good position, with or without you all got your eyes all glowy and whatnot." The mocking tones were clear, and the remaining warriors began to bridle beneath their impact.

A dull, muffled detonation sounded in the distance. A cloud of smoke, eerily lit from within by a snap of red flame, erupted off to White Tree's left, followed immediately by an angry streak of crimson light slapping through the leaves towards them. The missile briefly illuminated the forest around the war party in stark red tones, wild, dark-ruby shadows swinging in wild counterpoint as it slashed into the clearing.

The bolt flashed between two warriors, across the clearing, and struck another in the back. The poor boy's body was shattered by the impact, arms flown wide, the ghost of a cry emerging before the ravening fire of the blast consumed the breath from his lungs. The body tumbled into a still heap, streamers of red-tinged smoke rising from the ruin of its back.

"Well, seems you got some room there now, yeah?" The same voice, coming from another direction entirely, mocked them once again. "But you know what?" The voice turned thoughtful. "I do believe we'll just kill the lot of you and then have a seat when there's plenty o' room. What d'you say about that?"

Suddenly the forest was alive with fierce crimson bolts, smacking through the trees and striking warriors down all around. The rattle of demonic gunfire echoed from all directions as the warriors, shaken out of their astonishment, flung themselves into the darkness with ululating war cries.

Namid, Chatan's warnings forgotten, leapt after the others, leaving the elder alone with the gently-snapping camp fires. White Tree knew he would be less than useless trying to follow and so moved slowly to the bole of a giant pine. He crouched into the shadows and followed the battle from his hidden vantage point.

Crimson bolts were answered by the electrical flash of spirit energy as the braves fired their charged arrows at targets White Tree could not see. Streaks of red and blue passed each other in a chaotic mayhem of light and shadow. Many of the bolts blasted the thick trunks of trees in passing, filling the night with shattered splintering and firefly sparks illuminating roiling clouds of ash and smoke. Screams echoed among the trees as warriors died. Howls of victory were proof enough that the attackers were not having it all their own way.

As the combat moved deeper into the woods and farther from the clearing, White Tree lost any sense of what was happening. Distant flashes and muffled wails were the only indication that the elder was not completely alone. Carefully, he rose and began to move towards the fighting, the long knife held high and at the ready. He saw the twisted bodies of young Nation warriors who had been blasted by the demonic weapons the European had introduced to the land, their faces contorted with the savage pain of their last moments. A building anger caused the knife blade to tremble as the elder's mind registered the extent of the massacre.

Soon, however, the bodies of strangers were intermixed with the fallen warriors, and White Tree bent down to inspect these new dead as best he could in the shifting shadows. Worn leathers, old gear but well-maintained, and a mix of weapons showing hard use all pointed to one thing: outlaws. If these men had been fighters for the brutal Union they would have been in uniform, their gear more standardized and better-maintained. If they were deputies of the self-proclaimed men of law, there would have been glittering metal stars of office. And only a cursory investigation proved that they were not the abominations of Doctor Carpathian.

White Tree stood and continued to move carefully through the shifting darkness. The battle still raged ahead of him, the blue and crimson flashes like distant heat lightning on the rolling plains of his youth. He began to move faster as his heart perceived a slackening in the azure flames.

"Come on, ya damned savages!" It was the same taunting voice, coming out of the blinding swirl of light and shadow. "Ain't ya got no more fight in ya than that?"

White Tree came slowly out into a wide clearing, a shallow stream flowing away on the far side. Most of the braves of the war party were scattered across the grassy sward, bodies twisted in violent death. The number of dead outlaws here was nearly equal, but at least the same number, appearing unhurt, were standing along the tree line opposite. In their center stood a young looking scoundrel with a red kerchief tied around his neck, pulled to one side. He wielded two old-style six shooters that bore the obvious marks of upgraded weapons, the tell-tale red gleam from various components announcing the presence of the European's foul technology and the corrupting energy of his unnatural new energy source.

Nearer to White Tree crouched the remnants of the war party, their turquoise flames guttering in the darkness. There were not many left.

"Well, now, I guess we know who the curly wolves are, don' we, boys?" The young man laughed and his friends quickly joined in. "Figure we better clean this up, call it a night?"

A resounding shriek echoed from above and a streaking blur fell from the trees overhead. A creature out of nightmare dropped among the outlaws; a grotesque amalgam of man and some mysterious bird of prey. Hands hooked into brutal claws, glittering talons erupting from fingers, sank into the eyes of an outlaw. The man spun, screaming, down into the dirt. The nightmare vision's head slashed down again. Its vicious, hooked beak tore into another man's head, sending a shower of blood across his companions.

White Tree shrank back for a moment. He had never become accustomed to the changes wrought by the Great Spirit upon its most potent warriors. The familiar form of Chatan was scarcely recognizable within the twisted, violent creature tearing into the outlaws before him. But the elder was a warrior still, in his heart, and he gestured at the rest of the war party.

"Move forward! To Chatan!" And with that, White Tree ran towards the startled outlaw posse, the thrill of battle singing in his veins. Behind him, the remaining men and women rose up, the flames in their eyes and along their weapons roaring back to azure life.

The young outlaw leader grinned to see the renewed attack and waved one of his altered pistols into the shadows behind him.

"Guess you were right, Clem! Let'er rip!" The man's smile turned savage as a quick clattering from the darkness was followed by an explosion as if the world was ending. A seemingly unending spray of crimson bolts flew from the shadows, slashing out with the constant hammer-blows of an automatic weapon.

White Tree felt as if he'd been kicked by a horse and found himself flying sideways through the air. An alarming numbness spread out from his side, but not before he felt burning heat as a wash of blood ran down his ribs. His head was spinning as he landed in the soft grass, the ironic counterpoint to the violence and the pain resonating in his mind. All around him, the few remaining warriors were pounded off their feet, their spirit fires extinguished and their blood spraying across the cool grass.

Through the haze of pain and despair closing down around him, White Tree watched as the spirit creature that was brave Chatan slashed through the outlaws. The young outlaw leader danced among his own men, many standing still in shock, and cracked blast after blast against the young warrior. Chatan leapt into the air, spinning around as he soared over the heads of the outlaws, landing lightly behind one large brute wielding a massive meat cleaver. The talon-hands arced up, blood-spattered claws hooked to strike.

"Watch it, Smiley, somethin' behind ya!" The young man had spun around with the Warrior Nation scout, and as Chatan landed, ready to strike, the outlaw was bringing both of his pistols into line with the warrior's bare chest.

"Fly away, birdie!" The young man sneered, and then fired both pistols. The dual streaks slashed out, striking Chatan in the chest and blowing him backwards into the trees. The azure flame in his eyes, wide in surprise in the moment before the outlaw fired, were quenched before his body tumbled to a halt in the dirt.

White Tree slumped down, his vision fading and his mind beginning to wander. Who would recover the artifact . . . if there even was an artifact in Teetonka valley? His people needed him. The chiefs had entrusted the wellbeing of these young warriors to his care . . .

The elder felt the cool grass against his cheek and fought to claw his way back into consciousness. There was so much that needed to be done. But he was so very tired, and the leaden numbness from his side was spreading across his entire body.

"How many's that?" A voice on the edge of his awareness dragged him back. The voice seemed so young.

"Twenty, Billy. We got 'em all." Another voice, harsher and more grating. "Well, twenty one if you count the old one, but o' course we ain't got his yet."

The voices drifted back and forth, but seemed to wander closer. White Tree felt the Great Spirit summoning him, and was filled with a sudden desperation to answer the call. Something within him screamed that he needed to flee this life and listen no further to the voices closing in.

"Still," the young voice again. "These folks are pretty far afield. And they're all a lot younger than you'd expect, exceptin' pops, here."

White Tree's spirit tried desperately, but the voices called him back, and he was unable to deny them.

A burning pain flared in the body he had forgotten, dragging him screaming out of the shadow realm between life and death. He could see nothing but a red-tinged blur and the voices speaking above him were distorted and strange, but still he could not sink away.

"So, old man, what brings you so far from the new hunting grounds?" The voice lowered towards him, circling ever-nearer.

There were things White Tree must not say. Knowledge he dare not pass on to one so clearly tainted by the evil of the ancients. But what were they? He felt the most sacred knowledge slipping from him, and tried desperately to retain it. He felt his dry lips, salty with his own bloody, forming the words, giving shape to the sacred trust. Teetonka. The artifact. He remembered. He remembered, and his lips smiled as he felt a vague tugging across the throat of his body, and his spirit was allowed to drift downward once more, into the Spirit Realm, to continue his journey.

In a blood-drenched clearing far above, a young man's face creased in a very similar smile.

Chapter 1

The Union packet boat, Lincoln's Gift, roared up the wide waters of the Missouri River. It kicked up a frothing wake behind it. The massive RJ-1027-powered engines that took up the rear third of the small craft thundered out across the water as red-tinged flames shot from the exhaust pipes along the boat's flanks. It had the sleek, hard lines of a predator as it slid in an easy back and forth motion that tore the river into foaming waves that were left to pound the distant green banks as it past.

On the shore to either side, keeping pace with the boat, two outriders hunched over the control consoles of their armored steeds. Heavy iron bodies stretched over eight feet long from scooped nose fairings to flaring exhaust funnels. A pair of long metal skids hung below the trim bodies, skimming a foot over the grass and brush growing along the river's edge. The Iron Horses had made their first appearance nearly twenty years ago, but they were a common sight throughout the western territories in modern times.

Slung high on the front of each vehicle, to either side of the rider's dust fairing, hung a pair of heavy weapons. The lead 'Horse on either bank was armed with rotating Gatling cannons, RJ-1027 telltale lights winking among the boxy firing mechanisms of the weapons. Rocket pods nestled in the weapon mounts of the rearmost vehicles. Their massive bores seemed to scent the air ahead for trouble.

The crew of the Lincoln's Gift was sweating horribly within the armored confines of their crew compartment. The heat of the summer sun blazed down from above. Combined with the furnace bellow of the massive engines, the temperatures inside were barely tolerable whenever the boat was battened down for full thrust. All viewports were closed and sealed; cutting off nearly all circulation of outside air and leaving only the narrow vision slits to navigate by. The crew was out of uniform, wearing only soaked undershirts above their blue trousers. Only the most inhumane officer would hold any crew to standard codes of dress during the very rare Treasury run out to the territories.

The coin to run the territories was almost always transported by Union Heavy Rail; the enormous armored behemoths that growled along the railways of the continent. Occasionally, due to maintenance schedules, military movements, or some other, less-obvious intrusion on the status quo, one of the armored Union packet boats had to make the run instead. On those trips, the crews knew that more than the standard oversight would be in effect.

Each man's mind was never far from the heavy strongbox that sat in the boat's small, locked hold just aft of the crew compartment. Holding the bullion necessary to keep the western territories operating for a month, the gold would have been enough to set up the four men pushing the packet boat westward as petty kings for life. If only it were not marked by the government for easy tracking. And, of course, if only they could spirit it away from the Federal agent that accompanied each shipment.

There were rumors among the men and women of the packet boat that a crew had tried it once. No one could agree on what happened to them, but the details of every version were gruesome enough that no one had turned traitor in living memory.

The man in the dark suit stood calmly at the rear of the crew compartment, despite the horrific heat and the constant shifting of the boat beneath him. His eyes were hidden behind dark, smoky goggles. However, a gleam of crimson occasionally escaped, hinting at advanced augmentation of some kind. He wore a massive Union blaster strapped to one hip, and the weapon did all his talking for him. The agent had not uttered a single word since boarding back in St. Louis. The crew went about their work, casting an occasional daunted look aft.

Otherwise, took no notice of the large, dark figure in their midst. Lieutenant Truett kept his gloved hands tight on the helm and his mind focused on the river ahead. Each bump and shudder registered through the old wooden wheel. He read the signals like words in a child's chapter book. He had been aboard packet boats since the War Between the States, and had captained Lincoln's Gift for nearly five years. He never looked forward to his turn at the Treasury run, but his daddy had always told him when he balked at work as a kid that the soonest run was soonest done. He took that advice to heart each time he shut down the hatches and viewports on the old Gift and prepared to the run the gold to the hayseeds running amok out west.

The Lieutenant kept his hands on the wheel steady as he peered out the tiny slit to starboard. He could just see the two escorting Iron Horses soaring along on the bank of the river. Even after all these years, it seemed strange to watch such heavy machines floating on cushions of thickened air. The boat crews never knew the men and women who rode herd on these trips. They joined the boats just outside of St. Louis and flew along with her to Kansas City, where they peeled off and presumably made the return trip.

He shrugged; each to his own. When they got to Kansas City, the gold would be the agent's trouble, and Truett would be free to enjoy the entertainments barbarian society for a night before returning to civilization. If the cavalry boys were alright sucking dust for most of a day and a night, that was their lookout. Mama Truett had not raised such a dummy.

Truett's second in command, Engineer's Mate Hadley, waved a hand in the Lieutenant's peripheral vision to get his attention. The only way to communicate in the compartment, when the hatches were all secured and the engine was roaring out at top speed, was with gestures. With a rapid fluttering of hand signals, Hadley indicated that they should be stopping soon. Each packet boat running full out needed to stop every four hours or so; long enough for the engine components and hull seams to be inspected for wear and damage.

The Lieutenant nodded and flashed two quick gestures to Seaman Graff, the signalman. He moved to the signals station as Truett gunned the engine into a quick surge of power that sent the boat roaring ahead of the 'Horse escorts. There, the flickering signal lamps would be more easily seen. Graff worked the controls for a moment, slamming the handles back and forth several times, and then rushed to a starboard vision slit. He nodded to Truett as he turned and moved to a port slit, and then straightened up, giving the commander an "okay" sign with his fingers.

Truett pulled back on the throttle of the boat, easing the power down gently so as not to swamp the small craft with its own surging wake. He nodded to the fourth member of the crew, Gunner's Mate Travis Stint, who immediately moved forward and worked the anchoring controls. A shudder ran beneath their feet as the barbed iron dropped from the bow. The metal bower fell into the debris at the bottom of the river and snagged there. After a moment of gentle drifting, the Lincoln's Gift swung slowly to its anchor against the soft but persistent push of the current.

The commander brought the enormous engines down to a low idle and then cut them completely. The silence within the close metal chamber was heavy, the ringing in the crews' ears pushing in on them uncomfortably. The agent continued to stand, unmoved and unmoving, his face immobile behind the dark lenses.

"Alright, boys, let's get this done so we can get moving again. I don't relish the idea of sitting here with a fortune of gold for ballast." Truett nodded to Hadley and Graff. "See to the inspection, but keep it quick. I don't want us to shake apart before we get to KC, but I don't want to sit here all day either." The older man turned to the gunner. "Stint, stand your watch as usual. Man the cupola cannons and keep those cavalry boys honest. No napping while they're supposed to be babysitting the president's coin."

The men saluted and moved off to their areas. Truett turned to the agent and smiled grimly. "Agent, if you would care to conduct your midday inspection of the cargo and sign off?"

The agent nodded once and turned to a small hatch behind him. Spinning the lock wheel with practiced moves he knelt down to reach inside the hold and pull out a compact iron box. He grunted slightly at the weight, but the container slid out easily enough. He leaned in to open the lock with a key he pulled from around his neck. Truett tried not to watch over the man's shoulder, but the temptation proved too great. That much gold in one place was enough to make even a loyal man like the Lieutenant entertain impure thoughts.

The officer whistled and shook his head. He knew it would never do any thief any good, even if they could take out the escorts, peel open the packet boat, and kill the crew. Each of the heavy coins gleamed in the soft red light of the compartment's RJ-1027 bulbs, but he knew they would gleam with a tinge of red no matter what color the lighting was. Each coin was enriched with the mystical substance that had changed the world in the last months of the war. The government was jealous of its wealth, and it tracked these government coins with the greedy obsession of a miser. Without this gold, and the structure and stability it paid for, the western territories would soon devolve into utter chaos, threatening to drag the rest of the republic down with them. It was a sobering thought, and more than enough to quench the impure thoughts of a moment before.

"Are we just about ready?" Truett stood up and glanced around the crew compartment. Hadley was still trapped in the broiling confines of the tiny engine room while Graff had moved through a crawl hatch forward to check the seams below and to the bow. Stint gave an all clear, and the agent, pushing the strongbox back into the hold, nodded over his shoulder as he spun the locking wheel tight.

"Just replacing one of the coolant hoses, sir." Hadley's voice was muffled, buried within the maze of pipes, tubes, and arcane components that made up the enormous engines.

"Got a small leak at junction two, sir." Graff shouted from below. "Giving it a quick splash of sealant and we should be good."

Truett settled against the small pilot's seat. He wiped the sweat beading down his forehead with the back of one hand and tilted towards the vision slit, hoping for a slight breeze. Of course, there was none. The lieutenant rested his forehead against the warm metal anyway in the hopes one may come up before it was time to push forward again.

Hadley was backing out of the engine room and Graff had just scrambled back into the crew compartment, gleaming with sweat, when Stint tapped at the collar of the cupola. "Sir, something strange on the south bank - off to port, I mean."

Truett slid off the jump seat and to a vision slit on the port side of the boat. "A little more information, if you please, Gunner's Mate?"

"Sir, I don't know. The cavalrymen over there seem a bit jumpy. And I thought I saw—"

Truett swung his head back and forth in front of the slit trying to find the Iron Horses in the tight field of vision. He found them after a moment and could see that they were, indeed, moving about. One man had dismounted and was moving away from the river, a large blaster rifle raised in a firing position, but sweeping back and forth as if unsure of a target. The other cavalryman was still mounted, but his 'Horse was operational, hovering on a cushion of blurred, dense air and swaying slightly as he brought it around to face away from the river as well.

"Damnit, what do they think they're doing?" Truett muttered. "Stint, anything from the two on the north bank?"

"No sir!" Stint's voice had ratcheted up slightly with this change in routine. "They're watching those two, opposite, sir."

Truett, still bent to the vision slit, shook his head. "Hadley, prep the engines for restart. Graff, be ready with the anchor. If there's something going on out there, I want to be somewhere else as quick as possible."

The agent had moved to another vision slit and was watching the two cavalrymen as well. The man on foot was moving deeper into the trees along the bank, while the active 'Horse was pushing up after him, Gatling guns swiveling, searching for prey.

A furious detonation erupted on the north bank of the river. A dragon's breath of blast wave pushed out over the water and set the packet boat to rocking in the sudden, vicious swell. Truett rushed to the starboard bulkhead and pressed his eye to a vision slit there.

"Stint, talk to me!" The commander's eye roved over the bank. He could not to see what was happening within the restricting little rectangle. With a violent mutter, he stood up and began to spin the securing wheel to the larger hatch. "Toss this over for a game of soldiers." He rumbled. If he could get the larger hatch open he'd be able to see more clearly, better know what should be done—

The butt of a large pistol cracked against the hatch and snapped it shut under his fingers. Truett spun around, face twisted with anger, but came up short as he found himself staring into the warped reflection of his own angry face in the agent's goggles.

"Opening the hatches is against protocol." The man's voice was devoid of any tone or emotion, but carried with it a strength and authority that could not be denied. "We must move forward."

"Sir!" Stint's voice was ragged with shock and fear. "That blast took out one of the cavalry boys! He's – he's in pieces, sir! In the water! His 'Horse was torn to shreds! What could have—"

The young man's legs, standing on the firing platform below the cupola-mounted gun, gave a sudden, savage jerk and then relaxed. The body slumped back down into the compartment. Its head was a bloody, shredded ruin.

"Hadley, now!" Truett snarled aside at the agent as he jumped back into the pilot's position. The Engineer's Mate was frantically working the controls at the aft of the compartment, bringing the engines back to life. Graff slapped the switch for the anchor mechanism and the small motor growled into life. The deck beneath their feet began to shake slightly to a rattling sound forward.

The agent took Stint's body beneath the arms and hauled him back into a corner, sitting the grotesque figure against the aft bulkhead where it would be out of the way. He resumed his position in front of the cargo hatch, blaster held in one steady hand.

Truett brought the throttle forward and the engines behind him roared back into life. The boat surged ahead just as another explosion tore up the northern bank. Bits of burning wood, twisted metal, and other wreckage arced over the water into the lieutenant's narrow field of vision. He tried not to think about what some of the softer, more irregular pieces flying into the river might be as he concentrated on the course ahead.

"Sir!" Graff's shout could barely be heard over the roaring engines. "The anchor's not—"

The boat was wrenched quickly around, throwing everyone off their feet. The agent fell heavily against Stint's body as the howling of the engines rose several octaves. Truett dove back for the controls, bringing the bow of the boat back up in a wide turn into the current before it could be driven ashore. The engines struggled against the ensnared anchor, digging the boat deeper into the water, before the chain gave way and the Lincoln's Gift was launched forward, sending everyone but the lieutenant staggering back against the bulkhead. Truett, braced against the pilot's jump seat, leaned into the thrust and kept his eyes pressed to the vision slit.

"Get to the gun!" The commander's shout was lost in the deafening roar that shook the compartment, but his pointing finger was all that Graff needed. He jumped up onto the blood-stained firing platform, his head and shoulders thrusting through the cupola. At once, the gun collar spun around, facing back into their wake, and the stuttering concussions of the Gatling guns pouring fire aft growled beneath the heavier sound of the engines tearing away at the water beneath them.

Truett navigated the sleek boat around a lazy bend in the river and then pushed the throttle all the way down as he swept on into a straight section, making for the middle of the flow and away from the rocks along the banks. Above them the firing stopped, and the commander gestured for Hadley to check on their escorts. The young man stepped to the port vision slit first, and then hopped to the starboard side, before turning to Truett with a serious face, shaking his head.

The commander snarled under his breath as he concentrated on the river ahead. Constant slight corrections swayed the boat first one way and then the other as he wove between tumbled rocks. Behind him, the agent pulled Graff off the firing platform and took his place, scanning their wake for any sign of attackers. The signalman and Hadley stood uneasily behind the firing platform, grasping grip rings with white knuckles. Their eyes twitched from the commander's back to the agent's legs and back again. Time stretched on, no further attacks erupted from the blurring shorelines, and the three navy men began slowly to relax.

The agent continued to stand his watch in the cupola, muscles tense and legs unmoving.

*****

An hour had passed since they had lost Stint and their escorts, but no further assaults had occurred. Graff and Hadley had wrapped the Gunner's Mate's body in a rough blanket and wrestled it into a small unsecured hold forward. The agent had come down off the gun not long ago and was standing once again before the cargo hold, face inscrutable. The signalman had taken his place and was standing on the hastily-wiped platform, keeping watch behind them.

Graff had been on watch for a few minutes when the boat thrashed violently without warning, there was a tortured screeching of metal, and his body was yanked upward and out of the hatch. Any scream he may have uttered was lost in the continuous roar of the RJ-1027 engines.

Hadley crouched down in shock and surprise as his friend was sucked from the boat. The agent lunged for the firing platform and Truett shouted soundlessly over his shoulder, demanding to know what had happened. He was whipping his head back and forth between the forward vision slit and Hadley's pale face when the boat staggered beneath them, the noise from the engines rising in a crescendo of furious howls.

Lincoln's Gift careened around in a stuttering arc as the engines whined and screamed. The deck shook to the rhythm of the tormented engines, then jumped sharply as something crashed against the hull. The boat jumped away from the impact but then lurched the other way as something else crashed against the outer armor. An abrasive, grinding sound shook the entire boat and it came to rest, canted up at an odd angle. The engines screamed as if animals in pain and abruptly sputtered into silence.

The deathly stillness was haunting. Truett and Hadley looked to each other and then up to the cupola. The agent eased himself back into the boat, one arm cradled tightly against his ribs. His face was pale but still impassive.

"The gun is gone, torn away." With his good hand he pulled the heavy pistol from its holster. "You will need to open the arms locker."

"What?" Truett's voice was high with disbelief. "How—"

"A chain strung across the river, secured to boulders on either bank." The agent bent down to check on the cargo hold's lock. "It rode along the top of the boat and took out the gun and the gunner." He looked over his shoulder at Truett. "He's still hanging from it behind us. I'm sorry, but you will need to open the arms locker now. They will be upon us at any moment."

"Who?" The commander knew he need to shake off the confusion of his shock, but his mind would not cooperate.

The agent turned his blank gaze upon Hadley. "Can you open the arms locker?"

"I can do it!" Truett pushed past Hadley and the agent and knelt down beside another hatch on the aft bulkhead. He spun several dials on a large lock and then snapped the bar open, pulling on the hatch. He withdrew a long blaster rifle and handed it to Hadley. Another was handed back for the agent. He pulled an additional pistol for himself, then rose.

"What should we do?" The commander put every effort into keeping his voice steady. "We're in the middle of the run, hours from anywhere, and we've lost our escorts. How can we— "

The agent held up a small black object with a flaring red light embedded in it. "The Treasury offices in St. Louis know we are in difficulty. They will send help immediately."

"What—?" The Engineer's Mate's eyes were wide with awe.

"Never mind." The agent slipped the box back into a pocket and nodded towards the gaping cupola. "We need to secure the area so we can wait for recovery. This has been elaborate and well-executed." He tilted his head towards the secured hold. "We cannot allow that gold to fall into their hands."

Hadley nodded. "Right. Damn corn-husking dirt farmers."

The commander just shook his head. "We're sure the cavalrymen are down?"

The agent moved towards the firing platform, the rifle gripped by the barrel in his good hand. "Someone took out the ones on the north bank with heavy weapons. The southern team was hit with personal weapons." He tucked the rifle under his bad arm and reached for the twisted wreckage along the edge of the cupola. "We're on our own."

"Hey!" Truett rose and slapped the roof of the compartment with an open palm. When the agent ducked back down the commander shook his head. "You're wounded. I go first."

The agent thought about it for a moment and then simply nodded, easing himself off the platform.

Truett stepped up onto the platform, trying to ignore the dark stains still clinging to the edges of the metal's diamond texturing. He poked his head through the cupola, past the twisted wreckage of the weapon collar, and just high enough to scan the area around his crippled boat.

The Lincoln's Gift had come to rest up against the southern bank of the river at a relatively wide, shallow point. The bow of the boat was tilted upward against the shoreline, smoke pouring from the engines aft of the hatch. Truett noticed the sad figure hanging limply over the water about a hundred yards downstream and quickly looked away. There were areas of relatively thick scrub pine clumped along either side of the river. More than enough cover to conceal any number of ambushers.

The lieutenant lifted himself up out of the wrecked cupola and onto the tilted deck, drawing both pistols as he came to his feet. His weapons were standard-issue Union blasters, heavy weapons powered by clips of RJ-1027 that fired bursts of crimson fire far more devastating than any black powder weapon they had wielded during the War Between the States. With far more accuracy and range than those antiques he had grown up with, Truett knew that if a target presented itself, he would be able to take it down.

Behind the commander, Hadley lifted himself up out of the boat and onto the deck, a blaster rifle cradled in both hands. Truett gestured for the engineer to keep a watch out over the water and the northern bank as he started to sidle towards the bow, scanning the southern bank for danger. The agent threw his blaster rifle up onto the deck from below and began to crawl up out of the boat as well.

Truett moved to the bow of his boat and looked down. It was not a long drop to the shallow water below, but he was not sure he wanted to abandon the Gift quite so soon. Glancing behind him, the commander could see that Hadley was keeping a good watch out over the glistening water while the agent was settling against an intake fairing. The man cast his shrouded gaze all around, assessing their current situation.

The lieutenant looked back down and crouched, preparing to jump.

"That's a mighty fine rowboat you got yerself there, mister!" The voice came out of a cluster of low pines off to Truett's right. He brought his pistols up, arms straight and firm, but he could not see a target within the shifting shadows beneath the trees.

"Now, that's hardly friendly, is it?" The voice was light, and the old lieutenant felt his anger rising at its tone.

"Show yourself, or we're going to come in and drag you out!" Truett's pistols were rock steady. He edged back down the slanting deck towards Hadley and the government agent, both of whom were now watching the small grove.

"Well, I sure don't wanna be dragged nowhere, an' that's a fact!" The voice laughed. "Though, I'm not sure that I'm all that much concerned. You boys look like you've been havin' a bad day." Somewhere in the shadows, the smile widened. "Looks like you got ten or twenty nets caught up in yer little motor, there!"

Nets in the water. Truett's eyes narrowed as he considered the idea. If they were heavy enough, like the metal nets used by some of the fishermen working the Great River back east . . .

"In the name of the federal government, come out or we shall open fire." The agent may have been injured when the boat heeled over and threw him, but his voice was still strong.

"Oh! The federal government now, is it? Well, that there is certainly a hound of another litter, as they say!" The voice was harder now, and for some reason, Truett was suddenly very aware of how much colder it was outside the crew compartment of his little boat.

"You heard me." The agent eased himself to his feet. "Every minute of this inane chatter makes you look more suspicious to me."

"Well, I wouldn't ever wanna look suspicious to a man from the federal gov'mint, sir. An' that's a fact!" The voice was now a dangerous mix of hard edges and amused disdain, and Truett felt himself grow even colder.

The figure that swaggered out of the shadows was sneering through its beard. Heavy goggles, similar to the agent's, but tinted with a bright red shade, gleamed in the sun beneath the tilted brim of a battered stetson. The stub of a hand-rolled cigarillo hung from the corner of the man's mouth, and his thumbs were hooked nonchalantly in an elaborate cross-draw gun belt. His stance was aggressively casual, and Truett felt the heat rising once again in his chest at the man's clear lack of concern. He felt his hand lifting the pistol before he heard Hadley behind him whisper. "Oh, damn."

The lieutenant was brought up short by the fear and awe in his engineer's voice. His eyes tightened as he took a closer look at the stranger. The man was wearing a duster, common enough in the territories, although out of fashion back east for years. However, the arms of this man's coat had been removed, with fancy stitching around the sleeve hems showing that it was intentional and decorative. Truett's eyes widened as he saw why the arms had been cut away from the long coat.

The man's arms, fully revealed by this custom duster, were not flesh and blood. They were sculpted shapes of iron and rubber, armored sheathing protecting delicate-seeming components within that gleamed silver and gold. The telltale ruby-red glow of RJ-1027 power glinted from several points along each arm. As the man lowered one arm and raised the other to tip his hat to the men aboard the wrecked riverboat, the tiny parts inside of each whirred and spun in the sunlight, small bursts of smoke or steam flashing out and pulled away on the gentle breeze.

Only one man in the world had mechanical arms like that. Tales said they had been crafted for him special by the mad European: Doctor Burson Carpathian himself. Carpathian had discovered RJ-1027 and its many applications and changed the world, and the course of the American Civil War, in the process. The man who might have been viewed as a hero was a monster to nearly everyone in the Old States, as word of his terrible experiments and devastating inventions continued to spread. It was said that a savage, mysterious vendetta against the Union hero, General Ulysses S. Grant, had driven him to horrible deeds.

Now, back east, anything involving Carpathian or his inventions was looked upon with suspicion and dread.

None of the tales were as dark or fearful as the outlaw whose arms, nearly torn from his body by a Warrior Nation chieftain, had been interchanged with metal replacements by the great Doctor.

"Jesse James." For a moment, Truett thought he had spoken without thinking, but out of the corner of his eye he saw the agent step up to the edge of the tilted deck, rifle hanging loosely in his one good arm.

The man on the riverbank nodded. "The one and only, gentlemen!" His smile widened. "And now that the mystery is solved, if you might care to hop on down from up there, we can see about securing you all and liberating my gold?"

The agent had only moved a fraction of an inch, the barrel of his rifle swaying slightly, before those horrible metal arms had flashed down and two enormous weapons, gleaming with the crimson glow of RJ-1027, filled both iron fists. Each was pointing directly at the agent.

"Now, old son, I don't think you wanna be doin' that." James nodded. "You had a rough enough day as it is. Why not relax, make it a little easier on yerself?" But the smile had never faltered, and the first signs of emotion crossed the agent's face as it tightened up behind the thick goggles.

One of James' pistols floated out to his left, in line with the stern of the crippled boat. "Don't be a hero, son." His voice was flat. "There ain't nothin' or no one on that boat worth dyin' fer. Trust me."

Truett looked back to see Hadley lowering his rifle, a look of sheepish apology on his face. The commander looked back down at James.

"There's three of us, and even you only have two arms." The lieutenant's grip tightened on his pistols and he stood up taller. "You going to shoot all three of us at one time, before we can get a shot off on you?"

From the corner of his eye, Truett could see the agent and Hadley standing taller as well. He knew, whatever he did at this point, they were going to back his play.

James' smile just widened. "Three of you. You new in the territories, there, Billy Yank? You heard o' me, but you think three men at once is goin' to pose a challenge?"

Truett wished he could see the eyes behind those red goggles. The sardonic grin in that trim beard, the careless pose, and the curious tilt to the head were all playing havoc on his mind. The gold on the Gift was important. It was to keep men like this in check. It was to make the territories safer for decent folk. One month's loss would not cause the downfall of the west, but it was more than he wanted this nasty little road agent to get his filthy paws on.

"Roll the dice, bas—" Truett brought his pistols to bear on the outlaw's sneering face. He saw Hadley's rifle rise almost at the same time, and the agent's come up as well. All three of them were going to fire within a second of each other. There was no way—

The lieutenant did not hear the shot that hit him. He felt like someone had kicked his leg out from underneath him. He went down hard on the deck of his boat. His head slammed into the armor with a thick clang, and a sickening haze rose up over his vision. He felt himself rebound off the deck and fall.

There was a staccato string of detonations from terribly close by and yet somehow muffled. There was a strobing crimson light that flashed like summer lightning all around him. He heard a dull splash not far behind, and a gentle sizzle in the distance like rain on the surface of a lake. Then he hit.

Truett landed in the sandy shallows and his breath was knocked out of him. He rolled in the warm water, struggling to breathe, and fought desperately when he felt two hard arms wrap around his chest and begin to haul him backwards. His entire body was on fire, pain throbbing in almost every muscle and joint. Only his right leg was free from agony; cold and heavy.

The lieutenant coughed up a stream of water and rolled over onto his stomach, wrenching away from the arms that had dragged him clear of the river. He coughed with ragged breath, trying to struggle to his hands and knees only to tip onto his right side as his cold, heavy limb refused to support him.

"Now, now, kid." The voice was hovering over his head and maddening in its friendly openness. "Don't hurt yerself any more 'n you already did."

Truett felt a hard hand patting him on the shoulder and tried to shrink away. "Don't touch me!" He tried to shout, but it came out as a feeble whimper.

"It sure has been a bad day, now, ain't it." The voice spoke in consoling tones and the hand patted him on the shoulder again. Truett forced his eyes open and looked up into the grinning face of Jesse James. He tried to surge to his feet, but his body failed him, and the outlaw reached out and casually pushed him back into the warm sand.

"Now, son, I'd hate fer you to try to stand up and bleed out, now." James stood up and looked down at Truett, mechanical hands on his hips.

A terrible thought rushed into the commander's mind and drowned all the heat that had settled there. He struggled up onto his elbows and looked down at his legs. Or rather, he looked down at his leg. His right leg ended just below the knee. Ragged tatters of flesh and fabric trailed off into the shallow river where a swirling stain of red eddied away into the deeper water.

"Oh my sacred God . . . " The lieutenant's whispered words were not lost on the outlaw standing above him. James smiled down with an even broader grin.

"Well, you're a might better off than yer friends over yonder." One metal arm rose to indicate the boat.

Every element of Truett's mind shouted at him not to look down that articulated mechanical limb, but he could not stop his head from swiveling on his neck. His eyes searched along the side of his boat and out into the river.

Nearby, floating on its back in the shallows was the dark-clothed body of the agent. A massive red crater had been blasted out of his chest, and the water all around him was cloudy with his blood. The goggles had been torn from his head and crude ruby lenses flashed in the bright sun. Further out, beyond the stern of the wrecked boat, there was nothing to mark the passing of Engineer's Mate Hadley but a few bubbles and an ever-widening pink stain that rushed away downriver while the lieutenant watched.

Truett looked back up at Jesse James, hatred rushing through his body and mind. "You bastard . . . "

James crouched down beside the Union officer and all traces of his grin were gone. "Well now, that's hardly a complimentary thing to say, old son. Especially by a man wearing the uniform of the very folks who hanged my old man, and then whipped me in front of him, tryin' to get at the whereabouts of my big brother." The outlaw leaned back a little to look at Truett's gory wound.

"This looks like it's gonna hurt a whole lot more before it might start gettin' to feel a little bit better, boy." A ghost of the grin came back, but it was cruel and cold. "Which means I got some good news for ya."

Jesse James stood again and drew one of his sleek, custom-looking pistols. "You ain't gonna have to worry about sufferin' through the pain."

"Just kill me, you gray-back bastard!" Truett could feel the tears of rage and frustration coursing down his face. He cursed the weakness of his own body that denied him the dignity of facing this moment with a dry eye. He could feel James pacing around him.

"Oh, you were a dead man the day you named your damned boat, Billy Yank." Jesse James took the toe of one boot and gently settled it over the wounded officer's shattered leg. "Who you think you are, comin' into the territories sportin' a boat with a name like that?"

Truett screamed as the outlaw applied gentle pressure with the boot. James crouched down by his head again and the officer tried to muster the strength and coordination to spit. He only managed to dribble bloody liquid down into his own beard.

"You folks back east, you think you won yer war, but yer wrong." Hot breath brushed against Truett's ear. "Out here, that war ain't even close to bein' done yet. And you ain't even come close to winnin' it. Out here, you ain't just fightin' those of us left who remember the Confederacy. You're fightin' the Doc and his monsters; you're fightin' the savages of the Warrior Nation an' all their ghost story shenanigans; an' yer fightin' the people, old son."

Truett watched as Jesse James stood up once more. "Because the people out here, they ain't havin' none of it no more, soldier boy. The world's rollin' along, and it's gonna roll over you, an' yer Union, an' yer president too."

The lieutenant found himself looking down the wide muzzle of the outlaw's pistol. "When you see 'im, you thank Lincoln fer his gift now, ya hear?"

A crimson-edged flash was the last thing Lieutenant Joseph Truett ever saw.

*****

Jesse was stretched out on the canted deck of the wrecked Union packet boat. His mechanical arms were crossed casually behind his head, back resting on the twisted metal wreckage of the weapon cupola. The distant grumbling of Iron Horses had been growing for some time, and it was no surprise when his brother Frank rode up, his machine stopping abruptly in a sharp turn that threw sand and dirt across the body of the dead Union officer.

Another 'Horse roared up behind Frank. The youthful face of Bob Younger, the fledgling of the notorious outlaw family, smiled beneath its layers of grit and trail dust. The young man looked up at the ruined Union boat and whistled.

"Damn, if we didn't do a number on this ole girl! Eh, Frank?" Bob Younger leaned in over the control panel behind the wind fairing of his 'Horse to get a better look.

"Well, I'm damned glad those old fishing nets you got from St. Louis worked, Frank." Jesse stood up, brushing non-existent dust from his legs. "I wasn't lookin' forward to tryin' to take this thing down with that old rocket launcher you left me."

"Damnit, Jesse, you were supposed to wait for the rest of us before you took on the survivors! There was a damned federal agent aboard this boat!" Frank swung his leg over the saddle and dismounted, pulling an elegant, elaborate long rifle from its boot behind his seat. He careful sidled down the embankment towards the crumpled bow of the boat.

"Yeah, I know." Jesse grinned at his brother. "You wanna meet 'im? He's takin' a swim right over on the other side of the boat."

Frank shook his head. "An' you din't have to kill every livin' soul, neither. You are gonna get yerself killed one of these days, an' there won't be nothin' I nor anyone else can do about it."

Bob shrugged. "Looks like he did a pretty thorough job of it, Frank." He smiled up at Jesse and gave him a mocking salute.

Frank snorted. "Yeah, he did a great job. Your brothers blew up two of the cavalrymen, you an' I took out the other two, an' I took out the boat gunner with Sophie here." He patted the scoped long rifle. "Then the chain we strung up took out another one, hangin' yonder." He pointed the rifle at the figure hanging over the river not far away. "And the nets we all put out took out the boat's engines and sent it crashing into the dirt here so he could gun down the wounded folks who survived." He spit off into the sand. "But yeah, he did a great job."

Jesse grinned even wider. "Don't be sore, Frank. It's always your plans work out best." He jumped down into the shallow water. "An' now we got more gold'n we'd know what to do with! We'll be havin' ourselves a hog-killin' time fer months now!"

Frank frowned at his brother and shook his head. "You ain't got the brain's God gave a beaver, Jesse. I swear."

Frank tossed Sophie up onto the tilted deck then jumped up, grabbed ahold of the deck edge, and heaved himself up and onto the boat. He was still talking to himself as he jumped down through the wrecked cupola and into the metal chamber within.

"I thought you was awesome, Jesse." Bob Younger grinned at Jesse as the outlaw chief sloshed ashore.

"Thanks, Bob. You guys seen any sign of yer brothers as you rushed up here to save my virtue from the terrible Union?" Jesse walked up to the other man and stood with his back to the officer's sprawled body.

"Well, they was supposed to stay behind an' make sure no one was followin' along. Then they was supposed to get here to back us up backin' you up. But no, I ain't seen 'em yet."

Jesse nodded and turned, moving around the body to look out over the water. Over the constant rushing of the shoreline he could just here a distant rumble, almost like thunder that never ended but instead built slowly over time. He grinned at Bob.

"Bobby, I think this might be them makin' their heroic arrival already."

The sound grew louder and louder until there was no doubt. Soon after, three Iron Horses burst out of the brush on the far side of the river and rode straight into the water. Huge clouds of vapor boiled up around the three vehicles as they tore across the Missouri River. Jesse smiled to hear Cole's rebel yell as he shouted out, seeing the crumpled ruin of the boat.

The three eldest brothers tore up out of the river in a cloud of moisture that soaked Jesse, Bob, and the ruined boat. Cole Younger grinned hugely behind his thick goggles and hooted. "Man alive, that is some ride! You remember when we had to worry about bridges an' the like, Jesse?"

Jesse nodded as Cole and his brothers leapt off their 'Horses. The machines growled down to idle, hovering just an inch off the ground. "Yeah, I do, Cole. I hear you boys din't run into too much trouble takin' out the Yanks."

John Younger, older only than their little brother Bob, grunted. He was always putting on grave airs, trying to come over the big man on the scene. "Wasn't nothin'. They weren't even watchin' fer us. Jim took out the first one with rocket pods, 'n the other one, we got 'em with blasters between us."

"Weren't no one followin', neither. So it's a good thing you lot din't need no babysittin'." Cole grinned and leaned over to spit a stream of tobacco juice into the sandy soil.

Bob shook his head. "Weren't us t'all, Cole. Jesse took three of 'em out all on his own afore we ever got here!"

Cole laughed. "I'm sure that set Frank off into a tizzy, eh?"

"You ladies want to stop with yer afternoon tea and help me with this damned strongbox?" Frank called out from inside the boat. Soon the men were on the tilted deck, tossing small, heavy bags of coin up and then handing them along until they could be thrown onto the shore.

When all the gold coin was piled up in the sand, the outlaws stood around admiring their handy work. "This oughta keep us livin' the life o' Riley over in Kansas City for a while more, don't you think?" Bob's smile was as wide and open as a child's, as if there weren't dead bodies floating just yards away.

"Well, not exactly." Frank was crouched down on his haunches, frowning down at the pile. He had a small wooden box in one hand, several winking red lights flashing dully in the sun. When he did not offer any further comment, Cole knocked one foot against his leg.

"What you mean, Frank? By 'Not exactly'?"

Frank shook his head and waved a hand over the pile. "The coins're all shot with RJ-1027. This level, won't fade fer months. An' no way to get rid of the trace no matter what you do."

Jesse frowned down at his brother. "What?"

Frank tapped the top bag. "There's always been rumors they zap all gov'mint gold headin' west." He waved the wooden cube. "I ain't never been sure 'till now." Frank stood and stretched his back. "Nope, if we want face value on this plunder, we're gonna have to bury it and wait a few months at least. Probl'y as much as a year."

Jesse kicked at the sand as his mechanical hands came to rest on his hips. "Well that ain't all! We din't just blast this boat outa the water so's we could live like paupers fer a year!"

Frank gave his brother a tired, irritated look. "We ain't livin' like paupers now, Jesse. We got plenty of coin stashed away, we don't live too high on the hog. But we might not have to wait, neither."

The outlaw chief's lip curled in a barely-controlled scowl. "You see a trail clear o' this bein' fer nothin', Frank, you best speak up now."

Frank shook his head again. "No, I know some folks, back in St. Louis, can unload gold like this, even with the mark." He shrugged. "They work for the government, but they ain't too partic'ler about extra business they can pick up."

Jesse sighed and crossed his mechanical arms. "So, we don't just go back to KC and whoop it up, but we can get us the payola?"

Cole laughed. "You mean you don't go back to KC and whoop it up, kickin' yer heels with the lovely Miss Mimms don't you? I ain't noticed the rest of us moonin' over any dancehall girls lately that'd have us rushin' back to Kansas City any time soon."

Jesse shrugged, shooting the firstborn Younger a sharp look. "I mean, we ain't goin' back to KC?"

Frank shook his head. He picked one of the bags up and tossed it in his hand as if weighing it. "No, I don't think we all need to go into St. Louis. Besides," he looked up and gestured with the bag at his brother's arms. "You stick out like a nun in a whore house wherever you go, dressed like that. No, I think Cole an' me, we can take care of this."

He shot a warning finger up at the other men. "Now, you keep in mind, marked goods like this, we ain't gonna get even a solid part of what normal gold would be worth. We gonna have to settle with a beggar's share. But that's better than nothin'."

Jesse snorted and threw up his arms, spinning to walk away. "We gotta do it this way, Frank? We can't just unload this plunder in Kansas City?"

Frank gave his brother a pitying look. "Where's your brain, Jesse? We rode all the way out here so we wouldn't draw attention to us layin' low in KC. You wanna push queer gold right where we're livin'? That ain't no way to avoid the marshals, an' you know it."

Jesse kicked at the sand and swore under his breath. "Hey, it ain't all bad!" Bob Younger grinned. "I always wanted to go see St. Louis! Jesse, you get a coat with some sleeves on, the rest of us are good as we are, an' we all go into town and kick us up a good row in the big city!"

Jesse shook his head. "Naw. I wanna get back. I don't need to go into no big Yank city anyhow."

Cole chuckled. "I knows a lot of folks'd take exception to that remark, there Jesse."

"I don't care none. This is all a crock." Jesse moved back towards the trees where his own Iron Horse was hidden. "I'm goin' back to KC, you boys get what you can for the plunder, and I'll meet you back there. Maybe we do another job when you get back."

"Jesse," Frank's tone had a warning edge to it. "We don't need to do another job anytime soon. We got enough coin to set us up right nice for a while. We need to lay low for a bit.

Give the marshals some time to find another diversion."

"We'll see." Jesse did not turn around as he moved into the trees.

"I'll see you all in Kansas City."

"Say hello to Misty for us!" Cole laughed and his brothers joined in.

“It’ll be a few days, maybe a week before you see us.” Frank’s voice was sharp. “Don’t get into any trouble before we get back.”

Chapter 2

The sun beat down on the dusty streets of Tombstone, driving most folks indoors despite the close heat they found there. The bulky shapes of a few old civilian Iron Horses lined the streets, shimmering in the sun. Long landing skids rested on rubber recharge pads, shimmering waves of heat rising off the barrel-shaped forward cowlings and empty weapon mounts. Leather seats strapped above the powerful RJ-1027-fueled engines had cracked and dried in the intense heat. Beside each recharge pad an RJ-1027 generator hummed softly, winking crimson lights barely discernible beneath the sun's hot glare.

A single man in shirt sleeves and a tight vest ran from the protected walkway of a small building and into the headquarters of the self-styled Federal Bureau of Lawmen, formerly the Sheriff's office. He ran past an old crow hunched on a rotten hitching post. The bird barely ruffled a feather in acknowledgement.

Virgil Earp pushed through the creaking door of the office with one balled fist, pulling his hat off with the other and fanning himself desperately.

"Damn, it's hotter'n a whore house on nickel night out there!" He sat down heavily in a creaky old chair that was already host to the heavy uniform duster of a Federal Lawman. The room held several desks cluttered with chunks of rock, paperwork, and a strange array of mechanical parts including two RJ-1027 power cylinders, their glows a dull, pulsing burgundy.

Wyatt Earp, Over-marshal of the western territories and de facto leader of the Federal Bureau of Lawmen, looked up from the report he was reading with an exasperated sigh.

"Did they have anything?" He looked pointedly at the flimsy piece of paper clutched in Virgil's fist.

"Don't get 'em in a bunch, Wyatt, town ain't gonna burn down while I catch my breath." The older man carefully folded the paper flat against the desk top and handed it over to his brother.

"Your friend's been seen in Kansas City. No official reports yet, but I sent out specific inquiries, knowin' you'd want hard info before you stirred from here. The wires ain't that reliable out this far, but we should hear something before too long."

Wyatt sat back in his chair, ignoring the plaintive creak from the ancient wood. "What friend are you talkin' about, Virg? I got an awful lot of friends in that line, for you to be playin' coy." He glanced over the wrinkled paper and frowned when he came to a name. "Jesse James?"

Virgil smiled widely beneath his massive mustache. "The same. We been gettin' reports he'd moved out east for a few months now, but nothing certain. That there's from a local sheriff.Claims the word comes from one of Jesse's own men."

Wyatt snorted. "They all turn on each other if you give 'em enough time." He quickly read through the rest of the message.

"No Frank? No Cole boys?"

Virgil shrugged. "Not in that report. But I couldn't ask for much detail. You know how the connection can get." He looked around slowly, grizzled brows pulled together in mild discomfort. "We got anythin' to drink?"

Wyatt turned his chair around to face his desk and cleared an area for the message. "I think I drank the last of it before you came in." His voice was muffled as he bent down over the sheet of paper. "This says there hasn't been any major activity in Kansas City. You'd think if Jesse was there, he'd've felt the itch by now."

"Don't piss where you drink? There's been some activity within a day or so's ride of Kansas City. One big job, took out the Union packet. O' course, the government boys are claimin' it din't have anything onboard, but those ain't easy to take down. A lot of trouble for someone to take, to sink an empty boat." Virgil stood up with a groan and moved to the window looking out onto the barren street. "Damn, I don't want to go out there again. You ain't got nothin' to drink in here?"

"Comes to that, Jesse's never been the soul of discretion where it came to pissin' and drinkin'." Wyatt stood up with a shrug and joined Virgil by the window. "The boys have been keepin' a jug out back since the heat got up. Ask nicely, they might let you have a sip."

Virgil gave a quick bark of laughter. "They ask nicely and might be I won't drink the whole damned jug."

Wyatt smiled and shook his head. "Come with me first." He moved to a small side door and jerked it open with a quick pop. "You checked on 'em lately?"

Virgil followed his brother down a small hall. "Nah, they put my hair up, an' that's a fact."

Wyatt stopped at the end of the hall where a pair of wide doors stood closed. The raw wood made for a marked contrast next to the old, faded paneling of the hallway. The Over-marshal reached out and slapped down a locking bar. With a quick twist, he pulled one door open. Virgil stepped back, hand resting on the butt of his pistol.

The door opened to reveal a small, closet-like room where four human shapes stood stock still. Flickering red lights winked at several points on each body. Rigid metal armor was visible beneath mundane-looking riding leathers and wide-brimmed hats. Each figure sported a single crimson eye flaring from the center of its head, their light pulsing with an eerily synchronized rhythm. Each form wore a large metal star built into its armored chest.

"Well, they look alright to me." Wyatt stood, eyes running quickly along each figure, glancing with cool familiarity for the story the flickering lights would tell. Each form was connected to a large, barrel-shaped RJ-1027 generator by a series of rubber hoses and metal wires.

"Sittin' here in the dark, just waitin' for their next chance to raise hell." Wyatt's eyes took on a look that mixed equal parts pride and wary discomfort.

"Wyatt," Virgil's tone was casual but curious. "You been leadin' the charge for years to get one of these into every piss-ant town too poor for a decent whore house. You mind tellin' me why you keep yours locked in a closet?" His voice had picked up an edge of dark humor.

Wyatt turned to his brother with a grin as he swung the doors closed again. "Simple, Virg. Too many folks have been jawin' about these things spyin' for Washington and Grant's pet European Johnny-Come-Lately. Now, I don't know if that's happenin' for a fact 'r not. But I figure, we got plenty of real live human marshals and deputies hereabouts, we don't really need these metal brutes on a regular basis. I figure, we keep 'em in the closet 'till we need 'em, we take 'em out, shake 'em down, and set 'em off. Then, when we don't need 'em anymore, we put 'em back in."

As the door creaked shut Wyatt rested one hand upon the rough fresh wood as if feeling for a pulse. "Damn if these ain't interestin' times we're livin' in, eh, Virg?"

Recognizing his brother's mood Virgil spun slightly and rested his back against the hallway wall, kicking one boot heel up against the wood. "What you mean?"

The younger marshal knocked on the door twice as if calling the metal men within to open up, shaking his head with a rueful smile. "You remember what it used to be like, before Carpathian? Before Grant came chargin' over the hill? Before James and his filthy band of pirates took down that first Heavy Rail?" He turned to rest his own back against the wall. "You remember when none of this damned crimson gold existed? It was a man, standin' or fallin' on his own, and the speed of his arm was the difference between a tale worth tellin' and sloppin' for hogs on some dude's ranch?"

Virgil screwed up his mouth as if sucking through his teeth, then spat on the floor in a neat, studied movement. "Wyatt, I followed you out here cuz you've always been the man with the plan. Whether you were firing lead or bolts of hellfire from your shootin' irons, I been able to back your play cuz you always been good to me and ours. Now, we got fearsome weapons, and that's not mistake. But damn, you gotta have noticed by now, those of us who are packin' the RJ-1027 on a regular basis, we ain't getting' old nearly as fast as we should? And don' you forget

Doc, Wyatt. Without the Union tech they brought out with 'em, he'd a been dead several times over by now."

"Yeah, an' we gotta beg for every power cylinder, every gun, and you remember the dancin' we had to do to get Doc that fancy get up that breaths for 'im? Like I been sayin', I don't know whose team those Union boys are pullin' for half the time."

Virgil pushed off the wall and turned to face his younger brother. "Wyatt, Grant and his eastern pals mightn't have the best manners, and they sure's manure don't care about the little folk out in the territories, but we wouldn't be able to do our jobs without 'em. So, we beg when we gotta, we steal when we can, and we stand between the folks an' everythin' that'd roll over 'em, whether it's injuns, outlaws, or the damned Union itself. But right now, Wyatt, my throat's gonna burst into flames if I don't pour some water down it soon . . . "

Wyatt grinned at Virgil and nodded, spinning on his heel to walk back down the hall. He stopped at the door to the back room and gestured for his brother to go in ahead of him. "Well, you make a good point as always, Virg. And as far as the UR-30s go, if these reports of Jesse James in Kansas City are true, we're probably going to need to bring all four of those galoots out of hibernation before we're done."

In the back room, several younger lawmen were sitting around a large table rolling dice or playing cards under the disapproving glare of an older man in long, black leather robes. The conversation came to an abrupt halt as the older men walked in. The deputies shot each other several furtive glances. Virgil did not seem to notice, kicking one man's boots off the table as he passed, growling something about manners and pig sties. Wyatt pushed through a moment later and tapped the same man on the shoulder.

"Provencher, watch the front." The small man hopped up seeing the Over-marshal standing there, and Wyatt smoothly slid into his seat.

"Ah, boss!" The young man whined, his dark eyes pleading. "Can't I just— "

"The front, shave tail!" Virgil barked. "Or you want another smack up-side of your head you'll feel till next Tuesday?"

Provencher shot the Over-marshal's brother a spiteful glance and skulked out of the room

"Damn, that man's wearing a ten dollar Stetson on a five-cent head." Virgil shook his head in disbelief. "This here the lot that's gonna save civilization, Wyatt?"

Wyatt put the wrinkled report paper on the cluttered table, nodded to the man in the robe, and looked up at the rest of the men gathered there. "So," the lead lawman smiled wisely at his charges. "What were ya'll talkin' about when Virg an' I happened on in?"

One of the younger marshals looked at the others before clearing his throat. "Seems the Kid turned up in Yuma, claiming the bounty on twenty Injun scalps. Sounds like they had quite a little shindig up in the mountains."

Wyatt stared the younger man down over the tips of his boots, now propped up on the table. "Might you be a tad clearer, marshal?"

The man cleared his throat and sat up straighter.

"William Bonney, sir. Billy . . . the Kid."

The man in the robe snorted in contempt.

Wyatt snarled and turned to spit on the floor. "These animals and their pet names. G'damned William Billy the damned Kid Bonney! An' who the hell's paying out bounties for scalps in Yuma, for the Lord's sake? Didn't we announce we were stoppin' that?"

Another of the men nodded. "Yessir, we sent that out over the wire first thing after the meeting at the Cosmopolitan. But some's ain't followin' suit, sir."

"The warden over at the Territorial Prison, sir, he's got some strange notions. An' he's been known to back 'em up with gold he says is from the government. Word is, the Kid—"

"Can we please not call him by that ridiculous nickname?" Wyatt's tone was even, but he was clearly getting annoyed.

The deputy speaking swallowed. "Yessir. Bonney, sir. Word is, Bonney turned his twenty scalps in to the warden at the prison, sir, and got paid in good hard gold."

Wyatt stared off into space for several moments, his left hand playing with the end of his mustache. His eyes flashed as he scanned around the room. Many of the younger men were smiling at the news, some even muttering behind raised hands.

"Has anyone given any thought to what Sitting Bull and the other chiefs may well do when news of this reaches them?" The Over-marshal's voice was cold despite the room's oppressive heat.

The man in the robe shook his head. "You're askin' fer a bit much, Over-marshal. Thinking, and whatnot."

That seemed to put a damper on the men. "Well, sir, they're already savages, killin' innocents wherever they go."

Virgil shook his head and looked down at the younger men with contempt, wiping water from his lips with the hand that held the sweating metal cup. "The Warrior Nation hasn't wandered into civilized areas for over a year now. They're out there in the wastelands, in the hills, deserts, and mountains, running around bouncing off the army troops, Carpathian's nightmares, and anyone else stupid enough to go seeking them out. They haven't been a danger to normal townsfolk in a coon dog's age."

"Well, they weren't much of a threat to the K- . . . to Bonney, sir." Another of the young men tossed out. "I have a cousin in Yuma, said he and his men just threw twenty bloody scalps on the table, pretty as you please, and then tore the dock district up raisin' hell with the gold the warden give 'em."

"And that's interestin', Johnson, but it doesn't really address the issue at hand, now, does it." It was not a question, and the men at the other end of the table sat up to hear what Wyatt thought the real issue was.

"What was Bonney and his bunch of misfits doing out in the mountains in the first place? How'd they find a Warrior Nation war party in the first place? Those folks aren't the easiest to find when they're out in the boonies, and why'd they go lookin' for the savages in the first place? And what in the name of Sam Hill were the braves doing out that far west? Twenty braves, that's no walk in the park back east, if you follow me."

"Well, they were talkin' that they took some hits, sir. There was a lot of talk that they were splittin' the take on fewer shares than they'd expected."

Wyatt pinched the bridge of his nose with one rough hand. "But what pushed them out there that far? Either of them, for God's sake?" He looked over at his brother. "We ain't heard the end of this, have we Virg."

Virgil shook his head. "No, Wyatt. No, we ain't. Somethin' goin' on out there, and that's for sure."

The robed man nodded earnestly. "Going to get worse before it gets any better."

Wyatt looked at the robed man. "What do we have over that way? Are there any of our new-minted marshals out that far?"

"Slaughter ranges out that way, sir, but we ain't heard from him in months." He looked apologetic.

Wyatt pursed his lower lip and shot a gust of breath up into his mustache as he thought. "Any UR-30 units around Yuma?"

Blank stares and vaguely-shaken heads were the only responses, and Wyatt lifted up his boots, letting the chair slam back down onto the wooden floor. "Well fat load of good those damned machines have been, eh? Anyway, send a wireless out for Slaughter. Tell him to be on the lookout for Bonney or any of the men he's known to run with. That damned Johnny Ringo was running with him for a while, along with that injun outcast, and the big ugly guy with the teeth . . . what was his name?"

Virgil grinned around a thick toothpick. "Williamson. They call him 'Smiley' . . . " The old marshal grinned even wider at the younger men. "You don't want to know why."

Wyatt gave his brother a look before going on. "Anyway, yeah, send out a message for Slaughter to be on the lookout for any of these boys. I want to know what they're up to, if we can find out. It's about time we hit some of these larger outfits - Bonney, the James 'n Younger gang, the real players that have been causin' the most grief in the new order."

"Ah, sir, James ain't so bad, surely?" The youngest man in the room was smiling openly. "I mean, he's sorta like Robin Hood, ain't he?"

Another of the younger men perked up. "Yeah! I mean, I heard he took down banks, stages, and the like, but he's the Simon Pure when it comes to raisin' hell out in the territories!"

The younger men were laughing again, slapping each other and nodding.

"You remember the stories come out of Diablo Canyon? Before the UR-30 automaton got sent that way? Place was like a bandit's paradise, and Jesse James was king!"

"He was! He was! They say, before the metal marshal got turned loose on that burg, Jesse'd come an' go like a lord! Wasn't a workin' bank in the town, cuz'a he and his boys!"

"Bah, hobble your lip!" Another young marshal waved away that whole line of thought. "Jesse's yesterday's dime novel, boys! You heard about the scalps! Jesse don't hold a candle to Bil-- . . ." A look at the Wyatt brothers sitting blank-faced at the end of the table, then a quick resumption. "William Bonney, that's how he rides! Why, Jesse James is a coffee boiling flannel-mouth when you put him next to Bonney!"

"You ain't got nuthin' under yer hat but hair!" One of the young men stood up, fist on the table. "You gotta shut your shave tail, corn-cracker mouth! Jesse James'd— "

When the butt of Wyatt's massive pistol cracked against the surface of the table it sounded like an explosion in the small, close room. The heavy metal of the handle left a gauged scar in the surface, and every man, including Virgil, leapt up and stared at him. There was an array of emotions flaring in the eyes around the room that ran the gamut from angry to terrified. Most of the young men were deep into the terrified band.

"I see one of y'all smiling for Jesse James or any of these other yahoos, it'll be the last fool thing you do wearin' one of my stars. 'N the next thing you'll be doin' is sittin' in my calaboose for givin' aid and comfort to a confirmed enemy o' the people. Have I made myself crystal clear?"

The Over-marshal's voice was cold, his eyes blazing with radiant hatred. The younger men in the room could only nod as Virgil shook his head and resumed his seat.

"These men are nothin' but unreconstructed algerines, and they," he gestured out the back door to the rest of the town, "don't need us throwin' fuel on the fire of their so-called 'legends'. And as for Jesse James, the man's a foul little bully, a heartless killer, and an empty-headed blowhard playing to the gallery an' feeding off the gullibility of people too stupid to realize they're as much victims of him and his ego as any bank ever was."

Wyatt Earp's eyes were wild as he scanned the room, nostrils flaring. The young men, cowed back into their seats without a sound, could only nod again, eyes pinned to the Over-marshal in his red-faced fury. The robed man stared severely at the cowed youngsters.

Wyatt looked into each man's eyes before leaning back in his chair with a sharp nod. "I trust I won't have to speak on this again. I don't care how the gullible rubes out there feel about a man. Anyone who don't respect the law gets no respect from us. We've got to start reinin' in these bandits, show the people we mean it when we say we can keep 'em safe. First chance we get, we're gonna hit one of the big boys, and we're gonna hit 'em hard."

The Over-marshal reached out and picked up the wrinkled wireless report with a fist that shook with anger. "Jesse James is still the big bug as far as most folks are concerned, regardless of your little shindig here today, and especially if he was behind that boat job. You just know it was loaded with Treasury gold, too. He's been on the shoot the longest." He was calming down a little, and sat back into his chair, a thoughtful look on his face. "If we can put a spoke in his wheel, we can nail his legend to the counter and convince the rest of them to pull in their horns a bit."

Wyatt looked around the room again. Virgil was grinning around the stick in his mouth, but the younger men looked questioning; one of them even on the verge of speaking. The Over-marshal put up a single finger to forestall a potentially-career-ending gaff.

"Jesse was the mastermind behind the big train job that hit that first Union Heavy coming out of Kansas City for the border forts all those years ago. Before that, we had every bunko artist, four-flusher, hard case, and soaplock on the ropes, heeled with the army's castoffs. Not a one of them could stand against even the underpowered RJ-1027 weaponry we were getting' back then. But that all ended the day one man convinced every last knuck and road agent to band together and hit that supply train."

Wyatt's voice had lowered to a harsh whisper, and every man in the room bent closer to hear. "Ever since that day, every one of these low-lives has come at us armed with the heaviest tech around. They're wearin' the armor, they're packin' the guns, and they're ridin' stolen Iron Horses as free as they please." He waved a hand at the men, one of whom had opened his mouth to speak. "I know, they get a lot of their newest stuff from Carpathian now. But it was the plunder from that first job that gave them the stones to make a stand. Sure, they coppered their bets, they lit a shuck out from under James' shadow first chance they got. But it was him that sent them through the mill, put some iron in their spines, and set this all in motion. And you know and I know, they still come together to kick up a big row every now and then."

Wyatt stood up and stabbed each man there with a fiery glance. "Make no mistake, gentlemen, Jesse James is the root cause of almost every fallen marshal, sheriff, and deputy going on over a decade now. It don't matter if he's laying low now. Hell, he could be movin' to set up a homestead with some grass widow out in the prairie for all I know, an' I don't care. We take him down, we settle the score on hundreds of souls demandin' vengeance, we send a clear signal to the rest of those lawless bastards, and we take a big step towards cleanin' up the territories from this point onward."

He sat back down and held up the paper. "We have it on good authority that James is back in Kansas City. God alone knows how long he's been there. Probably tossin' back some tar water every night with the local mamby-pamby deadbeat sheriffs if they're anything like you lot, and couldn't be bothered to send in a report."

Wyatt cleared his throat and then spoke with the full weight of authority in his voice. "We're goin' down to Kansas City right now." He turned to the man in the leather robes. "Is yer Judgment wagon all set and ready to head out?"

The man nodded solemnly. "Fully fueled and armed. It's even got the new wireless unit packed away."

Wyatt grunted in satisfaction. "Good. We'll also want a full squadron o' Interceptors ready to go as soon as the afternoon takes the curse off out there. We're gonna need everyone we can take along, if we want to bring down Jesse James." He turned to Virgil. "We'll want to bring all four of the UR-30s." A look of discomfort passed over his face as he continued in a lower voice. "And we better let Morgan know as well."

Virgil nodded. "Might be time you rethought your decision not to deploy one or two into KC permanently." Virgil got up and moved to a battered sideboard to pour himself another cup of water. "They made good points when they first argued against it, but if they're failing to call in a report on a sightin' of the James 'n Younger boys, might be time we sent a metal man their way, watch over their shoulders?" The jug yielded a drop or two of lukewarm water. "Damnit. Provencher, get in here!"

The dark haired young marshal stuck his head in the door. "Sir?"

"Go across the street and get some more water from the Cosmopolitan, will you?" Virgil sat back down, gesturing to the sideboard with one casual hand.

"Sir? But . . . the front office . . . and . . . the heat . . . "

"You're makin' some fierce shirker-like noises there, Provencher." The elder Earp cocked a sardonic eyebrow at the miserable officer.

"Sir." The look Provencher shot the older man was ripe with frustration and resentment. As the front door banged shut with a dull sound, rendered flat beneath the heat, Virgil smiled at his brother.

"I'm tellin' you, Wyatt, that boy's hat's nine dollars and ninety five cents too big."

Chapter 3

The gentle swaying of the old horse, liberated from a republican couple too afraid to fight for him several days back, was lulling him to sleep again. The old wound, lack of food, and the hot sun blazing down all conspired against him, but they were old friends compared to the true enemy that sat behind his eyes, mocking his every breath. Defeat, cackling away at the lofty pride of man, rode with him everywhere now, and leached all the color out of the world.

The boy looked up suddenly. Something was not right. The old nag, the dusty Missouri road, even the heat of the sun beating down upon his high gray hat was all familiar to him. Too familiar, for he had never ridden this way before, and he had only stolen the horse a couple days ago. The taste of defeat, though, that was new. He had forgotten over the years how that had felt, how his heart had ached at every beat, knowing that everything he had loved and stood for was passing from the Earth.

The boy felt his chest, where some strange ghost of a memory told him he should find a still-tender wound, only recently healed. The wound that had put him on the sidelines of the great war's last moments, and stolen him from his brother's side just when he was needed the most. The wound was there, but the pain was dull, as if only half remembered, or much more healed than it should have been.

He looked around him, starting to grow wary. The occasional clumps of trees were familiar, although they swayed gently back and forth in a breeze that he did not feel. The split-rail fencing along one side of the road echoed similar images in his mind down to the last splinter or scuff. As the road rose up and curved down into a shallow valley, he somehow knew what he was going to see before the old horse had even topped the rise.

A group of men in faded blue uniforms sat on exhausted horses across the road, but they were all staring straight at him as if they had been waiting for his arrival. An officer was in front of the group, with a sergeant at his side, both smiling wicked smiles. This all seemed wrong, but the boy could not have explained why. He remembered the heartache; he felt the thirst, the exhaustion, the despair. But at the same time, he felt almost as if he were in a dancehall show, acting out a part for the amusement of some unseen audience.

"We been waiting for you, Jesse." The officer called, lifting his voice to carry over the wind in the trees. "You got something you want to say?"

The boy's eyes tightened. How did they know his name? They had not known his name. That last thought, carried through his mind as a whisper from the shadows, concerned him even more.

Who had not known his name?

Jesse shook his head and tried to think clearly. He was on his way home. The men before him, though hated and despised, representative of everything he loathed in the world, were the very men he was searching for. In a young life full of adventure and pain, he was trying to do the right thing, trying to offer his surrender to the men he hated most, so that he could return home and try to salvage what was left of his life.

"I want to surrender." Jesse tried to shout but his throat was dry and sore, and his chest was hurting worse now, as if the pain of his wound was intensifying with the thinking of it. He cleared his throat and tried again. "I want to surrender, like the flyers say."

The Union cavalrymen laughed among themselves, and the officer nodded over his shoulder to them, sharing in their joke.

"Not sure we're going to let you get away so easily, son." The man's face was twisted with hatred, looking less and less human with each passing moment.

This was all wrong. Jesse knew, on some deep, visceral level that he could not explain, that this was wrong. Those soldiers below were savage; they were fierce, but they were just men. They were tired and hungry, and they just wanted to go back to their own homes. It was not until—

"We know you're one of the savages that rode with Bill Anderson, one of those that killed Major Johnson and his entire command back at Centralia." The officer's face began to writhe, its color burning with rage.

Reality seemed to snap into place around Jesse, and he knew what was about to happen. The brave words that rose naturally to his lips died without breath, and he began to urge the old horse backwards up over the hill. He raised his hands, desperate to alter the scene, knowing that it was hopeless.

"Ain't no amnesty for savages like you, son. We only got one thing for you." The man who spoke looked like all the other soldiers, except that there seemed to be a flicker or reflection of red flame deep in his sunken eyes. The moment seemed to freeze in the young man's mind. Those eyes. Those eyes had haunted him for years. Wait . . . what did that mean, for years? He could not remember ever seeing them before! Except . . .

Jesse's head began to spin and he lowered his hands to the reins, desperately clinging to the worn leather, feeling their rough texture in his hands as he sawed them back and forth, trying not to fall. The old horse jerked beneath him.

The soldier with the flaring eyes turned to another and whispered something, his face twisted into a cruel grin.

Jesse, even as he swayed and shook on the horse's back, saw the flare of red pass from the one man to the next. The new man, listening with a harsh smirk of his own nodded once and brought his carbine up to his shoulder.

Something was wrong with the gun. He could see the blued metal, the worn wood, as if he were holding it in his hands. It was old, antique, without any of the gleaming dials or indicator lights of a modern weapon. The boy's brow wrinkled in confusion and fear. What had he meant by modern weapon?

The man with the fire in his eyes turned back to Jesse and nodded as they were old friends, his smile widening. "People die in war every day, Jesse. That's just the way it is."

When the carbine fired, it seemed to catch most of the cavalrymen by surprise. Horses shied and started, sending men pulling at their reins as the formation disintegrated.

But Jesse had no attention to spare on the milling, comedic scene. The bullet struck him right in the chest, as he knew it would. Bullet . . . not bolt. If it had been a crimson bolt he would be dead, but instead he was . . . what?

Jesse's world tilted with the impact. The bullet had slapped directly into the old wound, redoubling the pain but reassuring him in one way at least: he had already survived an identical wound. That got his mind to thinking further, what were the chances that the scruffy Union bluebelly, taking a snap shot from the back of a shying horse, would hit that exact same place?

Jesse felt himself lose his seat as the old horse slid sideways and down, frightened by the sudden blast and the smell of blood. The shifting saddle tossed Jesse off, spinning dully into the dust, his world shrinking to the flare of pain in his side. The fall seemed to take an eternity, however, and he began to notice that the world around him was again not behaving the way it should.

The trees behind him, lush and green a moment ago, now presented a kaleidoscope of browns and yellows to his spinning vision, the emeraldclarity fading before his shocked eyes, the trees wilting and withering away. The color of the sky deadened, the deep blue of the Missouri summer fading to the stark iron of a hot desert noon. Even the smells were changing, grass, mud, and dust giving way to a sterile, dry suffocating emptiness.

By the time Jesse hit the ground, landing on his wounded side, naturally, the entire world around him had changed. He found himself lying on the desiccated sands of an empty desert. There was no sign of the road he had travelled or the horse he had been riding. The trees were gone, the fence was gone, even the Union cavalrymen were gone, although one figure remained for a moment longer, the strange, smiling corporal with the burning eyes. And then, with a swirl of sand, even he was gone. Jesse was completely alone.

The boy looked down to his side where his hand was clutching at his blood-slick shirt. Something about his hand seemed wrong as well, but the pain flaring from the wound denied him the luxury for further analysis. He looked around, not understanding how he could be where he was, and yet, the pain from his wound, the dust in his eyes and throat, and the sun beating down upon his uncovered head were all undeniably real.

He shielded his eyes from the worst of the sun with one upraised hand, searching the horizon for any sign of help. The desert stretched away all around him, featureless and empty, for as far as he could see. Tears burned tracks through the dust on his cheeks and he tried to sit up, gasping as the wound was once again wrenched open, spilling more blood into the hot, dry air.

At the sound of his ragged breath he heard a harsh, hissing croak from nearby, his searching eyes found an enormous black vulture watching him with beady black eyes that flashed with a reflected crimson whenever it bobbed its head from side to side. The vile bird gave another croaking bark that sounded almost like laughter, and Jesse felt a burning desire to throttle the beast if only he could reach it.

With more effort than he had ever been called upon to make, Jesse first got one leg beneath him, then the other. Kneeling in the sand, he paused to catch his breath, hand once again pressed to the wound. He could feel the slick heat of his own blood on his fingers, and something about that bothered him more than he could have said. He flexed the other hand, looking down at it, trying to force his mind to focus, but there was nothing there but the dirty flesh of his own hand. For some reason, that was not right.

Jesse looked up again, casting his eyes all around for lack of anything else to do. This time, however, where before there had been nothing but the emptiness and the vicious bird staring arrogantly at him, an enormous structure now rose up into the burning sky behind him. With another grunt of effort, he pushed himself to his feet, blinking away the tears and the pain, and looked up at the mighty edifice. Even through the haze of his throbbing pain, Jesse could sense that the thing was ancient. Shaped like some kind of stepped pyramid, its sandstone construction was covered with strange symbols and carvings. It was like nothing he had seen before, and yet something about the place called to him. He could sense there was something inside, something that cried out to him. It was an ancient power that seemed to make his bones vibrate with its immediacy.

Not far away the vulture hopped away from him, hissing a harsh warning call.

Jesse ignored the bird and took a single step toward the structure, then stopped. The hand clamped to his side had tightened of its own volition, digging painfully into the wound and driving him to his knees with a bright new explosion of agony. The desert, the ancient pyramid, even the sun above disappeared in the blazing pain that drove him down, growing more intense as his hand continued to squeeze the tortured flesh. The boy stared down through fresh tears, desperate to understand what was happening. When he saw his hand, time froze once again. It was not his hand.

Jesse was staring at a sleek metal construct, all wheels and gears and pistons, tubes and cables and brass fittings. It was entirely alien, unknown to him, and with a mind of its own it dug deeper into his wound, driving upwards towards his heart. Jesse rushed to grab the alien hand with his other, and screamed in terror to see that this hand, too, was an artifact of steel, rubber, and brass. The second hand heeded his commands, however, and grasped the first, attempting to pull it away from the wound. The two arms struggled, causing even further pain as they mauled the injury, and Jesse howled up into the empty sky, his raw voice rippling out across the barren sands, the only reply the raucous call of the red-eyed vulture as it launched itself into the sky.

*****

Jesse James was fighting for his life. Something bound his limbs as he struggled, wrapped tightly around his sweat-slick torso as he thrashed in the parched darkness. His mind was a panicking blank, visions of empty deserts, grasping metal arms, and flaring red eyes swirling in his brain as he desperately wrestled with an unknown assailant.

"Jesse!" A voice called out to him, sounding far away. "Jesse, stop!"

The words did not sooth him, but rather drove him to greater effort. Stop? When some damned sonofabitch was trying to kill him? Not likely! He thrashed from side to side, trying to hold his attacker's arms back as he attempted to free his own.

His own arms.

The attacker's arms.

"Jesse, it was a bad dream!" The voice again, but this time it was barely a senseless whisper as he realized where he was, and what must have happened. Suddenly, his tense body relaxed, lungs still heaving from the struggle, but shoulders slumped in a mixture of resignation and relief. He was in his small attic room above the Arcadia Saloon in Kansas City, his body was wrapped in sheets drenched with his own sweat, and each hand firmly gripping the opposite forearm as tightly as the mechanical gears and servos would allow was his own.

Jesse forced his fingers to loosen their death-grip, wincing slightly as the rubber feedback pads on the inside of his grip peeled away from the hard metal of his forearm sheaths and pistons. He would not be surprised to see dents in the metal once he got a chance to inspect them in better light.

"Jesse, are you alright?" The voice was softer now, a mixture of concern and fear. "You were runnin' wild there for a little bit. Growlin', screamin' an' the like. Were you havin' a nightmare?"

Jesse smiled a bit despite his roiling mind. There was nothing like waking up to a woman's tender thoughts to set a man straight. He liked to fancy he knew more than most. He could just make out her shape on the other side of the bed, her skin glowing faintly from the ruby indicator lights along his arms and the spark from the bedside lamp's lowered element. But the fear in the girl's voice bothered him, and he reached out into the darkness in her direction.

"A humdinger of a nightmare, there Misty, an' no mistake." He tried to make his voice light, but even in his own ears he knew he was not entirely successful.

He felt the rubber pads graze the showgirl's bare shoulder; felt her shy away from the touch, and his face tightened in the gloom.

He and Misty had been an item since his posse had come to Kansas City a few months earlier. At first she had been just another girl, a roaring good time in a long line of similar experiences. A very pleasant byproduct of his fame, he found many women were drawn to the rougher crowd, and him in particular. Whether it was some instinct to save a bad man, change him, or more akin the fixation of the moth to the flame, the more a woman knew about his past, the easier it was for him to monopolize her time. And he had certainly been monopolizing Misty's. Women were fascinated by his arms, as well, mesmerized by their alien appearance, their hard metal armor, and the countless moving parts ticking away within. Thinking about his arms Jesse frowned again.

"Could you get a light, darlin'? I'm still a might jumpy." He unwound the sheet and settled it in a more comfortable position. Misty reached up to the lamp and turned the key, bringing the element up to a warm glow.

The illumination revealed a pretty face framed by wild honey brown hair falling in ringlets over her shoulders. She turned back to look at him with wide green eyes, and he tried not to notice the edge of fear that remained there, coloring the concern for him just enough that he could not ignore it.

"Baby, you were makin' the worst noises, an' your hands were smashin' against each other like you was workin' a forge right there in the bed!" Her gaze flickered down to the mechanical arms and the ember of fear burned a little brighter. "You sure you're okay?"

Jesse looked at her a moment, sheet pulled up tight beneath her chin despite the little garret's oppressive heat. He wanted to reach out and pull her into a hug, but he had no idea how she would react, given her fixation on his arms. With a frustrated sigh he spun his legs off the bed and reached down for the pair of denim pants he'd dropped there the night before.

"I'm fine. Just a dream is all. You twitch when you're sleepin', don'cha?" he looked over his shoulder at her while he fastened the pants. When she nodded, he nodded back.

"Well, this was the same thing. 'Cept my arms're tougher than yours, and harder, and make a lot more noise. Wasn't nothin'." He threw a shirt over his head as he rose and moved away from the bed.

"Jesse, I din't mean nothin' by it. I was just scared." She was scuttling down the bed now to sit at the foot, legs dangling over, eyes wide. "I din't mean to say nothin' 'bout your arms—"

Jesse felt the frustration and annoyance rising, and wanted to cut her off before she had his head spinning too fast for him to stop. He turned and held out the gleaming metal hands for her to get a good look.

"You mean these arms, Misty? Nothin' to worry 'bout, with these arms! Best tech money can buy, from anyone!" He gestured broadly with both arms as he danced towards her, a wide grin blossoming across his sharp features. As he moved the myriad gears, pistons, and counterweights moved with him, causing the various red lights to flash or dim with each movement.

"You know what these arms are capable of, honey." His smile turned a little sly. "You seen 'em drawin' a gun faster'n lightning, you seen 'em flippin' pasteboards at the gaming tables an' shootin' billiards to beat the band, and you din't seem to have any complaints about 'em last night, now, did you?"

He folded his arms in front of him, noting the play of pistons and gears beneath the bands of armor. The movement within was smooth and seamless, but he could not forget the sensations of the dream, or the waking nightmare of the two arms fighting against each other.

"Maybe I oughta go visit the doc though . . . " His words were soft, hesitation struggling against concern. "Just in case. Payson's a bit of a trek, but our gear's getting' worn anyway. 'Bout time we headed west for a bit."

"You gotta go to the doctor's baby?" She took a step towards him, and he smiled slightly at her concern. "We got doctors right here in Kansas City, you know."

"Nah. Talkin' about Carpathian; the ghoul who fixed me up with these arms. You ain't got no doctors like him 'round here, trust me. You'd know it from the smell." A shadow passed over his eyes and his nose twitched as if he had sensed something foul. He shook his head quickly and threw the dancer a wide smile.

Jesse swooped Misty up in the powerful arms and swung her around the room in a passable imitation of one of the moves he'd seen her perform with the other showgirls plenty of times before. She whooped in surprise as he picked her up and spun her around, a giggle escaping as her feet left the floor, kicking a little before they came to rest again. She held tightly to him after he had stopped spinning, and he tightened his grip, thankful that the episode seemed to be over.

"You got fine arms, Jesse, and no mistake. Ain't none of the local girls ain't jealous o' me, an' you know that." She spoke into the rough spun fabric of his shirt, arms tightening even further as if afraid he would disappear.

Jesse gently disentangled himself from the girl's arms with a grin and a laugh, but he turned away before she could get a good look at his face. Something about her sudden surrender bothered him, and he could not have said what it was. A moment ago he had been desperate to reinforce her affection for him, to distract her from her doubts and fears. And now that he had done just that, he could not shake a rising feeling of guilt.

Jesse moved to the bed and took his gun belt from the bedpost where he had hung it the night before. With quick, practiced motions he whipped the belt around his waist and fastened the buckle, leaning down to tie the leather thongs that would hold each holster in place. Out of habit he drew the hyper-velocity pistol riding on his left hip. His iron hand spun the weapon first forwards, then backwards, and then around in a flat horizontal spin around his trigger finger. The metal of the trigger guard clicked rhythmically against the metal of his finely articulated fingers.

Jesse stopped the gyrations of the pistol with a sharp clack as the pistol grip slapped into the feedback pad of his armored palm. He inspected the weapon quickly. The dull metal of the long, angular barrel thrust out from the cylinder of the RJ-1027 power core, which gleamed with the subdued crimson radiance of its constant standby setting. The enrichment cartridge, feeding from beneath the barrel, was fit snuggly in place, indicator light winking its own ruby reassurance.

Jesse flipped the weapon back into its holster with one studied motion. He would check the other later. He moved to the small window opposite the bed and pulled back a curtain to peer out at the street below.

Misty pouted. "You got yer smile, now yer just ridin' off, are you?" She did not try to hide the frustration rising in her voice.

Jesse kept looking out the window, giving no sign at all that he had heard her until he suddenly turned back into the room, his grin back in place, and shook his head.

"You gotta know, Misty, I ain't one to go givin' up what I taken off anyone." He swooped in for a quick kiss and then moved back to the bed, grabbing his heavy boots and dropping to the old mattress with a grunt.

"Where you goin? She wrapped the sheet tighter about herself and sat beside him. "It ain't barely light out yet! Ain't like no one's gonna be open for business at this hour."

Jesse gave a mighty pull with both of his mechanical hands and his foot slid smoothly into his boot. "Well, firstly, darlin', ain't like I much care what some shopkeeper's posted hours are, is it?" He grinned sideways at her before moving to slide on the other boot. "And secondly, ain't like I can go back to sleep now, that damned nightmare still rattlin' around in my skull. Frank an' Cole an' the gang're supposed to be comin' back in today, and I got an idea fer a job I wanna have lined up fer when they land."

Jesse rose once the other boot was on, planted a quick kiss on Misty's forehead, and moved back to the window.

"Frank don't like me." Her voice took on a sulking tone that set Jesse's eyes to rolling. "He don't!" she repeated, as if she could see through his head.

"That's just Frank. He's quiet, and smarter'n everybody in the room, an' no one knows it better 'n him." Jesse bent down to get a good view of the street. Misty was not wrong: it was too early for most civilized men to be up and about. The buildings lining the street were tall for the west, but then again, Kansas City was right on the edges of the territories. Not many lights twinkled in those windows, though, and the street itself would have been heavily shadowed if it were not for the lampposts rising out of the wooden sidewalks at regular intervals. The base of each was wide and fat, the glowing crimson telltales of RJ-1027 generators gleaming around them.

"Misty, you ever miss the ole' days?" Jesse's voice was soft for a moment, as his eyes focused on the winking red lights far below.

"What?" Her voice was muffled. "What ol' days?"

"You know," he gestured vaguely with his robotic arm at the street below. "Before RJ-1027 an' all this tech stuff. When a man on the road just had a normal gun by his side, and he knew the other guy only carried a gun the same kind. None o' these

Gatling cannons, or rocket pods, or Heavy Rails or Carpathian's monsters . . . Just seems sometimes like the world was a lot simpler back then."

"Well, I don' know about none o' them guns, an' I only ever heard o' Carpathian's craziness, but I don't remember ever playin' a house that didn't have RJ-1027 lights, or ridden in a horse-drawn cart instead of an auto-wagon run by one of them big motors. I reckon, for most of us, the world's a sight better with RJ-1027 than it used to be."

Jesse grunted. "How old you think I am, Misty?"

"I don't know, 'bout my age, prob'ly?" He gave a single harsh grunt of a laugh and her voice was tart as she continued. "You're changin' the subject. I know Frank's older'n you, an' I know he reckons he's smart, but that ain't it. He don't like me. Thinks I'm trouble." She was moving around behind him, most likely getting her own clothes on now that it was clear he was up for the day.

Jesse smiled and turned enough to watch her admiringly. "Well, you are trouble, ain't you, girl?"

She threw a small shoe at him and turned around to adjust her dress. "You got a lot of girls. I know that, Jesse, I ain't dumb. But your brother, he's thinkin' you been around KC too long, and he's blamin' me. I can tell."

Jesse was looking out the window again. The sky in the east was taking on a rough, almost burlap texture as rays of light reached into the west. The light gleamed off the massive glass and steel dome of the Heavy Rail station rising up above the buildings across the street. He imagined what sorts of technological treasures the trains pulling through that station were carrying west nearly every day and felt the feedback pads on his palms twitch.

"Misty," he turned and looked into her deep green eyes. "Frank and me, and the other guys too, I reckon, we seen a lot of people come and go. We seen a lot of friends die, or move on, or even get sick of our bilk and try to turn us in. This life we're leadin'? It's not always a happy one. Frank ain't tryin' to protect me from you, darlin', he's tryin' to protect you from all of us."

Jesse walked to the girl, now in a tight-fitting blue bodice and flowing yellow skirts, and hugged her to him once again. "An' when I'm not bein' selfish, I gotta say, I agree with him. There's paths that'll end much happier for the both of us, ain't got you an' me together on 'em, Misty." He kissed the top of her hair. "You deserve better'n I can give you, more security, and more o' my time. I just gotta grow up enough to let you go."

He held her out at arms' length, the mechanisms of the limbs whirring and clicking as he moved. His grin was back in full force. "But I ain't grown up yet, and I've had more opportunity than you'd guess from lookin' at me. So I'm thinkin', till I do grow up, you're stuck with me, whatever Frank says, or thinks, or feels."

She smiled up shyly at him and kissed him quickly. He ended the kiss first, pulling away from her before she had begun to loosen her own grip.

"I'm goin' over to the station, see what's comin' through over the next few days, an' see what I can hear 'round town. I reckon I'll be back downstairs in time for dinner." He moved towards the door, pulling his hat and coat off a hook on the wall. "You girls still playin' the Occidental?"

Misty nodded at his retreating back. "Yeah."

Jesse stopped in the doorway and flashed his gleaming teeth one more time. "Well, maybe, if Frank and Cole get back in, we'll swing by there, an' we'll see if we can't get Frank to loosen up a bit, eh?" With one last wink he let the door close behind him.

Jesse's heels snapped down the old, dry wood of the narrow hallway towards the steep stairs leading up from the saloon. As he walked he looked down at his arms, flexing the fingers and rotating the wrists. They seemed perfectly fine, but he could not throw off the memory of the two limbs struggling against each other in his dream. Or when he had awakened, he realized.

Jesse shook his head and tramped down the stairs, one hand lightly sliding along the old splintered rail, the feedback pads registering every nick and gnarl.

*****

Across the street two figures stood together in the darkness of a cheap room, the only illumination leaking in from the lighted window in the back of the Arcadia Saloon. They peered out at the window, watching carefully for any further sign of movement. A moment ago they had seen a shape look out the window, but there had been no movement since then, and they waited to see what would happen next.

"It's him?" A harsh voice with a northern accent asked.

"Yes. They were quite explicit. The arms and everything. It's him, and some woman." This voice was much higher than the man's, but still strong and heavy. A dusky contralto that matched well with the surroundings.

"I don't give a rat's ass about that damned gold shipment. They think he can lead us to the doctor?" There was doubt in the harsher voice, and the creaking of wooden furniture as the speaker sat down.

"Nothing else has worked, so they think this is at least worth a chance." The lighter voice moved off into the darkness. "And if it turns out he's got the stamped gold, we can pick him up on that, all the better." There was a pause, then a yawn. "I'm going to try to get a little some sleep. Wake me if anything interesting happens."

The heavy voice snorted. "Yeah, I'll do that. I just hope he doesn't do something stupid before we can see what he knows."

Across the street the light continued to burn softly, but nothing in the room moved.

Chapter 4

Jesse focused on the dusty road as it swept beneath the heavy weight of his Iron Horse. Scrub brush flew past on either side of the narrow track, and occasionally he could see the glittering surface of the Missouri River through the tracery of leaves off to his left. It felt good to be out on the trail again, away from the tall buildings and crowded streets of Kansas City.

The outlaw shot a glance to either side, nodding to the men riding there, their Iron Horses rumbling along beside his. He hid his clinging annoyance at Frank's refusal to participate in this latest job behind his ready grin. Frank had been mad enough to bite, and had not bothered to hide the fact from any of the other men. Cole Younger and his brothers had followed Frank's lead, as they usually did; leaving Jesse to ride out for the first time in months without any of the old gang beside him. It bothered him more than he was willing to admit, but he knew he could never show that to the men who had agreed to go with him.

Frank was angry, and Jesse knew he had had a good point. They had enough coin laid up in town; they did not need more right now. They had a good thing going in Kansas City, with most of the local law dogs fawning over them and everything the city had to offer laid out before them every night. Frank was also concerned that one of the damned marshals was eventually going to twig to their presence, and the whole lot of them would be on the run again. Frank was no slick city man, but he liked his comforts sure enough. He would not want to leave Kansas City until absolutely necessary.

Jesse had never been a creature of the city; he felt the call of no-man's land too strongly. He was most at home in the wild places, where a man defended himself, took what he wanted, and kept what he could. He felt the pull back into Missouri, to their old stomping grounds, and he had known he would not be able to deny himself that satisfaction much longer. And so he found himself roaring down an empty road accompanied by a posse he barely knew, but every one of which was desperate to earn himself a place in the legend of Jesse James. That brought a more natural gleam to the smile, and he settled back in his saddle, comfortable with his position, his decisions, and his life.

Frank had been upset when Jesse told him about the plan to take out the bank in Missouri City, a few miles down the river to the east. Missouri City had been a favorite target of theirs during the war, and most of the folks who had reestablished their businesses and their lives were still the same damned republicans that had been trying to lord over his family since before the first shots were fired. Although the coin would be welcome, this little trip was more about sweet revenge than anything else. When the young local back in Kansas City had mentioned the new bank going in down the river, it had seemed too perfect. When he had offered to lead Jesse James there, it was too good an opportunity to pass up.

Who needed Frank anyway? Or Cole and his damned family? These boys seemed plenty sturdy, and besides, it had been too long since he had tested himself under fire. If a man did not push himself every now and then, he went soft. And if a man went soft, someday someone would be coming up behind him when he least expected it, and that would be the end of that. And besides, since when did he ever need an excuse to take a chunk from some hayseed republican?

"Hey, Jesse!" The local boy, riding a borrowed Iron Horse at the rear of the group, called out over the growl of the engines. "You think we could stop for a bit?"

The boy had been getting steadier on his mount all day, although things had gotten off to a shaky start in the morning when he had almost knocked Harding off his feet. He was still swaying a bit from side to side like most new riders, getting used to balancing on the cushion of thickened air that the vehicles rode on, but he was doing alright.

"You need a piss already?" Harding, just ahead of the local, sneered over his shoulder from behind wide, blue-tinged goggles. "We ain't on some church outin', boy!"

The younger man frowned, glancing quickly between Jesse and the other outlaw while still trying to keep an eye on the road ahead. They had not slowed down during the exchange, and he was obviously not entirely sure in his seat.

"No!" His voice was firm. "I just gotta walk this off for a sec is all. Feel free to piss if you need to, though, Harding!" There was just enough attitude in that to get the rest of the men grinning, and Harding's hands tightened on the control handles of the Iron Horse, revving the engine and tearing off up the road ahead. The reddish flame licking out from the drive nozzle lengthened as he worked the engine, red lights flaring along its flanks.

Jesse smiled and nodded to the young man. "Sure, Ty, we can take a bit of a break. I could stand to get a drink myself, maybe take a few steps."

The rest of the men nodded in agreement, as they always did, and the party pulled off into a small clearing, the wide river rushing by not far away. Each vehicle gave a quick, angry snarl as the engine was cut, and then sank deeply into the soft ground beneath the trees. The men swung their legs up and away from the saddles with easy grace. Ty nearly mirrored them before the heel of his boot caught on the pummel and almost spilled him into the dirt, but he caught himself, grinning openly at the rest of the men.

"Ty, you're gonna have to get better with that thing if you wanna stick around with us." Another outlaw, Gage, shook his head with a quick laugh. "I wouldn't wanna be seen dead with you in public right now, the way you swing that machine all over the road like the worst kind o' greenhorn."

"Not bad for your first time out, though." Jesse hefted a canteen and took a healthy slug before throwing it to another man. "Although I gotta say, you keep ridin' Harding that way, only gonna be room for one of you in this gang, before long."

Ty shrugged as he stood beside his borrowed mount, clearly unconcerned. "Harding'll do what Harding'll do, an' I can't worry myself about it either way. 'Sides, I'm not here to ride with Harding."

Jesse laughed and almost missed the canteen being lobbed back to him. "Kid, you sure do have some balls, and no mistake. If you're right about this bank, and you don't embarrass us all when the penny drops, I think we might just have a 'Horse you can call your very own when we get back to KC."

Ty nodded in calm agreement. "That's the plan, Jesse. An' you can trust me about this bank. My cousin lives in Missouri City, and she was just sayin' last week that all the folks there were chipper as hell to be gettin' their own savings and loan. The reserves were supposed to be delivered by yesterday, so we should be all set for a mighty withdrawal today, don't you worry."

One of the older men coughed, and then looked sideways at Jesse. "Jesse, you mind if I ask again, how come Frank and them ain't comin' along?"

Jesse's eyes grew cold and he shook his head. "Frank's tired, Chase. He din't wanna go rushin' out after he just got back from bein' away."

"Um, okay." Chase nodded. "But . . . the Youngers?"

Jesse whirled on the other man, one hand floating by the butt of a hyper-velocity pistol. "You wanna ride with my brother and the Youngers, Chase? Or you wanna rid ewith me?"

Chase put his hands up and took a step back. "With you, o' course, Jesse! With you! Those other guys, they're coffee boilers next to you! No joke!"

Most of the other men were nodding fiercely, some glaring at Chase for even bringing the question up. Jesse shrugged, slapped the other man on the shoulder, and moved back towards his 'Horse. "They're tired, boys, an' I ain't. That's what it comes down to."

Most of the men chuckled at that, and everything calmed down. Jesse shook his head and turned around to shove the canteen back into his saddle bag. The rest of the men were leaning against their mounts, smoking quirleys. The blue-tinged coils of smoke from the home-made cigarillos were pungent in the clear country air. Two of the men had wandered back towards the road, watching for Harding's return.

"Jesse, you been doin' this for a while, huh?" Ty rested his hands on the worn leather of his saddle, straight arms supporting him as he leaned across to look at the outlaw leader. "Like, I remember hearin' stories of you back before I was hip-high to a horny toad, an' my daddy, he said there'd been stories goin' for years back to when he was little. I was mighty surprised when I met you. You don't look too much older'n me!"

Jesse shrugged. "A man's as old as he feels, kid. An' I feel pretty damned good." He grinned at the other men.

"Man, Jesse, me an' the other kids when we was growin' up, weren't a one of us didn't dream of ridin' with you someday, and look at me!" He gave the saddle a hard slap. "I'm the one who made it!"

"Well, we'll see, kid. Don't get your hopes up. Ain't no tellin' how you'll act once you've seen the elephant." Jesse tipped his hat back a little bit with one metal finger. "Some folks just ain't cut out for the sharp edge. No way of knowin' till you're there."

Ty shook his head. "Nope, this is for me. You ridin' wherever you want, not havin' to listen to nobody, takin' what you want whenever you want it! And the girls! Man, you guys have all the luck with the womenfolk! A kid like me? I can't even get a girl to so much as look at me by wavin' a greenback in her face!"

One of the other men barked a sharp laugh at that. "Kid, you don't wanna go judgin' how much action the rest of us get by watchin' Jesse here. He sort of has a reputation for that sort of thing that belongs to him all alone."

"Ah, keep a hold o' yer jealousy, Chase, kid don't need to hear that." But Jesse's smile was wide as he continued. "Hell, we all got talents we're born with, right? Besides, just because you lot o' trolls can't get a lady to look at you twice, ain't no reason to make the kid here feel like he'll live a life as empty of a lady's affection as you all."

Chase snorted. "Well, you don't seem to be makin' the rounds as fast as you once did neither, old man." The two men returning from the road laughed at that. "All the time you been spendin' with that new sweetheart dancin' girl, half the ladies of KC are pinin' away every night."

"An' so you'd think that'd make it easier for you boys to sweep 'em off their feet while they're distracted, yeah?" Jesse laughed. "But instead, ya'll just end up cryin' into yer joy juice come closin' time every night."

The men laughed good-naturedly, one of them scuffing at the dirt with a heavy boot. But Ty looked far more intense, watching Jesse's face with a steady eye. "She's a beauty, though, that Misty

Mimms. Half Kansas City's been in love with her for years, and they fall all over again every night. But you're the one she comes back to, eh, Jesse?"

Jesse nodded with an open smile. "Reckon she does seem smitten, now that you mention it."

"She must have a soft spot for rough n' ready boys, I guess." Ty smiled, but the expression seemed vaguely predatory.

Jesse's face stilled slightly. "Whataya mean, Ty?" He stood up straighter, and the rest of the men quieted, looking from one to the other.

Ty shook his head as if clearing it, his smile showing genuine again. "Oh, just that she was spendin' a lot of time with Bill Bonney a year or so back. Now, it's almost like she's workin' up a collection."

Jesse looked sour for a moment. "Misty used to walk with the Kid?"

Ty's face loosened in thought for a moment, then tightened with concern. "Um, yeah. I wouldn't guess it was nothin', Jesse. He ain't been near KC in almost a year."

Jesse's eyes grew unfocused for a moment, his mechanical hands tightening as he turned to look out through the trees and over the slowly rolling waters of the Missouri. The men exchanged looks with each other, none sure what they should do.

When Jesse turned back around he gave the young man a quick glance, then swung back up into his saddle. The Iron Horse gave out a throaty growl as he kicked it to life. It lifted up onto its cushion of thick air, wind tearing at the men still standing around him.

"I'm sure it ain't nothin' either, Ty." He pulled his red-tinged goggles down over his eyes. "Let's head out. Missouri City ain't that far away, and we want to get there before Harding decides to go in without us."

He gunned the 'Horse and sent it spinning in a tight circle back towards the road. The men reached for their hats as they jumped into their own saddles, the roaring of motors rising as each iron beast was thrashed back into life.

Ty was the last to jump onto his borrowed steed, watching as Jesse led the way back to the road. His face was blank as he mounted with casual grace, but his eyes, perhaps reflecting the flaring engine wash from the machines ahead of him, glowed crimson as they tightened slightly in amusement.

*****

Jesse pulled his Iron Horse up to where Harding sat, his machine idling roughly in the middle of the road. They were on the crest of a hill overlooking a bend in the Missouri River, and on the other side of the slowly moving water they could see the quiet collection of buildings that marked the center of Missouri City. Men and women, tiny in the distance, moved among the buildings, going about their daily business blissfully unaware of the gathering on the ridge above them.

Jesse stared down for a moment and then cast around looking for Ty. The young man, swerving slightly as he approached, pulled his 'Horse up beside the outlaw leader with a slight jerk and a quick exclamation of concern.

"Easy, Ty, don' wanna lose you this close to the bank!" Jesse reached out one hand, metal gleaming dully in the flashing sun, and grabbed the boy with a solid, steadying grip. Ty nodded his appreciation with an embarrassed grin.

Once the younger man was steady in his saddle, Jesse rocked back onto his own machine and rested his armored forearms across the control panel. He gestured down the hill with a jerk of his chin. "Which one's the bank, kid? They had to pretty much rebuild the whole town since the last time we was through, so it all looks new to me." His grin was wide and warm.

"Well, Jesse," Ty pointed towards the center of the cluster of buildings. "That there, the white one? That's the Missouri City Savings and Loan."

The men scanned the town, several using stolen Union monoculars bulky with RJ-1027 enhancements. Gage grunted once and passed his heavy piece of equipment to Jesse who immediately raised it to his eye and made some minor adjustments. He wished he had Frank with him once again. Frank's long-scoped rifle, Sophie, had the best optics he had ever seen. If anyone could twig to a law dog ambush from afar it was Frank and that damned gun of his.

Within the view of the monocular, the little burg of Missouri City sprang up at him out of a swirling confusion of colors. He panned the machine from one side of town to the other, trying to decipher from the shaky images what sort of opposition they might encounter if they made a direct run in. Beneath the dull blue of the monocular's bulk, Jesse's smile widened even more.

Not even half the buildings below them were sporting RJ-1027 generators, which was unusual for a town this far east. Most of the generators he could see, of course, were the bulky units being produced back in Washington and distributed through the government offices. There were a few of Carpathian's more streamlined pieces, but it was clear, even from the ridge across the river, that Missouri City was nothing but a bunch of mudsills; probably still holding a torch for old Emperor Lincoln, martyred to his unholy cause all those years ago. Jesse's smile widened just a little bit at the thought.

"I'm not seein' any law, Jesse." Chase muttered. "No sign of any 'o them UR-30 statue-men, neither."

Ty nodded, looking from one outlaw to the other. "No, it's like I told you, Jesse; ain't no real law in Missouri City right now. They's got a sheriff, but he don't like that new-fangled marshal's gang they put together over in Tombstone. He's an ornery old guy, and might not even be around on a day like today! He spends a lot of time riding between here and KC."

Jesse continued to move the monocular around the town, smiling widely. He was hoping someone was going to put up a fuss. Last time they had ridden through this way, Missouri City had been nothing but filthy turncoat republicans, and the James gang had charged the entire town a heavy price for that lack of loyalty. Today, itching for some action and annoyed by his brother's absence, Jesse was hoping for an excuse to burn the whole damned place to the ground.

One of the men behind Jesse murmured to another while they waited for him to formulate a plan. "D'you hear about Billy down Yuma way? I heard they claimed bounty on over a fifty injun scalps!"

"Nah, I heard it was more like ahun'erd," Harding, arms crossed, muttered over his shoulder. "He ain't no blowhard, Billy the Kid. I run with him a few times. He ain't no flannel-mouthed city slicker."

"I don't know, Harding." The first man said. "A hundred braves? That seems like it'd be an awful lot, even for the Kid."

"He ain't no blowhard," Harding repeated.

Jesse's grin faded slightly, his teeth grinding together before he realized it. He quickly relaxed his jaw, gave his head a quick shake, and continued to scan the town below.

Beside the outlaw leader, Ty watched, from the corner of his eye, and seemed to take satisfaction in the minute motion.

"Boys," Jesse lowered the instrument and gestured with it at the town. "Ain't time to be shootin' yer mouths off about the Kid with such a ripe peach waitin' to be plucked down yonder. Everybody loosen those holsters an' have the rifles at the ready. I don't much think today's a day for slow'n easy." The smile was back and the men responded to it with vicious smirks of their own.

"Now, you boys remember back when we used to have to worry about things like fords and bridges?" He looked around him with a laugh, but most of the men looked blankly back at him. Some shook their heads slightly. It seemed to take the wind out of Jesse's sails a bit, and his shoulders slumped.

"Would you wanna try to cross that river on horseback, without a bridge, you bunch of shavetail croakers?" He flicked the monocular downward again before tossing it to Gage in frustration.

"Forget it, let's just get down there and do some damage, eh?" He revved the mighty engine of his 'Horse, sending crimson flames flaring from the drive nozzle. He stood tall in his saddle, leaned his weight forward, and the machine tilted its nose downward. The rest of the gang followed quickly as he tore down the hill in a plume of choking dust. Even over the roaring of the motors he could hear the rebel yells of the men behind him, and Jesse's smile came back full force.

Jesse was hunched behind the control console of his Iron Horse when he took the machine off the road and aimed it directly at the glittering river ahead. When he hit the bank, a geyser of green water flashed up all around, sparkling in the sun and sending rainbow prisms dancing behind him. Each of the other outlaws crashed through the falling curtain of mist, their own plumes exploding out around them. To the men and women on the waterfront across the way, it appeared as if an enormous cloud had suddenly erupted from the far bank, rushing towards them like a vicious storm front. Ruby flashes from within marked the flickering afterburn of the engines and the pulsing lights of the RJ-1027 modules along their flanks.

The townsfolk stood staring numbly as the rushing wall of vapor rolled towards them, and Jesse, soaked to the skin by the roiling moisture, grinned evilly. He crouched down lower, peering ahead through the swirling crimson-stained chaos of his goggles. He could just make out the shapes of the people on the waterfront, and so he tilted his body slightly, bringing his center of balance over and throwing up a high white rooster tail of foam. The roar of his motor rose an octave as he gunned it towards a gap in the crowd.

Jesse's 'Horse threw up a bow-wave of churning water, flashing fish, and shredded vegetation as it erupted out of the river and onto the dry bank. The surge of muddy water broke the spell that held the crowd in thrall, and they began to run inland shouting and screaming. Jesse laughed as he pulled one of his hyper-velocity pistols and fired over the heads of the fleeing crowd. The shattering blasts struck against the walls of waterfront buildings and set small, vicious fire. .The crowd scrambled even faster, covering their heads with desperately up-flung arms.

Jesse took one quick glance over his shoulder and then gunned the 'Horse again, tearing between two buildings and forcing the stragglers in the fleeing mob to dive out of the way. One fat old man was too slow and the outlaw nudged him aside with the nose of the vehicle. Jesse hooted as the poor old muggins fell into the dirt, arms wind milling wildly.

Behind Jesse, the rest of the gang roared down the alley. Two of the boys revved up the Gatling guns on their machines and sent sheets of crimson bolts sleeting out after the fleeing townsfolk. Buildings detonated in red fury, sending burning chunks of wood, masonry, and shingling sailing into the air. A pair of rockets sailed down the street on twinned lines of white exhaust, punching through the front wall of a small two story business and exploding within. Fire and debris crashed back out through every door and window, while the chimney coughed up a column of dark smoke and then collapse d into the building.

Jesse gave an invigorated whoop of his own as he saw the building collapse in on itself, sending a plume of dust and smoke into the clear blue sky overhead.

Within the confines of the town center, the roar of the Iron Horses was nearly deafening. The terrified men and women were gone, still fleeing out the other side of town and into the hills, but horror-stricken eyes stared from many darkened windows as the outlaws slashed through town, their thunderous machines throwing up gouts of dirt and dust as they slid to a stop in front a neat, trim building sporting a freshly-painted sign, "Missouri City Savings and Loan."

Jesse leapt from the saddle and landed in a slight crouch, pulling his other custom pistol and scanning the surrounding buildings for targets. Most of the outlaws were quick to follow him, but two brought their mounts around to cover the approaches down either side of the street with Gatling guns still glowing from recent use.

"Okay, boys, just like we planned it!" Jesse did not even try to hide his wild grin. The rest of the gang, especially young Ty, were smirking and wild-eyed themselves. Jesse knew the feeling well, and he welcomed it. "Harding, you and Chase watch the street, any sign of one of them metal men, you give the signal and the rest of us'll come runnin'. Any sign of the sheriff, you start shootin', and we'll finish up our business right quick an' join you."

He turned to look at Ty, standing nearby and eagerly shifting his weight from foot to foot. "Ty, you come with me, the rest of you, follow behind and back my play. Ain't no need to end any of these folks today less'n they get ornery, but I'm in no mood to back down neither, so if you see me light one up, you consider it open season on dirty rat mudsills, and we'll start keepin' score."

The men nodded eagerly and Jesse turned back towards the building. He could just make out some movement from within, the windows now coated in the dust from the Iron Horses still rumbling in the street. He leapt up onto the raised walkway, his heels cracking against the fresh wood, and moved towards the doors. His duster flared behind him with the speed of his excitement.

The doors to the bank yielded immediately to the first savage kick, the wood crashing inward as the hinges gave way. Both doors fell off to the side with a clatter that caused the people within to cry out. The sight of the men in the door, brandishing RJ-1027 weapons and faces snarling beneath the dust of the road, set the entire crowd surging away. The mob did not stop until they were pressed to the wall, hands in the air. Some glared in anger, but most were terrified, emitting a low moaning sound heavy with fear and despair.

Jesse walked straight into the bank, noting quickly the folks huddled along the walls to either side, and lifted an unlit quirley to his grinning lips.

"Howdy, folks! This ain't gonna take but a second, and I'd be right obliged if you'd just do as I ask, no one playin' hero 'r nothin'." He lifted one heat gun to the end of his cheroot and lit it with a blast that cracked into the ceiling, leaving a scorched ring of shattered plaster and wood.

Jesse and his boys crowded into the room. Jesse lowered his pistols casually, grinning widely at the terrified clerks behind their barred windows. The rest of his men took up positions behind him, covering the small group of customers cowering against the side walls.

"Okay, boys and girls, let me explain real quick how this is goin' to play out. Ya'll know me," Jesse spun his two pistols in quick spirals around his articulated metal hands with smooth, deceptively slow movements. Silvered elements beneath the dull armor glinted in the bright bulbs overhead. Jesse smiled even wider, teeth clenched around the cigarillo.

"Ya'll know you're dealin' with Jesse James, and ya'll know this ain't my first visit to your little burg." He gestured with one hyper-velocity weapon at a grizzled old man crouched in the corner. "Hell, grandpa here probably remembers it his own self, don'cha, grandpa!"

The old man cringed, his head lowered.

"So," Jesse holstered one of his pistols and gestured vaguely towards the clerks. 'Less'n ya'll are plannin' on hidin' behind those bars all day long, I'm thinkin' we need to start passin' yer cash on through, so's my boys here can help themselves and we can be on our way before any of these nice folks out here start crampin' up."

The clerks stared, only the tops of their heads visible through the barred windows. They did not so much as blink, and Jesse's smile slipped with annoyance as they failed to move.

"Maybe you din't hear me, Billy Yank." He walked quickly towards the window and tapped heavily on the bar with the barrel of a gun. "Less'n you want me to decorate that back wall there with what you spent your life holdin' yer ears apart with, I wanna start seein' greenbacks flyin' through this window."

"Get down, ya little coot!" One of Jesse's boys rushed forward, a modified rifle gripped tightly in both hands, barrel jabbing towards a man staring up from the floor. Jesse's eyes never left the clerk's as his free hand flew to his holster, drew his second pistol, and brought it unerringly up at the face of the man on the floor.

"You gettin' some unhealthy ideas, Lincolnite?" The words were soft, all vestiges of Jesse's smile worn completely away.

The man raised his hands over his head, stammered out an apology, and scuttled backward through the crowd until his back was pressed up against a wall.

"My patience is peter'n out, folks. Now, if you don't get a wiggle on and start pushin' some coin our way, I'm about to kick up a row the likes o' which this bug hill ain't never seen before." Jesse's voice was low and even, his eyes flat as he stared through the bars.

"Sure thing, sir!" The blonde clerk nodded suddenly. "Sorry, sir." The top of the man's head began to bob as he reached beneath the counter, coming up with sheaves of cash that he pushed through the bars. He jerked his head, eyes wild, at the other clerk, but the man merely stood dumbfounded, unable to move.

"Alrighty, lads," Jesse tossed over his shoulder, eyes and pistol still on the moving clerk. "Why don't you all see what sort of financial support the kind folks of Missouri City would like to donate to the cause while our friend here empties the drawers?"

The gang started to move towards the crowd, stabbing barrels at folks moving too slow for their tastes. Watches, wads of cash, and jewelry were handed over and the outlaws grinned wider and wider as their pockets filled. The clerk, working under Jesse's calm direction, had begun to shove the cash into a bag he had grabbed from behind the counter. Several bags lay nearby, already bulging with money.

"Ty, any sign of the law dog out in the street?"

The young man was standing by one of the doors, a pistol clenched in one hand. He peeked out the small window and shook his head. "Can't see no one, Jesse."

Jesse's smile was slowly coming back and he began to toss stuffed bags at the men who had returned to the door. He spit the soggy cigarette onto the floor and gestured with his chin at a pin on the collar of a sullen man crouching nearby.

"Ty, scoop me that little broach on yonder Zu-Zu, will ya? I seen one o' them before, an' I been meanin' to pick one up."

The young man moved quickly while the man's face went through several painful contortions, blurring from terrified to indignant and back again faster than the naked eye could follow. In the end he merely sat completely still as the young outlaw reached down and yanked the pin out, tearing the cloth.

Ty looked at the little object quizzically then shrugged. "Some old guy's head?"

Jesse nodded, tossed the last bag of cash to one of the waiting men, and crossed the room, one of his mechanical hands outstretched. "You said it, Ty. Some old guy's head." He took the small token and held it up the light. "Howdy, Abe!"

If Jesse had been paying closer attention to the men and women on the floor he would have noticed the dark looks and shifting glances. His men were no more attentive, laughing as the legendary outlaw made an ironic leg as if bowing to a great man.

"Gentlemen, I give you the original big bug himself, Abraham Lincoln! Of course, in this partic'lar rendition, he's got a bit more head than the esteemed man himself currently sports . . . " With a chuckle Jesse moved to slip the pin into a watch pocket. As he looked down to the small opening the pin's original owner made his move.

"You southron knuck!" The man was rising from the pile of cowering civilians, a small enhanced pistol appearing in his hand. "Get your freak hands off that pin! You're not fit to lay a finger on—"

Jesse's face hardened as time slowed around him. The pin fell from his hand, tumbling end over end towards the hard wooden floor as the leather duster flared out with the outlaw's spin. The hyper-velocity pistol, already skinned, came up in a smooth arc as its twin seemed to leap out of its holster into his other hand. Across the small room eyes widened in horror, mouths dropped down to scream. The man with the holdout shooting iron tried desperately to bring his weapon up, but there was a look in his eye that Jesse had seen many times before; he knew he was dead, but the day just had not caught up to him yet.

As Jesse's muzzles settled on the man's head he snarled, "tell 'im I said 'hi'." With slow deliberation he pulled the triggers.

The crimson flashes from the two pistols snapped out as if reaching for the man's face. For a split second Jesse's world narrowed to focus solely on the man's eyes. Did they flash red for a brief moment? Was that just a reflection of the muzzle flashes in his terror-wide eyes? Was the man actually smiling?

The dual shots crashed into the man's head simultaneously. His entire upper body splashed backwards, showering the cowering townsfolk with gore. The murmurings and cries rose to a fevered pitch.

Time stopped. Jesse felt as if he had eternity to study the scene before him. The cringing men and women now dripping blood and viscera, the tellers diving behind their wall, the outlaws arrayed behind him, weapons half-raised to threaten the room. Blood drops glistened in the artificial light, hanging in the air like tiny balloons. Through it all, Jesse could not shake the memory of red eyes smiling at him before the face disappeared forever.

When time resumed, it did so with the deafening crack of gunfire erupting all around. Bolts of red energy slashed into the wall as the bank's unlucky customers flattened themselves on the floor. The blonde teller rose up behind his window holding a massive hand cannon, its muzzle gaping darkly.

"Die, you bastard!" Jesse's eyes widened as a cloud of crimson-edged smoke billowed out of the giant weapon, reaching out for him like a creature out of a nightmare.

With a grunt, Jesse hit the hard floor, the ravening blast roaring over him. He reached out with both of his pistols, blasting holes in the wall at knee height. A scream rose over the ringing in his ears and a confused jumble of movement flashed from the window as the gun-slinging teller went down.

Jesse leapt up, his anger high, and stalked towards the window, his right arm outstretched, his pistol slapping bolt after bolt through the bars. The far room was a chaotic confusion of debris and smoke, flames spreading out over the wall and across the floor.

"Jesse, we gotta go!" Someone shouted from the door. Jesse glanced back and was shocked to see three of his men down, bodies torn and lying in a spreading pool of blood.

"Damnit." Jesse looked up at the iron frame holding the bars. Teeth flashing in a snarl, he raised both pistols, mechanical thumbs flicking a small switch on each pistol grip. Both weapons flared crimson for a moment and then launched a beam of solid, furious heat through the bars. The metal kissed directly by the light simply ceased to exist, while the remaining bars and the frame itself sagged in place, the molten ends burning with eerie blue flames. The entire metal structure collapsed backwards into the teller's room.

Jesse stepped up to the window and leaned inside, one armored limb rising to shield his face from the heat. The two tellers were cowering in a corner, the blonde whimpering as he held a shredded leg with red-stained hands.

"Looks like it ain't my day to die, chiseler." He put one shot into the blond man's head without warning, then swept the pistol over to point at the other man. Just as the targeting blade settled on his forehead, however, the gun bucked beneath his hand and blasted a hole in the wall behind him. Jesse growled, looking down at his hand and the weapon, and shook his head.

"Well, if that don't take the rag off." He shook his head. "Someone up there shinin' on you, Jonah." He looked around at the building, its walls now fully engulfed in red-tinged flames. "You might wanna light a shuck before whoever it is loses interest."

He spit a heavy wad into the furnace heat and turned back towards the door. One of his pistols slid quickly into its holster as he bent down to grab a bag of cash.

"Get the rest of it." Jesse growled under his breath as he swept out the door.

The outlaw jumped onto his rumbling Iron Horse, his face set in grim lines of discontent. The excitement and the joy were gone, drained from him as if someone had burst a water skin. He turned to Ty as he and another man stumbled from the burning building loaded down with heavy bags.

"Ty, you get on Lyndon's machine, he ain't gonna be needin' it no more." Jesse drew one of his custom pistols and riddled the engine on Ty's borrowed mount before the young man could answer. "Chase, take care of the others before we skedaddle. We ain't leavin' nothin' behind these mudsills could get a lick o' use out of."

Jesse gunned his 'Horse in a tight circle, throwing out a wave of dirt and dust that rattled off surrounding walls and windows. He headed back towards the river without looking back, leaving his surviving men standing in the street watching his retreating back. As he leaned into a tight turn and disappeared from view, Chase turned to Ty with a shrug.

"He don't take kind to folks shootin' at him, 'specially in a loser burg like this." The big man cupped one hand around his mouth and yelled into the burning bank. "You folks know what's good for you, you'll sit pretty 'till you can't hear us no more! Believe you me, that fire's a lot less scary than you come out and meet up with an ornery Jesse James!"

Ty smiled with a sharp edge. He hopped up onto his new machine as if he'd been born into its saddle. The Iron Horse slid smoothly beneath him as he pushed it backwards into the street, bringing its forward cowling into line with the bank. Behind him, he could hear Chase slapping several bolts into the dead men's vehicles. Ty was not thinking about those rusty old hulks, however. He was bringing his new machine into line with the bank, where shadows were moving against the rising flames inside, the people trapped within gathering up the courage to emerge despite Chase's warning.

When the massive Gatling cannons on Ty's Iron Horse began to fire, Chase and the other outlaws ducked and skittered away, startled by the furious hammering after the fight had long gone out of the men and women trapped in the bank. Chase and Harding looked on in disbelief as the young man pumped bolt after bolt into the building, shattering the front wall, blasting the glass from the windows, and slaughtering the terrified, helpless men and women within.

"What in the name of Heaven are you doin', boy?" Harding raced to Ty and pushed him hard back into his seat, forcing his hands from the weapon controls. "You gone loco?" His eyes were wild as he screamed, gesturing behind him at the devastated building with one clawing hand.

Ty's face was twisted in a savage grin. "Well, somebody's gotta watch out for the big man's name, eh? Jesse's obviously too tired to care, but he's got a reputation, and we can't let him sully that, am I right?" He was breathing heavily as if he had just run a long way.

The rest of the outlaws stared at the bank as the upper floor collapsed into the inferno below, the blasted first floor now unable to support its weight. There were no more screams emerging from within.

Chase looked back at the young man, the light of the blaze reflecting redly in the young man's eyes.

"Damn, son, you are the very devil himself."

Ty erupted in a moment of laughter as if Chase had just said something particularly funny, then gunned his 'Horse around and roared after Jesse James.

Chase looked back to Harding and the other men, all scrambling now for their own mounts, knowing that they needed to escape before the townsfolk realized exactly what had been done. Chase shook his head in disbelief.

"The devil himself!"

Chapter 5

"Jesse, I swear to God." The older man sitting across from him in the Arcadia Saloon looked disgusted, his face twisted with frustration and contempt. "They're sayin' more'n twenty people died in that fire! You have any idea what kind of red flag that'll wave in front of the law? They can't ignore somethin' like that! Even the tame ones round hereabouts can't turn a blind eye to that kind of body count! An' after all that gold went missin'?"

Jesse stared into his whiskey glass with a scowl. "Twenty little coots, Frank. World's better off without 'em. Asides—"

"Asides nothin', Jesse!" Frank slapped the rough table with an open hand. His custom-scoped long rifle, Sophie, shifted slightly where it rested against his chair. At the tables around them men and women looked up quickly before turning back to their own business.

On either side of Frank sat Cole Younger and his brother Bob. Both men stared hard at Jesse, hands resting loosely on the table in front of them, empty glasses resting forgotten nearby. Cole's jaw worked slowly as he shifted a large wad of chaw from one side to the other and back again.

"Don't matter if they were the entire Lincoln family, Jesse! The law just can't ignore somethin' like that! What were you thinkin'? We got plenty of scratch, I told you we didn't need another job so soon!" Frank leaned back in his chair, gesturing for his brother to speak as if inviting a child to expand on stellar navigation.

"I told you, Frank, I wasn't there." Jesse glared and leaned towards his older brother, mechanical arms folded before him. His voice was a menacing whisper as he continued. "An' you don't dare dress me down like this, Frank. Not in front of the Youngers, an' not in front of nobody. I'm still leadin' this gang o' pie-eatin' knucks, and I won't stand for tryin' to dry gulch me here in the middle o' the day."

Frank waved the threat off as if it were an annoying fly. "I don't give half a rat's ass what you are gonna or ain't gonna stand for, Jesse. We all told you, that Missouri City job was a bad one. We had a good thing goin' here! An' we're gonna have to leave sooner rather than later now, 'less you were itchin' to decorate that sweet set o' gallows they got erected down by the waterfront?"

Cole Younger snorted and spat a wad of dark juice near a spittoon not far away. "I'm figurin' the law'll be followin' us as we leave, too, so's my brothers'n I, we're not too keen on the whole situation. Jim and John'r gettin' supplies together so we can light out of here quick as you please, soon as you two stop yer dancin'. "

Jesse picked up his whiskey with the faint ring of metal on glass and knocked back the rest of the amber liquid inside. "You an' yer brothers've been lookin' for an excuse to get outa KC since we got here, Cole. Don't play like you ain't been holdin' the same hand since the beginnin'."

"I don' see you rushin' out California-way, eager to hang a hat in that ratty little camp where your father coughed out his last breath, eh Jesse?" Bob Younger, his face pale, leaned towards the outlaw leader, his elbow resting on his knee. "Our daddy was done for in this very town, not half a mile from where you're sittin' there grinnin'. Gunned down by a rat bastard group o' Billy Yanks as he was walkin' in the street!"

The young man stood and sneered down at Jesse, whose eyes were focused entirely on his own brother. "So yeah, if we're not gonna shed no tears over those uppity Zu-Zus over in Missouri City, don't expect us to be throwin' you a parade, with you getting' all promiscuous with the tech and violence, neither. My brothers'n me, we ain't comfortable here in the city where they killed our pa, and no mistake. But we stuck with you, and we won't leave 'till it's time." He reached down for his glass and kicked back the contents with a jerky motion. "An' thanks to you and those shavetails you brought with you, I think I hear a clock tickin' while we sit here bendin' our elbows and catchin' flies."

The glass came down on the table with a crack and the young man stormed off, pushing past several people on his way to the door.

Frank and Jesse were completely still, eyes locked on each other as if there were not another soul for miles. Cole Younger sat back for a few moments pushing the tobacco around his mouth, then stood up, shaking his head.

"You two are a hoot, you know that?" He knocked his own glass over with the slow, deliberate motion of a single finger and then grinned at the two brothers. "When you two're done dancin', we might wanna think about ponying up and headin' west, maybe?" He chuckled once and moved towards the door. As he came up to the doorway he stopped, gesturing grandly for an attractive brunette to enter. As she swept past he looked over to see Jesse James watching out of the corner of his eye. Cole's grin widened, he waggled his eyebrows meaningfully with a jerk of his head towards the new comer, and slipped out the door, pushing past a large, finely-dressed man trying to enter at the same time.

"I'm sorry, Jesse, but you and those greenhorns have knocked this whole caper into a cocked hat, and no mistake." He leaned towards his brother again, his voice low and earnest. " You gotta see we can't stick around here. We gotta not be here when the law gets around to doin' its job again, Jesse, and there just ain't two ways about that."

Jesse sighed with a mixture of anger and resignation. "I din't mean for any of that to happen down river, Frank, you know that. We was just gonna rough 'em up a bit, ruin their day, you know?" He shook his head. "But those damned yahoos, they never know when to quit! Next thing you know, the bolts 'r flyin', we got folks droppin' on both sides, and everyone's got their blood up somethin' fierce. An' then, when Ty let fly with his Gatlings, and I wasn't even there to see."

"Ty, he the young local scrub, convinced you it'd be an easy mark in the first place?"

Jesse nodded, but his eyes were now tracking something across the room, moving behind Frank and into the region of gaming tables in the corner. "Yeah. Nice enough kid, for all that's the freshest fish you ever met in your life."

Frank looked skeptical. "Fresh fish? To hear Chase 'r Harding tell it, he's the coldest soaplock who never sucked an ice chip."

Jesse shook his head, his eyes still looking past his brother's shoulder. "Naw, he's a quiet kid, didn't know what he was getting' into. Just went a little salty in the moment, is all."

A shadow passed over the younger man's face. Jesse looked back down at his arms for a moment, turning the hands over against the table. "'N Frank . . . my arms . . ."

Frank cocked his head. "Yeah? What about 'em?"

Jesse shook his head tapped a rapid staccato rhythm on the table, his eyes drifting back over his brother's shoulder. "Nah, never mind. It was nothin'."

Frank nodded, his expression thoughtful. "Whatever you say, brother. They're your arms, after all. Or at least, they are now." He leaned back a little bit, watching his brother speculatively for a moment before asking, "Jesse, you gonna tell me what you're lookin' at, that's got your eyes just about ready to pop from your skull? I ain't got one of them metal marshals comin' up on me or nothin' have I?"

Jesse shook his head and gestured with his chin as he sat back. "No, just some swell, all dressed up in widow's tackle. Looks like he's got a right pretty friend, though."

Frank shrugged and turned his head just enough to get a glimpse out of the corner of his eye. Sure enough, there was a man in a very expensive-looking suit sitting down to one of the gaming tables. The man's face was hard, the stub of a cigar hanging from one side of his mouth, nodding to the other players as he took a seat at the table.

Behind the man in the fancy gear stood a stunning brunette in a fancy dress that revealed almost as much as it concealed. Her fine features were distant and uncaring as she scanned the room, as if she could not find a single item of interest within sight. Her smile was radiant as she nodded to the men around the table, however, obviously having been introduced by her companion, leaning down to allow each man to take her hand in turn, and laughing at some remark one of the men must have made.

"Damned dirty dude trick, that." Jesse snarled.

Frank turned back from assessing the newcomers and shot his brother a questioning look. "Trick?"

Jesse nodded and gestured back towards the gaming tables with a flip of one mechanical hand. "Card sharp like that comes in with a looker on his arm, and she's all smiles and light from word one? Yeah. She's there to distract the other players, scoop 'em into throwin' their money away, and the fella cuttin' a swell there, he'll pick it all up." He shook his head again. "Damned dirty trick."

Frank muscled his chair around so he could get a better view, and then settled back as if he were watching a wrestling match or a horseshoe tournament. He stretched out his long legs, crossing them casually at the ankles, and folded his arms across his chest with an appreciative smile.

"Well, if I ain't got no coin ridin' on it, guess I can just enjoy the view, eh?" Frank's grin widened even more.

Jesse watched as the cards were dealt around the table in the corner, the men settling back, fanning their hands and watching their opponents. He noticed the eyes constantly flicking towards the tall beauty standing behind the fancy-pants, and watched as she smiled and winked at each man as if he were the only one in the room.

"Damn, but I'd be forkin' over every cent in my pocket before the first hand was up." Jesse shook his head. "Frank, I'm goin' to get a beer before we head on over to the Occidental. You want one?"

Frank's face soured. "The Occidental? What're we doin', headin' over to the Occidental? Your lil' bed warmer dancin' tonight? I seen about enough o' her as I need to see, thank'ee." He grinned again and indicated the woman in the corner with his chin. "'Sides, your poor Misty don't hold a candle to that sweet thing over yonder. And I ain't getting' any closer to either one'o them, so's I might as well stay right here and enjoy the view."

Jesse scowled as he stood. "You're a right bastard and no mistake. You want a beer, or don'tcha?"

Frank smiled benignly up at his younger brother and nodded smoothly. "Why I do believe I would, brother, thank'ee kindly."

Jesse was muttering under his breath as he worked his way through the tables to the bar along the back of the saloon. He flashed two fingers at the harried looking bartender and then set his elbows against the wood with a hard thump. His head sank down towards his crossed wrists and slowly rocked back and forth in vague puzzlement.

"Those are some fancy pieces of jewelry you got there, mister." The voice was a soft contralto that sent a shiver up his spine, and Jesse snapped upright, turning quickly around.

The woman who had come in with the card sharp was standing behind him, her full lips pursed in a mischievous smile. Her deep brown eyes flickered down to his mechanical arms again and then back up into his, one delicate eyebrow arched questioningly.

Jesse felt his old grin sweep across his face without conscious thought and brought his hands up between them, turning them back and forth, looking down as if seeing them for the first time.

"You talkin' about my arms, darlin'?" He smiled even wider as he looked back into her eyes. "Most advanced tech you're goin' to find in the territories, little lady. Ain't nothin' these arms can't do, and that is a verifiable fact."

Jesse plucked a silver dollar from a pocket and held in up in front of the woman. The coin popped up onto his knuckles as if it was alive, and then began to dance back and forth across them as the fingers beneath rippled back and forth like waves on a burnished steel ocean. The coin bounced towards his thumb, which flashed out, sending it springing up into the air where the other hand swooped across, catching it with a faint click.

Jesse cocked an eyebrow at the woman as he slipped the silver dollar back into his pocket. "Did I tell ya? Ain't nothin' these arms can't do."

The woman smiled slyly at him, tilting her head down slightly and pushing her bare shoulder towards him in a faint mockery of self-defense. "Maybe you'll get a chance to show me just what those arms can do sometime?"

Jesse's smile widened immensely, threatening to reach right around and meet on the back of his head. In a moment, however, his look became tinged with doubt. His head moved back a bit, cocked to one side, and the intensity of his smile lowered slightly, but a deeper appreciation dawned in his eyes.

"Damn, but you're good, missy." He shook his head at her and leaned back against the bar, his elbows striking with a muffled thump. His entire demeanor was more relaxed, and his smile was easy.

The woman, too, seemed to sense a shift in the mood, and smiled more openly, mischief still glittering in her eyes. "Whatever are you about, Mr. James?"

Genuine pleasure washed over Jesse. "So, you know me, then?"

She reached out with one small hand and rested it on his shoulder. "Oh, please, Mr. James. As far as I've heard tell, there is only one singular pair of arms in the entire world like your own. And after that bravura performance with the coin, I could, of course, have no doubt!"

Jesse nodded, casting his gaze over the crowded room affecting a vague indifference. "Well, you've got me dead to rights, miss."

The woman gracefully slipped into a bar stool beside the famous outlaw, her hand never moving from his shoulder. "From what I hear, sir, that does not happen very often."

Jesse snorted, turning to face her. "You'd be surprised. Here, you've got me at somethin' of a disadvantage, miss. You know me, but I don't know you at all. Please tell me a girl as pretty as you's got a name just as handsome?"

She smiled again, her eyes never wavering from his. "My friends call me Lucy, Mr. James."

"Lucy . . . yeah, that'd do it." He nodded to the bartender as the man placed two glasses beside him, and pushed the silver dollar across the bar. "Oh, where are my manners! Would you like something, Miss Lucy?"

She smiled wider, but there was a canny edge, as if she'd caught him at some game. "No, thank you, Mr. James. I've my own means." She leaned across the bar and snapped a quick order that Jesse could not quite make out. When she turned back to him, she was smiling openly again. "Where were we, Mr. James?"

"Please, call me Jesse. Mr. James passed on a long time ago, and I don't have any thoughts o' followin' him for a long time to come."

Lucy looked concerned, her hand drifting from his shoulder to the back of one metal hand. "Oh, I'm sorry . . . Jesse."

He looked down at her hand for a moment, then shrugged. "No, it ain't nothin'. He passed on a long time ago. Plenty of time to recover from that particular heart ache."

"There have been others?" She leaned closer to him, giving him her complete, undivided attention.

Jesse retreated slightly from her. "Well, sure. You ain't livin' if you ain't bleedin', as they say."

She frowned slightly. "That strikes me as rather a dark way to live, Mr. James – I mean Jesse. Aren't there any other times you feel alive than when you're bleeding?"

He shook his head. "There's plenty of times I'm happy I'm not bleedin', Miss Lucy, but there been lots of folks through the years taught me real good that those times don't last, an' I'll be bleedin' again soon."

It seemed as if all pretense had fallen from Lucy's face, and she looked at him with clear eyes. "So you live every moment expecting violence to engulf your world? That seems like a very sad way to move through life."

Jesse barked a short laugh, shaking her head. "Lady, if you'd seen half of what I'd seen, you'd know there ain't no other way. I was sixteen when I was wounded in the war— "

She held up one smooth finger. "Wait, you fought in the war? The war between the states? I would never have thought you were old enough!"

His smile faltered and began to fade as he continued speaking. "Well, I'm aging well, let's say. And I was young. Joined up with the raiders when I was younger'n I was supposed to be. Got myself shot towards the end, spent the last few months of the war laid up in a bed recuperating from the wound. Eventually, I went home. I'd seen the flyers, promises of amnesty and forgiveness if you'd just give your word to the degenerate turncoats that had inherited the late great state of Missouri. On my way to give my parole, the bastards shot me, again, and left me for dead."

A warm concern wrinkled her brow and she leaned towards him again. "Shot you right where you stood? Without a warning?"

"Well, I was sittin' on a horse, but yeah, shot me without a warnin'." His grin came back, causing years to drop from his face. "'Course, I been a right thorn in the Union's side ever since, and no mistake. Next time one of them blue-bellies gets the drop on me, you can be sure they ain't goin' to half ass the job, neither!"

There was venom in his voice as he finished, and a crease appeared between Lucy's beautiful eyes. "You hate them."

"Northerners? Hell, miss, I ain't alone in hating those high-brow Yanks, not even in a burg as ignorant as this one is. There's plenty of folks holdin' a torch for those old northern states, waitin' for the day."

Lucy sat back in her stool, regarding him calmly, but with no warmth. "You truly hate them."

Jesse turned fully around to face her, taking both of her hands in his metallic grasp. "Let's not beat the devil around the stump, miss. I hate them. I hate everythin' the Yanks stand for. I hate what they done to my family, I hate what they done to my friends, and I hate what they done to my home and my way o' life." His voice got lower and lower, more of a growl than a speech, and his eyes bore into her own with an intensity that seemed to rattle her.

"I hate their high-handed way of dealin' with folks they don't agree with, an' I hate the way they'll stomp all over anyone who gets in their way."

Lucy put up a hand to stall his diatribe. "But that's the government, the military. Surely you can't blame the men and women of –"

"They vote up there in the north, Miss Lucy?" His face was twisted with loathing.

"I beg your pardon?" The apparent shift in topic had caught her flat footed.

"They vote up there, in those states we're talkin' about, right? Vote for their mayors, an' for their governors, for their senators an' for their dog catchers? They vote for their president, Miss Lucy?" The anger was building again.

"Well, to answer that last question, no, Mr. James, they do not vote for their presidents. As any school child knows, there hasn't been a presidential election since the assassination of . . . President Lincoln. President Johnson's held the post ever since. Congress declared a state of emergency over a decade ago, imposing martial law and all the rest . . . "

Jesse waved her response away. "I know all that, but you get my point. Those folks that sit in their little log cabins, those folks who you say are innocent? They're the ones voted in the men who sent those other men after me on that road all those years ago, shot me in the chest and left me for dead. Robbed my family of their means of support and left us to fend for ourselves. Gunned down my friends' pa in the streets of this very city. So no, Miss Lucy, I am sorry to say I do not hold out any warm feelin's for the innocent civilians of the northern states."

She stared at him for a moment before responding, "that's why you rob banks and such? For revenge?"

He laughed once again, and again the darkness fled before the humor and good-nature in his eyes, as if the cold killer staring out from them had never been. "Well, I rob banks 'cause I like money, and I got a right nasty aversion to honest work, Miss Lucy, to be honest. But do I take special pleasure in hitting a republican when I can? You better believe it!"

She shook her head sadly. "And does that bring you peace, Jesse? Attacking and stealing from men and women who had nothing to do with what was done to you?"

His own demeanor turned cold. "M'am, ain't nothin' brings me peace, but yeah, knockin' a mudsill republican on the head every now and then, yeah, that brings a smile to my face."

"You realize that will never bring any of those people you lost back? The way of life you're talking about, that went away a long time ago, and was fading long before the first shot was fired at Fort Sumter. You can't give your life meaning by striking out at people who had nothing to do with that. Are the men and women you ride with any better than the people you terrorize?"

He stared at her for a moment, blinking as if waking up from a hypnotic state. But when he spoke, his words were calm and clear. "Have you ever tried living off revenge?"

She stared into his eyes, her gaze not wavering at all as she answered without hesitation. "Yes. It brought me nothing but pain."

That brought Jesse up short for a moment. In the end, though, his old familiar smile returned. "Well, I find it suits me just fine. Just because a fine filly can't live off a fresh kill, Miss Lucy, don't mean that it ain't good for a mountain lion."

She looked at him for a long time without speaking. There was an almost imperceptible shaking of her head, and an almost unnoticeable hint of pity in her eyes. She reached towards him and he leaned away, his smile faltering slightly. But she reached past him, taking up two tall glasses that had been set on the bar beyond.

"I'm being summoned, Mr. James. This was . . . enlightening, to say the least." Her amazing smile flashed once again, and all of the tangled emotions running rampant through his chest eased immediately. But before he could think to make one final statement, she was gone, weaving her way gracefully back through the crowd towards the gaming tables. He could not help but notice every man's eyes following her as she past. He snorted, shook his head, and grabbed his own beers off the bar, moving back towards where his brother still sat, unmoving, an appreciative grin still firmly fixed in place.

"Damn," Frank said as he sat up and grabbed one of the beers. He tilted it towards where Lucy was handing her friend a glass, once again charming the men at his table. "D'you ever notice, the way they move when they put their mind to it?"

Jesse grunted as he sat heavily back into his own chair. "What?"

Frank gave a chuckle. "Women! When they put their minds to it, they move unlike anything you've ever seen before! All the parts moving in so many different direction all at once, and yet it gets them right to where they're going, and you can't take your eyes off 'em!" He made a face as he knocked back a slug of his beer. "Damn, Jesse, you couldn't of taken a second to run this over? Tastes like two week old mule piss and it's flatter'n a cow flap in August!"

Jesse's forehead was furrowed in thought and frustration as he settled back in his seat. He did not spare his brother the briefest glance. His eyes were fixated on the gaming corner, where Lucy was smiling and laughing at the players around the table as her dour companion, all but ignored in the glow of her beauty, proceeded to once again drag handfuls of cash back to his corner of the table.

His voice was vague and without force as he muttered, "shut up and drink your mule piss, you bastard."

*****

The streets of Kansas City were nearly empty as the roaring growl of Iron Horses swept up the waterfront from the west and into the center of town. It was a large gang, and the townsfolk could tell from the poorly-maintained vehicles and the wild variations in clothing, that despite the massive weaponry mounted on the 'Horses, this was no military unit coming in on leave.

William Bonney, known to most folks as Billy the Kid, rode at the head of the gang, his back straight, his smile carefree, and his kerchief whipping along behind him. He nodded mockingly to various men and women as he passed, reveling in the fearful looks and angry glares this earned him. He knew that if he wanted to take the time to circle back around, not a single man who had glared at him would have the sand to back it up. He smiled even more widely.

Billy throttled back his machine to allow the men just behind him to catch up.

"Now, don't forget, we're just here to talk!" He shouted over the reverberant rumble of the engines. "You know Jesse don't like to be baited in his own lair, and word has it he's been here in KC long enough, he's bound to be feelin' like he owns the place."

The men who could hear him nodded. Many of them had ridden with Jesse James in the past. It was inevitable in the fluid structure of loyalties and alliances that connected the various outlaw bands together. But as was often the case with Jesse James, the more a man knew him, who was not riding in his inner circle, the less he trusted him.

"We gotta approach this delicate like, okay? We come up on him like we're on the shoot, that's what we're gonna get." Billy shook a bag he held in his right hand. "And this ain't the time to be stirrin' up trouble amongst our own selves. There's too much ridin' on this, and Jesse'll make it all a whole lot easier if he's ridin' with us . . . for now, anyway." He grinned wickedly to the rest of the men, and they snickered and nodded their heads.

"Okay, so when we go in, I just want Smiley and Garrett with me. All the rest of you, go find somewhere to spend whatever coin you've got left, 'till I need you. I don't think Jesse'll want to start any trouble here even if he's of an ornery mind. But just in case, I don't want ya'll too far away, you got me?"

The men nodded, and in twos and threes the Iron Horses began to peel away from the formation in search of their various amusements until called upon. Two men stuck with outlaw leader, one greasy and obese with the flat, dead eyes of a snake, the other a pleasantly nondescript young man with a mean-looking gun slung over his shoulder.

Billy looked up at the buildings as they slid by on either side. "Word is he's staying up on Independence." He peered up at the signs, noting the wildly diverse types of architecture that helped make Kansas City one of the largest burgs in the west. Brick three story businesses stood beside the rough and ready timber construction of frontier settlements across territories. And everywhere, there was the red glimmer of RJ-1027 generators supplying power to nearly every building. He had not been in Kansas City for more years than he could remember, and he knew it was going to take a while for him to find Jesse, wherever he had dug himself into.

*****

Lucinda Loveless, assassin and secret agent for the president of the United States, wove through the crowd in the Arcadia Saloon holding two drinks high and smiling at every man who looked her way. Damn, she hated this role. When her partner, Henry Courtright, had suggested they assume the guise of a gambler and his professional girl, she had argued against it. But the situation in Kansas City was quite fluid. The dynamic energy of a frontier city clung to the place despite its more refined façade and the power and prestige of the Heavy Rail hub station. In the end, although she hated playing to the crowds like this, she had failed to come up with anything with an equal chance of success, and so here she was, smiling until her jaw ached and carrying drinks to Courtright. It only made it worse, knowing that he loved it.

"Well, gentlemen," Courtright was blurring his accent a bit, hiding its deep northern roots behind a slight twang that seemed to recall the Carolina coast more than anywhere else. He leaned back in his chair, one elbow thrown over the back, raking in the pot with his other hand. "I'm amenable to a cessation of hostilities until you can replenish your funds, if you are willing?" He smiled a rare smile that seemed more of a challenge than a friendly gesture, and the men around the table looked grim and uncertain. Grim and uncertain, that was, until Lucinda came gliding up behind Courtright and gently placed a drink at his elbow. She swirled around to stand beside him, her smile bright and her eyes shining. The men, instantly changing their attitude as she sailed back into the picture, were all smiles as well.

"Well, sir," one older gentlemen said, his eyes never leaving Lucinda's neckline. "It's right neighborly of you to give us the pleasure of a further game." He looked back up to meet Courtright's eyes without any awareness that he'd been staring. "Shall we say a quarter of an hour before we reconvene?"

Courtright smiled again at the rest of the men. Lucinda noticed that several of the smiles her return had solicited faltered slightly at the prospect of continued play.

"It is so nice of ya'll to make us feel welcome, boys." She leaned over slightly to pick up a few coins from Courtright's pile, pretending not to notice the effect it had on the other men. She straightened and then slowly walked around the table. "I wouldn't want you all to go dry while you prepare yourselves for valiant combat once again, and I so do want to watch more of your game! So, please, take back some of Henry's ill-gotten gains for a drink on us, to replenish your strength for the renewed battle." With a smile she pressed a coin into each man's hands, being sure to maintain the contact with a lingering motion for each. It was as if she were casting a spell, and each and every one of them were following her with their eyes, dumb smiles on their faces, when she returned to stand beside Courtright once again.

The men stared at her, dumbstruck, and nodded slightly to the cadence of her voice. "Now, boys, you go do whatever it is you have to do, so you and Henry can continue this fascinating ritual in, what did you say, Mr. Stanfield? A quarter of an hour?"

The distinguished older man took her hand and bowed low over it. "Indeed, young lady. More than enough time to prepare for another skirmish with your imposing companion, but far too much time to be away from your radiant beauty."

The others nodded rapdily, and then followed Stanfield away, muttering to themselves. Lucinda could not quite make out what they were discussing, but it seemed to involve the source of the capital for their next attempt.

"I hope you're planning on filing a report for that money." Lucinda sat down beside Courtright. Her hand rested teasingly on his shoulder, her face was bright with open admiration and warmth, but her voice was coldly amused.

"For what they pay us?" Courtright leaned closer, his northern accent seeping through. "They can raise taxes, if they need more cash." He flicked his eyes towards the table where the James boys still sat, trying not to stare at Lucinda now that the game had broken up. "That them?"

Lucinda laughed as if her companion had made a hilarious remark, tapping him lightly with the hand on his shoulder. Her voice, however, was still cold, and she leaned in close, pitching her response beneath the room's general chatter. "With those arms? Who the hell else would it be? I swear, Courtright, sometimes it feels like I have to do all the thinking around here."

He smiled wickedly at her and flicked a golden coin up in the air in front of her. She jerked back slightly but caught it readily enough with her off hand. "Buy yourself somethin' pretty, little lady. And you don't worry your lovely little noggin about the deeper thoughts."

She let a bit of her sour response leak through her kept-woman demeanor before smiling brightly at him again. "Keep it up, you'll be waking one night missing a party or two I know you, anyway, look upon as essential. I know where you sleep."

He snorted and tossed back half his drink. He grimaced at the taste. "Christ, Luce, what'd you do, sit on this for an hour?"

She kissed him fondly on the cheek, eyes twinkling. "You got complaints," she whispered, "get your own damned drink next time. Now, what are we going to do about the James boys?"

Courtright looked over at the back table again with a speculative eye. "Well, we think those were Coles we bumped into on the way in, right?"

She nodded, easing back into her own chair and taking a delicate sip of her drink. It was clearly an effort for her not to react visibly to the taste.

"Well, if both the James boys are here, and at least two of the Younger brothers, then that means they're probably all here. Did you get anything out of him about Carpathian?"

Lucinda shook her head. "No."

Courtright looked at her sharply. "No? He didn't say anything about the old man?"

She shrugged. "I didn't ask." There was a sharp edge of guilt beneath her response. Usually she was much better at getting the information she needed from a mark, but she had somehow lost her way while talking with Jesse James.

"You didn't ask?" Courtright sat back and stared at her in dismay. Coming back to himself he looked around and then leaned back towards the table. "You were over there for God knows how long, Luce, and you didn't bring up the one thing that brought us here in the first place?"

She shrugged again, trying to hide her embarrassment. "It didn't come up."

Courtright leaned back in his chair and stared at Lucinda speculatively. "Hmmm," was his only response a moment later.

"What do you mean, 'hmmm'?" Her eyes were now flinty, and she leaned forward in a way that could easily have been seen as threatening.

He waved it off. "Nothing. You're going to have to go back and talk to him again, though, you realize that, right? I mean, we didn't come all this way to stop off for a quick flirtation before getting back to the real job, you know."

The anger in her eyes flared. "I was not flirting. Understanding what makes that man tick could open up the whole outlaw organization to us. I don't have to explain to you what that would mean to all our efforts out here, do I?"

He put his hands up in mock surrender, shaking his head but smiling still. "Hey, hey! I was just having fun with you. You're a professional, I get it. Laying the ground work, it's all standard. No problem." He lowered his hands to pick up his drink, thought better of it, and folded them before him on the table. "That doesn't change the fact that you have to go back over there and talk to him some more, however. We have to find out where the damned doctor is, or the president will have our hides."

She nodded, looking down at her own hands, sneering slightly at the paint and polish that adorned her nails like some common dancehall girl. "I'm giving him a few minutes to miss me, then I'll go back in. Is that damned brother of his still at the table?"

Courtright glanced back and then nodded. "Yeah. Can't keep his eyes off you either." He smiled slyly again. "Looks like you may just have bagged yourself two James boys for the price of one." The smile faltered. "Now go and bag us a doctor."

Lucinda shook her head faintly. With a look her partner could not interpret, she stood again. Anyone who did not know her would have missed the transition from resigned acceptance to graceful playfulness as she rose. She gave Courtright one last look and then turned on one high heel, swaying her way back through the crowded tables towards Jesse James.

As she moved through the crowd she reflected on why she had been so distracted with the outlaw in their first encounter. It had certainly been a strange path that had brought them together here in this filthy little dive in Kansas City.

She saw Jesse watching her approach. He had been watching her since she rose, she realized, and summoned her most alluring smile. She glided up to the outlaw's table and indicated a chair beside him. "Mind if I have a seat, Mr. James?"

The older brother, Frank, jumped up and pulled back the chair for her. "Certainly, miss! Glad to have you!" He gave her a bright smile of his own as he settled back into his chair. "Might I say, you have certainly brightened the premises of this poor establishment today?"

She caught Jesse giving his brother a dark look and wondered if it was jealousy or just annoyance at his forward older brother.

"Ain't you got someplace you gotta be, Frank?" the sour tone matched the look, and Lucinda smiled a little more genuinely to think that it might just be a tinge of jealousy after all.

Frank looked at his brother, his smile slipping a little, before he shook himself, smiled even wider, this time equal parts charm and amusement, and stood with a nod. "Certainly do, little brother. Gotta see a man about a horse."

Frank James nodded at Lucinda and took her hand, glancing at his brother with a grin before gently brushing the back of it with his lips. "You don't tucker the lad out now, little lady. He's got work he's gotta do." He stood back up and gave his brother a glance that Lucinda could not interpret, but it had a dark edge. "Don't forget what we were talkin' 'bout, Jesse. We got pressin' business that ain't gonna press any less the longer we hang about KC."

Frank lifted the elegantly-scoped long rifle from where it rested against his chair and began to walk away and then turned, a downright vicious glint in his smile. "Oh, and remember, we're all meetin' up at the Occidental for the show. Wouldn't want to disappoint Misty, right?" With a quick chuckle, he turned again and was gone.

"Misty?" Lucinda pretended to be unaware of the name.

Jesse shot his brother's back a dark look, shaking his own head in disbelief. He looked back at Lucinda. "A girl. Frank's just shootin' his mouth off again. He does that a lot."

Lucinda nodded. For some reason, the fact that he had not identified Misty more clearly annoyed her.

"So, what brings you back to my table, Ms. Lucy?" His smile was back as he leaned into his chair in a relaxed pose. His eyes flicked over to the gaming table where Courtright was organizing his winnings with a slight smile of his own.

"Well, I just wanted to talk some more, and my . . . friend," she nodded over her shoulder to the gaming tables, "won't be needing my help for awhile."

Jesse smiled at that. "Friend. That's rich. Tell me, you get a cut of his take? Or does he just pay you a flat fee? Or maybe you do it for true love?" His voice was a little bitter, and she decided she needed to go forward with a little more caution.

"It's purely a business relationship, I assure you, Mr. James." She tried to put a little chill into her words to convince him he had wandered close to a line.

Jesse smiled again. "Well, ain't nothin' stoppin' a lady from conductin' her own business, that's for sure."

Lucinda's shock at his words caught her by surprise. She made a show of lowering herself into a chair, masking the momentary lapse with another smile. Haunting words from her unhappy childhood rang in her ears. It had not been pleasant, after he farther was killed at the Petersburg siege. Her mother, bitter and resentful, had tried to fill the gaping hole he had left behind with alcohol and a succession of gentlemen callers who made the house a living hell for little Lucy. She had escaped as soon as she could make her own way, and had struggled against perception and expectation as much as any other obstacles as she established herself in one of the most competitive arenas in the world. She brought herself quickly to the present and shook her head slightly.

"Well, back in Georgia, it's not everyone that shares your view, Mr. James."

He smiled wider. "Georgia! I thought you was a bit of a peach, miss. An' I believe I asked you to call me Jesse?"

Lucinda lowered her eyes demurely, trying to reestablish her equilibrium. "Of course, Jesse."

"So, Georgia. Well, you can't feel none too charitable towards the Union either, then, can you? After what Grant and his pet pyromaniac did to Atlanta?"

Lucinda shrugged. "That was a long time ago. If you want, we can trace every little grudge back to Cain and Abel, and just all kill each other and leave it to the birds and lizards. Does that sound about right?"

Jesse stared at her without responded, then laughed. "Yeah, we could do that. But Cain and Abel, that was a powerful long time ago. Atlanta, that seems a tad closer. When you lost as many folks as I did—"

"You're not the only one who lost folks, Jesse." The façade of easy grace and beauty slid from her face and she stared at him, anger and pain very real in her eyes. "We all lost people. And if there weren't bigger problems in the world then I'd say sure, let's keep fighting that war until we all felt satisfied. But you can't do that, Jesse, not with all the problems we got nowadays. We all stand together eventually, or they're going to hang us all alone in the end."

Jesse cocked his head to one side. "Who's 'they', sweetheart? Who's got you all scared?"

Lucinda cursed herself for losing focus again. What was it about this man? "The natives are getting restless, Jesse, and they're on the warpath. And everyone has been talking about nightmare creatures, and walking dead, and lights that set fire to the desert sky. What do you think is happening, while you sit here and nurse your cheap beer?"

After she snapped she pulled back, not sure how he would react. When she saw his smile grow a little wider, it made her even more angry. His words, however, brought her back to the task at hand.

"I don't know about the Injun magic, Lucy, but you don't have to worry about those walkin' corpses. They smell to high heaven, and they ain't much good for much as far as I can see, but there ain't nothin' biblical about 'em, I can tell ya'."

Lucinda schooled her face to casual attention. "Really? You've seen them? I thought they were never far from that Doctor Carpathian?"

Jesse gave a jerk of his head. "Yeah, they're usually around the doc. But they're all over, now, really."

She folded her hands on the table before her. "Why do you say they aren't 'Biblical'?"

Jesse waved that question away with an annoying lack of concern. "I don't know the specifics, but they're just like those UR-30 law mechanicals, just made out of flesh and bone instead of metal an' rubber. They aren't like folks comin' back from the dead 'r nothin'. They don't have any recollection of who they were or what they done before. They're just like machines, runnin' on Doc's crimson gold, is all."

"But they don't scare you?" It was a question a woman in her supposed position would have asked, so Lucinda forced herself to ask it even though she was fairly certain of the answer.

Sure enough, Jesse laughed. "Scared? Nah. They ain't so fast, an' most of 'em ain't so big, and if I wouldn't a been scared of 'em when they were alive an' fast an' thinking fer themselves, what'd I be worryin' about now that they're all dead and rottin' and slow?"

He grinned at her broadly. "How 'bout you, darlin'? Do they scare you?"

Lucinda knew what her answer should have been. She began to formulate it in her mind, with the requisite shiver and fetching wide eyed look, but she heard herself respond before she even knew she had taken a breath. "No. They don't frighten me either. I'm just curious."

Jesse seemed pleased by that response, and she felt a genuine answering smile on her own face. She cursed herself in the silence of her own mind. The smile, however, remained professionally in place.

"No, I didn't figure you'd be scared of too much, actually."

They found themselves staring at each other. The silence stretched on. Lucinda could feel Courtright's eyes on her back. She tried desperately to summon up some thought or statement that would break the lull, but all she could do was smile.

All he seemed to want to do was grin back at her.

*****

Henry Courtright watched as Lucinda and James fenced back and forth. Every gesture and look she employed was masterful. He had seen her use it all before. She was deploying her full arsenal on the poor copperhead, and the secret agent had no doubt the rube would not know what hit him.

But at the same time, Courtright felt a touch of nerves. Lucinda was usually focused to a fault and would never let a mark go by without getting the answers she needed. The fact that James seemed to fluster her at all was reason enough to feel concern, despite the fact that she seemed to have marshaled her efforts back to the task at hand.

A whispered doubt crept into his mind, however. She had never acted like this before. How would he know if she was back on her game? If she started to use her talents on him, would he be able to puzzle out her true intentions beneath the layers of falsehood and illusion she had spent a lifetime learning to weave?

Courtright eased back into his chair, elbow once again hooked over the back, and stared openly at a Jesse James too caught up in Lucinda to even notice. The freak's artificial hands were clasped behind his head in an attitude of complete relaxation. The dull metal of the arms contrasted sharply with the brighter metal of their internal components and the flat black of the tubes and wires. And of course the flickering gleam of RJ-1027 cells and indicators winked here and there along their lengths.

What were the chances that any man, no matter how good he had been with the arms God had given him, was as good, never mind better, replacing them with gears and pulleys, wheels and pistons? There were many stories, told and retold across the territories, about Jesse and the speed of his draw. Most of the tales sounded fantastical, painting a picture Courtright found it impossible to fully believe. And yet there seemed to be a path of dead bodies behind the man, and the agent wondered how many of those had thought the same thing.

Courtright patted the blaster pistol riding on his hip and thought fondly of the mini Gatling in his room. He felt a smile tug at the corner of his mouth. Their orders were to find Carpathian wherever he was hiding, and to get that information back to Washington. But everyone knew that Jesse James had ties to the mad inventor. If their paths should cross in the wilds, things might just develop on their own. And maybe, just maybe, Mama Courtright's little boy would get a chance to see what Mrs. James' little piss-ant was capable of.

Chapter 6

Jesse stared at the cards in his hand without seeing them. There was no forgetting those dark eyes and that wide smile. He could not deny, Lucy had made quite an impression on him. She had left when a few of his posse came in, and even after she had gone back to her card sharp friend, Jesse had been sitting there trying to remember their conversation. He could not recall much, and for some reason that did not bother him. When Harding, Chase, and a couple of the other men asked if he wanted a game, he just nodded and they sat down, oblivious to their leader's lack of focus.

Despite his inattention, however, his stake was still healthy after several hands. His eyes kept drifting back towards Lucy, although he never caught her looking his way. Even though his heart was not in the game, his luck was bearing up better than usual. The same could not be said for Harding.

"Who brought this tainted deck o' pasteboards into this parlor?" Harding threw down his hand and spat off into the corner. "I swear, one more hand goes 'round that way I'll know one of you is bilkin' the table." The other men were not trying hard to conceal their amusement.

"Well, you know what they say, Harding: Unlucky at cards, lucky in . . . what are you lucky in?" A red haired outlaw chuckled as he went back to looking at his cards. Jesse smiled as Harding sputtered.

"Bryce," Harding growled, low in his throat. "You wanna make it out of here to spend any of that coin you're hoardin', you best hobble your lip before I beat you within an inch of the Almighty, and we'll see if your luck'll save you then."

The men laughed as Harding organized the coins and notes in front of him, ignoring the continued banter.

"Hey, isn't that Billy the Kid?" Ty's voice was curious and soft as he whispered into the considering silence of the game. "I think that's Billy the Kid, right?"

Jesse looked at the youngster with a blank face, all of the warm confusion draining from his mind. When he spoke, he did not take his eyes off Ty. "Gage, William Bonney just step into the establishment?"

In a moment Jesse's mind had gone from a pleasant, relaxed state to a vicious tension as Ty's words about Bonney and Misty on the trail to Missouri City came back to him. There was no sense of guilt or irony as he shifted from idle speculation concerning one lady to a building jealous rage over another. He had entirely forgotten the beauty sitting not twenty feet away. As the heat began to rise in his chest, he could only think about Misty, and Ty's innocent words.

It had been years since the big train job that had ended the brutal persecution of the men and women living on the edge of society, putting them on an even footing with the soldiers and lawmen who had been trying to exterminate them. Nearly a decade since those seemingly hopeless days when RJ-1027 tech was new, and Carpathian's weapons had suddenly shifted the balance of power forever. Since then, he had worked a couple jobs with Billy the Kid, but it had been a couple years since he had seen the Kid in person.

Jesse contemplated all the different ways he could welcome the Kid into Kansas City, from a hug to a handshake to a hole in the head. Instead, he decided to ignore him and continued to look at his cards, waiting for Chase to make his call on the current hand. Conversation around the saloon died down, however, and Jesse could feel William Bonney coming towards him through the room.

"I'll see your whole pot and raise you one of these, Jesse!" The voice was pitched high with excitement and anticipation, but he refused to turn. When an object sailed over his shoulder and landed in the pile of coins and notes in the center of the table, however, he could not ignore the Kid any longer.

Jesse leaned forward a bit to look at the thing in the middle of the pot: a piece of poorly cured leather trailing a tuft of long white hair. Jesse looked over his shoulder to where Billy the Kid stood with a wide grin, and jerked a thumb at the object.

"What is that?" Jesse kept his voice flat, knowing the anger building in his gut could get the better of him at any moment.

"Why, don't you recognize it?" The Kid's voice was mocking. "Well, that there is a bona fide Injun scalp, that is! And ain't no normal brave, neither. That there's the scalp of a gen-u-ine medicine man!"

Jesse looked at the sad, pathetic thing with a curled lip. "Get it outa my pot before I lose my manners."

An enormous fat man beside Billy gave a wet chuckle and reached out with a long, wickedly curved knife, picking the scalp up by its white lock with a neat twist. He swung the thing wide and offered it back to the grinning young outlaw leader.

"Thanks, Smiley." Billy took the scalp and gently put it back in a cloth bag. "You remember Smiley, Jesse? He was in on the train job." Being in on the train job was often a way of dividing the innumerable outlaws throughout the territories between the established and respected and the inexperienced and green. It did not always work like that, however, and Jesse remembered the man most folks called 'Smiley' for a violent lunatic who enjoyed disfiguring the faces of his victims. He grunted without a smile and looked back at Billy.

"Is there a reason you come lookin' for me, Billy?" Jesse's tone indicated that the younger man was beneath him within the obscure outlaw pecking order. "Or am I just lucky today?"

Billy's smile never faltered as he swung an empty chair around, bringing his leg up and over to sit down backwards. "No, sir. I came here to find you.

"Ain't exactly like you been hidin' yourself out this way, you know, living like a bunch of city swells." The younger man on Billy's other side muttered.

Billy grinned at the boy and wagged a finger at him, still swinging the bag. "Now, Garrett, we're all friends here, right?" He looked at Jesse. "Right, Jesse? All friends?"

Jesse grunted and put his cards down. "Sure, Billy. We're all friends. Now you care to tell me why you're lookin' for me? I got places I gotta be, and you're seriously queering my luck."

Billy nodded, his pleasant smile still firmly in place. "Sure, Jesse, I get it. You're a busy man." He looked at the cards in front of the other outlaw and his grin widened slightly. "We're all busy men." He gestured broadly towards the bar and then signaled for the man standing there to bring three whiskeys. "You heard what went down out in the mountains, a couple weeks ago?"

Jesse nodded sourly. "Yeah.Heard you ran into some squaws and cut 'em down from behind." He pointed to the bag still swinging in Billy's hand. "That a bit o' one of them poor ladies?"

Billy's smile darkened a bit before coming back full force. "Squaws. You're funny, Jesse. I always said that about you." He turned to the fat man now sitting beside him. "Don't I always say that about Jesse, Smiley? That he's funny?"

The man's small eyes tightened. "Yeah. You say that."

"See? Jesse's funny. I always say that." Billy leaned back, relaxing in his chair as if he owned the Arcadia. "No, they weren't squaws, Jesse. We hit ourselves a Warrior Nation war party, wanderin' around out there in the wilds, way past their usual haunts. An' we dry gulched 'em somethin' fierce. Din't we, Garrett?"

The young man, still standing behind Billy, nodded.

Jesse nodded, mechanical arms folded over his chest. "Okay, so, you got lucky against some Injuns. An' that lands you all the way back here, in Kansas City, sittin' at my table?"

Billy frowned and shook his head. "You're missin' the point, Jesse. What was a war party of braves, led by this white haired bug himself, doin' kickin' around up in the mountains? Almost all of Sittin' Bull's savages are back this way, gettin' fancy with Grant and the Union slugs." He met Jesse's disdainful glare with a steady look. "Why were they that far west, Jesse?"

The older outlaw shook his head. "This ain't my tale, Billy, it's you'rn. So why don't you tell it?"

Before Billy could continue, one of the barkeeps stopped by and dropped three heavy whiskey glasses on the table, standing stubbornly by until Billy nodded to Garrett, who pulled a couple coins out of a pocket and handed them over. The barkeep looked as his palm, sniffed, and turned to walk away.

"Okay," Billy sat back, resuming his nonchalant pose and idly picking up his drink. "They was lookin' fer somethin', Jesse. Somethin' big. Twenty braves, led by one o' their white-hairs hisself?" He waved the bag again for emphasis. "You don't see that kind of weight out that far for nothin'."

Jesse's mouth quirked into a tight grin for the first time since Billy had walked into the saloon. "That's what you got? Injuns don't go that far, so they must'a been lookin' fer somethin'?"

Billy's smile dropped completely from his face and he shook his head. "No, Jesse, that ain't all I got. Before we sent Senor White Hair to the happy hunting ground, we got some words out'a 'im. He was singin' like a showgirl afore Smiley finally did for him. So yeah, we got a lot more to go on." He smiled again, leaning back in his chair. "Way I figure it, we got a real hog-killin' time comin', and I'm the only one knows where to start lookin'."

Jesse stared at William Bonney for a moment, eyes flat and blank, before he said, "So, what were they lookin' for, Billy? You ain't mentioned that."

Billy's smiled faded again. "Well, we din't get that out'a him, but we know where they was headed! An' we know it was real important-like, cuz'a they had a medicine man with'em!"

Jesse nodded. "So, you don' know what it is you're lookin' for, or why even the savages would'a wanted it, you're hell-fire sure you wanna go hairing off into the wilds after it? And, since you dropped your sorry ass here on my doorstep, half a country back in the wrong direction, I'm assumin' you wanna drag me in after you?"

Billy nodded, ignoring the sarcasm. "They was good, Jesse. It took everything my posse had to take 'em down, and even then, I lost half my guys. Half of 'em, Jesse, and that was with we had the drop on 'em! Sittin' Bull and the other chiefs, they never woulda sent that many o' their best young braves, led by a white hair, out that far, in the middle of a war where they need every one o' their boys an' girls close to home, lessen there was a damned good reason."

Jesse shook his head. "That ain't necessarily true, Billy. Coulda been they saw a shape in some smoke, or a bird crapped on the wrong man's head, and they thought it was their Great Spirit jawin' at 'em from the Big Beyond, and off they go, gallivantin' into the wilds, to get chewed up by the likes 'o you, who then comes runnin' back to civilization with this tall tale an' your eyes all full o' gold, 'r gems, 'r God knows what you think is out there."

It was Billy's turn to shake his head sharply. He leaned over the table; his hands pressed wide to either side, and tried to force belief into the skeptical outlaw across the table. "You weren't there, Jesse. You weren't lookin' into that old man's eyes as he died. He was terrified, man. He was terrified we was gonna find this thing. Whatever it is, it meant enough to them to send some of their best, with one of their elders, an' you know how they guard those old men, Jesse. They sent their best, an' this old man, far away lookin' for this thing when they needed 'em most against Grant. It's big, Jesse, its mighty big, whatever it is."

Jesse stared at the younger man for a long time. When he spoke, he was careful to keep any tone of agreement or warmth out of his voice. "You know where we'd have to go to get it?"

Billy's eyes dropped and his hands started to tap randomly on the back of his chair. "Well, not exactly—"

Jesse barked a laugh. "Not exactly!" He slapped the table and then looked around at his own men. "Not exactly! Well, hell, Billy, what does that mean, exactly?"

Billy's eyes flared at the tone. "I know what the Injuns call the place. I figure, we get closer, out into the desert, we start talkin' around, there's always some folks out that way, half breeds an' whatnot. Probably, someone'll know where it is we're tryin' to get to."

Jesse watched him squirm. "And leavin' aside for a moment the location of this great treasure of yours, you're thinkin', if this is so all-fired important, you're figurin' you'll need extra bodies to go get it?"

Billy shrugged. "They sent twenty of their best braves, Jesse. An' those folks near-wrecked my crew. I'm figurin' they was expectin' a fight, an' we better expect one too, if we take up their trail."

Jesse grinned. "Or coulda been, they were expectin' the fight you gave 'em, Billy, and they lost that one. Maybe all the fightin's done, and you just gotta walk into this fairytale place an' grab whatever it is they were headin' for!" Jesse could see that possibility had not occurred to the younger man, and he shook his head. "Course, it's probably two dusty old buffalo hides and a spittoon of squaw piss that you'll be grabbin', blessed by the Great GoogelyMoogely, or whatever."

Billy brought his hands down on the table, ready to push off with anger, and beside him Smiley and Garrett were frowning as well, hands on their weapons. Jesse raised one finger to stave off a fight.

"But let's assume there is somethin' worth havin' out there, Billy. An' let's assume we're gonna have to fight to get it. That still don't answer my original question: why've you come lookin' fer me? You ain't never lacked for lads to fill up yer posse whenever you were on the shoot."

Billy settled back down, fingers steepled across the back of his chair. "Well, Jesse, first, I'm figurin', for somethin' this big, I really need someone I can ride the river with, you know? Someone I can trust to watch my back, an' everyone knows, that's gotta be you, right?" His smile was as wide as it was false.

Jesse watched him with lidded eyes, knowing full well that there had never been any great trust or faith between them. However, he merely waited, a growing curiosity as to Billy's true destination growing in him. He gestured with one lazy hand for Billy to continue.

Billy was ready to charge right in and continue the flattery, but something stopped him, he paused to take stock, and then with a sharp nod, he said, "I figure, once we find whatever it is, we gotta get rid of it. Find someone to buy it. Ain't nothin' any good to ya if you can't find someone else who wants it." He flipped a hand towards Jesse. "You got a lot more inroads with folks that could pay big, when we gotta unload it."

Jesse watched him fidget for a moment and then said, "You gonna tell me the rest, or you gonna make me guess?"

Billy sighed, but then lurched forward, his eyes glowing with an idea he had kept close to his vest, from even his closest men, until now.

"Well, Jesse, the Warrior Nation is fightin' for its very life against the Union, right? So I figure, they're lookin' for somethin' that desperate like, it's gotta be somethin' they think they can use against the Union, am I right?"

Jesse nodded for him to carry on. He could tell that this was the first Billy's men were hearing of this new wrinkle because all of a sudden Smiley and Garrett were watching their boss with growing interest and confusion.

"Well, I'm thinkin', if they could use it against Grant and his bully boys, what's stoppin' anyone else from usin' it the same way, right?" Billy's mind was racing now, his eyes bouncing around the table, and Jesse could almost taste his excitement. There was doubt there too, however. Billy did not have full confidence in his conclusions, he was following blind impulse, or advice that he did not fully understand, and it was clear that he was riding full tilt without a map.

"Sounds like that might not be completely mad, Billy. But so what, you plannin' on goin' up directly against Grant and the whole Union, now?"

Billy looked around the table, his eyes sly again. "Well, no, not me, exactly." His eyes slid sideways back to Jesse. "But it struck me, we got some mutual friends that might not mind gettin' their hands on somethin' powerful enough, the Nation thinks it'll help against the Union. Strikes me, we know some folks got their own grudge against Grant and the rest of those damned Lincolnites, an' they might be more'n willin' to entertain some generous thoughts for the folks who brought 'em a little treat like that."

Jesse's brow furrowed in confusion for a moment before clearing, and then rising in disbelief. "You mean the Rebellion?" Since Grant's armies had crushed the Confederacy, the remnants had been skulking around in the swamps of Florida and Louisiana, calling themselves the Confederate Rebellion, swilling rotgut and singing Dixie at the moon. Jesse was disgusted with what had become of his former comrades in arms, and he let that distaste show now.

Billy, either because he was more of an idealist or, more likely, because he'd been too young himself to fight in the war, did not share Jesse's disdain. "Yeah, the Rebellion! Those boys're just waitin' for their chance, Jesse, an' we could give it to 'em!"

Jesse looked at Harding and Gage, the only other men at the table who had fought in the war. "This strickin' you boys as a good idea?"

Harding spit a plug onto the floor nearby with a snicker. "Rebellion don't have a pot to piss in, literally. They're down in those swamps, chasin' gators and getting' eat by gallinippers. And besides, they ain't got two copper pennies to rub together, neither."

Billy leaned in again. "But Jesse, if this thing the savages were after, if it's all that, don' you think it could make a difference? Don' you think those ol' gray backs out in the swamps, they're just lookin' for some way they can get their own back?" He leaned even closer. "An' don' you think, they'd jump at the chance to follow whoever it was that showed 'em that way?"

Billy leaned back, his hands grasping the chair back on either side, a smile forming once more on his face. "You see the possibilities now, don'cha? Two gents like you an' me? Showin' up in the swamps with a way to put Grant down, and the South can rise again? Hell, Jesse, we'd be writin' our own ticket at that point!"

Jesse stared at the bag still dangling from Billy's wrist. Although he could not tease it out right now, Billy's whole scheme had a lot to recommend it. It was not like the war leaders of the Warrior Nation to send a party out under the command of an elder on a frivolous mission. There could very well be something out in the desert, and if so, it was something Sitting Bull, Geronimo, and the other chiefs who now led the unified Warrior Nation were keen to collect. It could be some sort of weapon, the way new and alarming things kept popping up ever since Carpathian had arrived towards the end of the war. If someone were to appear down in the swamps with some new super weapon, to rally the shattered forces of the Confederacy, reshape them into a fighting force once again, wielding whatever it was that Sitting Bull seemed so eager to recover . . .

"Most o' those I rode with in the war come up a cropper a long time ago, Billy." Jesse leaned back, the picture of regret.

"Those that ain't, most o' them are still ridin' the trails up here with us. I'm not sure who all ended up down in the swamps, but I'm not sure they'd give a lick for me or what I thought, if I was to suddenly appear down there. I wouldn't even know who to ask for."

Billy nodded at this renewed interest. "I get it, Jesse. I do. But you knew a bunch of folks! Gotta be some of 'em 're still down there, an' if we could bring'em somethin' big, somethin' they could use to get back on top? I'm pretty sure, we follow it through, we could end up big bugs ourselves, one day soon."

Jesse noted the excitement in Billy's eyes. "These are pretty grand plans, Billy. You're thinkin' mighty big all of a sudden, ain'tya?"

"Well, ain't nothin' says we gotta stay in the shadows forever, now, does it?" Billy gestured to the saloon around them. "Kansas City gets 'emselves some decent law, an' they will, we're out in no-man's land again. As long as the Union is in charge out here, we ain't gonna have nowhere to go. We're gonna be stuck on the fringe. But if we can tip that balance? If we can bring back the Rebs? Why, then, Grant's gonna have a whole lot more to worry about than us, eh?"

Jesse nodded slowly. "Might be you're onto somethin', Billy. I'm willin' to give you that. An' you say you got an idea of where we'd be headed?"

Billy's energy dimmed slightly with suspicion. "Yeah, I got a name. I figured, though, we'd share that sort of details when we got a bit closer."

Jesse laughed. "You don't trust me, Billy? That hurts. That really does a number on my insides. Okay, well, that'll come. Can you give me an idea of what types of terrain we'll be lookin' at? If my boys an' I go with you, what're we gonna need?"

Billy shrugged. "Desert, I think, like I said. An' the white hair said it was buried. So we might need to be diggin' it up."

Jesse was blank. "Dig? How deep?"

Billy shrugged again. "I don't know. But the Injuns, they were carryin' an awful lot o' spades, axes, an' things like that.

They looked like they were plannin' on some serious excavation."

Jesse tapped the table, his eyes unfocused slightly as he thought. "Well, if we're gonna have to be doin' a lot of diggin', I 'm thinking maybe we wanna stop somewhere along the way an' get some serious equipment, do it right."

Billy brightened. "Carpathian? You think he could help us?"

Jesse shook his head. "No, not the Doc. I'll go see him anyway on our way west, my boys and I need to see him about a few things." He looked down at one mechanical hand, opening and closing the fingers quickly. "But I was thinkin' we swing through Diablo Canyon. We need heavy equipment, there's enough there, pretty much all we'd have to do would be to throw it in a wagon--"

Billy nodded, smiling, but Garrett and Smiley shared a hooded glance as soon as Jesse mentioned Diablo Canyon, and Jesse stopped.

"What?" The older outlaw's face was blank as suspicion flared again in his heart.

"You ain't heard about Diablo Canyon?" Smiley was not smiling.

The suspicion built. "Yeah," Jesse kept his voice even. "Diablo Canyon. Best place in the territories to kick up a fuss if you're feelin' the need. Ain't been no law down there since those odd sticks ran the railroad tracks right to the edge of the cliff with no ideas on how to get across. Place is a pirate's paradise, with all that equipment just sittin' there, waitin' for someone to shoot or get off the pot."

Jesse twisted to look over at Gage and Ty. "Boys, if we're goin' to Diablo Canyon, you all are in for a right good time."

"They got themselves a 'bot." Garrett's voice was flat as he spoke, and his words brought Jesse's head snapping back around.

"They got a 'bot? You mean a UR-30?" His tone rose incredulously. "How in the name of Hell did one o' them metal marshals get down to Diablo Canyon, for God's sake?"

Billy looked grim and shrugged. "The townsfolk were bein' bled dry. They sent a telegram to Tombstone, an'—"

"Damned Wyatt Earp." Jesse collapsed against the back of his chair. "Damned Earp and his damned fool Lawmen, stickin' their noses in where they don't belong." He looked up at Billy. "The thing any good?"

The younger outlaw nodded. "Ringo and the Apache Kid got caught by it, the thing cleaned their plow somethin' fierce, left most of their boys pushin' daisies before they could skedaddle."

Jesse pursed his lips. "Ringo and the Apache, eh?"

"They ain't no slouches, Jesse." Harding muttered. "Johnny Ringo and the Apache Kid ain't no slouches."

Jesse nodded. "So, they got themselves a 'bot . . . "

Billy nodded, and then added, somewhat sheepishly, "That might be another reason I need you to ride along, Jesse. The way Ringo talked, this thing's a killer, and no mistake."

Jesse's smile returned. "Well, now everything makes a lot more sense, Billy! I was worryin' you'd gone all mamby-pamby on me all of a sudden! So, you knew we'd need to go to the Canyon."

Billy shrugged. "Thought it might come up."

Jesse thought for a second and then nodded. "Okay, I think I can work with all this. Tell you what, you an' your posse head on over towards Diablo Canyon. We'll follow you, and we'll meet just above town, where the tracks go through that cut in the hills?"

Billy nodded, a slight smile returning to his own face.

"So, we meet up in the hills, an' we'll come up with a plan on how we're gonna get around the metal man." Jesse paused and then gave Billy a sharp look. "Your boys are all heeled with the latest, right? Crimson gold all around?"

Billy took out one of his modified RJ-1027 six-shooters and gave it a quick twirl around his trigger finger before sliding it back into the holster. "'Course, Jesse."

Jesse nodded again. "'Course. Well, then. You boys be on your way, an' we'll meet you in the hills, bout seven days from now?" They all nodded. "We take care of the UR-30, we go find this mysterious oasis, dig up our treasure, and see if we can't raise the South once again, eh?"

Jesse reached out for his glass and raised it towards the other outlaw boss. "You wanna drink on it?"

Billy smiled and raised his own glass, and the two gave a heavy clunk as they hit over the center of the table. "Seven days from now, just above Diablo Canyon." They shot back the warm remnants of their drinks and nodded to each other.

Jesse held up one gunmetal finger. "An' you don' go rushin' in without us, now, you hear? 'R lightin' a shuck ahead of us an' leavin' us seven days from civilization and nothin' to show for it."

Billy waved with both hands, his smile firmly in place. "Jesse, we're in this together, thick or thin. I won't let you down."

They reached over the table again to shake hands, and Jesse gripped tight when Billy expected him to let go. The older man pulled his younger compatriot closer and stated, "I know you won't."

Billy pulled his hand away with a start, and a cloud moved over his face before his smile came swiftly out again. "That's you, Jesse, always funny!" He nodded to the other men and then moved towards the door, Smiley and Garrett following behind, not breaking eye contact with Jesse's boys until they had to, their faces grim.

"So," Harding muttered, playing vaguely with his cards. "We headin' west?"

Jesse smiled and shook his head. "Not necessarily."

The men all leaned forward. The boss held up his mechanical hands, still smiling widely, and gestured with a thumb over his shoulder towards the door. "That little corncracker ain't ever gonna tell me 'r mine what to do, first off. So, if'n I see's fit to let him stew in the hills for a few days, he's gonna grin and take it. He knows it, an' I know it. But if we do wanna throw in with the Kid and his mob of misfits, well then, we're all set to do just that." He wove his hands behind his back with a series of soft whirs and clicks, his grin growing wider. "So, we either got the Kid stuck in the middle of nowhere waitin' for us for God knows how long, 'r we got us partners in what might or might not be the damned-foolest thing I ever heard of."

Gage chuckled. "Secret Injun weapons, raisin' up the damned Rebs outa their fool swamps, save the world, and damn the Union!" He downed the last of his own drink. "Sounds like a good enough ride to jump on, just to see where it takes us!"

Harding grunted. "I don't trust Bonney. He ain't nobody's baby, and those soaplocks he rides with are all of 'em worse."

Jesse did not disagree. "Well, there's nothin' sayin' we gotta ride with 'em. Plenty of time for us make that call later. Billy'll wait for a few days, anyway, afore he goes chargin' in or runs off with tail tucked. Ain'tno rush."

Jesse flipped his cards over, a quick glare daring any of his men to say something. "Well, this game's dead, boys. I'm gonna head up to my room for a sec, then move on over to the Occidental. Who's with me?"

Although most of them had the grace to look sheepish, all of the men around the table muttered something about other plans. Jesse's smile hardened. "Well, that'd be your loss, ya'll. I think I want ya'll with me anyway, in case I need to get a hold of you. Meet you all over yonder?"

He picked up his hat, settled it on his head, and tapped a single mechanical finger to its brim before turning and heading for the door.

It felt as if he'd been hearing William Bonney's damn fool nickname every day for a year. And he knew that his own men were starting to feel that they had spent too much time in Kansas

City. The cockup in Missouri City hadn't helped that at all, either.

Harding and the other steady hands had come to him and recommended they lose Ty after the Missouri City job. But there was something about the kid that made Jesse feel more comfortable with things, and he had denied them. He knew Harding had talked with Frank, though, and he knew his older brother would be watching the young kid like a hawk, and there was nothing wrong with that.

Jesse knew that Billy's whole story seemed absurd, and he was trying to convince himself there was nothing to it, and the best he could hope for was a good laugh next time he ran into the Kid, after leaving him with his britches around his ankles out in the bad lands above Diablo Canyon. But something about the whole thing would not let Jesse go. He had friends in the swamps far to the south, and although he had played it cool with Billy, he would like nothing better than to see them emerge and confront Grant and his galoots, now that the Union was fighting on a couple different fronts.

He thought back to what Lucy had said, about killing random Yanks not leading to a fulfilling life. What if he could somehow bring the Rebellion something it could use to bring Grant down? And not only Grant, but maybe the whole damned Union?

His eyes were dark and his brow furrowed as he took the steps to the second story rooms two at a time. He was far too preoccupied to notice Lucy and Courtright watching him as he disappeared onto the second floor.

*****

Wyatt stood amidst the wreckage in the center of Missouri City with a blank face, his eyes flicking from detail to detail, absorbing the entire scene. This was worse than anything he had imagined when they followed the column of smoke seen from the road to Kansas City.

In the middle of the street was a double row of bodies covered in sheets and blankets taken from nearby houses. Most of the shapes beneath their coverings were shrunken and contorted; the sign of an excruciating death by fire. These were the casualties of the bank job, as well as two women and a man who had been killed when a building down the street had collapsed. Quite a death toll for a single visit to this poor, sleepy town.

The bank itself was completely gutted. The corner posts and a few charred remnants of support beams were all that remained standing. A thick cloud of greasy smoke continued to rise into the clear warm air, and an oppressive heat still radiated from the wreckage as if, somewhere in the ruins of the once-grand building, there was some sort of portal straight to hell. Wyatt's mustache twitched at the thought, or maybe at the sickly-sweet smell in the air.

There were three poorly-maintained old Iron Horses in front of the shattered bank. Each had been riddled with RJ-1027 shots rendering them inoperable. The blasts had been carefully placed and, as far as Wyatt could tell, the machines probably would not be moving again anytime soon. Wyatt's eyes flicked to the row of bodies again, particularly the shriveled bodies from within the bank. He was willing to bet that careful inspection would reveal at least circumstantial evidence indicating that three of those bodies were perpetrators, not victims, in the previous day's events.

Behind Wyatt stood his brother Virgil, silent as the grave, and Doc Holliday, standing unmoving except for the constant whisper and hum of his re-breather. Further behind them, across the street and keeping folks at bay by their mere presence, was a line of figures menacing in their utter stillness. All four of Tombstone's UR-30 Enforcer units, activated for the hunt, stood in a line like statues from some ancient temple. Their armored forms were visible beneath their standard riding leathers; both clothing and metal skin scorched and soot stained from recovering the bodies from the seething hell of the bank.

There were five figures in the line, Wyatt knew without looking, and the fifth figure, the hulking form of his brother Morgan, was what truly kept most of the townsfolk of Missouri City back. Wyatt shook his head slightly and continued his methodical examination of the scene. He hated brooding over Morgan's condition, and often hid behind the needs of the moment to avoid doing so.

A little further away from the robots and the massive, armored form of Morgan, sat the brooding hulk of a Judgment support wagon. The enormous vehicles were usually assigned to circuit judges moving through the territories, and made perfect mobile courthouses and jails, as well as fortresses in times of serious trouble. For this foray, Wyatt had grabbed one as a mobile headquarters and a way to transport his brother and the Enforcer units. He also knew bringing the judge along with him might grease some wheels, the deeper into trouble he got. A squadron of marshals and deputies on Interceptors, the small personal transports his men called Hogs, rode along as outriders and scouts, and added gun hands if things got ugly. The Hogs and their riders were now scattered around the town collecting statements and looking for other witnesses.

"So, there were eight of 'em." Wyatt's drawl was low, and the town officials had to lean forward to hear.

"Yessir," the old sheriff, Casey Stillman, said. The old man had been mortified by the devastation visited upon his town in his absence. He was a broken man, something inside him had died with the folks lined up in the dust behind them.

"Eight, including Jesse James?" Wyatt turned his head to look down at the slope-shouldered sheriff.

"We think so, sir." He shrugged. "They hit the town from over the river, their 'Horses throwing up a terrible fog. Most folks ran. Those that didn't . . . " he gestured weakly behind them, and Wyatt nodded.

"And you were in the big city whoopin' it up." Virgil's voice was low but filled with contempt. The old man could only nod, and the big marshal snorted and looked away.

"Any of the bodies identifiable as the outlaws?" Doc spoke over the hissing of his breathing apparatus, and another man, the town manager, shook his head. "By the time most of us come back, the bank was completely goin' up. There weren't no way we could stop it at that point. It was lost, an' . . . all those folks that hadn't gotten out."

Doc leaned towards Wyatt and murmured, "Taking another gander into the bank might prove useful. Morgan'd be game."

Wyatt grunted over his shoulder at his friend, one hand smoothing his mustache in a habitual gesture. He hated asking anything of Morgan because of his younger brother's special status. With a quick shake of his head, however, he bowed to necessity. No one else was going to be able to go into that hell except a UR-30 unit or Morgan. And the UR-30s were not known for their delicacy.

"Morgan," Wyatt pitched his voice to be heard over the muttering crowd behind the marshal's line.

The Over-marshal felt, more than heard, the impacts of his brother's footsteps as Morgan approached. There were always moments when Wyatt allowed himself to forget what had happened to his younger brother, but those footsteps always brought it all rushing back.

"Wyatt." The voice was toneless, buzzing with the inhuman resonances of the UR-30 vocal interface.

Wyatt schooled his face to stillness and turned to regard the hulking form of his brother. Morgan had nearly died over a year ago, the victim of an assassination attempt, gunned down while playing pool at Campbell and Hatch's. The bastards had fired right through the back door, catching Morgan in the side and throwing him across the table.

Wyatt's eyes were firm and still as the scenes played again in his mind. The desperate rush for doctors, the bleak diagnosis from all that came, and Virgil's refusal to abandon their little brother. The sharpest memory he had, however, was the bitter disappointment in Morgan's voice as he grabbed Wyatt's collar with failing strength and spat, "I don't see anything". Morgan had always shared Wyatt's fascination with life after death, and had often speculated on what he would see as life ebbed away.

They were the last words Morgan ever spoke with his own voice.

Virgil, refusing to stand idly by while Morgan passed, had bundled their brother in a cloak and rushed out the door. No one knew where he had gone, although many had strong suspicions. He returned late the next day, exhausted and travel-stained, but had never spoken of where he had gone or what he had done. Morgan was not with him, but he reported that he believed they would see their brother again. And he had been right. Nearly a month later, Morgan had returned, after a fashion.

Wyatt nodded to Morgan, forcing himself to look into his brother's blood-shot eyes. Morgan's pale face was completely framed by the iron support structure that held his head erect. The supports were affixed to the bulky suit that sustained the young marshal's life and held him upright, bypassing his severed spine and allowing him to walk. The supports and braces incorporated a comprehensive array of armored plates, as well, offering him a great deal of protection from further harm. Wyatt did not know how much of his brother's own body still existed within the armored suit, as Morgan was unable to remove even parts of it and survive. The armor moved with the natural grace and flexibility he had possessed before the attack, however, rather than the more rigid, jerky movements of a UR-30 Enforcer, but its bulk and weight forever set him apart from normal men.

"Morgan," Wyatt's voice betrayed nothing of the guilt that rose in him each time he thought of his brother. "Do you think you might take a look inside there, see if there's anything worth seein', before we continue on to Kansas City?"

"Sure, Wyatt." The pale lips quirked in a slight smile that was not even the ghost of his former jovial self, and he turned towards the smoking pile of rubble. As he walked towards the ruined building Morgan lifted his helmet to his head and settled it in place, armored fingers deftly securing the latches on either side of his throat. He looked back at Wyatt through the distorting lenses of thick glass and nodded once.

"This really necessary, Wyatt?" Virgil's tone was neutral, but it was obvious by the way his heavy brows lowered that he thought the answer was clear.

"Virg, if there's anything in there that can help us, either link this more firmly to James or, God help us, give us an idea that he might o' gone elsewhere, can we afford not to look?" Wyatt was watching Morgan's heavy bulk push past the wreckage of the bank's front doors and into the terrible heat within.

"What the hell you think would still be in there that might help at all?" Virgil always got protective where Morgan was concerned. "The animal's been stayin' in Kansas City for months. He's in Kansas City. Anything we do that costs us so much as a minute, will be somethin' we regret for the rest of our days, if he gets away."

"Damnit, Virg," Wyatt snapped. "How the hell do I know what we might find in there?"

"If we don't look, and we miss somethin' that would lead us in a different direction, we'll have even longer to regret it." Doc's calm voice, muffled as always by his leather breathing mask, eased through the brothers' frustration.

The three of them watched as Morgan's armored form, obscured by smoke and the intense shimmer of the brutal heat, moved through the wreckage. He walked in an awkward, hunched position as he scanned the floor for any signs or clues. The young marshal was slow and methodical, and for his colleagues, time seemed to crawl as they waited in the street for what seemed like hours.

When Morgan emerged he was covered in soot but otherwise none the worse for wear. He held something clenched in his armored fist, and as he approached his brothers he held up his arm, servos whirring, and opened the fingers.

In his palm was a metal pin of some kind, deformed and partially melted by the intense heat. Wyatt took it carefully, shifting it quickly from one hand to the other. After a moment he held it up to the light, grasping it carefully between thumb and forefinger. He could just make out a familiar silhouette mostly hidden within the smudged metal.

"A mourning pin." Wyatt muttered.

Doc, looking over his friend's shoulder, sniffed. "A Lincoln mourning pin. Damn, you Yankees never get tuckered out from worshipping that man."

Wyatt gave the former Georgian a sour look a then went back to the pin. Sure enough, the familiar nose, the top hat, and the beard were clearly visible despite the damage. He looked back to Morgan.

"Where was it?"

Morgan's emotionless face looked out from its metal cage and spoke with his soft, buzzing voice. "The floor, near the tellers' windows."

"If anything would set that bloody-minded bastard off, Wyatt, it'd be findin' one o' these on somebody." Virgil soft voice was intense.

Wyatt nodded, then looked again at his younger brother. "Nothin' else in there?"

Morgan's head shifted slightly from side to side, all the movement his restrictive supports would allow. "No."

Wyatt looked at the pin for a moment longer and then shrugged. "Okay, gents. Then it's on to Kansas City." He looked up into the sky, noting the position of the sun. "We should be able to pull in not long after nightfall, if we push on through."

"Or it might be better we stay here for the night." Doc Holliday offered. "Leave with the crack of dawn, hit KC early enough in the morning, we got a whole day's worth of light to root 'em outta wherever they're hidin'."

Wyatt looked from Virgil to Doc, then to Morgan. Each man's face was impassive, allowing the Over-marshal to make the call.

Wyatt shook his head after a moment. "Doc's right. We been riding hard already, and now this." He gestured disgustingly at the ruins of the Missouri City Savings and Loan. "We'll bunk down here, get up before dawn, and hit them as soon as we can. Take the Judgment just outside of town, have the deputies and the outriders sleep there. The rest of us will find beds in Missouri City."

Virgil nodded and turned to say something Morgan, then shouted to one of the deputies standing near the Enforcer units. "Provencher, take first watch, through midnight."

The dark-haired young lawman looked sourly at the robots, then flicked a bitter salute from the brim of his hat.

The Over-marshal turned to sheriff Stillman and leaned in close. "If any word beats us to Kansas City, I'm comin' back here first thing, and I'll be lookin' fer you."

The diminished man could only nod in numb fear. The townsfolk watched silently as the senior Lawmen gathered their equipment and moved towards a tall hotel on the waterfront, speaking quietly among themselves as they moved away.

Chapter 7

The Occidental was the fanciest establishment in Kansas City. Every aspect of the place screamed class at the top of its frontier lungs. The floor was carpeted with an intricate, and ironic, oriental pattern. The tables and chairs were dark, polished wood, and the lights overhead were draped in dark red shades and hoods, giving the entire dancehall a shadowy, exotic atmosphere.

Jesse sat at a card table towards the back of the room that still afforded him a decent view of the stage. Ty's story about Misty and William Bonney had continued to haunt him, and he had no interest in sitting near the front as he usually did. His men sat around the table, most not trying to hide their resentment at being forced to come to the Occidental. They stared down at their cards or took sips from glittering glasses. Even springing for a bottle of genuine bourbon had not softened anyone's mood, and that just tossed grease onto the cooking fire for Jesse.

"She sure is purty, Jesse." Ty was the only man at the table paying any attention to the show, and he was enjoying it with an openness that underscored the sullen set of the other men. "Any man'd feel like a king, standin' next to her!"

Jesse grunted and tossed two coins into the pot. The cards were not being kind, which had added to his dark mood. He wished Ty would shut up about Misty.

Play moved around the table, with coins arcing into the pot or cards flopping down onto the felt-topped table, but Jesse was not paying particular attention. He looked at the men still holding cards, glanced down at his own sad hand, and shrugged, tossing in another coin to follow the raise. As he moved to lower his cards, however, his thumb gave a slight jerk, and the cards shifted in his grip. He clutched at them, but they slid out and flipped onto the table, revealing his pathetic hand.

The men all stopped playing, staring down at the revealed cards; all low numbers and off-suit, and then up at Jesse's dangerously still face. An awkward silence stretched out as everyone around the table waited to see how the outlaw boss would react.

Jesse looked down at the hand that had betrayed him, turning it over to stare at the palm, each finger curling and relaxing in turn. Everything seemed fine, and Jesse shrugged slightly, his shoulders lifting with a heavy sigh.

"You know, boys, some days it just doesn't pay to get outta bed." He gathered up the money that was still in front of him and jerked his head at the pot. "You boys keep that, it wasn't doin' me any good anyway."

Jesse stood up and grabbed the bourbon by the neck of the bottle. "Sorry to've dragged you boys away from your fun. I do think I'll be takin' this with me, however, to keep me company on the long walk back to the Arcadia." He looked up at the stage where Misty was moving sinuously with the other girls, large feathered fans waving to the swirling piano music. He shook his head and looked down at Gage.

"When she's done, tell her I've gone back to my room, will you?" His voice echoed his flat, empty eyes.

"Sure thing, Jesse. You want me to walk her back over when she's done?" Gage's young face was worried, and Jesse knew he did not look good. His men were already concerned that he was losing his edge, and all this talk of Billy the Kid had them thinking about their own situations, riding with Jesse and the Youngers. The older outlaw summoned up a smile and shook his head, pushing as much bravado into his voice as he could muster.

"No. Anyone who thinks they can mess with Jesse James' girl, any time o' the day 'r night, is gonna have another think comin' at 'em faster than they can know." He pulled one of his hyper-velocity pistols and sent it spinning and whirling around his hand before it leapt back into the holster, forcing a grin for moral. "Am I right, boys?"

The men around the table agreed with energy that seemed just a little forced. It struck Jesse that they were putting perhaps a little too much effort into being agreeable, but he decided to let it slide. He tipped his hat to the table, gave one quick glance at the stage where Misty was watching him out of the corner of her eye, and turned towards the door.

Maybe with a little time alone, he'd be able to calm himself down enough to talk some sense.

*****

Jesse stared at the small lamp on the little table in his room. The empty bourbon bottle lay on its side nearby, a glass upside down a little beyond. His dark eyes peered into the depths of the lamp, searching out the swirls of ruby highlights present in all RJ-1027 lighting. The flecks of color within the lamp's illumination seemed to dance, suspended in the glow. He had lost track of time, slumping down at the table, mechanical arms folded before him, chin resting on the hard armor of his forearm.

His mind had been running through the same familiar paths all night. He could not remember being as happy as he had been in Kansas City with Misty these past few months. But still the constant need to throw himself into the fire was always overpowering. And now, with the return of Bonney . . . Jesse had gotten so used to being at the top of the pile, he had forgotten what it was like struggling to get up there in the first place. He knew Bonney, Ringo, hell probably even folks like Carpathian and his little stooges, were struggling every day to make names for themselves.

All Jesse had ever wanted, since he was a little boy back in Clay County was for folks to know his name. Sure, he had joined Frank fighting the Union because he believed in the Confederate cause, and because he had hated those treasonous jayhawkers with every fiber of his soul. The filthy bastards had strung up his stepfather trying to get to Frank, and when that failed they had whipped Jesse himself until his back had bled. Those scars were more than enough to drive him into joining his brother's unit as soon as he was able. Even then, however, it was the lure of fame and notoriety that drove him to his wildest exploits.

When he had first thought up the train job, to seize back the initiative from the law, to salvage the position and prominence of the renegades of the western territories in the face of the new weapons and power the European brought with him, he knew he had established his name in the histories for all time.

But time was like a river, as the saying went, and she kept on flowing even after you docked your boat in the big city. With Carpathian, the Injuns, and now Grant flooding into the western territories, his greatest exploit seemed to be disappearing into the mists of history before he could really revel in the victory. Years had passed, he knew, but somehow it still seemed like only yesterday. And it seemed terribly unfair that folks were forgetting so soon. Without him and his train job, every one of them knucks, hard cases, thieves, and road agents would be dead by now, victims of the new law and the new weapons. The fact that most folks had forgotten that was the hardest thing to bear.

That old frustration and the happiness he had found with Misty were crashing together in his mind over and over as he sat in the small, warm room with Ty's words churning over and over again through his sluggish thoughts. The idea of Billy, the boy who had risen among the outlaw elite to be his foremost competition, spending time with Misty, the source of the greastest peace he could remember in many years, was plaguing his mind.

Jesse shook his head and lurched up, pacing back and forth as he tried to focus his thoughts. Misty had been besotted with him since they had first met, and she had been nothing but devoted to him through their months together. They had spoken of his past many times. In all that time she had never mentioned Billy the Kid, or in fact anyone else within the outlaw brotherhood. Ty was almost certainly mistaken, despite his confident manner.

The outlaw stopped at the window, grabbing the sill with both iron hands, and looked out into the streets. They were almost empty. Still, there were men and women, usually walking in couples or small groups, moving along on whatever business had them out so late. One large cargo wagon, a ghostly crimson glow flaring from beneath as its RJ-1027 engine sent fat red sparks sailing through the night, rumbled down the street, pausing for pedestrians trying to cross through its harsh white headlamps.

Nothing in the street offered any insight, however, and Jesse sighed and returned to his pacing. The floor creaked beneath him, the heels of his boots cracking harshly in the silence of the night. Most of the lodgers staying in the other rooms of the Arcadia had gone to bed over an hour ago, and those that were not sleeping were quiet, only faint, muffled mutterings showing that they were awake. Jesse suddenly felt very much alone, and wondered where his brother might be. Frank had taken a room at another hotel, smaller than the Arcadia but much closer to the edge of town, right near where the Heavy Rail line ran out into the western plains.

Jesse heard a scraping at the door as a key went into the lock, and without thought one of his pistols was in his hand, pointed rigidly at the door. Whoever was on the other side was having a hard time with the knob, and the outlaw sidled slowly towards the bed in case he found a sudden, overwhelming need for cover. When the door swung open, however, it was only Misty standing there, a look of frustration on her pretty face.

The girl looked up and her deep jade eyes widened as she stared down the bore of Jesse's massive pistol. He immediately lowered the weapon, but the damage to the poor girl's calm had already been done.

"Jesse, are you okay?" She bent down to pick up her key from the floor where she had dropped it, and eased into the room carrying a couple of bags with her. "Were you expectin' someone a little more intimidatin', maybe?"

Jesse was caught on the verge of two reactions. He wanted to scoop her up right then and there; she looked so pretty and so vulnerable, but Ty's words, and the image of Billy the Kid's smug face, kept rising in his mind. He stood there, pistol lowered but still out, arms heavy, hanging at his side. He knew the bourbon had not helped his situation any, but could not, for the life of him, clear his head of its fog.

Misty put the bags down on the little table and turned gracefully, her hands on her slender hips. "Why did you leave the show early, Jesse? To come up here and get full as a tick all on your own?" Her tone was light but her face was pursed in disappointment.

Jesse gaped at her for a moment, his mind running in too many directions at once. He stood there mute, staring at her with dull eyes, swaying slightly as she sat down at the table, pulling pins from her elaborately piled hair. "I swear, Jesse, if you don't put that gun away I'm going to slap you." He could see, in the mirror in front of the table, that annoyance was giving way to anger and disappointment.

Jesse looked down at the pistol in his metal hand as if seeing it for the first time. He looked up at the back of her head, tilted as she washed the makeup from her face. She looked at him through the mirror and her eyes tightened. "Jesse, put the gun away."

Almost without thinking about it, the gun rose, and then softly slid into the holster. After he took his hand off the butt, however, he stopped moving again, staring at Misty's back. The girl was now combing through her honey brown hair with an ivory-handled brush he had given her. He stared at the brush, watching as the crimson-tinged light reflected softly from its curved surface.

Sensing him standing there motionless, Misty eventually stopped brushing and swiveled around daintily in the chair. She stared up at him, one eyebrow quirked, and asked, "Jesse, is there somethin' on your mind?"

He stared at her face: that beautiful face that had captivated him for so long. He could not remember the last time a woman had kept him in thrall this way. The long, wavy hair that swept down her neck, the big green eyes, the soft, clear skin; she was truly a beauty by any measure. Something in his chest seemed to crack slightly, and he blurted what had been plaguing his mind.

"You been with William Bonney?" It came out harsher than he had intended, the tone accusatory, but he straightened his shoulders and raised his chin as if daring her to take offense.

Misty sat staring at him in blank confusion for a moment before her head tilted to one side and she said, "are you drunk, Jesse?"

Jesse shook his head and snapped around on his heel, pacing once again. He had taken that first dreadful step; it was too late now to go back.

"Answer the question, Misty. You been with the Kid?" He could not look at her.

Misty stood slowly, hands on hips, and stared at him incredulously. It was clear she was caught between rage and laughter. "Jesse, are you jealous?"

He continued to pace. "Tell me, Misty. I need to know."

"Jesse, was I the first girl you were ever with?" Her tone was flat and uncompromising, and it stopped his pacing in its tracks.

He turned to her, his look comically confused. "'Course not."

She nodded and gave him an arch look. "An' did I at any time give you the impression I was a pure 'n pristine unplucked flower when we first met?"

He smirked despite himself. "Ah, no, you didn't . . . "

She nodded firmly. "There you go."

The shadow returned immediately to his face at her tone of dismissal. "Now, hold on, Misty. Billy the damned Kid?"

She put up a hand. "Din't we just agree it don't matter?"

He shook his head. "No, we didn't. The Kid?"

She huffed angrily and turned back to the table. "Forget it, Jesse. I was never with Billy the Kid, I've never even met Billy the Kid. I wouldn't know Billy the Kid if he walked into this room right now and shot you. Satisfied?"

He found himself once again staring at the back of her head, at a total loss for words. "But . . . but you said . . . "

She did not turn around. "I said we weren't neither of us virgins, is what I said, Jesse. An' you agreed. So it don't matter if I was with Billy the Kid or not. I'm just sayin', I wasn't."

His confusion deepened. He felt like a child lost in unfamiliar territory. "But why din't you just say — "

She clapped the brush down on the table. "Because it don't matter none, Jesse! And we both agreed it didn't." She stopped moving for a moment, still and silent, and then spun to meet his searching gaze. "Why're you suddenly so concerned about Billy the Kid, Jesse?"

He shrugged, feeling even more like a boy caught in some foolish act. "Ty was talkin' — "

"Ty?" Her voice rose, an angry note rumbling beneath its usually soft tones. "That little pie eater from Missouri City? That little cretin? What the hell do you care what that little offish tick has to say?"

Jesse struggled to convey to Misty the confused jumble of emotions he was feeling, about his place in the world, his feelings for her, and his fear of sliding into insignificance. The thoughts and images swirled in his foggy brain, but the words would not come. Over all of the images, William Bonney's face rose like a mountain looming over a darkened landscape.

"Jesse, what does it matter what that worm of a boy had to say? Some jailbird-in-waiting mouths off about me, an' your first thought is against me?" She stood up, her back straight and her shoulders back, and looked him directly in the eye. "Jesse, if you don't trust me, why am I even here?"

He shook his head, emotions rising up to engulf him. But now over everything was the fear of losing her. He reached out with his mechanical hands, and tried to ignore the slight flinch she gave before making the conscious decision not to pull away. Was it the fight, or was it the damned arms that she was flinching from?

"Babe, you know I trust you." He muttered the words, and even in his own ears they sounded weak. "It's just the boys, you know. An' damned William Bonney always comin' up." He tried to pat her hair, but at that she pulled away.

"No, Jesse. You gotta put Bonney, and Ty, and whoever else has gotten into your head aside, now, before you're touchin' me again." She leaned towards him, her eyes earnest. "I ain't never lied to you, Jesse James, I ain't never jabbed you in the neck over nothin', and I ain't never walked out with anyone behind your back. An' I never would."

He looked into her eyes and everything else seemed to fade away. He felt safe. His head started to shake back and forth. "Baby, baby, I'm so sorry." He held a hand out but did not take hers until she offered it. "You're right, Misty. Completely right. This was all me, babe. It weren't you, it weren't even Billy or Ty or any of the other guys."

She slowly allowed him to pull her into his arms, burying her head in the crook of his neck. "This is real, Misty. I know. I'm sorry. I'm gonna make it up to you, I promise. I'm gonna—"

He held her out at arm's length so he could look at her, drink in her beauty, and the returning warmth of her eyes. There was nothing there now but trust and love. The suspicion, the anger, and the frustration were all gone. He felt answering emotions rising up within him as well.

"Next time, Jesse James, you better just trust me, or —"

When his arm lurched back he did not understand what was happening, but when it slashed across his body, the armored hand taking Misty full in the face, he staggered back in horrified disbelief. She flew backwards, spiraling hard into the wooden floor. Jesse stopped, arms out-flung as if to keep his balance. He stared at her in complete shock. He had no recollection of reaching out with his arm. He looked down at the offending limb. There were no feedback pads on the back of his mechanical hands, so he had felt nothing but the jolt up his arm upon contact, but there was a garish splash of blood across the armored plate. Far too much blood, he thought as he stared.

A whimper from the ground brought him back to the stuffy little garret, and he rushed towards the huddled shape in the corner. Misty was crouched down as if expecting another blow, one shaking hand raised up over her head to defend herself. Her face was pressed against the wall, cradled in the other hand, and her shoulders shook with terrified, silent sobs.

"Honey, I'm so sorry!" Jesse reached out towards the cowering woman. "Baby, I don't—"

"Stay away." Her voice was muffled and slurred, but the stone beneath it was unmistakable. She slowly curled around herself to bring her head up and around, her mouth and nose hidden behind her raised hand. Her other hand, still shaking, was brandished before her as if it were a weapon, one finger wagging towards him. "Don't you come near me, you monster."

He stopped, the words twisting in his gut. "But, Misty, please—"

"Get. Away." The fire in her eyes froze him in his tracks. She gingerly pushed herself to her feet, swaying slightly as she rose. Her finger was still raised like a talisman, the only thing holding a ferocious beast at bay. The fear in her eyes was harder to bear than any burning anger.

"I want you to leave. I want you to leave an' I don' want you to come back." She was now standing, her back pressed to the wall, one hand still pushed to her face.

He shook his head, not believing how swiftly things had turned. "Misty, please. It wasn't me, it was –"

"Stop talking!" she screamed the words, closing her eyes to the pain it obviously caused her. "I don' wanna hear another word, Jesse, I jus' want you to leave, and never come back again'. I seen those other girls, let men hit 'em, an' that ain't ever gonna be me." The finger now pointed towards the door. "Leave."

Jesse felt completely empty. He felt exhausted, as if he had gone the full three rounds with a raging bull. He stood there, his arms hanging limp at his sides, staring at the woman he would have done anything for.

He looked more closely and his eyes widened to see the extent of the damage hidden by her upraised hand. That hand was now soaked in blood, and he could see torn flesh behind. Her eyes were blazing even as tears poured from them, fear and fury mingling in their jade depths.

Jesse took a halting step backwards, and then another. He could not take his eyes from the wreckage of Misty's cheek. He could see her strength failing her, could see the sick anguish rising in her eyes as the shock began to subside and the pain truly made itself felt. And his heart took another blow as he realized that, despite his immediate impulse, he was the last man on earth who could comfort her now.

His back came up against the door behind him and he stopped. He had to force himself to move sideways, his hand reaching out behind him for the knob. He searched for some words, something he could say that would make her feel better. He could not salvage this for himself, he could see that now. Whether it had been a bitter remnant of his emotional pique or his damned arms acting all on their own, all of the trust that she had held for him was gone. Between his thoughtless accusations and this last, fateful blow, he could feel any ties between them severing forever. Still, there was a desperate need in him to bring her even a shred of comfort.

But nothing came to his mind.

"I'm sorry, Misty." He shook his head, bitterly feeling failure of his own mind. "I'm so sorry."

She stiffened, standing straighter again, and her hand reached out to jab that finger at him one last time. "Out." She said it in a flat voice that carried a finality he knew he would never forget.

Jesse bowed his head, slipped out the door, and muttered "I loved you," in a broken voice as the door closed softly behind him.

The sound of her suddenly released sobs made him feel worse than he had ever felt in his life.

*****

Frank sat in the Arcadia enjoying the peace and quiet. The men around him were all old timers with the James and Younger gang, men he knew he could trust to watch his back, because they had been there too many times to count. Ty and the rest of the shavetails Jesse had been bringing into the group lately were absent. Probably past their bedtimes, he thought with a slight smirk.

The bottle at his elbow leached the smile away again, however, and he grasped it by the black fabric tied around the neck. He and the men with him were drinking to the three old hands that had fallen with Jesse at Missouri City, the bottle bought with coin from that job for this express purpose. Frank shook his head sadly. He knew that Jesse had not so much as said some words for the fallen men, and after waiting all day, Frank had taken it upon himself to arrange for this late night drink. They were chasing some coins around the table too, of course. But then, the boys who would not be coming down for breakfast again would never have begrudged them a little poker at a time like this.

Frank looked through the amber liquid in his glass and thought again of his brother. Jesse had been happier with this new dancehall girl than he had been in a long time, but Frank knew his younger brother would be itching to move on eventually, and when he did that, the closer the two had grown, the harder it would be for him to leave. It would be infinitely harder on the girl, though, to have been left by the legendary Jesse James. He had broken hearts across the western territories, and this girl just seemed too sweet to let his randy little brother wreck her life.

Somewhere upstairs a door closed with a firm bang. Frank could tell that he was the only man at the table who had heard, and as he turned to see who was coming down, he lost the thread of the conversation around the table. As soon as he saw the boots thumping slowly down the stairs he could tell that it was his brother. What was more, however, he could tell that something was wrong.

Jesse walked down the stairs like a man in a fog. As his head came into view Frank's frown deepened at the pallor of his brother's skin and the empty look in his eyes. Ever since Jesse had slinked back into town after that Missouri City job yesterday, he had not been acting like his old, confident self.

Jesse took the steps slowly as if he were carrying a massive weight on his shoulders. Each step jarred his entire body, sending his listless arms swinging aimlessly. His face, an empty mask that seemed to radiate a dangerous mix of loss and hatred, was downcast, eyes staring into nothingness.

Frank was shocked to see his brother so diminished. He knew the men saw his brother as an indomitable force of nature; his wry grin and his glinting eyes were known across the territories. He also knew how fragile a legend could be. The wrong person seeing the shuffling wreck moving down the stairs could well damage his reputation for years to come. Frank knew how important his brother's reputation was to him.

The older man looked sharply around the table, saw that the rest of the boys still had not noticed Jesse, and rose to intercept his brother. Jesse was moving faster than it appeared, however, and when Frank stopped him, they were close enough to the table that Jesse could make out the general point of the conversation. Frank turned to look at them, realized what they were saying, and cursed under his breath.

"I'm just sayin', Billy's one hell of a curly wolf and no mistake. That boy shows up on the street, you know he means business." Chase's voice was pitched low, even unaware of Jesse's presence. But not low enough.

"Sure 'nuff. D'you guys hear what he did to those deaders of Carpathians awhile back?" Gage's eyes were alight with the fire of a storyteller with a good tale to tell. "Ripped one of 'em's jaw right off, and rammed a note into its mouth, blamin' the whole thing on ole' Jesse!"

The men snickered, but came up short as they realized that Jesse was standing not far away, his brother's hand on one shoulder. The men stopped laughing and turned in their seats to look at their leader. Frank could tell that all three were shocked at what they saw.

Jesse's face was slack with grief and shock. Deep within his eyes, a flicker of the old flame ignited as Gage's words registered. Those eyes snapped from man to man around the table as he ignored his brother's hand. The light within guttered and rose as if his mind were engaged in an intense inner battle. Frank could only imagine what sorts of things had happened upstairs to push his brother so close to the edge. The calm, cold outlaw, with a reputation as wide as the territories and frightening as death, looked like he had been run over by a freight wagon. That fire was coming back again, however, and it was burning hotter than ever.

"That one was a hoot, Gage." The smile twisting Jesse's thin lips did not reach his fiery eyes, and the boys around the table sat back, looking at each other sideways.

"Didn't mean nothin' by it, Jesse." Gage's smile was hesitant.

"Nah, 'course not, Gage." The ghastly smile was still in place, the eyes still flat, as Jesse grabbed a chair by its back, spun it around, and sat down backwards with a mocking tilt to his eyebrow. "An' that was a ripper, that note in the ole animation's brainpan. Had Carpathian lookin' to wind me up but good, 'till I could convince him it wasn't me. I think we lost, what, five guys, cuz o' that note, Frank?" Jesse's eyes stayed firmly on the three men at the table as he addressed Frank, who had walked up behind him.

"Yeah, Jesse. 'Bout that." Frank's voice was cautious.

"Yeah. Five o' my boys, all up the spout cuz o' that little joke. You guys twig to that? Five o' my guys, bleedin' out into the dust, all ripped up with RJ-1027 fire, 'r worse, at the hands of the Doc's animations, afore I could convince him it wasn't us had done for that entire column in the woods."

His smile widened as his eyes grew flatter. "Guys just like you, Gage . . . 'n you, Chase."

"Jesse, honest, we was just talkin'. Frank was with us!" Fear had seeped into Gage's voice now, his courage failing him in the continued pressure of Jesse's blank stare.

"Gage, you ain't got nothin' to worry about."Jesse leaned back, one arm still wrapped around the chair back as he took his hat off in a grand gesture. "You was jus' talkin'. I get it."

Jesse stood and turned back to Frank. "Frank, I need you to go get the Youngers. We're headin' out o' town now. We got a meetin' out in Diablo Canyon, an' we better get a wiggle on afore were late."

All four other men stared at Jesse for a second. "Jesse," Frank leaned in to speak low in his brother's ear. "It's after midnight. Most o' the boys'll be unconscious, this time o' night. Maybe we can wait till first light, anyway— "

Jesse cut his brother off with a chopping motion that set the inner workings of his arm buzzing and purring. "We ain't waitin', Frank, we're leavin'. An' anyone who can't drag their sorry asses out o' their bunks can damn well stay here an' wait for the law."

All three of the other men were standing now as well, and Gage coughed. "Jesse, it's really late, an'—"

Not even Frank, who had been watching for something like this, saw the gun leap from its holster, or any more than a rushing blur as the armored arm snapped out, hyper-velocity pistol filling the metal fist, and angular barrel pressing up against Gage's forehead.

"Word one, an' it'll be your last, boy." The false smile was gone, and only the hard, dark eyes remained to communicate what was going on in the outlaw's mind. Frank had seen that look once or twice, but not more than that, and it had never ended happily for anyone.

Gage backed away, his hands raised to either side of his head, his mouth slack.

"Jesse, I think maybe," Frank began, his own hands upraised to fend off any aggression thrown his way. Jesse's pistol wavered slightly in his direction, but settled back on Gage's forehead. "Jesse, I think maybe you wanna put the smokewagon down, an' have a seat? This seems to be somethin' we should all be talkin' about, rather than you throwin' yer weight aroun' when somethin's got you all riled up."

Again the hand moved faster than anyone could follow, this time to flip the pistol around so Jesse was holding it by the barrel and then bringing the heavy gun down onto the table with an echoing crack. The sleepy bartender snapped awake, looking around blearily as he reached beneath the bar for a weapon. The rest of the men and women jerked upright at the sound, but Frank noticed that they made no move towards their weapons. They just watched the famous outlaw from the corners of their eyes.

"You dictatin' actions to me, Frank? You wanna be leadin' this gang?" He glared over his shoulder at his older brother. "You sick o' followin' your little brother? Time to reach for the brass ring on your own?"

"'Course not, Jesse." Frank raised his hands a bit higher, trying to find a neutral expression for his worried face. "Gang's yours, Jesse. Always has been, always will be. You make the call, I'll back your play, same as always."

"Same as Missouri City?" Jesse sneered, and Frank felt a pang of guilt, his eyes flickering towards the black-draped bottle.

"Missouri City was a mistake, Jesse. You knew it. I couldn't of—"

"It was a mistake, I know that." Jesse spat at him. "I went off half-cocked, and drug some good boys with me." He nodded at the bottle. "An' yeah, some of 'em didn't come back. An' that's been eatin' at me since we rode back into town. But you know what, Frank? If you had been there, if you'd o' just ridden along anyway? You might'a saved those men, Frank, just by bein' there." His empty hand jerked towards the bottle. "You and that damned rifle Sophie might'a saved 'em, and you might'a saved those people down in Missouri City, too."

The pistol whirled around, almost as if by magic, and he slashed it back into its holster with a slap. "So, when you start thinkin' you're gonna start tellin' me what to do, or where to go, or when, I want you to think about that, okay?"

Frank knew the argument was not a fair one, and knew that Jesse's own guilt was a major source of the anger and frustration being thrown his way, but something had happened upstairs to bring this all to a head, and things did not look like they were going to be easy to defuse, now that he had his dander up.

"There's some fair words, there, Jesse, and that's the honest truth." Frank tried to strike a reasonable tone, but he saw that he had lost before he had begun as Jesse's eyes flared again.

"Nothin' you're gonna say is gonna matter, Frank!" Jesse's mouth was twisted into a snarl. "You're right! You wanna hear me scream it? Wake up half this bug hill? You're right! Frank James is right!" A mechanical arm lashed out, latched ahold of Frank's vest, and pulled him close. "You're right, Frank," Jesse whispered. "The law is comin'. They're comin' because we sat on our asses here too long, an' their comin' because of what we did down the river, and when they get here, they'll be loaded for bear."

One metal thumb jerked towards the stairs and for a moment Frank thought Jesse was going to choke on his words, but he twisted his neck, never breaking eye contact, and spat, "Ain't nothin' holdin' us here, we got the law bearin' down on us from God knows where, an' we got us an appointment out in the hills we're gonna be hard pressed to meet if we don't leave soon."

Frank looked from his brother to the three men, none of them willing to speak, Gage nearly drowning in his own sweat. Frank looked back to Jesse and lowered his hands. "What is it you want us to do, Jesse? You just say the word, an' we're there."

The tension in Jesse's face eased slightly, although the anger and the pain still burned in his eyes. He nodded. "I – We, need to leave. We need to round up as many as we can, an' we need to leave here tonight." He tapped Frank on the chest with the back of one heavy hand. "You're right. They'll be comin', an' I've had an itch between my shoulder blades since ridin' out o' Missouri City." His eyes flicked up the stairs. "An' I just wanna go, Frank. I just wanna get out of Kansas City, hit the trail again, and leave this damned manure pile behind."

Frank gave an answering nod. "Okay, boys, you heard 'em. Roust up as many as you can, an' have 'em meet us all on the edge of town, where the tracks run out west. I'll get Cole an' them, an' we'll be gone in less than an hour. That sit right with you, Jesse?"

The three men nodded and walked towards the door, casting backward glances at their shaken boss. Gage could not stop rubbing the center of his forehead, a wary look in his eyes.

Jesse collapsed back into another seat, right way around this time, and Frank sat down next to him. "Thank you, Frank. I really gotta get out of this burg, 'r my head feels like it's gonna explode."

Frank nodded. "Um, Jesse," he did not know how to proceed, but knew that he must. "Your plunder . . . is it upstairs still?"

Jesse looked at his older brother, eyes haunted again, face pale but blank. "Yeah, Frank. It is."

Frank looked at the stairs and then back to his brother. "An' you can't go up an' get it?"

Jesse looked down at the table, his hands lifting up to fold before him with studied calm. "No, Frank. I don't think I can."

Frank nodded. "An' it prob'ly wouldn't do for me or one of the boys to go fetch it?"

Jesse shook his head in silence.

Frank looked around, then pushed away from the table. "I'll be right back." He moved towards the bar, casting a couple looks over his shoulder to see his brother still slumped there, exhausted. The rest of the men were gone, and the other folks in the room studiously avoided looking at Jesse.

At the bar, Frank made a quick inquiry about the old lady that worked most nights, and then turned to wait, back resting against the rough wood, while the bar tender went to drag the poor woman out of bed. Frank could feel the exhaustion of the day pressing down on him and did not relish the thought of riding out into the dark of the night like common thieves. The thought brought a smile to his face, however.

When the old woman dragged herself out from a small back room Frank apologized and passed her a coin, asking if she would be willing to do him a favor.

Frank waited by the bar while the old woman went upstairs, keeping an eye on his brother's stooped, still form. When she returned, lugging Jesse's worn leather bags, duster draped over one arm, and horrified, accusatory heat burning in her eyes, Frank gave her another coin and a shrug, pulling the things away from her. Something told him he did not want to hear anything she might have said. If there had been a dead body up there she would have already raised a stir, but from the look on her face, what was up there could not have been much better.

The old woman muttered something to the bartender, who turned back to Frank. "There's a broken mirror, cost more'n a dollar to replace."

Frank shook his head and handed over another coin before turning away. He moved through the room holding the heavy bags high. He needed to get Jesse up and moving before he went searching for the Youngers. Another duty he was not much relishing in a night that had really just gone all to hell in a matter of moments.

Chapter 8

"So you're telling me he's gone." Courtright's voice was even, but there was something in his eye that set the bartender back a step.

"Yeah, skedaddled in the night. He'd been paid up through the end o' the month, so weren't no reason' to make 'em stay." The man's voice shook slightly, but his eyes darkened as he continued. "Shame what happened to the girl, though."

Loveless rested on the bar, leaning towards the shaken man. "The girl? What happened to the girl?"

The bartender shook his head. "He roughed her up somethin' fierce, miss. Struck her in the face with one of those arms o' his. There were folks, told me I shouldn't o' let no outlaw freak like him board here. But din't seem too bad to me, you know? And he was so personable. There's folks tell he's like a Robin Hood outa the old stories, right?" The man's face darkened again. "'Cept he was pretty tight with his coin, if you want the truth. And 'course, when he run off, he left that poor girl from the Occidental all beat up. The missus, she had to go up and get his stuff, and she found the girl sobbin' her heart out on the floor."

"He hit her?" Loveless could not believe the urbane man she had spoken with the day before could have beaten a defenseless woman. Then again, talking to him it was easy to forget that he was a known criminal with an impressive trail of bodies behind him. If the army found out she had been within arm's reach of him and not taken him into custody, there could very well be hell to pay.

"I'm not sure what else he could o' done, miss. My missus, she said the girl was bleedin' like a stuck pig all over the floor." His look soured even more. "The mirror was broke into a thousand tiny pieces too. Took my idiot boy most of the day to clean it up."

Courtright turned away from the bar, leaning against it. He rolled his head towards Lucinda with a fixed smile. "So, there goes our only lead in this latrine trench of a town. And he managed to assault an innocent girl on the way out, too. The president will not look kindly upon the results of our latest outing."

Lucinda snorted. "Since when do you care about the wellbeing of some fast trick from the territories? No one in Washington is going to care about Miss Misty Mimms either, so you can quit your carrying on over the poor innocent and her blood and tears."

Courtright smiled and turned back to look out over the saloon's common room. "Well, fair enough. But that doesn't change the fact that James was our only lead on Carpathian, and he's gone."

"He's not the only one who's gone, Henry. His brother left his room, none of the Youngers are in town, and none of the locals that had been taking up with Jesse have been seen all day. The entire gang's cleared out. And it can't have been because he roughed up some dancehall girl." She was still facing the bar, looking at her hands as her fingers tapped softly on the scarred wood. "There must be a reason they all left in the middle of the night like that."

"They're corn cracking road agents, Luce. Ripping out in the middle of the night is sort of central to who they are." He threw an elbow up on the bar and turned to face his partner. "The real question is what we do next? I don't relish the idea of going back east empty-handed. The president won't like it. And it's not going to make us look like very good agents if we let this country rube hightail it out of town in the night, taking our only leads with him."

She could only nod, her eyes unfocused. "I didn't get any sense yesterday that he was planning on leaving."

Courtright leaned towards his partner, his face wrinkling slightly in concern. "Luce, where's your head? You need to get back in the game before we find ourselves taken out of things completely. Half the towns along the Missouri are sporting Carpathian Industries generators and tech. The lunatic is strengthening his hold over the whole region and stretching eastward every year. If we can't pinpoint his position for a major strike, he'll own the west before Grant can push through with the army and take care of things." He shook his head. "If I didn't know you for the ice cold bruja you are, I'd swear that filthy cowboy got into your head." He sneered slightly, "or someplace lower."

She snapped a dirty look at him and snarled. "My head's right where it should be, chiseler. Worry about your own; I'm fine." She shook her head trying to clear it of the vaguely melancholy fugue that hung behind her eyes. "Anyway, I know what it'll mean, but maybe if we talk with the girl he left behind? Maybe he told her something before he took off."

Courtright's smile was hard and without humor. "Sure, maybe he was keeping up with the light banter between slaps." He shook his head. "A guy who's hard enough to hit a woman and draw blood is not going to be taking the time to pass along his itinerary." His face darkened again. "You don't tell a woman you're hitting where you're going to next."

Lucinda looked sharply at her partner. "You got a lot of experience with that sort of thing, Henry? Roughing up girls?"

Courtright's smile widened. "I haven't ever roughed you up, have I? So don't worry about it."

She snorted. "If you ever tried to rough me up I'd be days filling out the paperwork explaining to Washington about your tragic and untimely death at the hands of a passel of prairie school girls."

"School girls, would it be now?" He completed his turn and rested his elbows on the bar. "Wouldn't be doing the dirty work yourself?"

"No, that sort of thing is really beneath me at this point in my career." She sniffed primly and then looked at him again. "Seriously, though. Any other ideas, if you don't think Miss Mimms will offer any hope of tracking James down to his next destination?"

Courtright's expression turned grim. "Sadly, no."

"Well, since that's what we've got, I'd say we would be remiss in our duties were we to not, at the very least, check in on the girl and get her statement." Lucinda pushed her way from the bar. "Damn, but this report is going to read like a flipping tragedy."

Courtright nodded and turned towards the door. They were just moving away from the bar when a seedy-looking local stepped in front of Courtright. The man seemed loath to make eye contact, but stood like he meant to stop them, one hand braced as if expecting them to push past.

"You talkin' 'bout Jesse James?" His voice was hoarse, his eyes flitting around like skittish wild animals.

Courtright casually put a hand on the butt of his pistol. "Not sure you were invited into the conversation, friend. Maybe you should see yourself back to your seat, now, before you upset the nice lady here." He indicated Lucinda with a jerk of his chin. "She's not nearly so pleasant when she's upset."

"I's in here last night," the reticent man continued. "I heard 'em talkin'."

Lucinda put one graceful hand on Courtright's, pushing the blaster back into his holster. "Wait a second, Henry. It's quite possible this nice man can help us. Sir, did you happen to hear Mr. James or any of his companions talking about where they might be headed?"

Courtright grudgingly stepped aside, but there was something strange about the man's face that he could not quite put a finger on. He examined him carefully while Lucinda continued speaking.

"We're friends of his, and his sudden departure caught us by surprise." She was employing her most ravishing smile, but she could see it was having little effect on a man that refused to meet her gaze. "We would be ever so thankful if you could give us even an inkling of where to look?"

The man snapped sidelong glances at Lucinda and Courtright. "Well, I'm not sure how much I remember . . . it was late, I mean . . . "

"Would a slap up the side of your head jar your memory at all?" Courtright snarled as he took a step towards the cowering man.

Lucinda put a hand on her partner's shoulder and drew a coin from her purse. "I'm sure a drink would refresh you and restore your memory. Perhaps after we talk you can treat yourself to a bottle of something nice?" She handed him the silver coin and the man smiled a thank you. The coin swiftly disappeared, although neither Lucinda nor Henry would have been able to say where it went.

"They mentioned some canyon out west aways. Devils canyon? Demon canyon?" He muttered as if unsure of his memory.

"Diablo Canyon?" Courtright snapped. Whatever it was about the man, it was getting harder and harder to stop himself from slapping him.

"Yeah, that was it. Diablo.Canyon. Means devil, though, in Spanish . . . don't it?" The man's vague bearing was getting worse.

"Yes, it does mean devil in Spanish. Very good." Lucinda tried one more of her smiles, but again the man's flitting eyes rendered her efforts useless. "Thank you, sir. Jesse and his friends will be very happy to see us."

"Who wouldn't be, miss?" For a split second all the fuzziness and jittery energy seemed to settle, and the strange man looked right into Lucinda's eyes. She blinked and drew back away slightly from the sudden directness of his eyes. She was staring straight into them, but she would not have been able to say what color they were.

"Well . . . thank you . . . " Lucinda attempted to regain her bearings.

"Thanks again, folks." The man ducked his head again and turned away from them. "A right pleasure doin' business with ya'll."

Lucinda and Courtright were left standing in the middle of the floor, watching the man push quickly through the doors and out into the morning air. For a moment, they just stared at the doors as they slowed in their swinging. Courtright's head swiveled back to his partner's.

"Was that guy's eyes red?" He said the words hesitantly; as if not sure he wanted to ask.

Lucinda shook her hear. "I'm not sure. There was something . . . I don't know."

Courtright stood up straighter and sniffed loudly. "Anyway, Diablo Canyon.That make any sense?"

Lucinda nodded. "The place was a ruin for years. One of the railroad companies had commissioned a line to go through there, take a bridge over the canyon, and continue on to the west coast. But everyone forgot to plan for the bridge, and so things stalled. All the engineers and workers were staying in tents, waiting for the equipment. When the equipment got there, they started to lay out the foundations for the bridge, and then the government began its Heavy Rail program. All the funding for new civilian lines dried up as the situation out in the west got progressively worse. No one ever cancelled the Diablo Canyon project, but no further work got done, either. The tents gave way to wooden structures, all the various folks went about trying to make a living until the bridge started up again, and then continued on out of habit long after it should have been clear that there wasn't going to be any bridge." She shrugged. "For a long time it was a bandit's paradise. No law at all, since the town didn't officially exist. Outlaws basically made it their own, treating it like one of those pirate's lairs from the old stories."

Courtright was staring at her with puzzled admiration. "How the hell did you know all that?"

She smiled and shrugged. "I did some research years ago, when it was obvious this is where someone with my . . . talents . . . would most likely get sent, in the event that I was hired."

Her partner shook his head. "Damn, but the stuff you've got shoved into that brain pan of yours." He gestured back to the door. "You think there's anything to what the old coot said about Diablo Canyon? What the hell would James need with construction machinery?"

Lucinda shook her head. "It's not just the machinery. The whole town was a chaotic den of thieves and barbarians, and Jesse James fit right in. In fact, there were a few years where he basically ruled Diablo Canyon, before he decided he'd rather be closer to civilization. The place is completely isolated."

"Great, sounds like a lovely place for a holiday. But if it is the machinery they're after . . . why?"

Lucinda pursed her lips. "James has never been famous for an eagerness for hard labor. If they're planning on using machinery, it must be something big."

A dark cloud lowered over Courtright's face. "Like they might be trying to dig something up?"

His partner nodded. "Maybe."

Courtright's brows lowered further. "Would this not fit into the latest bulletin from Washington, requiring immediate report?"

Lucinda's eyes met his. "If this has anything to do with that last bulletin, and the James gang is heading for it, then yes, one of us will need to make an urgent, personal report."

"Well, we can draw matchsticks on that. You really think we should split up?" He gestured towards the door and she nodded her thanks, moving towards it.

"I think we should probably complete an interim report here and get it sent off to Washington over the wire. We should check on Miss Mimms, see if there are any other leads, and then both set off tomorrow when we'll be fresh." She pushed her way through the doors and then stood on the other side waiting for him on the rough wooden boardwalk.

He followed her out into the shade of the saloon's overhang, his eyes dazzled by the brightness of the sun in the street. "Well, hell. I was thinking, this lead's hot enough, maybe we had to rush off before we got a chance to complete any written . . . bloody hell."

She looked back at his sudden shift in tone. He was staring out at the street, shielding his eyes from the glare of the sun. A massive freight wagon had pulled up across the street accompanied by a formation of low-slung one man vehicles. The entire entourage glided to a stop nearby, their engines roaring with the full-throated fury of an RJ-1027 power plant in hard labor. The smaller machines had two wheels and were ridden like ground-bound Iron Horses. The men were dismounting, long tan dusters flaring out as legs came up and over. Most of the men wore shining silver stars on their chests or hats, and she shook her head in disbelief at the bad luck. Realizing she was seeing a large band of federal marshals, she looked more closely at the larger vehicle and her mouth fell open in disbelief.

Lucinda had heard of the big circuit court support vehicles that been sent out west, but she had never seen one. She understood now, given the reputation of the circuit court judges, why most folks had taken to calling the vehicles 'Lynch Wagons' despite the official government designation, 'Federal Judgment.'

The vehicle was massive, a wall of riveted armor carried along on three enormous iron wheels on each side. It cast a long shadow across the dusty street. Small firing ports dotted the flanks, while two long slits perched at the front must provide the driver with visibility from within his armored protection. On the roof of the monster was a socket large enough for a man, housing an imposing Gatling gun. Obviously this was for supporting fire during particularly salty legal debates. The strangest feature of the vehicle, however, was the armored box built into the rear. Barred windows looked out over the street. The thing had its own jail cell built directly into its armored bulk, for transporting prisoners who had not suffered the ultimate sanction. And for that, the government had provided as well.

The mechanisms of the retractable gallows were stowed for transportation, but Lucinda had heard rumors, and could see the armatures, hydraulic pistons, and winch system that would deploy to provide immediate and irrevocable judgment should the circuit judges and marshals deem it appropriate.

It was nothing if not dramatic.

The smaller vehicles, however, must have been the Interceptors the marshals were always complaining about. They seemed quite sleek and vicious to her. They looked less bulky than the Iron Horses, carrying less armor, but they made up for that with their understated, low-slung lethality. They were a perfect match for the methodical men who were now gathered around the side of the support wagon.

One of the men in the small group pointed at the Arcadia. From Lucinda's vantage point on the long porch, it appeared that the men turning in her direction were focused on only on the building. She quickly pulled Henry aside, catching him off balance and having to steady him before he toppled them both into the dust.

"What the—" Courtright growled as he pushed off Lucinda and gave her a hard look.

She gestured with her head towards the Federal Judgment. "That's no standard circuit court."

Courtright looked back at the vehicle and saw two of the new UR-30 Enforcer units moving smoothly down the hull ladder from the access hatch. Two more moved around from the far side. "Four of those chiseling automatons?"

Lucinda gripped Courtright's arm with painful intensity. "That's not all." Her eyes were riveted to the back of the vehicle, where a massive armored door was unfolding to provide a ramp up into the cell compartment. A rumbling hiss escaped from within the wagon, and then a loud clank echoed across the street. Another metallic clang sounded, and then another. The vehicle shook slightly with each sound, despite its size. A huge hand reached out and gripped the side of the doorway in grinding metal fingers. Another emerged on the far side, and then a hulking form pulled its way out of the hatch. It stalked out onto the ramp and down to the street. Each footstep resounded with a metallic clash, shaking the Judgment.

"What the—" Courtright repeated, but this time his voice was soft with awe.

"It's Morgan Earp. Gotta be." Lucinda's eyes would not move from the enormous figure now standing in the street. A pale face, tiny amidst the armor and iron, blinked in the sunlight. It was a colossal form, armored plates and support braces melding together like a bulky statue come to life. The only flesh visible from her vantage point was the man's face, peeking out from an elaborate framework that almost completely enclosed his head.

"They reported an attempted assassination a year or two ago, and then a couple weeks later reported that it had failed, and that was it for official reports." She flicked a finger surreptitiously towards the armored man, her voice still hushed. "There's been a lot of speculation, and unconfirmed reports that Carpathian was somehow brought in to repair the damage, but no one knew for sure."

"Are you telling me that the Federal Bureau of Marshals has known where Carpathian is for years?" Courtright's voice rose, his eyes widened and his color darkened. It was clear from his tone what he thought of the self-styled Federal Bureau of Marshals. Lucinda agreed with him, as did most federal agents working in the western territories. The federal government continued to deal with the marshals, providing them with material support and the damned robot Enforcers. Although there was no officially sanctioned Federal Bureau of Lawmen, the very fact that they were allowed to continue to function without any legal sanction from the federal government made them the de facto law in the west until someone in Washington did something about it.

"I swear, if we've been kicking around out here in the sand and the scorpions for months, and Earp and his damned merry band of hooligans knew where the mad European has been all this time—" His growl was rising to a roar, and Lucinda's fingers tightened painfully around his arm.

"Earp doesn't know, and neither do most of the other marshals. Word is that Wyatt's oldest brother, Virgil, grabbed Morgan on his death bed, threw him in a wagon, and disappeared with him." Her mouth stopped moving, assuming a vapid smile as the lawmen approached, but she continued to speak in a husky whisper. "Two weeks later, he's completely encased in steel, breathing, folks think; alive, apparently; and back in the saddle, so to speak."

Lucinda pushed Courtright farther into the shadows with an empty smile and nodded towards the group of lawmen clumping onto the boardwalk. Courtright grunted in offended surprise but tipped his hat towards the group.

Most of the marshals moved past the pair without a second glance. One of the men, wearing an elaborate set of black leather robes, eyes completely obscured behind dark, smoky goggles, looked them up and down with an impassive face and continued on into the saloon behind his companions.

"What the hell was that sand head supposed to be dressed like?" Courtright straightened his gambler's clothes, mustering what dignity he could.

"Circuit Judge. Sort of a liaison between the Federal Bureau of Marshals and Washington." She shook her head. "Pretty odd sticks, from the reports I've been reading. Some have even taken to wearing wigs like the judges back in merry old England like to sport."

"Well, damn. That fella ain't gonna be standin' long in this heat, he keeps traipsin' around in all that leather." He shrugged. "What you think's brought Earp and his traveling circus into Kansas City?"

Lucinda rested against the warm wall of the saloon and produced a lacey fan. She began to work it back and forth in front of her face while smiling at one of the marshals that had been left behind. The man tipped his hat to her and then turned back to the UR-30 units and the hulking Morgan Earp. Behind the fan she continued. "Well, pretty much what brought us here, Henry, if I had to venture a guess."

"They're after Carpathian as well? Well then, why they hell wouldn't they just hold down that gray-haired old sod and force 'em—"

"Not Carpathian. Our ultimate goal is Carpathian, but we did not come here to Kansas City thinking to find the great man here walking the streets, did we?" Her face was still empty and smiling, but her tone was cold behind the fluttering fan. "His animations haven't been seen within a hundred miles of KC, and he never goes anywhere without them, as you know. Why, oh Henry dearest, were we submitting ourselves to the provincial mercies of Kansas City in the first place?"

Courtright turned to face the wall, pretending to check his boots by kicking them against the worn wood. "So they're here looking for Jesse James?"

"Or for his gang, or someone in the gang, would be my best speculation, yes."

Courtright grunted around a cruel grin. "Well, looks like we won't be the only ones had our whole day ruined by their late night withdrawal." He spit a solid plug out into the sunlight. "At least we didn't drag a freak show into town in our wake. They really aren't going to be happy when they—"

"What!?!" The shout from within the saloon was harsh, and several folks walking along the street were distracted from their fascination with the Judgment wagon. They cast cautious glances at the saloon before hurrying along on their way.

Courtright smiled tightly at Lucinda as the shouting continued inside, muffled just enough to mask the words. It looked as if they could add the bartender to the list of folks who were not having a good day.

Earp and his gang pushed through the doors with enough force to send them crashing into the wall with a resounding crack. Lucinda and Courtright once again assumed their roles, empty smiles in place, and nodded to the retreating lawmen. Henry could not quite keep the edge from his smile, however, and he realized he may have overplayed his hand when one of the marshals hesitated in his stride, looking right at him. But the man shook his head slightly and continued after the Over-marshal and the judge.

The two agents watched as the lawmen conferred by the flank of their massive wagon. Almost immediately the four UR-30 units snapped into motion, moving off in four different directions, bodies moving smoothly down the street while heads began to swivel continuously, scanning everything in sight. One unit moved down the street past the Arcadia, and Lucinda and Henry watched as it strode by, head swiveling with every step. It was past them already, moving down to the east, when its pivoting head stopped suddenly, followed almost immediately by its entire body.

The body of the Enforcer was still for a moment, standing in the shining sun, staring into their shadowed retreat. When it began to move towards them a ruby beam lashed out from its single eye, scanning them up and down several times before winking away again. When the metal man was about ten feet away it stopped, and in a buzzing, unnatural voice, began to speak.

"Federal agents Lucinda Loveless and Henry Courtright, currently on assignment for the President in the western territories. Please accompany me to the Over-marshal."

Courtright looked at Lucinda with an upraised eyebrow, but she was staring at the machine, real anger flaring alight in her brown eyes.

Lucinda snapped her fan closed and stalked off the boardwalk and into the blazing sun, not flinching for a moment under the brilliant heat. She walked past the android and directly into the circle of lawmen standing beside the looming wagon. The men all turned to watch her approach with faces that ranged from expectant to appreciative to surly. One of the men was wearing a bulky rebreather mask that covered the lower half of his face, but his eyes seemed to crinkle with amusement. The man at the center of the circle, however, with long flowing mustaches and hard, flat eyes, merely stared at her with cold calculation.

"Over-marshal Earp, I assume?" Lucinda's voice was harsh. With a jerk of her head she indicated the android that had followed her back towards the lawmen. Henry, following a little way behind the robot, watched the proceedings calmly with a hand casually hooked into his belt near his blaster. When Earp nodded once in recognition, she snapped, "and who do you think you are, endangering federal agents like this?"

Earp's head tilted slightly at the attack, but otherwise registered no reaction. "I'm sure I don't know what you're talkin' about, young lady."

She pivoted slightly to stab a finger at the robot. Now her voice was harsh but low, hissing with anger. "Your creature, here, just called my partner and me out in the middle of the street! We are currently working in the territories under cover for the president himself, marshal! If our work here has been jeopardized, the president will—"

"Which one?" The mild tone of the question caught her off guard and Lucinda stuttered to a temporary pause.

"What?" Her anger was still boiling, and it was clear she did not like being forestalled this way.

Earp shook his head with a slight smile. "Never mind. I apologize for the actions of the robot, however." His eyes flicked to the machine now standing behind the agent. "They ain't known for their subtlety, and half the time, I don't know what they know. They sure as Sam Hill weren't supposed to go pulling you out of your lair, though, miss. So again, I apologize."

The apology took much of the steam out of her approach and she paused again, attempting to rally her thoughts. While she struggled, however, Henry stepped up, hand still near his weapon, eyes tight with suspicion.

"Well, an apology is all nice and good, marshal, but it doesn't do us any good now if our cover has been blown."

Earp smiled even more broadly, hooking his thumbs into his vest pockets and rocking back on his heels. "Well, folks, you do have my sympathies, but if your real concern was maintaining some sort of fictional cover, it don't strike me as you're doin' yourselves any good, comin' at me guns a'blazin' in the middle of the street. Am I wrong in that, though? Is this some sort of secret agent trick, maybe an honest lawman wouldn't know about?"

Lucinda's anger blazed anew, and her own hands balled into fists as she leaned closer to the Over-marshal. "Why you bastard pissant!How dare you lecture us— "

Earp raised a hand, head cocked to one side. "Now, don't get your bloomers in a bunch, there, Miss. I'm just makin' a point. But maybe it ain't the best time nor place to make it, as the milk's already been spilled."

An older marshal standing by Wyatt Earp's shoulder snorted. "Don't make his point any less relevant, miss. Weren't more'n a soul or two could o' heard the mechanical man's words, but you rushin' this way . . . that weren't none too smart."

A muffled laugh quickly followed. "Virg, always makin' friends with the ladies." The man in the breathing mask shook his head. "Anyone else curious as to why the metal man called 'em out in the first place?"

Earp nodded. "Unit AZ-21, why did you stop the agents here?"

"And how the hell did it know they were agents?" One of the marshals muttered under his breath, shying away from a dark look from the Over-marshal's brother as soon as the words were out of his mouth.

"Federal information indicated agents Loveless and Courtright are currently on assignment in Kansas City region." The machine's voice, with its unpleasant buzzing, was at the same time hard to hear and hard to ignore. "Recent reports indicated the agents were currently searching for Jesse Woodson James in the same region. Federal asset requisition protocols indicate immediate contact with agents authorized and advantageous under current circumstances."

Lucinda scowled at the inhuman metal face with its single eye and round, grill-like mouth. She looked back at Earp without changing her expression. "What circumstances?"

Wyatt Earp coughed apologetically, looking down for a moment and kicking a small stone aside with his boot. "Well, miss, there was an incident down the river aways, in Missouri City. A bank job, saw over twenty people killed, more'n that injured. Don't know how much money they made off with, as there weren't no one left to ask."

Lucinda looked confused, her hands falling at her sides. "Over twenty dead? Was it a battle? Did they fight back?"

Virgil Earp snorted. "Did they fight? No, miss, they didn't fight. What they did, mostly, was die. James and his gang burnt the bank down when they were done, most of the customers trapped inside to burn like animals."

The circle of faces turned bleak and angry. "Miss, if you'd a seen what we seen down Missouri City, you'd be angry, for sure, but it wouldn't be us you'd be cussin' at."

Lucinda was still distracted, turning to look at Courtright with a questioning tilt to her head. "Over twenty people?"

Courtright stepped up and made a big show of offering his hand to Earp and then the other marshals in the circle. "Over-marshal Earp, sir, my name is agent Courtright, sure enough. Sorry for the earlier misunderstanding. We have been, in fact, seeking contact with James, but not as a direct part of our investigation. He was a source of intelligence in our current assignment, is all."

Earp stared at him, the smile gone from his face. "By that flannel-mouthed response, agent, I'm going to assume you met Jesse James, but did not apprehend him or his men?"

Courtright's own eyes flared. "Sir, it is not our job to apprehend petty criminals. If we had been aware of the events down in Missouri City, then we may well have taken a different tack. But we had not heard anything about it, and we are in the middle of our own assignment."

"You know for a fact it was Jesse James that killed those people, marshal?" Lucinda's voice broke in on their conversation and both men turned to look at her. "It could't have been some other gang? Perhaps one of the unaffiliated groups working out of the badlands?"

Earp shook his head. "No. We had several folks down there who recognized him. It's been awhile since he's been active, but there wasn't any doubt, this was his job."

Lucinda's thoughtful gaze passed beyond the circle of men and robots, focusing on some distant object. "But Frank James and the Youngers were all in Kansas City the whole day." She turned to Courtright. "He almost never does a major job without his brother and one or two Youngers with him. And he's never put up numbers like that before. Twenty civilians?"

Earp shook his head sharply. "Sorry, miss, but that just ain't so. During the war, Jesse James and his brother took part in more than one massacre, killing scores of unarmed soldiers. He's capable, and he's done it in the past. And we know he was in Missouri City, in the bank, with a force of men on their damned Iron Horses." He gave her a closer look, and she could feel his eyes boring their way beneath the façade of her role. "And what I'm wonderin' right now, if you don't mind my speculatin' out loud, is why it is that a Federal agent seems to be lookin' for excuses that this atrocity can't have been perpetrated by a man who's been known to commit worse crimes." His eyes flicked to Courtright. "Am I wrong, Agent Courtright? Or is your agency, perhaps, working along a different set of assumptions than us lawmen, scratchin' along on the sharp edge out here?"

"I'm not looking for excuses for anything." Lucinda snapped, and she tried to reign herself in, knowing she would not be doing herself any good if she let this Podunk yahoo get under her skin here in the middle of the street. "Jesse James puts on a good act,

Over-marshal, and he's got quite a reputation. But you're going to see, as you continue to track him, that he's a lot smarter than you'd think. You'll also see, I believe, that he's done a lot of growing up since the war. I have no doubt this atrocity you're speaking of took place, and that those poor people were killed. I have no doubt that Jesse James was there." She shifted her gaze to take in all of the men around the circle. "What I am saying, however, is that there is more here than what you are reporting. Something about the events in Missouri City does not add up, and you'd do well to take that into consideration before rushing off into the wilderness after them all."

The men were momentarily taken aback by her harsh words, but even as she allowed herself to think that maybe she had gotten through to them, that they were looking at the evidence before them with clearer vision, Virgil Earp leaned forward and muttered through his mustache. "No, look here, miss. That was a nice little speech you just gave, but it sounded a lot more like a wife arguein' for a guilty husband than a Federal agent giving a concise field report."

Wyatt Earp's eyes tightened at his brother's words, and his gaze remained steady on Lucinda. "Gotta admit, miss.Virg's got a point. Is there any chance you ain't lookin' at this whole thing with a complete lack of bias?"

There was no warning as Loveless' hand suddenly plunged into the slit of her dress and whipped up, holding a long, slim knife. Even the UR-30 unit was only beginning to react when her arm hurtled back down again, sending the knife tumbling through the air.

The knife glittered as it spun through the harsh sunlight, and when it smacked into the packed dirt of the street directly between Wyatt Earp's dusty boots, it was as if a brief electrical current had run through the entire group. Every marshal around the circle tensed at the exact moment, hands on gun butts or reaching for knives of their own. Doc Holliday already had his weapon out and pointing straight at Lucinda's head at the end of an arm as steady as bedrock. Virgil Earp was crouching down, a hand on either pistol grip at his waist. Only Wyatt had not moved.

"Well, that was mighty fine knife work, miss." Wyatt lobbed a gobbet of spit out of the circle and into the dust. "Don't really address the issue at hand, however."

Courtright grabbed Lucinda by the shoulder and forced her behind him, his other hand raised in a placating gesture that took in all the marshals but focused primarily on Holliday and the bore of his RJ-1027 pistol.

"Now, Over-marshal, to be fair, I think Luce meant that for being in the way of addressing that very issue." His voice was steady and calm, but Holliday and the robot were particularly unnerving, neither moving but both focusing hard on the two agents. "We been together a long time, and we've been together on this assignment the whole time. No one's been compromised. She just took exception to your tone, I think. Ain't that right, Lucinda?"

The snarl was still firmly on her face, but she thawed it through a force of will and gave a bright smile to the Over-marshal and his brothers. "Absolutely."

Earp nodded with a grin. "Well that's good. I'd hate to think that we were all workin' at cross-purposes on something this important." He scuffed the street with his boot again, then looked up with a purposefully vague expression. "Now, did you folks already mention where James and his gang had scarpered off to?"

Courtright looked to Lucinda to respond and the weight of his gaze was crushing. She flicked her eyes from her partner to Earp and back again, and was hurt and irritated to see the sudden doubt in Henry's eyes. She sighed, shook her head, and looked back to the Over-marshal. "An old man in the bar told us he'd overheard them talking about Diablo Canyon."

"Makes sense, go back to hide in his old stomping grounds." Doc Holliday nodded.

Virgil looked puzzled, however. "Don't they still have AZ 20 in Diablo Canyon? Ain't gonna be like nothin' he'd be expectin', he heads back there right about now."

Wyatt nodded. "First UR-30 we sent out from Tombstone went down that way, been keepin' the place quiet as a crypt ever since. That ought 'a be a nice surprise to tide them over till we come ridin' down their backtrail, eh boys?"

The other marshals had already begun to mount their Interceptors while Morgan Earp and the robots were making their way back into the Lynch Wagon. As Wyatt was climbing up the access ladder to the high hatch he stopped and tipped his hat to Lucinda. "Now, miss, if you're assignment should happen to bring you up towards Diablo Canyon, I trust you'll have the professional courtesy to let us know we're all playin' in the same sandbox again, okay?"

Lucinda said nothing, her jaw clenched tight, but forced herself to give a single jerky nod.

With low, growling roars the Interceptors moved out, taking up an arrowhead formation and roaring down the street into the west. The Judgment support vehicle, its tone a much lower, subterranean bellow, rocked into motion and followed behind at a more dignified pace.

Lucinda and Courtright stood alone in the middle of the street watching the monstrous vehicle disappear around a corner. Lucinda reached down to retrieve her throwing knife, wiped the dust and dirt off the blade, and then slid it back into her dress.

"Well, that could have gone better." Courtright looked at his partner with a lopsided grin. "It's a good thing Washington doesn't care much for the marshal's service's opinion, or we'd be getting our hides tanned over this." He nodded to the disappearing knife. "Now, am I remembering correctly, or did you just throw one of your little party favors directly at the Over-marshal of the western territories?"

Lucinda was still in no mood for joking. "If I had thrown it at him, he'd be dead, instead of making foolish accusations and riding off into the sunset."

"Well, setting aside the immaterial article of evidence that it's hardly past noon, I agree with your assessment of the situation, anyway. I don't think I've ever seen you miss something you meant to hit, so, excellent bit of inter-office relations, there, then." His smile was wide, but his eyes were serious as he assessed his partner.

"His words did seem to strike a nerve, though." He leaned in towards her. "Enough to make some folks who might not know you as well as I do wonder some things we'd rather not have them wondering, no?"

She forced herself to snap out of the fugue state and shot him a look. "I just didn't want to be giving too much away, was all. Do you think Grant or the president would thank us for letting the Earps in on all this drama swirling around the good doctor?"

Courtright went back to looking down the road. "Well, one thing's for sure. Dragging that enormous contraption with them wherever they go, there ain't no way they're going to be able to get to Diablo Canyon before whatever James and his boys have in mind has already gone down." He let a moment's silence stretch on for a while before looking at her out of the corner of his eye and whispering. "He's an outlaw, Luce, ain't no two ways about that."

Lucinda nodded silently. Jesse James was an outlaw, and the body count he had racked up throughout his extended life was enough to make any peace officer blanch. And yet, while they talked the other day, she knew, against all reason and right-mindedness, she had seen something in his eyes that mirrored something in her own mind. He was a man hounded by his past, doomed to make the wrong decisions until he found the strength to break the cycle. It had taken a great man, who also happened to be a good man, to help her break the cycle in her own life. Was there any hope for Jesse, out in the middle of the badlands, hunted down by an army of lawmen itching to make a point?

Lucinda sniffed, shook her head, and gestured for Courtright to follow her back to their room. "We better get going. I think our best bet will be to split up at this point. I know some folks might be able to get me to Diablo Canyon quick as a wink, and you've always been better with those office types back east."

He grunted in reply, not looking up. Lucinda continued, "We've got too much ground to cover, and not much time, if we want to get useful information from James before the Earps and their traveling Wild West show catch up to him."

Chapter 9

The town was tucked into the dark forests in the northern edges of the territories, and no one left there remembered what its original name was. The place had been called Payson for decades, named by the world-renowned Doctor Burson Carpathian. It was a dirty town in the middle of once-beautiful country. Filthy brick buildings of almost entirely utilitarian aspect lined the streets, granting no decoration or ornamentation of any type. Factories, mostly, spewed red-tinged smog into the crystal blue sky, giving everything for miles around a sickly, pink pallor.

Jesse and his gang rode into town along the single dirt road connecting it to the rest of civilization to the far south. Everyone was exhausted from days of hard riding, but this would be no place for them to recoup their strength. There were no signs on any of the buildings, and the streets seemed all but deserted. Jesse raised a single fist into the air, and the Iron Horses of his posse drifted forward on their roaring engines, settling down around him.

Most of Jesse's men had never been to Payson before, and these were in some danger of damaging their necks as they swiveled from side to side trying to take it all in. The sickly-sweet smell that was always Jesse's strongest memory of the place had made itself known nearly a half hour before. It was even stronger than he remembered as they sat in the middle of the main street, wondering what they should do next.

"Jesse, you reckon there's anyplace we can get a drink, recharge the 'Horses, maybe, while you talk to the Doc about new equipment and weapons?" Frank was leaning against the control panel of his machine, his hat in one hand. "I don't relish the idea of going into the lion's den myself, an' I'm wonderin' if it ain't best for the rest of these boys to be keepin' a bit of distance as well?"

Jesse did not stop scanning the street, but nodded. "The saloon used to be down that alley to the left. It's as far from the main row of factories as the folks who have to live here could get the Doc to put it. Every now and then they move everything around, though, so it might not be. I better get a move on or we're gonna miss Billy at Diablo Canyon."

"I hope this side trip was really worth it, Jesse." Harding's voice was grim, his tone frustrated. "We went straight past the turn off for The Canyon more'n a day back. The way you was pushin' us, we woulda beaten the Kid there by a few days at least. Now, we'll be lucky if we get there on time."

"You got any pressin' need to see Billy the Kid, Harding?" Jesse turned a severe glare on the older man. The look was rendered more effective, however, by the ruby lenses of his goggles, reflecting shards of light back into Harding's face.

"Just don't wanna have to ride any further than we gotta, is all," grumbled Harding.

"Jesse, you go on down and see the Doc. I'll let these dirt farmers in on the great and mysterious secrets of Payson while you're gone. Who knows, maybe they'll see an animation close up. Bryce's been havin' a bit of trouble moving his bowels. That oughta set you right as rain, heh, Bryce?"

The young kid snorted and flipped a middle finger in Frank's direction, causing Frank to chuckle, shaking his head.

"You keep those foul Eye-talian gestures out of my face, Bryce, you hear? Or Sophie'll have somethin' to say to ya" He reached around for his gun as if threatening to pull it on the boy.

Jesse shook his head. "You lot of numbskulls go find the damned saloon while I go see what I can't pry out of the Doc's warehouses for this little shindig."

"What's it called, Jesse?" Ty had been quieter since leaving Kansas City, mirroring Jesse's own dark silence.

"What's what called?" Jesse goosed his machine forward a bit, drifting off down the street.

"The saloon?" Ty yelled after him.

Jesse called over his shoulder as he gunned the rumbling vehicle forward. "They call it the saloon, ya silly cracker. Payson ain't got but one."

As Jesse moved further down the main street he could hear Bryce say, "Town this size only has one waterin' hole?" It made him smile.

The main street of Payson wound its way down a moderate incline in a slow turn that eventually left even the echo of his men's Iron Horses behind. The echo of his own, bouncing off the plain brick buildings, was familiar enough but offered no comfort. He knew they had been under observation for days, and he knew that if Carpathian had wanted to keep him away, they would know it by now.

The fact that there were no animations present was a pleasant surprise. Every time Jesse had visited Payson before, he had seen many of the disgusting things shambling about on one errand or another. He knew the town was lousy with them; that they were, in fact, the source of the smell that troubled his dreams for days after every visit. Their absence, however, was almost as troublesome as their appearance would have been.

The main road continued down, side streets reaching away on either side almost at random. Eventually, the road leveled out to a wide, straight boulevard, and the first buildings with some style made their appearance. Along either side of the broad street intricate building fronts featuring dizzying arches, shaded promenades, large windows, and even gargoyles made out of some substance the color of the ubiquitous red brick rose into the sky. Large buildings marched down towards an edifice that looked like it had been dropped right out of a fairytale, except that rather than the smoothly polished, dressed marble of a castle, this one was built, once again, out of fired red brick. Flying buttresses, crenellations, turrets, and other archaic features completed the appearance. The presence of the bricks just made it all seem as bizarre as the rest of the town.

Jesse gunned his 'Horse forward, watching, with his peripheral vision, all of the shadowed nooks and crannies in each building that he passed. He kept his head rigidly forward, however, and his chin up. It would never do for any of Carpathian's creatures to read weakness or hesitation in his manner. He took a deep breath and banished the heartache, confusion, and anger of the last few days to a corner of his mind. He would be able to deal with all of that later. Right now he needed to have all his wits about him, dealing with the Doctor.

The Iron Horse rumbled to a halt in a grand parade ground before the castle-like main house. Jesse allowed the machine to rumble into silence and slowly swung his leg up and over the saddle, standing in an assured and easy pose beside it. The heat from the exhaust pipes radiated through his riding leathers and warmed the backs of his legs. He stood completely still, mechanical hands confidently on hips, and looked up at the big house, waiting for a sign.

The sign was not long in coming, as the large double doors in the center of the massive, intricate façade opened with a slow, dramatic movement. A large man in dark clothes and a grim face hiding behind a massive black beard stepped out and gestured with an abrupt wave of his hand for Jesse to approach.

Jesse forced the cocky, self-sure grin onto his face and began to saunter forward. He raised one arm and gave a quick wave to the figure at the top of the steps. "Howdy, Ursul. How's things goin' behind that awful thatch of brush you call a beard?"

The man scowled but made a slight bow. "Domnule James." His accent was so thick that Jesse could never be entirely sure he understood every word. There was a grudging respect there, however, and Jesse had found himself in desperate need of that lately. One of the many reasons he had been hesitant to make this journey was a very real fear of his own reaction should Carpathian be in a foul, sharp-tongued mood. He had no doubt, if it ever came to it, he could shoot the old man ten times before the body fell and the old coot would never know what happened. He also knew he would never make it out of Payson alive if he did it.

"Ze Doctor iz busy now. Eef you vill come vith me, I vill zee that you are provided vith refreshments unt somevere to zit down." The big man gestured with one hand into the cool interior of the castle.

Jesse nodded his thanks and moved past the imposing guardian. "Thanks, Ursul. Mighty kind of you an' your boss. You have any idea when he'll be free, though? I'm in a bit of a hurry, with an appointment I gotta make back east. I really need to talk to him 'bout some stuff afore I feel comfortable makin' the trip."

Ursul led the way deeper into the castle. He answered with a tone completely devoid of pity or concern. "Ven zee Doctor iz busy, he brooks no disturbance. Zis you know, Domnule James, yah?" The man did not turn around, but Jesse could hear the shrewd smile in his voice.

"Yeah, whatever you say, Ursul." Jesse looked around at the wide hall with its dark wood paneling and gothic decorations. There was even an old suit of armor standing on a pedestal in one waiting area they moved through. They were almost past when Jesse noticed the two men lounging in the shadows. They both sported dark goggles, considering they were indoors, and both wore sleek black leather dusters of a strange design. Their hair, too, was strange; long like a woman's hair, and blacker than a mineshaft at midnight.

One of the men looked up at Jesse and smiled, nodding slightly and raising a glittering knife to tap at his own forehead in a salute Jesse could only interpret as ironic.

"Couple o' new pets, Ursul?" Jesse followed the large man down the hall and away from the strange pair. He forced his body, against every impulse, to move straight and not turn to look over his shoulder.

"A couple uv young men from zee old country, Domnule James. Zee Doctor prefers, ven possible, to provide assistance and guidance to such as they." It was even harder to understand him as he powered down the hallway, heels clacking on the wooden floor.

"Ah, Europeans then?" Jesse called out for lack of anything better to say.

Ursul paused for a heartbeat in his stride, casting an astounded look over his shoulder. "Ah, yes, yes. Europe." He nodded, then turned away, shaking his head, and hurried on at a greater pace.

*****

Frank led the men into the building they assumed was the saloon of Payson. A nondescript brick building like all the others, this at least had the look of constant use, and the windows along the front of the building were at least slightly larger than the rest that looked out onto the street. The door had a knob rather than the freely-swinging batwing doors favored by most establishments that might require the speedy eviction of a patron in the heat of battle. Frank had tested the knob, felt it give, and then nodded to the rest of the men, pushing the door warily open.

Inside the room was much more in keeping with saloons across the west. There were tables, a long bar running across the back, with a wall of bottles and glasses behind it. One thing they all noted with some relief was the fresher air within as the door closed behind them. Probably another reason to avoid the batwings, Frank thought as he surveyed the darkened room. A barkeep stood behind the bar polishing a mug with a clean white towel; however, he gave it one last brush and then placed it on the counter behind him when he saw the small crowd enter.

He stared at Frank and the other outlaws guardedly, taking in their dusty, trail-stained clothing and weary gaits. He nodded to Frank, who nodded back, and then gestured with one hand to any of the unoccupied tables.

Frank had been to Payson before, and as the saloon had not been moved since last time, he had even been in this very bar. He was not surprised to see that most of the tables were empty. In fact, he was moderately surprised to see any patrons at all. Only a couple of the tables were occupied, and the men sitting around them were sullen and quiet as they slouched in their chairs in the semi-darkness.

Frank gestured to the men to take a couple large round tables in the corner and then waved at the bartender, although the man was still staring at them as they moved through the room. "Barkeep, send over a couple bottles and enough glasses for the lot, will you? And good bottles, real whiskey, now, none of that ole Red Eye you push off on the locals, you hear?"

The man sneered slightly but reached under the bar and produced two dusty old bottles. He put them on a tray and loaded it up with enough glasses for the whole band. He pushed his way around the bar and to their tables, depositing the lot with a rattling crash. He held out a palm. "That'll be ten dollars." The man's voice was harsh as if he was not used to speaking.

Frank's eyebrow shot up. "Ten? You gonna kiss us each afore you go back to settin' there, doin' nuthin'?"

The large man's hands balled into fists that he rested on his hips. "You want the Simon Pure, you pay for it, son. You want the same tar water the locals here suffer through, you can save yourself some coin."

Frank smiled at the men with a shrug. "Well, nothin' but the best for these boys, I guess." He dug a few coins out of his pocket and made to hand them over, dropping them to the floor just as the bartender was about to grab them. "Oops. Sorry, barkeep. Guess I slipped."

The smile Frank gave the bartender was lethal, and after a single glance the man quickly looked away, ducked down to grab the money, and backed off with a nod and a mutter of thanks.

"Damn hayseeds." Frank sat down heavily. "Don't know who the hell they think they are, way out here in the middle of nowhere, puttin' on airs."

The men nodded while Bryce opened the bottle and began to pour generous glasses for his table. "Hey, Frank, how come Jesse calls this place The Town That Death Built? I ain't seen anythin' too scary here 'bouts."

Cole Younger snorted from the other table and lobbed a healthy gobbet of tobacco juice onto the floor. "You ever face any animations on the trail, kid? Ever stared into the dead eyes of one of those walking corpses the Doc uses for all his dirty work?"

Chase nodded. "Doc's animations ain't nothin' to shake a stick at, Bryce. If you'd 'a seen a bunch of 'em in action, you wouldn't be havin' any doubts now. You'd be just as happy they don't seem to be hangin' around today."

Frank snickered as he took a sip of his whiskey, sighing harshly with satisfaction. "Now that is the good stuff. But yeah, what these old hands'r sayin', kid. Folks say, once Doc scared the those who used to live here off the land – or convinced 'em to join him – or killed 'em all, depending on who's tellin' the story, he raised up a whole army of the dead with his RJ-1027 tech, an' they went straight to work rebuildin' the town. First thing he had 'em build was a bunch o' kilns, an' then, digging up clay from the canyon up that'a way, they just started churnin' out bricks to beat the band, an' the buildings just kept goin' higher and higher, day'n night. Pretty soon, faster'n any living men could o' built it, Payson was as big as you're seein' it now. Some say he went through a thousand Boot Hills full o' the dead before he was done, and ain't a grave with a body in it for miles in any direction. Folks round these parts, they've taken to burnin' their dead when they pass." He took another sip. "Well, those that don't up and sell 'em to the Doc, that is."

Gage looked around at the quiet men, and put his own glass down. "Well, if these dead folks are so good at workin', how come there's any live folks at all shufflin' around?"

Frank shrugged. "God alone knows what the Doc needs these folks that ain't done breathin' yet for. There ain't a lot of 'em, but there's enough. Jesse once tried to explain to me, the animations don't have any brains o' their own. They're like idiot dogs, gotta be led around nonstop. They're not as smart as those crazy metal marshals. So, could be, you need live folks to tell 'em what to do."

The outlaws focused on their drinks, occasionally shooting sidelong glances at the other men in the room. Most of the younger men had heard the stories but never seen an animation. Frank knew from personal experience that those creepy bastards were hard to believe in until you had seen one for yourself. He shrugged. They would see some soon enough, he had no doubt.

The men were muttering quietly, speculating on how long they would have to wait, when the door banged open and a smell worse than a charnel house wafted through the saloon. The outlaws all turned as one and stared as a figure shambled quickly in through the door, closing it clumsily behind.

As soon as Frank saw, he turned to look at his companions' faces, especially the young ones. He watched for their reactions at the animation that had shuffled into the room, carrying with it the unmistakable stench of death.

The men stared as the thing moved slowly towards the bar. The bartender, looking slightly paler than he had, stood up straighter to receive the thing.

The walking corpse was dressed in ratty working clothes that would have been common on any unskilled laborer throughout the western territories. Beneath the clothing, the body seemed as if it must have been a very robust figure in life, with muscles straining at the ragged shirt. The flesh of its face hung loosely, its mouth gaping partly open, its filmed, milky eyes staring fixedly ahead. A collection of metal supports and leather straps served to hold the thing upright, and a dark metal collar was fitted around the back of the corpse's neck and head. A small cylinder, glowing with the crimson light of RJ-1027, was rammed into a socket in the contraption and into the thing's skull.

The animated body moved to the bar where it raised one desiccated hand, a wrinkled piece of parchment grasped loosely by the lax fingers. The bartender took the paper and unfolded it, read it with a jerky nod, and then reached under the bar for another dusty bottle. He wrapped some sort of netting around the bottle, looking sourly at the table of outlaws, and then draped the netting, now snagged around the bottle of premium alcohol, over the corpse's head.

The bartender said something to the corpse, again with a sheepish glance at the newcomers, and then had to repeat it several times before the animation nodded once, turned ponderously around, and shuffled back out the door. The stench of the thing lingered for quite a while before it faded into the general background stink of the town outside.

The outlaws stared at the door for a moment before they turned back towards each other, the younger men with faces pale with disbelief.

"He weren't that fast, though . . . " Gage muttered. "Fightin' 'em can't be that hard, can it?"

Frank snorted and picked up his drink. "That was a laborer, boys. Not made for speed 'r fightin', just fer liftin' and carryin'." He nodded at the door. "The fighters the Doc makes, they're sometimes even bigger than that boy, an' fast as you can think, some of 'em. An' they have all sorts of 'emselves cut off, replaced with blades 'n guns 'n other weapons. Doc's a pretty odd stick, but he's a cracker when it comes to makin' up ways to kill folks from a distance."

"But . . . how come the thing was fetchin' and carryin' for a bottle o' rotgut?" Harding muttered to Frank. "I ain't never seen 'em doin' stuff like that before."

Frank smiled knowingly. "Well, boys, unless I miss my mark, I'm thinkin' that poor galoot was sent traipsin' through here strictly for our benefit." He looked at each man in turn. "Well? Everyone feel special now?"

Gage cleared his throat. "When you reckon Jesse'll be comin' back? I'm not eager to be here if that thing has to come back in lookin' fer seconds."

*****

The room to which Ursul had led Jesse was very comfortable, but he had already developed an itch to leave. The walls were darkly paneled, the furniture covered in luxurious supple leather, and the window looked out over the canyon behind Payson. The outlaw chief paced back and forth in the small room, occasionally stopping to puzzle out the titles on the spines of books in the various shelves, or to look out the window at the wide-spread mining and refining works built up all throughout the canyon.

Jesse knew the Payson canyon works had been under development for decades. Nevertheless, he was surprised at how extensive they were. He knew originally the work had been for clay along the riverbed that meandered below. Since then, far more elaborate works had been sunk into the canyon walls. He thought most of it looked like gold or silver mining, but the massive silos of glowing crimson fluid at the far end were clear indications that whatever they were pulling out of the ground, it was being converted, somehow, within the long low brick buildings, into RJ-1027.

Jesse knew that the secret of the mysterious Crimson Gold was one of the primary sources of Carpathian's power. Speculation abounded throughout the territories on what the substance could possibly be. Theories ranged from some fetid, naturally occurring mixture like the oil bubbling up across the arid plains of Texas, to the captured souls of innocents, trapped by the doctor's arcane machines. Jesse did not think they were souls, or spirits, or whatever, but he did not pretend to know what it was, either. He knew, however, that what he was watching through that high window was a good hint towards where the stuff came from.

The outlaw stared out the window at the bustling industry rushing from one end of the canyon to the other. It sent a creeping sensation up his spine to realize that nearly all the figures moving around down there were the corpses of men and women who had once moved around just like him. He looked down at one mechanical hand, flexing the fingers, and realized that in one way, at least, he was even less human than most of the workers down below.

"Zee Doctor vill see you now, Domnule James." The large door had opened without a sound, and Ursul was standing there, glaring at Jesse as if he was convinced the outlaw had somehow managed to steal every coin in the doctor's vaults while he had been waiting.

"Thanks, Ursul." Jesse tipped his hat with a jaunty metal finger towards the massive, hairy man, and walked past him into the hallway again.

"Vee vill be moving up to zee Doctor's receiving room. Vee vill be taking the lift. This way." He moved smoothly in front of Jesse again and led the way down a side-hall and into a large chamber that featured several sets of double doors. Each set of doors had a fan-shaped arrangement above it, with elaborate, wrought iron arrows pointing to numbers or symbols arrayed across the top of the arch. The arrow over one set of doors was moving steadily downward from the far right-hand symbol, what looked like a very ornate 'A', to an equally elaborate 'P' at the far left.

"Wait, lift?" Jesse's eyes widened as his mind finally reshuffled the muffled syllables into an order that made sense. "We're gonna get lifted all the way . . . up there?" He pointed at the 'A'. "Wherever that is?"

Ursul nodded without looking at the outlaw. The arrow finished its journey to the 'P', and there was a series of cracks and hisses behind the doors. They suddenly flashed open without warning or obvious assistance, revealing a chamber far smaller than Jesse would have guessed from the size of the doors themselves. The room was paneled in more dark wood, and Ursul moved quickly inside, gesturing for Jesse to follow.

Jesse looked at the other sets of doors, down the hallway, and then back into the small chamber. Ursul looked at him with a snide grin and gestured for the outlaw to enter and stand beside him.

After taking one more look around, Jesse stepped gingerly into the room, eyes roving over the paneling. A cluster of glowing red knobs was arranged in a double column to the right of the doors, and Jesse saw that one of the buttons, towards the bottom of the left-hand column, had the same 'P' symbol, while the bottom-most right-hand button was decorated with the same 'A' character. As soon as Jesse was completely in the room, Ursul reached out and pressed the 'A' button with one blunt finger.

"Da."Ursul's voice rumbled with amusement as he straightened, shooting Jesse a look out of the corner of his eye.

The doors to the tiny room slid closed, again without any apparent reason. The floor beneath Jesse jerked. A grinding sound seemed to reverberate all around him. The outlaw reached out with one mechanical arm, slapping the wall and digging metal fingers into the woodwork for stability as the room began to shake and rattle. Something within Jesse's ears told him he was rising. Without windows, however, there was no way to tell what was going on outside the little room. Jesse's stomach gave a lurch.

"Zee Doctor vill not be pleased that you damaged the paneling." Ursul gestured towards Jesse's death grip with another nasty smirk.

Almost before Jesse could process what was happening, the floor shuddered again, lurched once more, and then the doors slid open. The dark-paneled corridor was no longer there, replaced by what looked like the stone walls of an ancient castle or palace. The floor was polished wood, and Ursul gestured for the shaken outlaw to precede him out into the new hallway.

Jesse was in no mood for further verbal knife fighting, so he just nodded and moved out. They soon reached an intersection and turned right. The hall was flooded with bright sunlight from windows along either side, showing a soaring view of the valley far below. Ahead of them stood another pair of double doors, this time thick, old wood, intricately carved, with an ornate 'C' in the middle of each.

"He eez in there."Ursul pointed at the door and then pivoted on one foot, moving back down the gleaming hall.

Jesse rallied himself for a quick "Thanks a bunch, Ursul!" before the large man was gone around the corner and the outlaw leader was alone, staring at the elaborate doors at the end of the corridor.

Jesse moved up to the doors and looked for a place that would be safe enough to knock. He had settled on a small flat area in the center of the left 'C' when the door creaked open without warning.

"Come in, Mr James. " The voice was cultured, with rich tones that hinted at a foreign land without drowning the ear in strange sounds that robbed the meaning from the words.

Jesse stood by the open door for a moment before walking in, leaving the brightly-lit hallway with its panoramic views behind.

The room he entered was a large round chamber, with tall, wide windows stretching almost entirely around the circumference. A great fireplace dominated one side of the room, the only area that was not graced with the large, clear windows. The walls were the same stone as the rest of this level, and adorned with a staggering collection of weapons, old and new, as well as tattered flags and pennons that seemed to be ancient. The furniture, like in the parlor far below, was covered in supple leather, interspersed with dark wood tables. Opposite the fireplace was a long desk cluttered with a mess of mechanical bits and pieces, RJ-1027 cylinders, and a small collection of shapes covered with a shiny black cloth. The persistent sweet undertone of Payson hung over everything, as it always did. Although Jesse remembered, from his last visit, that the smell was usually less offensive in Carpathian's castle.

In the center of the room stood a man Jesse had not seen in several years. He was taller than the outlaw remembered, standing straighter. His face, a mask any grandfather would be happy to have, was still framed with billowing white hair, glorious muttonchops reaching down towards a smiling mouth. The entire effect was only slightly ruined by the ungainly metal prosthetic that clasped around his left cheek, housing a large glowing ruby of an artificial eye, and the flexible black tubing that entered a similar mechanical housing at his right jawline. Relics of the doctor's first moments in the New World, Jesse knew that the facial augmentations were the mildest of the surgical scars the old man bore.

Although Jesse was never sure how much of the Doctor was reconstructed or supported with metal parts or replaced completely, he knew that Carpathian's legs and at least one of his arms were heavily modified. No one knew exactly how the doctor had come by his extensive injuries, but they must have been nearly fatal. Only one thing was known for sure throughout the territories: Carpathian blamed the famous Union general, Ulysses S. Grant, for all of them.

"I trust my brother-in-law was more polite this time around, Mr. James?" Carpathian moved around the furniture and reached out with a hand that seemed equal parts flesh and metal reinforcement.

James looked back to the doors, which had closed silently behind him, and then nodded. "Ursul? Yeah, I can stand Ursul's gaff. In small doses, anyway."

The doctor nodded. "You have to forgive him, of course. Veronica's death hit him hard, and he came all this way for vengeance, as is our cultural obligation. But he feels that I do not move fast enough, of course, and so, much like an over-eager thoroughbred, things appear to be moving far too slowly for his tastes."

Jesse walked around the room, looking at the various objects on the tables or hanging from the walls. "Yeah, I get it, Doc. If anyone ever tried to off Susan, you better believe Frank and I'd be out to beef 'em by hook 'r by crook!"

"Please don't' call me that." The older man's voice was flat, his hands firmly grasping the back of one of the high chairs.

Jesse looked around, his eyes slightly surprised. "Eh? Oh, sorry, D-- . . . sorry, Doctor Carpathian. No disrespect intended."

The doctor nodded and gestured to one of the chairs by the cold fireplace. "Now, Mr. James. Care to have a seat? I'm sure you've got plenty you'd like to discuss?"

Jesse looked at one of the wide windows, the desk with all of its technological clutter, and then the offered chair. A small table beside the chair had a dusty bottle of amber liquid and two glasses. With a smile he sat down and popped open the bottle. He looked at the faded label and his smile grew even wider.

"Real Kentucky bourbon, sir! That's not easy to come by!" He poured himself a healthy dose and then settled back in the seat, holding the glass up to the light.

"It is not. I had that particular bottle brought up especially for you, however. I hope you enjoy it." The doctor lowered himself into the large seat opposite. He sat stiffly, back rigid, hands folded on his knees, looking expectantly at the famous outlaw.

Jessse crossed his legs, dangling one dirty boot off the beautifully carpeted floor, swinging it back and forth as if to some music only he could hear. "That's a pretty fancy magic room you've got there, Doctor Carpathian, that 'lift' of Ursul's? I can see how that'll save you some walkin', over time!"

Carpathian smiled politely but did not speak.

Jesse looked at the doctor for a few minutes, nodded, and then sat forward, both feet firmly on the carpet. "Okay, sir, I can see you're busy, so we'll jump straight to the point. I've got a notion of headin' out into the badlands, an' I've got an idea that we're gonna be meetin' up with some stiff resistance. Might be Injuns, might be Union, might be God knows all. But I'm thinkin' we might need some more heavy firepower to copper our bets, just in case."

Carpathian nodded, pursing his lips thoughtfully. "Interesting, Mr. James. Tell me, before we spend too much time and energy on such discussion . . . do I perchance have an outstanding balance towards you and your energetic little band?"

Jesse looked confused but tried to hide it behind a sip of bourbon. "Not sure I follow, Doctor."

Carpathian smiled thinly. "Well, it sounds to me as if you are asking for equipment, weapons, power, perhaps even upgrades? Such things do not come cheaply, Mr. James. Am I indebted to you in a way I was unaware? Do I owe you, say, enough to justify you coming to my home and asking for such dear gifts?"

Jesse's answering smile was as open as he could make it. "Well, no, Doctor, o' course you don't owe me nothin'. I was thinkin' I'd pay you, maybe half now, half in services down the road, once we agreed to a figure?"

Carpathian's smile widened. "Ah, now we are talking, as you say. Well, Mr. James, what exactly would you be looking for?"

Jesse's smile darkened slightly as he thought. "Well, we're heading into the wastes, an' our Iron Horses haven't seen a repair dock in a good long while. Most of 'em have developed some mighty queer habits lately. An' of course, we always need RJ-1027." He jerked a thumb towards one of the windows. "An' I couldn't help but notice you got plenty o' that, just lyin' around."

Carpathian's eyes were flat as he responded. "Plenty is a subjective term, Mr. James. And I assure you, it is not merely 'lying around,' as you say. What else do you envision needing on this expedition?"

Jesse pushed his feet out in front of him, cradling his glass in both hands on his belly and looking up at the ceiling, lost in thought.

"Well, not knowin' what we're gettin' ourselves into out there, I guess whatever you could spare that you'd think might be useful. RJ-1027 weapons, o' course. And anything you think might be of help." He raised one hand to look at the back of it, working the fingers and watching the pistons and wheels move beneath the armor. "Might be good for my piece o' mind if you'd take a gander at my arms, actually, while I'm here. It's been awhile."

Carpathian shifted his weight forward slightly, peering at Jesse's arms from a distance. "Is there something wrong with the arms, Mr.James?"

Jesse's confidence slipped a little as he continued looking at the arm, then over at the doctor. "No, not really. Just curious. You've done a lot of work like this, rebuilding bodies and such . . . have any of the parts ever failed completely? Or begun to move on their own notions?"

Carpathian sat back in his chair and gave the outlaw chief an appraising look. "Not that I know of, Mr. James. Why, have your arms begun to take on a . . . life of their own?"

"No!" Jesse raised both hands up as if to prove their power. "Not at all." The guilt rose in his chest as an image of Misty's face peered at him from the back of his mind. "Nothing like that.

Just curious, is all. Just wonderin' if somethin' like that could happen."

Carpathian's smile was predatory. "Not that I know of, Mr. James, no." Jesse nodded. "But would you still like me to look at the arms? It has been quite a while since I first replaced your own shattered limbs with these priceless augmetics, after all."

Jesse nodded, lowering the arms back into his lap. He could not forget the wrenching jar to his shoulder as the metal hand connected with the poor girl's face. The other instances where his arms seemed to have failed him, or acted on their own, paraded past his inner eye. In a more subdue voice he muttered, "Yeah, I think maybe that'd be good."

"Excellent, then." The doctor stood and gestured for Jesse to follow him over to the desk. As the outlaw moved towards the windows, he was shocked again to see how high they were. The workers down below seemed smaller than ants. A chair sat next to the desk, and the doctor pointed him towards it. Soon the armored shrouding of his left arm was lying on the table while the doctor tinkered with the intricate mechanical workings with long, silver tools.

"So tell me, Mr. James, what is pulling you so inexorably out into the wastelands so precipitously?" The tool moved deftly from component to component, causing the fingers to jerk rhythmically in response.

"Not much, Doc . .tor." Jesse looked quickly at the doctor out of the corner of his eye. He was not afraid of any man, including the mad European, but with the Doc up to his wrists into Jesse's arms, it did not seem like the time to push the man. "Just felt like it was maybe time to see somethin' new, push out into the unknown for a while. See if there weren't some shots to take out that way."

The doctor nodded while continuing to work in the arm. "William Bonney chomping on your heels, is it, Mr. James?"

Jesse's head jerked around to look at the doctor, but the old man was entirely focused on the components of the mechanical arm. From the slight smile twinkling from between the imposing muttonchops, Jesse could see that he had noticed the outlaw's reaction. "Don't know what you're talkin' about, Doctor."

Carpathian chuckled. "That's alright, Mr. James, nothing to worry about. Every now and then the leader of the pack must prove his dominance. It is nature's way." He tapped on the armored side of Jesse's arm with a musical chiming sound, then gestured for him to spin the chair and present the other arm.

As Jesse moved, he shook his head. "Still don't know what you're gettin' at, Doctor. Me an' the Kid, we ain't got no unpleasantness between us."

Carpathian's smile was so condescending it was everything Jesse could do not to slap it off of him. "I understand. Well, your arms look to be in tip-top shape." He lifted the sleeves of Jesse's shirt and prodded at the flesh where the metal was connected to his body. "Connection points seem healthy and robust. I would not imagine you should have any further troubles." He looked up quickly with a look of apology whose sincerity was entirely suspect. "I mean, I do not think you should have any troubles at all."

Jesse could feel the guilt burn behind his face while the feeling of loss and anger he had been living with for days threatened to engulf him all over again. While he struggled with these feelings, however, Doctor Carpathian was already moving on.

"Now, Mr. James, let us further discuss this adventure you are planning. You are wishing for me to look into your transportation, and I think I have just the thing for you. As for weapons and power, again, I think I can do more than you might have wished. But as for any additional assistance, I would need to know what type of work you are contemplating. I am guessing you are not just looking to stir up mischief. Your demeanor suggests there is something . . . extraordinary about this expedition."

Jesse shook his head trying to clear it of the guilt, fear, and confusion. "Well, we reckon we might be havin' to dig. If you've got anythin' fer diggin'—"

"You have looked out the window, I know, Mr. James?" Carpathian sat back with a wry smile.

Jesse was even more flustered. "Sure. 'Course. You got a huge mine back there. You got any diggin' tools we might be able to . . . borrow?"

Carpathian shook his head, smile firmly in place. "Sadly, no. As much as I would love to let you . . . borrow, expensive excavating equipment, I'm afraid nothing I have would be portable enough for you to take with you. All of my workings are designed and built on-sight. Unless you would like to take some of my modified Animations, to save you some manual labor?"

Jesse answered quickly. "No, no, that's okay. We'll just pick up some shovels and picks along the way."

Carpathian's eyes drifted towards the window and he pushed himself back up out of his chair, moving around the desk. "I must admit, however, that you have piqued my interest, Mr. James. Buried treasure not being among your usual repertoire, not to mention the tantalizing mention of the Warrior Nation, the hated Union, and so on. What, if I might make so bold, is it exactly that you are designing to dig up?"

Jesse stared down at his right hand, opening and closing the fingers into a hard metallic fist. Everything seemed to be moving smoothly, but then, everything had been moving smoothly, for the most part, before his arrival. He looked up as the expectant silence registered in his distracted brain.

"Hmm? Oh, I don't even know, Doctor." He shrugged. "Someone got a line on somethin' big, maybe, buried out in the desert. We're thinkin', maybe if someone else thinks it's big, maybe it's somethin' we might want to look into." He shot the Doctor a grin. "See what the market will bear, you know?"

Carpathian smiled and nodded, but he seemed distracted as he sat down behind the desk. "Yes, well, excavation, still, does not strike me as being strongly placed within your bailiwick, if you do not mind my saying, Mr. James." He folded his hands in front of him and gave the outlaw boss a warm smile. "Whereas, I was thinking, perhaps another train job? I have been tinkering with a new weapon system that I think is about ready to test on a major target, and I cannot think of a better subject than a Union Heavy Rail train. What would you say to another joint venture, Mr. James?"

Jesse shook his head. "'Fraid not, sir. I've got an appointment in Diablo Canyon that I better not miss." Carpathian's reaction to the buried object, and Jesse's interest in it, was ringing false to him, and he suddenly realized he needed to tread carefully with this man who was not a friend. The doctor was a sometime-ally, and a sometime-adversary, and unfortunately necessary to keep sweet in case anything ever happened to his arms, but he was no friend.

"Are you quite certain? I believe my Ion Energy Net device will be capable of catching all manner of RJ-1027 vehicles and technology in its web, and there could be no better test than the Heavy Rail. We could choose almost any target. Some of them are coming down from Washington absolutely laden with gold and notes, I hear." The smile grew wider.

Jesse gave the doctor a look he hoped seemed speculative. "Well, Doctor, I have to admit, you're makin' a pretty good case. If we do go after a Heavy, though, we're still gonna need this new gear. What say, you give me a price on the new plunder, I talk to my boys, an' we make the call later. I still may need to make a quick stop if we're headin' back east."

The doctor's smile widened slightly. Jesse marked this sudden release of tension for further thought. He wanted to hear what Frank might have to say about the Doc's reactions. "That sounds excellent, Mr. James. Now, let me see." He looked down at a sheaf of papers on his desk. "Judging from reports, you rode into town with roughly twenty companions?" Jesse nodded, no longer surprised at the information the doc always seemed to have at his fingertips.

"Excellent. Well, refurbishing weapons and vehicles, providing replacements and energy cylinders for the lot." His finger moved down a column of numbers on one piece of paper. "Let us say, twenty thousand, for the entire group?" His smile was predatory again, and Jesse tried not to let the shock show in his face.

"Twenty." He kept his voice flat. "That would leave us with a tad less than we were hopin' to walk away with, to tell you the truth, Doctor."

The smile widened. "Well, remember, that we have said, half now, half in services at some later date? And of course, if you should choose to assist with the Ion Energy Net test, that would certainly go a long way towards equaling this particular debt." The grin grew downright smug as the doctor's eyes flicked down to Jesse's arms and back up again.

Jesse thought for a moment. He knew they could pay half immediately, although Frank would howl to the heavens about it. But they had the coins and the notes to do it. The last bit, about paying for the second half in services in the future . . . exactly what would Carpathian think would be equal, in the services of Jesse's gang, to ten thousand dollars in hard currency?

Jesse knew there was no way they could face down Billy's gang with the equipment they had available. If Billy was right, and somewhere along the trail there was going to be someone mean enough that Billy really did need Jesse and his boys . . . well, it was not going to go well for Jesse if he decided to go it alone and they did not have the latest the doctor could provide. Yet, twenty thousand was a lot of dinero to be throwing around.

"I don't know, Doctor. That's a hefty bill, to be honest." He watched Carpathian for his reaction, and was happy when the old man leaned forward, eagerness to strike the deal flaring in his eyes.

"Well, Mr. James, let me see if I can entice you perhaps a little bit further. I have been designing a new transportation, something perhaps more robust than the Iron Horses so graciously provided by the Union and your first train job. I have not yet decided what to call it, but it can cover difficult terrain more easily, is faster in overgrown areas, carries more armor, and has a greater carrying capacity." His smile broadened and he gestured widely with both arms. "Not to mention that it is the latest technology I have to offer."

Jesse looked at the old man for a moment. It never failed. Carpathian always knew what a rube he was for new tech, and even knowing that, Jesse was always scooped in by the latest shiny. "I wouldn't mind seein' somethin' like that for myself, Doc . . . ter . . . if you've got one layin' about."

Carpathian smiled even more broadly. "Excellent! And let me show you something we have just put into production today." He pulled the small sheet from the objects on the desk, revealing several small, sleek-looking pistols, each of similar design.

The doctor picked one of the weapons up and held it out to Jesse. The thing looked almost like a child's toy. Its sleek lines were clearly made of some light metal from the weight and feel, and yet there were no cylinders for the RJ-1027 cartridges. He flipped the small pistol easily in his hand to look sideways down the barrel, only to see that there was no real bore. The barrel ended in a clear chunk of crystal or glass. He looked up at the doctor with a questioning eyebrow.

The doctor's responding smile was almost childlike. "Is it not fantastic? It is something that Thomas has been working on nearly since his arrival. We call it an ion pistol. Fairly short range, I'm afraid, but any RJ-1027 technology you shoot with this pretty little thing will immediately cease to function. It fires an agitated stream of ions . . . but never mind, you do not care for the technical minutia, I know." The smile took on a slightly patronizing edge. "Anyway, suffice it to say, you fire this weapon at anything carried by the Union, or anyone else bearing modern weaponry, and you will swiftly have them at a severe disadvantage!"

Jesse looked quickly down at his own arms and up again, not trying to hide the dismay. Carpathian immediately reached out to pat the outlaw's armored forearm reassuringly. "Do not worry, Mr. James. Your arms are only moderately powered by the RJ-1027 within them. Most of their power comes from your own body's electrical field. Even should the unthinkable happen, and someone fire one of these weapons at you, your arms would still function. You would not be helpless."

Jesse tried to imagine what it would be like, in the middle of a fight, if his arms suddenly stopped working. Many of his hidden fears came surging up at the thought. To be helpless before the enemy, to be at the mercy of anyone, never mind someone actively seeking to do him harm?

The outlaw came back to himself when the doctor patted his forearm again with a dull thud. "Please, Mr. James, do not fret. There are only four of these weapons extant throughout the wide world, and I am giving you two of them. The other two remain here, where myself and Mr. Edison will continue to perfect the technology. For now, look upon them as nothing more than a great advantage being proffered to you and you alone."

Jesse nodded vaguely, unable to completely shake the terror that had been rushing through his mind. "How much would these add to my tab, Doctor?"

Again the old man's arms were thrown magnanimously wide. "Why, included in the original fee, of course, Mr. James! I am not trying to render you destitute! In fact, for field testing these new weapons for me, I will reduce the balance somewhat. Shall we say, upon receipt of ten thousand dollars, you will only owe me eight thousand more in services? And the return of the ion pistols, of course. And, should you decide to keep the new vehicle, I would make that a gift, for loyal service in the past, and continued friendship in the future?"

Jesse found his brain starting to tie up in all the numbers and conditions, and nodded before he could work himself into a paralyzing bout of self-doubt. He reached out across the desk and Carpathian took his hand, shaking it vigorously. "I think you have yourself a deal, Doctor Carpathian. Our cash is with my brother right now, so let me head down to the saloon, meet back up with the boys, and I'll get you your money."

Carpathian rose from behind the desk with a broad smile. "Excellent, Mr. James! I shall walk you to the lift and see you on your way. Ursul should be at the bottom to guide you out."

"Thanks. I'm not sure I could make it on my own. These new digs are pretty impressive, Doctor." Jesse allowed himself to be led out of the turret room and across the bridge hallway, bright sunlight still streaming through the long windows.

"Thank you. Yes, it was designed as homage to my ancestral home, abandoned under duress many, many years ago. Its halls and rooms provide great solace when my work threatens to overwhelm me with its scope and weight." They walked down the corridor and stopped before the strange double doors. "Will you need assistance with the lift controls, Mr. James, or do you feel capable of finding your way down to the ground level?"

Jesse forced himself to give a smile that could, charitably, be considered friendly. "No, Doctor, I reckon I'm good. I just press the button with the 'P' on it, right?"

The old man nodded with a gracious smile. "Indeed, Mr. James. The button with the 'P' will bring you safely down to the ground level. Good day, to you. Ursul will arrange for a way you can communicate with us, when you decide the time has come for another great train heist to enter into the Jesse James legend. I hope will be hearing from you very soon."

Jesse shook the extended hand again and walked cautiously into the tiny room behind the double doors. He turned around, forcing his back to remain straight, and gave a sidelong smile to the doctor before reaching out and gently pushing the correct button. The door slid shut on Carpathian's smiling face, and Jesse signed with relief.

He looked at the array of buttons, wondering what all these disks above the 'P' might mean. He had puzzled out the basic structure of the control pad, and so he was fairly confident that the buttons between the 'P' and the 'A' were the levels from the ground floor to the tower room he had just left. But what were all of the other buttons? Basement levels? He counted them. Ten? He did not want to even contemplate what Carpathian might have going on ten levels below ground.

As the floor rumbled away and the walls creaked and hissed, Jesse tried to recall everything that had happened while he had been speaking with Carpathian concerning Billy's mysterious object. The doctor had seemed most eager to change the subject, trying to divert Jesse from this particular job. Was there a reason? Did he know something about more about the whole affair than Jesse or Billy?

Jesse felt a smile spread over his face at the thought. If Carpathian knew, or thought he knew, what was out there, it could very well be that Billy was right, and it was something important after all. If it was something important after all, it was possible that this caper could do everything he wanted and more.

Now he just needed to convince Frank the price was right, stick around for the repairs and refitting, and get out of Payson without tipping his hand.

The smile faltered slightly before flaring back full force. Well, what was life without some challenges?

Chapter 10

Jesse hunched over the controls of his new mount and thrilled at the growling roar. He had been calling it a trike after the three wheeled vehicles city swells had tried to introduce into Kansas City. His men, however, following the lead of damned Cole Younger, had taken to calling it a Blackjack, because, as Cole was swift to point out, the twenty other men riding in the posse were moseying along on the same old Iron Horses that had been seeing them through for well over a decade now. However, for Jesse, the twenty first of their number, it was nothing but the absolute best. There may have been a small touch of frustrated bitterness behind it, as there often was when Cole got clever about something Jesse had going, but it was plenty rich for the rest of the boys, and at this point even Frank was calling the big armored brute a Blackjack. Jesse had stopped trying to fight it.

With two large drive wheels in front and a smaller stabilizer wheel behind the driver, the Blackjack was far steadier in high-speed maneuvers than the top-heavy Iron Horses. The big craft was locked to the ground by its heavy wheels as opposed to riding on the blasts of heated air that suspended the 'Horses, but the Blackjack was actually faster on the straightaway. The broad armored nose provided more protection from a wider arc to the front in battle, as well. The four blaster muzzles that thrust from fairings in the front promised that it could rack up the pain when it had to as well.

Jesse cranked the power higher and gloried in the change in pitch from the RJ-1027 engine beneath him. The thing vibrated like there was a demon from hell trapped inside, and the image pleased the outlaw to no end. Behind him his men struggled to keep up, their own machines grinding out an even louder, thunderous bellow that echoed off the low hills and scrub pines around them. Each of those machines had been completely refurbished by the best engineers the doctor had on hand, but still they were no match for the Blackjack.

Blackjack. Lucky 21. Jesse grinned savagely behind his red-tinted goggles and gunned the engine again, reveling in the feeling of freedom that only such a burst of power along an empty open road could offer. Maybe he would let them call it a Blackjack after all.

They had been riding nonstop since Payson, and he knew the relentless pace was once again taking its toll. After riding all last night, the blazing sunset was a stark reminder of the exhaustion that plagued them all at this point. Still, they needed to get to Diablo Canyon if Jesse was going to have any chance of getting the lay of the land. He wanted to prepare something clever for the Kid. Most of the men still believed they would be joining Billy and his gang at the canyon, but Frank and the Youngers knew better. They knew Jesse had no intention of sharing whatever was at the end of the trail Billy had stumbled upon up in the mountains, and he certainly had no intention of sharing the glory and the influence, if any was to be had, with the no account little sand lizard.

Jesse had not formulated any concrete plans for Billy yet, but the wheels of his mind spun nearly every minute of the day, looking at every angle and trying to decide the best way to set events. It had been years since he had been to Diablo Canyon, and he had heard some nasty rumors about the metal man that had been lawing it up in the town recently. At the same time, his last couple of days in Kansas City still haunted him. The knowledge of how wrong things had gone in Missouri City, along with those terrible last moments with Misty, were never far from his thoughts. Every time he closed his eyes, he knew the image of her, face torn and bleeding, hatred and fear blazing in her red-rimmed eyes, would be waiting for him.

Frank and Cole had been trying to jolly him out of his dark depression, but even his brother's efforts had slackened over the last day as Jesse's mind refused to give ground. He was either thinking about Diablo Canyon and how he could euchre Billy the Kid, or he was obsessing upon those last moments in the little garret apartment above the Arcadia Saloon. He schooled his face to an impassive mask, smiled when the boys joked around during stops, and nodded as if he were listening whenever Frank or the Youngers had something to say. Yet, within the silence of his own mind there was only the whirlwind of images from Missouri City, The Arcadia, and the desperate hope that whatever was buried out in the badlands could somehow make it all better. He needed to believe that whatever it was, it was big enough to put the polish back on his name, heavy enough to convince himself that he was still on top.

None of this was fully formed in his conscious mind. He knew only that he felt the terrible guilty weight over what happened with Misty, and a ravenous, driving hunger to be the man with his boot on the treasure chest when this latest adventure reached its conclusion. He knew there was no line he would not cross to see himself on top. A part of himself was obscenely happy it was Billy the Kid who would be left holding the bag when all was said and done.

As Jesse's mind had rumbled along these familiar tracks, the rest of the posse caught up to him. He was only aware of this as Frank waved a gloved hand towards his unresponsive face, shouting something that was drowned out by the Blackjack's demonic roar. That was another thing Jesse liked about his new vehicle: it was nearly impossible for anyone to speak to him on the road, so they tended to leave him alone until it was time to stop.

Jesse nodded to his brother and looked up ahead to the trail that stretched out before them. A small stream had been running parallel to the track for several hours now. A nice flat meadow ahead seemed as good a place as any to walk some of the stiffness out of their legs and replenish their water. He pointed to the meadow with two metal fingers and Frank nodded in turn, raising one hand in the air to get the attention of the men behind him. They thundered onto the field, the Iron Horses blasting dust and yellow grass into the air as the Blackjack rolled to a halt beside a couple of low trees that offered what meager shade there was to be had.

As the others cut the power to their engines, allowing the Iron Horses to settle into the brittle grass of the field, Jesse pulled his goggles down under his chin and took a quick look around. There were clumps of low bushes and stunted trees dotting the entire region, but not much else that afforded any kind of cover. The shallow depression that channeled the stream would never hide a force large enough to challenge the outlaw gang with all of their overhauled firepower. The men were swinging down off their vehicles, many moving towards the stream or off to find a bush of convenience. Frank and Cole spoke together briefly, Frank nodded, and the two men approached Jesse. The outlaw chief braced himself. It was never good news when Frank and Cole came at him paired up this way.

"Hey, Jesse, we been thinkin'." Frank's voice was casual, but Jesse rolled his eyes at the opening salvo.

"Yeah? Must o' missed the smell, on account of the vehicles." Jesse stretched his arms out, noting the clicks and whirs as the machinery within slid smoothly from one position to another without a hitch. Whatever the Doc had done, it seemed to have worked.

Frank smiled thinly at Jesse's retort and then continued. "We been ridin' for almost a day and a half now without much of a break. The boys are all dragged out, an' we should be back on schedule, after the way you rode us all to get to Payson in the first place." Cole stood off Frank's shoulder, nodding. His mouth worked around a solid plug of chaw.

Jesse looked at his brother for a moment and then flung his arms wide to indicate the barren landscape. "So, you wanna throw a roll down and take forty here in the scrub, Frank? You so tuckered out you wanna sleep on the ground for a bit?"

Frank shot a sour look at Cole, who shrugged. "Jesse, you don't have to come over the tartar with us. I'm just thinkin', you want the boys ready for a shindig when we get to Diablo Canyon, you might wanna think about givin' 'em a chance to take a least a little rest afore we get there."

Jesse turned away from his brother and spat trail dust off to the side of his Blackjack. He looked back at Frank with an annoyed expression. "You might have missed it, when I said we needed to get to the Canyon as fast as we possibly can?"

Frank shook his head, with Cole behind him echoing the motion. "No I did not, Jesse, an' you know it. But if we pull into the Canyon half shagged and dull-minded, it ain't gonna matter that we made it in time, is it? Now, Garland over yonder says there's a small town, 'bout a couple more hours ride from here. Place called Sacred Lake, even has a small lodge for travelers. We roll into town, get some shut eye, we're up at the crack of dawn an' gone faster'n a milkmaid's virtue."

"Boys could really use some shut eye in a real bed, Jesse." Cole's voice was respectful, but his gaze was steady, almost challenging the outlaw boss to contradict him.

Jesse thought about it for a second. "Sacred Lake, eh?" He made a show of looking all around them at the rolling fields as far as the eye could see. "You figure there's a lake out here somewhere?"

Cole said, "It ain't always there, Jesse. It sometimes is and it sometimes ain't, accordin' to the seasons. Like a lot of things out here. But some religious folks, awhile back, came in and set themselves up some dairy farms." He spat into the dirt. "There's some as see it's sometimes bein' there sometimes not as a bit of a miracle. They been there a few years now. They got a nice little village an' everythin'."

"Garland says it ain't fancy, Jesse, but it don't need to be. We don't lose much time for stoppin', and it would mean an awful lot to the boys. They're ridin' as hard as they can, brother, but you'll be drivin' 'em into an early grave you keep this up. When you need 'em the most, they ain't gonna be worth a tinker's fart."

Jesse scowled, but he considered what his brother and Cole had said. He still could not figure out Billy's angle. It was unlike the younger outlaw to share in any major score like this. Billy was either scared of what he was apt to find out in the badlands, or he was working at something Jesse had not been able to figure yet. The last thing Jesse wanted was to get it in the neck from Billy, though. Knowing as little as he knew, the best way to get the bulge on the Kid would be to get to Diablo Canyon as early as possible and see what could be seen.

But Frank made a good point, also, that no matter what Billy's scheme was, he would need his boys in the best shape possible if he was going to have any chance of turning the cards on him.

"This lake is a couple hours ahead?" He knew he sounded angry, and he did not much care.

"We just take the Lake Mary trail, up ahead aways, an' we should be there before full dark." Frank looked to Cole for confirmation and the other man nodded.

Jesse looked back over the men as they moved about, taking water from the stream or resting against their 'Horses. They were clearly all exhausted beneath their forced bravado, but they were all also clearly watching the exchange between their boss and his brother as closely as they could without being obvious.

Jesse nodded. "Okay, if you boys think we need it, we'll take the time." He scowled at his brother. "But I swear, Frank, if things get knocked into a cocked hat in Diablo Canyon because I didn't have enough time to scope the lay of the land —"

Frank held up a hand to stop his brother's words. "Jesse, you push on through now and ain't none of us, including you, who will be able to catch a case o' scabies in a bawdy house at the end of the ride."

That brought Jesse up short and he could not keep a grin from twisting his lip. "Well, I don't know about that, Frank. Cole ain't never had a hard time catchin' scabies."

Cole snorted and hooked his thumbs beneath his holster belt. "Just cuz you boys don't like to live on the edge o' danger ain't no reason I ever seen I should settle for the tame fillies."

Jesse shook his head, one hand raised in surrender. "Okay Frank, you win. " He pitched his voice to be heard by the rest of the men. "Alright, you coffee boilers, listen up. Frank here has convinced me you rough'n ready algerines need your beauty sleep afore we ride down on Diablo Canyon. Appears some gospel sharps have set up shop on some magical lake just north of here, and they got themselves a lodge. You boys wanna sleep in some beds afore we brace whatever we find in Diablo Canyon?"

There were many smiles and nods, most weary, and Jesse could not stop a pang of frustration. If even a few of the men had put on a brave front he could have faced down Frank's suggestion and pushed the men through. Still, if every one of them was ready to settle down for a night, maybe it was for the best.

"Alright, then. We'll ride on up to Sacred Lake and see what's there. But don't you lot be thinkin' of sleepin' in, now!" He scowled at them and they grinned back, some raising their hands in mock surrender. "First yahoo among you don't get up, we'll be draggin' him the rest of the way to Diablo Canyon, see if that don't wake 'im up!"

As Jesse and his gang rode down the dusty trail, the grassy fields along the left hand side slowly gave way to the tall, dark Ponderosa pines of the Coconino forest. Majestic peaks reared up out of the west, blocking the last rays of the sun and providing dramatic silhouettes for the final shimmering colors of sunset.

The muted rumble of their mounts bounced from the trees, and as they pulled into the township of Sacred Lake, lights were already appearing in many of the houses. Jesse noticed something strange about the nature of the lights without really thinking about it. It was soon clear, however, that something was very different about Sacred Lake.

"There ain't no RJ-1027." Jim Younger, the second oldest of the four brothers, muttered as the posse pulled up on the edge of town. "No generators 'r nothin'."

Jesse realized the lights lacked the reddish tinge of RJ-1027 lighting, and there were no winking tell-tales anywhere to be seen. Sacred Lake, in fact, looked exactly like a town out of his distant youth, without any of the technology or equipment Carpathian's Red Renaissance had introduced to the western territories.

A two story building, larger than any other in the town center, had a shingle-sign hanging from a post in front, and as the roaring machines came close, their road lights flaring, Jesse saw the name Sacred Lake Lodge emblazoned on it. There was a rough image of a lake in the middle of the sign, and floating above it a strange symbol he had never seen before.

"No recharge stations, Jesse." Frank pulled up beside his brother and leaned over to shout into his ear. "Some of the boys'll be coastin' into Diablo Canyon at his rate."

Jesse nodded to his brother and pulled the Blackjack nose first against the hitching post in front of the lodge. The others slotted themselves into position as well, and soon the last Iron Horse stuttered into silence. The silence was oppressive, and he realized it had been a very long time since he had been in a town with no generators at all.

The tall door of the lodge opened, throwing a soft yellow fan of light onto the front lawn and its flagstone walkway. A man in an apron and a wide smile stepped out onto the stoop and waved to the group gathering at the gate.

"Welcome to Sacred Lake, strangers!" He stumped down the steps and as he came closer Jesse saw that the man had the heavy, muscular build of a farmer. His hair was cut in a strange fashion that left the sides long, hanging down past his ears, but the top was a rough bristle. "You boys need some vittles? I'm afraid we don't have any alcohol, but we've got good honest food, milk and clean, cool water, and clean beds a plenty for the lot of you."

The man stopped a couple paces from Jesse and a vague look of recognition came over his face before smoothing away. Jesse wondered if he had imagined it.

Cole stepped up to the fence, one hand on the rough wood. "You ain't got no generators or recharge stations hereabouts?"

The man smiled warmly and shook his head. "No, I'm afraid not. We aspire to a simpler lifestyle here in Sacred Lake. We do not allow any of the newest technologies to come between us and the soil."

One of the younger men, Bryce, grunted. Jim Younger stepped up to his brother's side. "You got a problem with what we're packin'?"

The man shook his head again. "Of course not. Travelers cannot be expected to adopt the deeper philosophies of every small town at which they sojourn. Might I entice you all to come in and lay down your loads, however? It is pleasant inside, and our prices are fair."

"Fair." Another of the boys snorted. "Old man don't know from fair yet."

Jesse stepped from the pack and put out his hand. "We'd be most obliged to you, Mr. . . . ?"

The man's hand came up automatically. "You can call me Elijah, son." He raised a finger with another of his honest smiles. "And don't feel you have to pass along your name. I'm no stranger to the wider world, and I can tell by your clothing and your transportation that you all are travelers on the verges of life. We of Sacred Lake will not pry."

Jesse tilted his head at this forward statement, but looked around at his men, reading nothing but hunger, thirst, and exhaustion there, and nodded. "Thank you, sir. We'd be much obliged, as I said."

Jesse followed the grey haired man up the steps, looking back to give his men a stern glance. If the folks of Sacred Lake were not going to give them any trouble, then it was best to play along. They could decide in the morning if they wanted to pay or not.

A flicker of movement across the street caught the outlaw's eye as he was about to turn to go into the lodge. A curtain or drape over a window had been dropped, muting the soft glow of a lamp within. The fabric still shifted slowly back and forth as he watched, settling into stillness. Jesse shrugged. Just a local, curious at the crowd of vehicles. It was surprising there were not more gawkers, really, considering this little burg did not have so much as an RJ-1027 warmed out house.

Jesse shrugged and went into the lodge. His band tramped in after him, quickly filling the small common room inside.

"Feel free to have a seat, gentlemen," Elijah waved to the empty room, full of mismatched tables and chairs. "Let me speak to my wife, see what rooms would be best for ya'll." He disappeared through a small door, going deeper into the building.

Frank looked around as the men settled down at tables all around. Some were rolling worn dice, others dealing tattered cards, but most were just sitting wearily, little more on their minds than the promised beds.

"This is a pretty nifty joint, eh, Jesse?" Frank nodded to the fireplace across the room. "That's quite a pigsticker for a bunch of doxologists, wouldn't you say?"

Jesse picked his way through the tables to get a better look at the weapon. The blade was a shining silver sweep of steel, nothing like the dark metals used by the Union in its charged blades. The handle of the thing continued the graceful curve, with supple black leather wrapped around two different sections, suggesting it was to be used two handed. All the metal work on the handle, including the butt end, the cross piece, and a fancy, fluted bit that divided the two areas of leather, were all done in gleaming silver. Jesse did not know much about swords, but he could see that the silver alone on that weapon would probably buy an Iron Horse if the owner was willing to part with it.

Jesse grunted at Frank. "Mighty fancy."

The outlaw chief was reaching out to touch the soft leather of the handle when Elijah came back in through the heavy door. His voice stopped Jesse's hand in mid-motion despite its casual tone.

"Ah, you've noticed Isten, I see." The man's smile was still in place, still open and honest as it had been since he had opened his door to the outlaws.

Jesse looked at the older man with a quirked eyebrow. "What now?"

The innkeeper gestured to the sword. "The scimitar on the wall. A family heirloom my father called Isten Kardja. No idea what it means, I'm afraid. It's been on one wall or another since before I was born."

Jesse turned back to look more closely at the sword. Frank was still staring and gave his younger brother a quick look before purposefully moving away from the wall. With a small shrug, Jesse did likewise.

"It's a lovely piece, and no mistake, Mr. Elijah." Jesse moved back towards the innkeeper.

"Please, just call me Elijah. My wife and sons have gone upstairs to get the rooms there ready. We've plenty, as we don't often receive guests. There is only one man upstairs now, a victim of an unfortunate accident on the road, I'm afraid. We've been taking care of him since some friends of his left him behind yesterday."

Cole and Jim exchanged looks and then Cole shot a glance at Jesse, who nodded before turning back to the innkeeper. "Well, that's great, Elijah, thank you kindly. My friend here," he gestured to another of the Younger clan, John, giving the man a quick glare. "He's a bit of a frontier sawbones, if you think it might help to get something of a professional opinion on the situation?"

The man's smile did not fluctuate at all. "Oh, I'm certain he's in as good hands as will be possible, never fear. Nothing to worry about. His friends had dressed his wounds quite well, and left plenty of money for his care and lodgings."

The man's smile did not shift. Jesse noticed, as did Frank and Cole, and their eyes grew suspicious. "They had plenty of money, these friends of his?" The outlaw chief's voice was casual.

"Well, I can't speak to one man's definition of plenty, son, but they had enough for me and mine to offer what help we can." Elijah's smile widened. "Now, would you boys like me to show you to those rooms before some of you peter out right here in the common room?"

The stairway was narrow, the stairs steep. The upper level of the building was stifling, but cozy. A small chair on the upper landing held a well-made afghan that sported the same symbol as the sign out front, and the walls of the upper hallway were decorated with paintings of far-off exotic locations that featured many strange trees and animals. Jesse was a little startled to realize that the strangest things of all, however, were the mundane oil lamps hanging from the ceiling.

"My wife made the last ten rooms at the end of the hall ready. I'm afraid the five at the far end are none too big, we don't usually get more than a couple visitors at a time here at the lodge." The innkeeper's voice was apologetic as he spoke over his shoulder, gesturing down the long hallway.

"No problem, Elijah, thank you very much for your kindness." Jesse was about to move around the man and down towards the rooms when a thought occurred to him and he turned back. "Which room is the wounded man in, sir, so that we might not disturb him?"

Elijah smiled and nodded. "That's right kind of you, son. The young man is in the room at the top of the stairs, so as far from you and your friends as possible. But judging from their demeanor, I'd venture to guess that your friends won't be kicking up too much of a fracas tonight."

Jesse shook his head. "No, probably not. Thanks, sir. We'll see you in the morning?"

"Indeed, young man.G'night. Feel free to lower the lamps when you're ready to retire." Elijah nodded once more and turned back down the hallway.

Jesse waited until the old man was gone before he gestured for Frank and the Youngers to join him in the nearest room. They went in to find a single bed, nicely made, and a small bedside table. A small desk with a pitcher of water and a basin was against the far wall. A well-made chair sat before the desk. Jesse gestured for the men to relax as he looked out the door and made sure his men were settling into their rooms. There was a quick, whispered commotion over who would be sleeping where, and then things settled down. Jesse carefully closed the door and turned back to the five other men.

"This place strikin' anyone else as strange?" He scanned their faces and found in every one a disquiet matching his own.

"What kind'a hotel has this many rooms, this far out into the middle o' nowhere?" Bob Younger, the youngest of the brothers, had leaned against the wall behind the desk.

"An' I'm not buyin' the soft solder the old man's given' us, neither." Cole, as the eldest, was usually the most outspoken, although his vicious sense of humor also meant he was probably taken the least seriously.

This time, however, Jesse could only nod. "Yeah, an' I'm not sure about this yahoo down the hall, but I'm thinkin' we need to at least peek in on him before we vamanos in the morning."

Frank nodded, but his face was worried. "I don't think we want to raise a fuss here, Jesse. Somethin' about this little burg don't add up, an' I'm not thinkin' things go in our favor if they go south."

Jesse rested a boot on the chair, articulated wrists crossed over one knee, as he stared out the small window at the silent street below. "I'm feelin' exactly what you're feelin', Frank. We gotta flow smoothly through this little bug hill, settle quietly, and move on. We still don't know what's waitin' for us out at Diablo Canyon, an' we can't get wrapped up in this no whorehouse town and its peculiarities." He looked over at his brother and the Youngers. "I'd say we bunk down, get up with the cows, visit our friend down the hall, and leave a nice pile o' notes for old Elijah before we skedaddle."

The men nodded and began to file out of the room. Jesse's arm struck out to snag Frank's sleeve before he left, and Cole, in the back of the pack of Youngers, nodded and closed the door behind them.

"There's somethin' more than strange about this whole place, Frank. Go back 'round to the boys and set up a watch through the night. I need you and Cole and the boys sharp, so keep the watches two men, by room, and keep it to the younger men." Frank nodded and turned towards the door, but Jesse jerked gently on the sleeve to turn him again. "The younger boys we can trust, though, Frank. None o' the shavetails."

Frank shook his head. "You mean like young Ty? Why we got boys we can't count on to watch our sleepin' backs at all, I don't know, Jesse. But you're the boss." He turned to go, then looked back at his younger brother. "See you in the mornin'?"

Jesse gave one sharp snap of his chin. "No doubt. See you in the mornin'."

After the other men had left Jesse shrugged off his duster and draped it over the chair, moving towards the small window. Below, the street was still and dark. Most of the houses around them still had the odd window lit, but there was no movement to be seen.

Despite his exhaustion, Jesse spent a long time at the window before settling into the bed with his boots still on.

*****

The interior of the Judgment wagon was not conducive to clear thinking, and as Wyatt braced himself against the constant rolling motion by grabbing an iron rung near his jump seat, he shook his head in frustration. The passenger compartment was small, and when you took into account the four UR-30 units that usually sat immobile in their harnesses along the walls, alongside Virgil and Doc, and the emotional crowding of Morgan's immense form taking up the cramped jail cell, he did not think the conditions could have been much different from those suffered by the slaves brought over packed ass to teakettle in the slaver ships from Africa.

The fact that two of the UR-30s were currently pacing along in front of the Judgment made the crowded situation slightly more tolerable, but the sound still pounded in his ears, the nearly unbearable heat churning up from the engine beneath them still steamed up through the air, and the placid look on his younger brother's pale face behind the heavy iron bars drew his constant and distressing attention. One good thing about the infernal machine, however: it was so loud inside, there was no way anyone could try to engage him in casual conversation.

They had been dragging the heavy machine across the trails for more than four days now. Wyatt knew any band riding Iron Horses would be making far better time, and so the chances of the lawmen getting to Diablo Canyon in time to stop whatever was going to happen there was slim. But he also knew something he believed the outlaw scum did not know about their own agile vehicles: all RJ-1027 machinery left behind a trail when it was used at high power. Not a trail visible to the human eye, and not even something that a normal person could smell, or feel, or track on their own. It turned out there was something that could track that trail, though, and that was the UR-30 Enforcer units.

Right then, two of the units were ranging ahead of the Judgment and its flanking Hogs. Their cyclopean eyes had been adjusted to see the faint RJ-1027 trail, slashing bright columns of visible red light out in front of them like the lighthouses of his childhood on foggy nights. Wherever the red beam made contact with an RJ-1027 trail, the trail suddenly became visible as a glittering ruby path hovering eerily about a foot off the ground.

Wyatt pulled himself up to peer out one of the forward observation ports and checked the Enforcer units at work. Sure enough, the trail ahead of them was still glowing with heavy red tracks left behind by a large band riding RJ-1027 vehicles. He grunted in satisfaction and sat back down on the wooden seat. He flashed a quick grin at Virgil, who was keeping busy cleaning a large hand cannon he had acquired from a Union officer a while back. Doc was sitting upright against the iron wall of the compartment, swaying with the motion of the vehicle, and gave Wyatt a slight, tired smile from above his breathing mask. Wyatt nodded and then settled back to his own meditations.

It seemed like it was only a few minute further down the trail before the Judgment rolled to a halt and the driver let the engine idle down to a dull rumble. Wyatt leapt up to thrust his head onto the driver's deck and shouted, "Why the hell've we stopped? Don't you boys know nothin' 'bout the concept of hurryin'?"

"Sir, the UR-30s have stopped. I . . . I don't think they're sure what to do." The driver shouted down at the Over-marshal, his thick goggles giving him an alien look.

Wyatt cursed under his breath and threw his weight against the closest side hatch, throwing it open to crash against the armored flank. He swung himself through the hatch, grabbed the access ladder half way down, and leapt the rest of the way, landing lightly on his feet with his duster flaring around his legs.

"What in the Sam Hill is going on out here?" Wyatt stalked forwards to where the two robots had stopped moving nearly altogether. Only a slight swaying from side to side differentiated them from strange ancient statues set to guard the road from otherworldly threats. At the Over-marshal's voice, both metal heads swiveled to home in on his approaching figure, their bodies pivoting to follow the alignment.

"Current trail has deviated from expected parameters." The buzzing voice of one of the units said. Wyatt felt his shoulders rise slightly. He could never abide those strange voices, or the uncomfortable harmonics they seemed to set up in his chest.

"What does that mean?" Speaking with the Enforcer units often took more patience that dealing with Virgil's least gifted deputies.

"It means these wily coyotes are slippin' north instead of continuing up the straight trail towards Diablo Canyon." Virgil leapt down off the access ladder, catching himself with slightly less grace than his younger brother. Virgil pointed to where the trail diverged just ahead of them. "Point your damned headlamps back that way."

Wyatt watched as the lamp beams switched back on and tracked across the intersection. It was clearly visible where one trail, the heavier of the two, moved off onto the overgrown trail to the left. Another trail, weaker or more faded, continued up towards Diablo Canyon.

"Damn." Wyatt stared at the revealed trails, hands on hips. "Well what the hell does that mean?"

"We knew there was something odd with the trail for the last couple of days, Wyatt." Virgil turned to his brother. "You remember, there was a clear trail moving out of Kansas City towards Diablo Canyon, but then, two days ago, a trail came up out of the west and joined this one?" He nodded towards the intersection. "Looks like some of them took a sharp left here."

"But which is which, damnit, Virg?" Wyatt flung one arm towards the enigmatic trails. "And where the hell does this left hand fork go?"

Doc emerged from the side hatch to sit on it, one leg dangling out, while he unfolded a faded old map. "Well, Wyatt, that there looks to be Mary Lake Trail. Nothin' up that'a way but a little settlement o' religious folks, calls itself Sacred Lake."

Wyatt scuffed his heel against the dust of the trail. "Godamn whoreson sumbitch! So, whoever it is, they're headed straight for a bunch of gospel slingers?"

Doc folded the map swiftly and jumped down to the ground. "Looks it. And from the trail, looks like it was either more recent than the other group of tracks, or much, much larger."

All of the men were completely still as they all stared at the Over-marshal, waiting for him to process the situation and make the call. Would they be continuing on after Jesse James, or would they be taking the left fork, and face whatever unknown threat had headed down that way so recently? Wyatt cursed again as he realized there was only one real choice.

"Damnit!" Wyatt ripped his hat from his head and smacked it against his hip. He stood still for a moment, bringing his breath back under control, and gestured to the left hand trail. "Well, we can't leave those folks to whoever left those trails. Virgil, get five of your deputies into the Lynch Wagon. We'll be takin' their Hogs and the rest of the Interceptors and go on ahead at top speed. Two of the UR-30s will come with us. We need to try to get as much force there as possible, as quickly as possible."

Virgil rattled off five names and four deputies dismounted. The old lawman sensed something was amiss and turned back to find the fifth man looking at him stubbornly, refusing to release the steering handles of his Hog.

"Provencher, get down off your vehicle as ordered." Virgil's voice was hard, his eyes steady.

The deputy shook his head. "No, sir! This here's my vehicle! I ain't getting' off it, an' you can't make me! I earned my place on this mission, an' —"

Provencher hit the dirt before the blow that put him there had even registered. He scrambled up onto his backside, dragging the back of his hand across his mouth. It came away bloody. He looked at the crimson smear in disbelief.

"You hit me! You can't—"

"Provencher, you are the worst excuse for an officer of the law I have ever seen." Virgil towered over the whining man, hands on hips. "You will go where you are ordered to go, you will do what you are ordered to do, and we will not be sharing these words again. Have I made myself clear?"

The young man looked up at the legendary lawman and sputtered. He pointed at the other deputies still mounted on their vehicles. "But how come they don't—"

Virgil crouched down beside the cringing figure so fast the man cowered back, fearing another blow. "You wanna know why they ain't givin' up their rides, son? You wanna know why I'm puttin' you in the big iron box? Because if things go south when we hit this little town up ahead, there ain't a single one of them that I wouldn't trust at my back. An' you? You're no better than a player piano at a round up when it comes to thirsty work." He looked up at the four men who had moved towards the Judgment without comment. "And before you think about sowing dissent among the other four men that'll be joinin' you, they're there to keep an eye on your sorry behind, an' make sure you don't cock anything up in the big iron box. You got all that, deputy?"

Provencher nodded, his eyes dark with resentment.

"Good. Now, you go on back, mount up, and follow behind. Maybe we can forget this little unpleasantness ever happened, eh?" Virgil stood and walked away without offering a hand up.

Provencher watched the old man, his head shaking slightly. He pushed himself up out of the dust and moved sullenly towards the wagon.

The deputies shuffled themselves quickly, with Wyatt, Virgil, and Doc joining the two lamp-eyed UR-30s on the newly-dismounted Interceptors while the deputies clambered up the access ladder, a sullen Provencher pulling up the ladder last.

"Man that fire hose, boys," Wyatt gestured at the massive Gatling gun mounted on the copula of the vehicle. "Anything other than us comes down this road as you're followin', you light 'em up. You got that?"

One of the deputies thrust his body up through the top hatch and gave the Over-marshal a thumbs-up as he did a quick check of the weapon's mechanisms and feeds.

"Okay, boys, no restin' till we fetch up on Sacred Lake, right?" Wyatt pulled a pair of goggles from a wide pocket in his duster, slipped them over his head, then returned his hat to its customary place. "We can't go slow enough for the UR-30s to be on the lookout for the trail, so we gotta use our old fashioned eyes till we get to town. Let's go."

The Hogs rolled out, the roar of their engines rebounding off the low hills as Wyatt and his men opened them up, tearing down the trail at full speed.

Behind them, the Judgment rolled back into motion, its own engine setting the entire landscape to rumbling with its power.

Chapter 11

The RJ-1027 pocket watch in Jesse's vest beeped gently, dragging him out of the abused torpor of exhausted, haunted sleep. He snapped awake, staring blankly at the cold white ceiling before he rolled off the bed. He rested his forearms on his knees, reorienting himself with his strange surroundings. The window showed nothing but black emptiness; the distant sound of crickets the only noise he heard. Moving as quietly as he could, Jesse gathered his things and crossed the hall, knocking gently. The door opened silently on the second knock and Cole and Frank stepped out, nodding as Jesse raised a single finger to his lips.

The three men moved carefully down the hall. The air was still warm, but much cooler than when they had arrived. They came to the door at the top of the stairs and the intricate metalwork of Jesse's hand wrapped softly around the knob, testing it. The knob turned with a soft click, and the outlaw boss looked back at the other two men, nodded, and turned it the rest of the way.

Inside, the room was much the same as the others, with a single bed and a few small pieces of furniture. There was an elaborate cross on the wall that recalled the symbol from the Lodge's sign again, but Jesse had no time to spare for the oddity of the decorations as his eyes settled on the man asleep in the bed.

"I'll be damned . . . " Frank's whisper was harsh. "Bennett Vaughn."

"The rat bastard." Jesse moved up to the wounded man's bedside and glared down at him.

"Well, you warned him what'd happen if you ran into him again, Jesse." Cole's voice was soft but his eyes were alight with anticipation.

Jesse shook his head. "Bastard's been riding with Billy the Kid for more'n a year now, Cole." His eyes flicked up to the other two men. "'N no one else. How much you wanna wager, these friends Elijah was talkin' 'bout last night was Billy an' his boys?"

"Well, you was wonderin' what to do next, Jesse." Frank tipped his chin towards the wounded man. "Ask and ye shall receive, as I don't doubt Elijah would say."

Jesse grinned at his brother and took a knee beside the bed. He reached out with one mechanical hand and clapped it suddenly and firmly over the wounded man's mouth. Above the armor the eyes popped open, a cry stifled by the metal and rubber shoved against his face.

"G'mornin', sunshine." Jesse's smile was fierce as he leaned down over the wounded man. "Fancy meetin' you out here in the middle o' nowhere, eh?"

There was a sudden sharp click and a buzz as Frank activated his blaster pistol, its red tell-tales flaring in the dark room. Over the skeletal hand, the man's panicked eyes darted from Jesse's face, to the pistol, and back again.

"Now, Bennett, my friend, this can go one of several ways," Jesse's voice was reasonable and steady, still pitched too low to carry into the hall outside. "But I'm only goin' to give you one option. You're gonna talk, an' we're gonna listen, and then we're gonna leave you here with these nice Biblical folks, cuz we don't want no trouble with them, right?"

Bennett's eyes were wide with terror, the whites visible all around. Still they flicked occasionally back to the pistol in Frank's hands, but mostly they stayed fixed on Jesse's grinning face.

"That's good, Bennett. We're gonna start with a couple yes or no questions, alright? Ease you into the whole process?"

The man tried to say "yes" but his efforts were foiled by the ironwork clamping his mouth shut. Cole slapped him across the top of the head contemptuously. "You nod or shake your damned fool head, you idjit." The growled words were loud enough to raise Jesse's eyebrow, and Cole nodded in apology. "Sorry, Jesse."

Jesse shook his head and looked back down at Bennett. "Okay, Bennet. Let's try this again. You understand?"

Bennett nodded with desperate energy, moving roughly against the metal hand.

"Good. Now, you come through here with Billy yesterday?" A nod. "Nice. I knew you weren't as dumb as Frank says you were. Billy goin' to Diablo Canyon?" Another nod. "Good boy. I'm proud o' you. It's like you got the hang o' this. Billy got his whole gang with 'im?" A nod, with a desperate flick of the eyes towards the unwavering pistol. "Good, good. And that would be what, after his little shindy in the mountains, about twenty fellas?" The eyes flicked back to Jesse, there was a pause, and then a slight shake of the head.

"How many boys he got ridin' with 'im, Bennett?" Jesse's tone was flat and left no room for discussion or debate.

"Fifteen, Jesse." The man's voice was high with terror, and he scrambled up with his back against the headboard, as far from Jesse as he could get, as soon as the metal hand released him. "Well, twelve, now. Twenty two, I guess, not countin' me."

Cole rolled his eyes. "Oh, Lord preserve us. Billy had to leave his idiot step child behind."

Jesse ignored the comment and leaned back in to Bennett, pushing the man farther up the wall with the force of his own fear. "So you all ran into some difficulties on the trail, then?"

Bennett nodded. "Ran into a Union advanced patrol coming out of the Coconinos. We fought 'em off, but we lost three men, and they got me pretty bad." His eyes flicked down to the bandages wrapped around his chest.

"You're just shootin' your mouth off," there was more hope in Jesse's voice than certainty. "What the hell would a Union advanced patrol be doin' out in the middle o' nowhere?"

Bennett shook his head. "I don' know, Jesse, honest! Billy, he was totally caught flat footed. They came out of the woods, guns blazin', and we just went right at 'em, Billy in the lead."

Frank spoke up, his voice gruff. "What'd the Union have on the ground, deadbeat?"

Bennett's eyes flashed again from Jesse to his brother and back. "Don't know that either. I'm sorry, Jesse, I really am! I got hit right at the beginnin'! Somethin' blew up nearby, took out my 'Horse, and I was out!"

Jesse sat back on the bed and stared at the cowering man without seeing him. When he spoke, the change in topic was enough to catch all three other men in the room off balance.

"Where's Billy goin' after Diablo Canyon, Bennett?"

Bennett's face paled even further in the ruby light of the pistol's tell-tales. "I—I don't know." This time his terrified eyes flicked all over room, looking anywhere but at Jesse.

"I don't believe you." Jesse's voice was flat, his entire body still.

"What d'ya mean, Jesse? I don't know! We was goin' to meet you in Diablo Canyon! I don't know more'n that." His head shook back and forth slowly as if it had a mind of its own. "I don't, I swear."

Jesse nodded, then looked down again at the bandage. "Your wound opened up again."

Bennett looked down in surprise and fear, then relaxed. "No it didn't, its— "

The man's scream tore through the room like a banshee wail, echoing off the clean walls, the cross glowing dull red. Jesse's face was impassive , but one mechanical finger pressed against Bennett's dressings, a dark crimson circle beginning to seep through the fabric.

"Where's Billy goin' after Diablo Canyon, Bennett?" The words were the same, the tone was the same, but the man panting on the bed was now shaking in pain as well as fear.

"I told ya! I don't— " Again the scream. This time there were muffled shouts from other parts of the house. Jesse's men were being roused from their sleep, flooding into the upper hall to see what was wrong. Cole went to the door to calm things down and get everyone ready to leave.

"Bennett?" Jesse's voice was calm and reasonable.

"I don't know! No, no!" Bennett scrambled to escape the clutching metal hand, pressing himself against the headboard with all his failing strength. "I swear! Billy don't even know! Just what that damned medicine man let slip afore Smiley slashed him! Some canyon out west! Billy don't know where it is! He's hopin', after he gets out closer, he'll find folks who recognize the name!"

The metal finger began to move towards Bennett's side again and the man's sobs became desperate and ragged. "I don't know, I told ya! I don't know. He never said!"

Jesse rested his hand in his lap, regarding Bennett with flat, dull eyes. "I believe you, Bennett. It's ok."

The man's gasping breath, half relief, half disbelieving fear, escaped him in a shuddering wave. However, he came up short when Jesse raised the finger again.

"But you gotta remember, that last time we saw each other, what I said?" Jesse's eyes were hard now, drilling into the terrified man's mind. Bennett shook his head violently back and forth.

"I didn't mean nothin' by it, Jesse, honest! I was just movin' on! I just don't know . . . " His hands rose in a futile attempt to defend himself.

Jesse sat back on the bed, his hands raised in a gesture of peace and acceptance. "I know that, Bennett. Folks move on. I get it." Bennett relaxed slightly on the bed. "But I did say—"

The metal arm sailed across Jesse's body and connected with Bennett's face in a vicious open-handed slap that sent the man sprawling out of the bed and onto the floor. His screams ended abruptly as he landed badly, one arm twisted beneath him. Low sobs shook his shoulders and he remained on the floor, hunched there as if waiting for the final blow.

Jesse stood up and stared down at the pathetic form. "We'll start the count down over again now, shall we, Bennett? The next time our paths cross, this time, I'm not gonna leave you enough breath left to cry like a little baby."

Jesse swept past the huddled form and Frank followed. He stopped by Bennett and leaned down. "I hope you realize how lucky you been today. My brother's in a righteous mood. If I see you before he does next time, you Jonah, your own sweet momma ain't gonna be able to recognize you."

They left the man sobbing on the floor of his room in total darkness.

In the hallway, the gang was gathered, gear in hand and ready to return to the trail. At a nod from Jesse, they moved out and down the stairs. At the bottom of the stairs the outlaw chief was surprised to see Elijah sitting at one of the tables, Bob and John Younger standing over him with blaster rifles at the ready.

"Boys, I'm sure you can let our host up." Jesse took a wad of notes from a back pocket and deftly thumbed several of them flat, pulling them away and tossing them onto Elijah's table. "I'm sorry for our premature departure, sir, and for the untoward disturbance." He pulled another note and dropped it. "I hope that will cover any cleaning required."

Elijah stood as Jesse moved towards the door after his men. "I won't be trying to stop you. From the continued sounds of distress upstairs I can see that you left the young man alive. But there will come a time in your life when you need the compassion of a stranger, and you might want to think to your behavior today, regarding your expectations for tomorrow."

Jesse stopped in the doorway for a moment and then looked back. "Sir, if anything had ever led me to expect anythin' comin' close to compassion from any stranger, I might not o' turned out to be quite the hard case I assure you I am." He tipped his hat brusquely and closed the door behind him.

In the street, several men were moving around, going about the business of the day. All of them were strong-looking, and each wore the same strange hairstyle that had caught Jesse's attention last night.

"Okay, boys, I hope you enjoyed our little stay, but we gotta pick up the pace now." Jesse shouted to his men as he jogged down the walkway towards the Blackjack. "Seems we're not the only ones in this race now. Union's got a pony runnin' too."

The men muttered to themselves but Jesse put up a hand to forestall the grumbling. "Now, it's just an advanced patrol, and as long as we know they're out here with us, we ain't got a thing to worry about. But I'll tell you what I am worried about, and that's Billy havin' time to prepare a surprise for us before we get where we're goin'. So we gotta ride hard, and we gotta ride fast."

He gestured at the sweeping plains off to the north and east. "I'm sure ya'll have noticed the local terrain. Ty made a good suggestion, sayin' we go overland, down around the south end of the lake, and shoot north over the plains. Frank and I agree. It should cut some serious time off our travels. You boys think you can take your sorry ass machines off the trail?"

Cole grunted as he pushed a bushel of tobacco into his mouth for the trail. "You think you can take your shiny new toy off the trail, Jesse? I'm pretty sure our flyin' 'Horses'll be able to make it without a hitch."

"We're still goin' to Diablo Canyon though, right Jesse?" Ty's high voice was clear in the morning air.

Jesse turned sharply to stare at the young kid in disbelief. Many of the townsmen around them had stopped to watch the outlaws depart. "Ty, I swear, you are hell-bent on makin' me regret takin' you in on this."

The boy raised his hands. "Sorry, boss! I didn't know . . . we still . . . yeah, Okay, Jesse!"

The outlaw leader shook his head in disbelief and swung his leg over the barrel of the Blackjack.

"C'mon, boys, before I decide I'm better off leavin' half of ya behind."

Jesse gunned his machine back down the main road the way they had come, back towards Mary Lake Trail. They were behind schedule even more now, with even more need to hurry. It was bad enough, knowing that he was up against Billy, not even knowing quite what for. Now, with the Union in the region, and Carpathian's acting strange, even for that strange old man, Jesse was starting to feel a might crowded. If you included the Warrior Nation that Billy had run into that put the whole kit and caboodle in motion, there were not many players in the territories that were not somehow tied in now.

Jesse snarled, echoing the sound of his rumbling Blackjack, as he tore out of Sacred Lake heading south. The growling thunder of twenty Iron Horses leaping into the air and rushing after him bounced off the houses and outbuildings all around. Still, another benefit of going overland that he had not told his men was the fact that the trail they'd laid down up to Sacred Lake would now take anyone tracking them far off course. If anyone was tracking them, that was. He could feel the phantoms drawing in from all around him, and he knew that there was every chance most of them did not even pose a real danger. Still, better to take care now and not need the extra slack than to need it and not have it.

In the street, the men all stood and watched as the outlaw band sped down south, leaving the town once again silent except for the disconsolate sobs from the upper hall of the lodge.

*****

Wyatt knew, as they pulled into Sacred Lake, that something was not quite right. He also knew that whatever it was, it was not anything he had been expecting.

The marshals looked at the small collection of buildings. Groups of men worked the fields or stood silently in the road, watching the approaching lawmen. Wyatt brought his Hog rumbling down the center of the packed-earth street and pulled up in front of the largest building, a long two story structure with a sign proclaiming it Sacred Lake Lodge. The building was set apart from the street by a split rail fence, with hitching posts for real-live horses spaced along it. Wyatt shook his head. He could not remember the last time he had seen real hitching posts in a town.

With a practiced flick, the Over-marshal shut off the engine of his vehicle, and soon the rest of the Interceptors grumbled into stillness.

"Damned if this ain't the quietest burg I've ever seen." Virgil muttered to his brother. The other marshals were standing in a wide circle around their leaders, watching the townsfolk with calm, professional faces. Wyatt nodded and looked around, surprised to see that there were no RJ-1027 recharge stations in front of the tavern. In fact, as he took a more careful look around him, he saw that there was no sign of any RJ-1027 tech to be seen, anywhere.

The UR-30 units stalked into the street, playing their crimson beams across the area in front of the lodge and revealing many interwoven Crimson Gold trails hovering above the dust of the street. They had been moving far too quickly for the robots to track the residue on their way to Sacred Lake, but clearly, the men they were following had been here, and judging from the intensity of the trails, not too long ago.

Wyatt pulled his gloves off and stuck them into his holster belt as he stood at the gate looking up at the lodge. The door swung silently open and a large man with iron-gray hair stepped out, an honest smile on his broad face. The man's hair was cut in a strange pattern, nearly shaved on top with long locks down the sides and back. Looking around, Wyatt noticed that the rest of the men he could see wore similar haircuts. He filed the curiosity away for later scrutiny as he moved toward the large man, hand outstretched.

"Welcome, gentlemen, to Sacred Lake Lodge!" The man's handshake was firm without being overbearing. He looked over Wyatt's shoulder at the lawmen standing behind him, the deputies fanning out across the street, and the UR-30s walking the perimeter of the parking area, heads tilted down and coherent beams sweeping back and forth over the ground. Wyatt was curious to see a look he could not quite decipher cross over the tall man's face at the sight of the robots.

The man did not miss a beat, however, and his smile never slipped, as he focused back again on Wyatt's face. "My name is Elijah, proprietor of the Sacred Lake Lodge. Can I get you and your men refreshment, sir? It seems a little early to be stopping for lodgings for the night."

Wyatt nodded, turning slightly to scan the streets again. He assumed a consciously casual pose. "Yeah, no, we're right as rain, sir." He looked at the gray-haired man out of the corner of his eye. "That accent of yours, ain't from around here, no?"

The man's smile widened even further. "Very perceptive, Mr. . . . ?"

Wyatt smiled. "Marshal, actually. Over-marshal, in fact, if we're getting' technical. But you can call me Marshal. Marshal Wyatt Earp."

"Ah!" Elijah's smile grew even warmer. "We have heard good things of you, sir, and the work you have done. It is truly an honor to welcome you to our little enclave!"

Wyatt could not have said why the man's words made him uncomfortable, but for a moment he had a hard time meeting Elijah's gaze. "Yes, well, thank you very much. Actually, we're following a band of wanted criminals, headed by Jesse James. Maybe you've heard of him as well?"

That saw the smile fade from Elijah's face, but even in its new, neutral configuration, there was a pleasant openness to it. "Well, no, Marshal, I can't say that I have. We do take in travelers, of course, and we never turn folks away who aim to behave. But once they're gone, they are no longer our concern here. We cannot allow ourselves to be sucked into the conflicts and struggles of the world outside."

Wyatt nodded, looking back at Virgil and Doc by the gate. "But a group was here." He looked back at Elijah. "We know they were, so please, think carefully before answering."

Elijah nodded. "You will find no duplicity here, Marshal. Those questions we answer, we answer honestly."

Wyatt grimaced, looking down at his boots for a moment. "Would there happen to be any other guests here currently, Elijah?"

Elijah smiled. "There is one sojourning wayfarer currently with us, yes. A poor man who seems to be the very personification of ill luck. Jonah returned, if you will."

Wyatt looked quizzically back at his brother. It was Doc who answered, his eyes smiling over the mask. "This boy must have powerful bad luck indeed, Wyatt."

Wyatt nodded thoughtfully again, then looked back at the man standing on the stoop beside him. "I'm going to have to see your guest, Elijah. I believe he may well be helpful in following our current trail."

"I'm afraid I can't let you do that, Over-marshal." Elijah's stance was casual and relaxed, but something about the man's demeanor registered as a threat in the lawman's mind. He also noticed the gray-haired man look out into the street, giving a minute shake of his head.

Wyatt turned to see several strong-looking men approaching from various angles. The deputies were pulling back slightly, pistols and rifles rising in warding gestures. The RU-30s had abandoned their lamp sight, crouching slightly in gunfighter's poses, metal hands hovering over the butts of their massive pistols.

"Boys, stand down!" Wyatt barked to his men, and they reluctantly lowered their weapons. "AZ-24, you're with me." One of the UR-30s immediately pivoted and approached the front of the lodge. Wyatt turned back to Elijah.

"My metal deputy and I will be going into the lodge, and we'll be in there for a few minutes, and then my men and I will be leaving." For the first time since the front door opened, Elijah's face assumed a dark aspect. "Now, if you or your people are feelin' uppity, sir, I'm afraid things won't be goin' that smoothly. We will be questioning this man. Other than that, there is all sorts of unpleasantness we can avoid."

Elijah stared at Wyatt for a moment, then looked out again at the street. He nodded slightly to his people. The large men all faded back, standing like trained soldiers ready for a fight despite the gray-haired man's signal.

"Thank ya kindly, Elijah." Wyatt tipped his hat and then pushed through into the lodge. The robot followed close behind.

As the door swung shut, Elijah was left standing alone on the top step. The man slowly put his hands on his hips and looked out at the marshals, his face schooled to an empty coldness.

Time seemed to have frozen, and when the door banged open again the lawmen in the street jumped at the sound. Elijah and his men, however, did not so much as twitch. Wyatt hurried out, taking the stone steps two at a time, the UR-30 hurrying along behind him. The Over-marshal flipped a silver coin into the air over his shoulder and Elijah deftly caught it.

"I'd recommend a pauper's funeral on the edge of town. That ought to pay for the necessaries." Wyatt's voice was cold as he called over his shoulder, his eyes fixed on his Hog. "Anything more you want to spring for, you can pay for it yourself."

Wyatt hopped onto his Interceptor, the rest of the marshals and deputies jumping on their own vehicles.

"It was James, and Billy the Kid too, apparently." Wyatt shot his brother a sour look. "And it looks like Grant's got some boys in the area as well, so things just got even more interestin'."

"Back to the Judgment, we'll turn it around as soon as we can and get back on the main trail. This is all goin' down in Diablo Canyon, and we've wasted too much time here already."

The lawmen roared off down the road, leaving a pall of dust and smoke in the air. As the grit settled, the sound was swiftly replaced once again with the village's peaceful silence.

Elijah was still standing on the top step of the Sacred Lake Lodge, eyes fixed on the road to the south where a dark plume of dust marked the lawmen's retreat. Another of the village men stepped up, turning to watch the road with a dark scowl.

"Three times in two days. Events are threatening to overtake us, Elijah. And every one of them tainted with the foul stain of the Great Enemy." The man's voice was soft but insistent.

Elijah shook his head. "The time is not yet ready. The Holy Council is not prepared to make themselves known, and many of these men know not what path they walk. Many will choose otherwise when the time comes. Have the men take care of the body upstairs, and then go about their business." He looked down at the other man and put a comradely hand on his shoulder. "We will be farmers and innkeepers for a bit longer, my friend, before we may once again take up the sword of our lord."

*****

The Judgment wagon had not quite travelled half the distance to Sacred Lake by the time Wyatt and the outriders returned. He waved for the giant vehicle to stop and then rolled up beside it, the other Hogs rumbling to a halt nearby.

Wyatt pulled down his goggles and took his hat off, wiping the dust and grime from his face. He looked up to the access hatch as it opened, the judge poking his head through, and waved him down.

"We need to set up the wireless. This is getting ridiculous." Wyatt dismounted his vehicle and strode towards the Judgment. Behind him Doc Holliday hurried after, while Virgil followed at a more sedate pace. The rest of the marshals and deputies stayed with their Interceptors.

"Wyatt, you sure you want to bring the feds in on this? They'll hog tie us sure as sure, and we'll be left with nothin'." Doc's voice was low but intense.

"We've now got two damned outlaw gangs running through the same stretch o' dirt, and on top of that, we've got the damned army running through here shootin' eveyrthin' up!" Wyatt's anger was barely contained. "You saw the trail head overland clear as the rest of us did. At least one of the gangs isn't even takin' the trails no more. We need to get in touch with someone, and we're out in the middle o'nowhere. Somewhere out east there are people who know more than we do,damnit! And we need as much information as we can get before we go ridin' into Diablo Canyon guns a blazin'!"

Virgil nodded as he came up to his brother. "Wyatt's right, Doc. We need to know what we're ridin' into. The James and Younger gang, that's bad enough. But we gotta deal with Billy the Kid and his boys too? If there are Union troops around here, we should know why, and we should know if they can help us."

Wyatt shook his head. "That ain't it, Virg. They know somethin's goin' on out here, those blue-belly bastards. Why else would they have an advanced force out this far, when they're facing down Sitting Bull and the Warrior Nation off east?" He rested up against the leather seat of his Hog and wiped his forehead again. "No, this is bigger than we thought. An' those damned Union agents in Kansas City? They weren't just there whippin' up biscuits, you can bet."

The judge and several deputies were wrestling a large canvas bag from one of the storage compartments along the rear of the vehicle. Clearly it was heavy, and jangled when they dropped it as if it were filled with pots and pans.

"Careful with that damned equipment!" Wyatt barked. "God alone knows how much that would cost to replace. And He also knows that General his High and Mightiness Grant the First would order us to replace it if we broke it." He finished in a mutter.

The bag was dragged away from the trail into an area of flat grass. A confusion of metal struts, beams, and tubing were dumped out onto the brittle grass. A large black iron box was taken out and placed beside the jumbled mess, a single red light twinkling on its side.

"Alright, get that set up pronto, and we'll see what we have to see. I don't wanna waste any more time than absolutely necessary, you hear me?" Wyatt pushed himself away from the Interceptor and moved into the shade of the Judgment's flank. Holliday and Virgil followed, and one of the marshals standing there offered them a canteen.

"Thanks." Wyatt took a quick swig and wiped his mouth with the back of his hand, tossing the canteen to Virgil. "You know, there's gotta be an easier way to contact Washington than this."

Virgil nodded before taking a sip. "You know we ain't gonna be able to hear half of what they say. An' we're gonna be lucky if we can understand every other word, the way those things work. An' you also know, half the time they don't work at all."

Doc, who had declined a sip of water, nodded towards one of the UR-30 units standing guard nearby. "Folks whisper as how your little tin soldiers, there, can sneak reports back to Washington without anyone knowin', spreadin' their secrets far an' wide. Maybe they can contact 'em for us?"

Wyatt snorted, shaking his head. "We been tryin', Doc, you been there." He turned towards the robot. "Hey, metal man, get over here." The head of the machine tracked to the sound of the Over-marshal's voice, then the rest of the body revolved to orient on the men in the shade. With regulated precision it stalked over to them.

"AZ 21, reporting as ordered." The robot stood stiffly in front of the lawmen, its single, baleful eye staring straight at the iron flank of the wagon.

Wyatt stood up and addressed the robot in a loud voice, as if speaking to a deaf person. "Okay, 21, can you communicate with Washington?"

There was a momentary pause before the eerily still figure spoke through its vibrating voice grill. "Query cannot be processed."

Wyatt's face twisted slightly in bitter amusement. "See? Hell, I don't even think they're speakin' English half the time." He turned back to the robot. "21, tell Washington we need to know what's goin' on out here."

Again a pause, before, "Directive cannot be processed."

"Send us some girls from Washington!" Doc's voice was quite loud despite the leather mask, and his eyes crinkled with amusement.

"Hell, send that little piece from Kansas City, she was a stunner." Virgil chuckled along with Holliday as Wyatt shook his head.

"Directives cannot be processed," the still figure replied.

"Go back to sentry duty, await further instructions." Wyatt did not try to keep the disgust from his voice. As the thing turned away, he sighed. "An' you just know they're a heck of a lot smarter than they let on, too."

"Well, they can't be a heck of a lot dumber than they seem, 'r they wouldn't be much use." Virgil was still smirking, but he shook his head in bemusement.

The men working on the communications assembly were just about finished as the UR-30 returned to its position. Three tall legs, articulated like the limbs of a giant insect, were affixed to a much taller pole that stabbed up into the sky, a strange ball glowing faintly red at the very top. Tubes and wires were spiraled around the pole to the box at the bottom. Another of the deputies came back from the wagon holding a wooden package the size of a small valise.

"Sir, we're ready for you." Another of the deputies opened the package and took out another black box, and something that looked like a thick wand, a black ball at one end and a tangle of cables and wires connecting it to the smaller black box by the other. This new contraption was held by one deputy while another handed the wand to Wyatt.

"You just speak into the ball, there, sir, and anything we get back will appear here, in this window." The young man indicated the smaller box. A square about the size of a dime novel had begun to glow faintly red when it had been plugged into the larger case on the ground.

Wyatt took the wand and shot his brother a quizzical look. Virgil just shrugged his shoulders. Wyatt cleared his throat and spoke, loudly, into the ball. "This is Over-marshal Wyatt Earp, is anyone attendin' the network?"

Doc gave Wyatt a wry look. "Ain't gonna follow procedure?"

Wyatt snorted. "You mean all that stoppin' an' rogerin' an' such? No. They can figure out what I'm sayin' just fine with me talkin' straight."

The ball at the top of the staff glowed more strongly, the box buzzed in the deputy's hand, and a series of red characters began to burn deep within the box's frame.

"THIS IXXXARSHALXXXXXLER IN TOMXXXXXE STOXXXXESTION WXXX DO YOXXXEED OVEXXXXRSHAL STXX"

Wyatt stared at the glowing characters with rising frustration. "Now you see that? What in the Sam Hill is that even supposed to mean?"

Holliday looked over Wyatt's shoulder at the box. "Marshal Miller back in Tombstone, mannin' the board, Wyatt. He's asking you what you need."

"Don't see that that's so tough, Wyatt." Virgil smirked beneath his sweeping mustache.

Wyatt gave them both a sour look and then addressed the wand again. "Miller, go up the network and get me someone from Army HQ."

A pause, and then the earlier message disappeared, replaced with another.

"SORXXXXIR I COXXX NOT UNDEXXXXXD THXXXUESTION PLEASXXXXPEAT STXX"

"God damn this contraption straight to Hades!" Wyatt took a turn and kicked at the unoffending grass underfoot, then turned back to the machine, holding the wand in both hands.

"Get me Army HQ now." He said the words slowly and loudly, every muscle in his body tense with annoyance.

The men waited a moment for the box's message to change.

"YEXXXIR ARMXXHQ PLEASXXXXXT A MINUXXXXTOP"

"I swear, I'd rather be using smoke signals at this point." Wyatt paced back and forth while the rest of the men watched him from the corners of their eyes. Most of the deputies had never seen the far speaking machine used before, but all knew that the Over-marshal got downright ornery whenever he had to resort to it. There was a reason most communication still went over the wires.

"Sir, I think it's Army HQ." The deputy holding the box jiggled it slightly to get his attention.

Wyatt walked back to the box and looked into the window where, indeed, the letters had changed again. He looked up at Virgil and Doc. "Well, trust the Army to have a stronger machine than the one they sent to Tombstone." The letters were much clearer.

"THIXXIS UNION AXMY HQ STOXXPLEASE IDENXXFY YOUXSELF STOP"

Wyatt sighed with frustration and yelled into the wand. "This is Over-marshal Earp. I need to speak to someone in authority of Arizona Territory Operations!"

The letters almost immediately faded out and were replaced in a new configuration.

"OVEXXMARSHXL PLEXXE STAXD BY STOP"

"Hmmm," Virgil straightened up from reading the words. "Looks like you might'a hooked a big bug with that one, Over-marshal, sir."

Wyatt growled wordlessly and waited for the reply. When the letters rearranged themselves again the three men all bent down. Doc whistled low and muttererd. "Damn . . . "

"THIX IS GENXXAL GRAXT WHAXXSEEMS TO BE TXE PROBXXM OVERXXARSHAL"

"He don't much cotton to the procedures himself, looks like." Doc was smiling.

"He's a blue-belly, they don't much cotton to anythin' if you think about." Wyatt jabbed an elbow into his brother's ribs. "This thing ain't half bad when you got the power of the whole Union Army behind you." Once again spoke into the wand.

"Good afternoon, sir. I was wondering if you could tell me if you have any operations currently active in the north eastern quadrant of the territory, around the Coconinos?"

This time there seemed to be a very long pause before the words in the box changed.

"THE SITUXTION IN ANXXAROUND THE COCXNINXS IS UNDER COXTROL OVER MARSHAX PLEAXX STAND DOWX AND RETUX TO TOMBSXONE FOR FURXHER INSTRXXTIONS"

The men straightened and glared at each other in disbelief.

"Did that bastard just order me to stand down?" Wyatt's voice was high and incredulous. The flare of disbelief in his eyes was matched by every other man watching.

"Damned if he didn't do just that." Doc seemed more amused than disbelieving. "Never trust authority, Wyatt. Isn't that what I always tell you? Especially when you are authority." It was clear that his smile was enormous behind the ornate leather mask.

"Well, he can just take his orders an' drown 'em in a spittoon! I ain't in his damned outfit, and he can't tell me nor my men what to do!"

Wyatt was grasping the wand with white knuckles as he shouted into the black ball. "Listen, Grant, my men and I are conducting our own operation, and we will continue—"

"Sir, the box is . . . General Grant must still be talking . . . "

Sure enough, the words continued to form.

"CEAXE AND DXXIST ALLXOPERATIXNS IN THE DIXBLO CANYXN AREA XNDER PXESIDENXIAL AXTHORXZATION"

"Damn," Doc repeated.

Wyatt looked down at the words as they swam in their crimson-tinged darkness. Presidential authorization meant something truly momentous was occurring. Or Grant thought there was, anyway.

"You think he's really got President Johnson on the hook for this?" Virgil looked at his brother, then to Holliday, then out to the deputies and marshals watching from a distance. He could not keep his gaze from lingering on the robots as they stood motionless at their posts.

Wyatt was still staring at the words. "Damned if I know, Virg. Still an' all . . . are we plannin' on backin' off, even if it is the president his own self tellin' us we're done?"

Virgil looked down the road, then back up towards Sacred Lake, and then over to his brother again. "Well, Wyatt, if there's anyone can tell us to stand down, it's Johnson."

"But it's not Johnson." The buzzing voice brought them all up short. They had all been so wrapped up in the conversation over the far speaker that they had not noticed the rear ramp being lowered, or Morgan coming down to join them. That said something for their depth of focus, anyway.

Wyatt nodded, forcing himself to look into Morgan's placid face. "Hey, Morg, thanks for joining us. What're you sayin', now?"

The enormous metal arm rose to point at the far speaker's window. "That is not President Johnson." There was a little more emotion in the voice than in a UR-30, but not much. "That is General Grant claiming the president's authority."

"Still, sir," one of the deputies looked pale. "The man's a general. If he tells us to back down— "

"Provencher," Virgil's voice was gravelly with anger. "You wanna add coward to the list of words that pop into my mind when I see you?"

The man backed down, but he was looking at Wyatt with grey determination.

"No, Virg, the little shavetail's right. Grant's a general, hell, he's the General of the United States Army." Wyatt took a few steps away from the box until the cords brought him up short, then turned and paced a few steps back the other way. "He can't have got that much out here to stop us, but at the same time, if we go against his word, he's got plenty he can send after us after the fact."

"Easier to ask forgiveness than beg permission, Wyatt." Doc's smile was still there behind the leather.

Wyatt's look at his old friend was sour. "That ain't no way for a grown man to live his life, Doc." He gave the robots a speculative look. "But still, that don't mean it ain't true. And I'll tell you what else is true, the Army ain't been there to help with the outlaw problem much at all either way. So, if they come farther into the territories, thinkin' their comin' after us, maybe that ain't such a bad thing neither. "

Wyatt smiled and went back to the box. The window was shifting as he looked into it.

"OVXR MARSXAL EARPXPLEAXE ACKNXWLEXGE STAND XOWN OXDER"

Wyatt cleared his throat and then raised the wand to his mouth again. "Sorry, General. Your last messages have been garbled. We will try to communicate with you again at a later date."

The Over-marshal tossed the wand to one of the waiting deputies and started walking back towards the Judgment wagon.

"Alright boys, let's pack up and move out! We've got us an appointment in Diablo Canyon we ain't about to miss. I want all the interceptors topped off from the wagon so we're all goin' in on full burn. We gotta take the roads, so we're gonna be late to the party anyway, but that don't mean we ain't gonna be bringin' the real entertainment!"

The marshals snapped back to life and began to gather the equipment. Wyatt noticed the robots standing hesitant for a moment longer than usual before following the orders, but he just shrugged it off.

The men working to take down the far speaker all stopped and the deputy holding the small box called out. "Sir, it's the general again! He's askin' you to confirm the orders!"

Wyatt smiled and called over his shoulder. "Just take it down, son. He got the message."

Chapter 12

Through the monocular, the town of Diablo Canyon looked much like any other town in the western territories. It had not changed much, in fact, since the last time he had visited, almost ten years ago. Sure, it was in better repair, many of the buildings were sporting big, new RJ-1027 generators, and there was even some new construction towards the center of town, but it still looked fairly normal.

The gang had parked near a set of railroad tracks that looked frail in comparison to the modern Heavy Rail tracks the Union was dropping down all over the place, but Jesse remembered when they marked the cutting edge of transportation technology. The tracks ran down a gentle slope towards the town, right through the middle, and then, of course, stopped abruptly at the dark scar of the canyon on the other side. Jesse did not know what the plans had been, all those years ago, to complete the rail line. He knew there was supposed to be a bridge, of course, and over time a great deal of equipment had been brought in to assist with constructing, but for some reason it never had completed. From his vantage up on the hill Jesse could see the shrouded forms of construction equipment parked up against the cliff, tarps billowing in the warm winds coming out of the canyon.

Somewhere in that maze of giant machines would be tools to dig, he knew. The plans to sink the massive iron suspension pylons deep into the canyon floor would have required more than just dynamite or whatever RJ-1027 equivalent construction crews were using these days. They would have digging gear for sure. And more importantly, due to the strange nature of the town, they would have folks who could operate it.

Many engineers and skilled workers had followed the high tech equipment out to the construction site. For years, they had been kept on retainer in the small camp that had grown up around the equipment and the rough barracks. Home had sprung up while they waited, and then a tavern, and then stores. Other people came to the area to provide food, entertainment, and willing company. Soon a thriving town had formed around the camp. When finally the retainer checks had petered out, many had felt right at home, and stayed. Most of them had developed other businesses or skills over the years in an effort to stave off boredom.

Because it had developed organically, with no plan or engineering, civil or social, there had not been any law, either. The place had become an outlaw's paradise, where the only rule was the commandment of strength. The place had been a playground for Jesse and folks like him. He had lived here for several years, in fact, during the little burg's heyday.

And so there it was: Diablo Canyon, where a man looking for the best excavating machinery from ten years ago could find it in abundance, along with the men and women to run it. It now only remained to liberate some of the machines and persuade some of the workers to accompany him.

Jesse's lips frowned in the shadow of the raised monocular as he remembered that this was not, in fact, all that remained. He had heard the rumors about the UR-30 unit that had been sent to Diablo Canyon. He had heard the story of Johnny Ringo and the Injun runaway that usually rode with Billy, The Apache Kid. They had apparently come rolling into town to break some heads and collect some coin, like in the good old days. The stories of what happened next differed, some said they had only been riding with a few friends, others said they rode in with twenty men beside them. All the versions agreed on one thing though: Ringo and the Apache Kid had been the only ones to make it out alive. Apparently it had been a slaughter, and every dead outlaw had been credited to the metal marshal.

There was no sign of the robot lawman now, however. As Jesse and Cole Younger looked through Union monoculars at the sleepy town, Frank sweeping the place with his rifle Sophie's high-tech scope, it looked as if folks were going about their business like folks did in most towns. The place looked like an idyllic little community, and something about that aggravated Jesse more than he could say. The damned Union, once again swooping in and taking his home away from him. Never mind that he had left years ago. What sat before him now was nothing less than the rape of his memories, again, before his very eyes.

Jesse spat into the dirt at his feet. "An' no sign of damned Billy, neither."

Jesse lowered the blocky monocular, his face set as a grim mask. "Well, it looks all peaceful-like, but you've all heard what

Ringo and the Apache Kid had to say about their last visit here. There's a metal marshal down there that's really acquired a taste for the blood of us folks who like to live on the fringes." His mouth twisted with contempt as he spat out the words. "Way I heard it, Ringo and his boys rode in free and clear and only saw the thing when it pounced on 'em."

"Sounds like we need some bait, Jesse." Cole smiled brightly as he said the words, spitting juice into the dust. "We gots plenty of new blood needs testin', eh?"

Most of the younger men shared nervous glances, and some giggled in a high-pitched nervous reaction, hoping the outlaw was joking. The giggling stopped abruptly as Jesse spoke.

"Yeah. Can't be wastin' proven hands on somethin' like this." He looked back over his shoulder at the men standing around him. He pointed to two. "Gage, Randall, you two got enough RJ-1027 to get into the center of town down yonder?"

The two young men swallowed hard, glancing down at the indicator panels on their Iron Horses. Gage spoke in a voice he was obviously struggling to keep steady.

"Just enough, Jesse."

The other new man, Randall, nodded. It appeared his mouth was too dry to speak. He kept working it but no sound came out.

Jesse nodded and gave both of the men a brief smile. "Nice. Don't worry, boys, we'll be right behind you. You'll have the best shot in the west watchin' yer back, as Frank'll be takin' Sophie fer high ground." He looked around to where his brother was bringing his storied rifle out of its holster. "Frank, 'bout time the ole girl saw some action, you reckon?"

Frank nodded to his brother, then to the pale young men. He patted his massive rifle affectionately. "You bet. Boys, don't you worry none. Once I got that thing in my sights, it won't be but a moment before I clean its plow but good."

The young men nodded, but they did not seem overly comforted.

"Alright, here's the real deal," Jesse gestured with his whirring arms to gather his men closer to him. "Gage and Randall will drive down to the center of town. Just havin' the guns on their 'Horses should be enough, illegal weaponry 'r some such. But just in case, I want you guys to go in, smoke wagons in hand, and launch some shots up at the sky like you was celebratin' at some wild shindig. That ought to get the metal man to come runnin'."

He then addressed the rest of the men, pointing with one hand at several negligently holding rifles over their shoulders. "Before you go in, though, the rest of us'll get into position. I want you rifle boys with Frank. He'll put you in the best positions to take advantage of the terrain. The rest of us'll approach on foot from the front and sides, weapons hidden from view and actin' like civilized folks." He gave a sly wink, and added, "Cole, you an' yer brothers'll have to just watch the rest of us an' follow along best you can."

Cole snorted with indifferent amusement, although his younger brothers all looked mildly annoyed.

Randall finally found his voice, speaking in a hoarse croak. "Why ya'll gonna need to be backin' us up if Frank's all we need?"

The chatter among the men died away as they all looked at Randall and then quickly looked away. Jesse gave them a short glare and moved to the young man, resting one metal arm across his shoulders. "Randall, you'll be glad we're there. Ain't nothin' to worry about, right? Soon as the metal marshal shows his eye, Frank's gonna put it out for him, and that'll be it. But what if other folks start gettin' ideas? Or what if the thing goes haywire when Frank takes its head off?"

Jesse raised his voice to speak to the whole group again. "Don't forget, boys, this thing ain't no man. It might have the right number o' arms an' legs an' such, but it's metal, not flesh 'n bone, and it prob'ly ain't built like a man inside. We gotta be ready for anythin' when we go down there."

The men nodded at the words, and Jesse could sense they were as ready as they would ever be. "Alright, then boys. Frank, take your long-shooters off first. The rest of us'll filter down in a few minutes." He turned to Gage and Randall, both mounting back up onto their 'Horses. "You boys wait 'till I give you the signal, then you come down directly, right?"

"We twig, Jesse." Gage had his chin higher lifted higher than normal, but the outlaw chief just nodded and patted him on the back, then did the same to Randall.

"You boys'll be right as rain, don't you worry none." He put all of the confidence and assurance he could into his smile. He immediately felt a twinge of guilt as he saw how well it worked on the two greenhorns.

It took a bit more than fifteen minutes for Frank to infiltrate the riflemen through the edges of town, walking casually with their rifles flat against one leg beneath their dusters. Once Jesse, following their movements through the monocular, saw them in place, he nodded to Cole who returned the gesture and started down the tracks towards town. Jim Younger had another group that moved out to the right, and their brother John, often rumored to be the toughest of the four, led a small group out to the left. Jesse waited for the groups to get about halfway to town before he turned back to the two young men who had been chosen, tipped one metal finger to the brim of his hat with another confident grin, and then turned to make his own slow, casual approach.

Jesse watched the last of his men disappear behind the outermost buildings of Diablo Canyon and was glad he had not yet heard any disturbances. There was no telling where the metal marshal was in the town, and he had been half-sure that one of his flankers would roust the thing from its hiding place long before Gage or Randall ever had time to leave their starting positions. He had figured, even if that happened, that Frank and his riflemen would be able to nail the thing anyway, so the plan had seemed pretty sound coming and going. That did not make his slow, lazy walk any more bearable.

Everything was peaceful, and so he turned slightly, raised one arm straight up to heaven, gave two quick shakes, and then dropped it again. He heard the sudden roar of the 'Horse engines as his two young greenhorns gunned them to life. Jesse casually moved to the side of the trail as the sound got louder behind him.

Jesse made sure he was even with the first buildings on the main street when Gage and Randall burst past. He grinned with honest affection as he heard their rebel yells over the howling of the engines. It was nice to see they had some fire in their bellies, even after hearing the stories.

Gage and Randall tore down the street, a ragged wake of dust and grit flaring out behind them. They were each brandishing an RJ-1027 pistol in the air as if they were posing for the cover of a penny dreadful novel, launching bursts of ruby fire up into the clear sky. The few folks who had been out and about in the heat of mid-day jerked crazily at the sound of the shots, covered their heads, and ran, crab-fashion, for the cover of the surrounding buildings. Jesse could swear he heard Gage shout out as he entered the center of town, "We're here fer yer whisky an' yer women!"

The outlaw boss smiled under the shadow of his hat brim, shaking his head. Had he ever been that young?

The smile faded quickly as a shape walked calmly from the darkness of an alley across the center of town. Despite the vest and riding leathers, Jess knew from the angular lines and the unnatural shape of the head beneath the straight-brimmed hat that he was looking at one of the UR-20 Enforcers. The same one, he knew, that had almost killed two of the most formidable men in the territories, and had managed to kill all their companions. It looked like a man as it sauntered out of the darkness, but Jesse knew it was nothing of the sort.

Gage saw the thing first, and deliberately put a bolt into the building behind it, just above its head. "C'mon over here, you tin can! Let's see what kinda beans they loaded you up with!" He fired again.

A strange, buzzing, inhuman voice echoed through the street. "Discharge of contraband military hardware and weaponry excessive to personal protection. Summary provisional sentencing."

Time slowed to a crawl. Jesse knew he had men sown all through the town by now, but for a moment he felt completely and utterly alone as that alien voice droned through the streets.

The robot's arm blurred and rose with a massive hand cannon clenched in its metal fist. "Relinquish your weapons and dismount. Prepare for summary provisional sen—"

A vicious crack exploded from above, like thunder from a clear summer sky, and the robot was sent reeling backwards, arms flailing for balance, weapon flying wide. It had happened so quickly, that Jesse could not be sure of the shot. The thing's hat was certainly shredded, fluttering into the street like a rag. The structure of the hat was gone, and for a moment, Jesse was sure his brother had leveled the thing with a single shot. He raised his arm in triumph, ready to give a resounding rebel yell, when the machine steadied itself, stopped the wild milling of its arms, and stood tall once more.

There was a huge dent in the UR-30's temple, and several of the elements of its face were clearly misaligned, knocked out of place by the shot. The skull itself was intact, however, and the eye still glowed a menacing red. A second pistol lashed upwards in its left hand.

The robot did not move like a man, there was no apparent processing or thought connecting one motion to the next. It flowed through a series of positions, the gun rising, blasting as it came in line with one of the mounted boys, continuing to float upward with the movement of the entire body, and then fired again when it was aligned with something high and away on Jesse's right. The outlaw chief was not paying attention to that second shot, however, as he stared in horrified fascination at the results of that first shot.

The gunshot was like nothing Jesse had ever heard before, a sharp, humming sound that lasted only a moment, but seemed to echo eerily in the air for a spell after the shot had been fired. The muzzle blast was a hellish eruption of crimson fury, rich with traces of RJ-1027 swirling within it. The shot took Randall in the chest, blasting most of his innards out across the street behind him. A grisly framework of glistening bone and gristle remained to connect the poor kid's arms and head to the rest of his body. Not enough to support him, however, and the whole disgusting mess collapsed back into the saddle. As he fell forward, the boy twisted, his face just becoming visible to Jesse's horrified eyes. The mouth was working frantically as if screaming for help or vengeance or death, but all that emerged was a faint red mist. The kid's pistol dropped from his jerking fingers and clanked off the footpad of his vehicle, floating slowly forward with no one at the controls.

And then Jesse realized where the second blast from that demonic hell cannon must have been aimed. "Frank!"

Jesse jerked out both hyper-velocity pistols, his arms swinging seamlessly through the motions. His face was twisted into a mask of fear and rage as he began to fire un-aimed shots at the thing standing before him. Part of his brain knew there was no way he was going to score a hit at this range, not while running. But he could not bring himself to care.

The UR-30 was swinging back into line with Gage, the poor kid staring gape-mouthed at the gory remains of his friend. The giant weapon was sliding into firing position and Jesse knew there was no way he would be able to stop it in time.

From another roof farther to the right, another thunder crack echoed off the buildings. This time the robot was thrown off its feet and into the dust, its head deformed from a blast that had hit it directly above its single eye. Even then, on its back in the dirt, the thing was not finished. It began to rise, once again bringing its pistol to bear up and to the right. Another shot rang out from overhead, and then another. Each struck the robot in the center of its metal face, driving it back time and time again into the dirt. The limbs began to jerk spasmodically as the twisted iron ruin took impact after impact.

Eventually, the gunshots from above stopped. The thing was still in the dirt, its head completely blasted away, a collar of springs, tubes, and wires erupting from its savaged neck.

The entire event had taken only moments, and Jesse slowed to a stunned walk, and then stopped completely, looking at the still-twitching metal man in the dust. He looked off to the right and saw Frank rising up from his firing position, nodding in satisfaction and propping Sophie on his hip. Frank jerked his chin towards his younger brother and then tilted his head towards the smoking hole in a sign that had once said "Dry Goods" one building over.

"Garland couldn't hold his water, shot before I tol' 'him to." The voice was harsh, but Jesse knew his brother was troubled by the Garland's death. He nodded back at Frank, smiling despite his heaving breath, and then started to walk again towards the downed robot.

"Damn, d'you see what it did to Randall?" One of the outlaws emerging from the surrounding alleys muttered to another.

"I'll venture a guess Garland ain't much better, up there on that rooftop yonder." Another pointed up at the smoking sign.

Their reactions were familiar to Jesse. He had felt them countless times himself. There was a savage thrill at being alive when others had failed to survive. There was a guilty twinge knowing those that fell had been friends and comrades. There was also an unspoken feeling of relief that the violence was over. He smiled and shook his head. No matter how many times he faced violence, it was always the same.

As each man processed what had happened, staring at the terrible proof of their own mortality slumped in the saddle of Randall's Iron Horse, none of them were watching the RU-30 unit, knowing that it had been completely destroyed by Frank's well-placed shots.

Every one of them had forgotten Jesse's words. Jesse had forgotten his own words. They were not facing a man.

The robot jerked upright without warning, ghoulish as it cast around without a head. Its movements were jerky, no longer smooth or choreographed. The massive gun was still gripped in its hand, and despite the utter destruction of its eye, the weapon slid smoothly into line with its next target – Gage. The young outlaw was numbly wiping blood from his face, breathing in shallow gasps as he tried to cope with everything that had just happened.

The robot may have been able to move again, and it may have been able to wield a weapon, but whatever drove it, whatever lent it the deadly accuracy it had shown earlier, that power was gone. The blast from the thing's weapon took Gage's Iron Horse in the flank, ravening crimson energy devouring the metal and unleashing the RJ-1027 stored in the vehicle's fuel tanks. The boy's leg, brushed by the devastating beam, was splashed away before the explosion, throwing him away like a limp rag just before his mount erupted in a ball of dazzling fire He was dashed against the side of a building over ten feet away. The bike's destruction threw ragged bits of metal and bone in a wide circle that caused most of the approaching outlaws to dive for cover, some screaming as the bits and pieces struck home.

"Kill it!" Jesse's pistols rose again, almost of their own volition, and this time his shots were deadly accurate. The hyper-velocity pistols ripped off a double stream of red bolts into the rising robot's chest. The metal man was sent flying back into the dirt, but the headless creation was not finished yet. It began to fire its terrible weapon in a wide fan of destruction, clearly lacking any rational direction. The blasts struck surrounding buildings, punching glowing holes in some, clearly starting fires inside. One collapsed in upon itself as soon as the blast struck, the roof slumping in to fan the fires within as it fell.

The outlaws were not standing motionless now, however. They were running for cover, directing a withering rain of red darts at the writhing metal machine in the middle of the street. Most of the shots were striking the thing, on its arm or leg or body. Some, however, were sailing right over the flailing target to slap into buildings on the other side, starting more fires.

"C'mon, you deadbeats! Beef this thing!" Two more of his men were down, their bodies twisted and torn, smoke rising from their smoldering clothes. Jesse spat again and ran across the street, keeping at an angle, both of his pistol's tracking with the robot's aimless movements. Each shot struck home, his arms guiding the devastation masterfully. The blasts tore through the things torso, shoulders, arms and legs, but it continued to fire, flailing around with the force of its battering.

"Gotta be the chest, Jesse!" Frank shouted from a rooftop. The angle was too severe now for the older brother, and he could not get a shot at the monster's body.

Jesse nodded. He had figured as much himself. He stopped, digging the heels of his boot into the dry dirt of the street, and brought both of his arms together with a sharp clap. The pistols cracked together, the energy in their power cells reaching out towards each other with ghostly crimson tendrils. Jesse gritted his teeth, flipped the switches on each gun with his thumbs, and then sighted down the gap between the two barrels directly at the robot's battered and dented chest. He took a slow breath and pulled the triggers as one.

The catastrophic wave of heat and force that blasted from the two pistols was unlike anything either of them could have achieved on their own. It struck the staggered robot in the chest and lifted it bodily up into the air. The blast wave pushed a storm of dust and dirt before it, driving the robot and the collected filth of the road against the side of a building ten feet away. Every window shattered as the wall bowed beneath the pressure and the heat, then collapsed backwards into shadow.

As the tidal wave pushed the robot into the building, it seemed to disintegrate beneath the ravaging heat of the joined pistols. The tatters of its clothing burned away in the blink of an eye, the remaining color bleached from the metal. Wires and hoses melted to black liquid streams that steamed away into the furnace heat. By the time the UR-30 disappeared into the building, the headless body was falling apart, limbs dropping from the shattered torso with a din that was lost in the raucous destruction of the wall.

Jesse stood in the ensuing silence, breath coming in ragged gasps. His pistols were still gripped in rigid arms, pointing at the smoldering hole. The wood all around the hole was scorched and blistered, and an alarming amount of smoke was pouring back out, rising in a dark column into the sky.

The outlaw chief shook his head to clear it, keeping his weapons at the ready but casting his eyes from side to side while he assessed the situation. The devastation that had been wrought upon the center of Diablo Canyon was staggering. The rain of fire the outlaws had called down upon the robot had shattered several buildings on the far side of the street. Each sent up a gyrating column of smoke and ash up into the sky. And despite having had its head removed, the Enforcer's blind shots had torn through the buildings on the other side of the street. Hardly a building in the center of town, in fact, appeared to have escaped unharmed.

There were three more bodies in the street as well, boys from Jesse's gang who had been unable to reach cover or were unlucky enough to avoid the random shots. Jesse slowly became aware of the looks he was getting from the rest of his men, and he lowered his gun to stare back into the smoldering hole. He knew what had his men spooked, and he did not want to think about it.

He had stood in the middle of the chaos, actually running towards the rabid metal man, while everyone else was hell-bent on running away. He had stood in the middle of the firestorm and had walked out the other side without a scratch. It had happened so often before that he almost took it for granted now. Often at night, staring into a campfire, he wondered if a person who felt no fear could even be considered to have courage anymore. He had never even spoken to Frank about these dark thoughts, and he knew that he probably never would. Shaking himself again, the street came back into focus, and with it, the sound of muffled sobs coming from behind the wreckage of Gage's 'Horse.

By the time Jesse fetched up beside the overturned vehicle, a circle of his men was already standing there. Pushing through the crowd, Jesse crouched down beside Gage's head, resting on a rolled-up coat Frank had put beneath him. The kid was a nauseating pale green color, and a growing pool of blood beneath the ragged stump of his left leg was all the evidence the outlaw chief needed to know that Gage would not be leaving Diablo Canyon alive.

"It's okay, kid." Jesse grabbed a canteen from one of the other men and twisted off the cap, offering to pour a little water into Gage's blood-rimmed mouth. "It's not that bad. This burg's gotta have a decent sawbones. We'll get you looked at, set you up with a nice shiny replacement like mine." He flourished his empty hand back and forth in front of the fluttering yes. Those eyes were fading fast, and Jesse knew it would not be much longer.

"Randall . . . " The voice was thin and whispered, pulsing strangely with the heart that labored to keep him alive.

"That was bad, Gage, real bad." Frank pushed a lank sweep of dirty hair from Gage's face. "That ain't you, though, son. You're gonna be ridin' again in no time."

"Randall . . . " Gage coughed weakly, his breath speeding up, each one more shallow than the one before.

"Gage, hobble that lip o' yours, kid. Randall caught it, an' he's gone. But you're still with us." Jesse was at a complete loss for what to do. Most injuries in the territories were either immediately fatal, or with some good medicine, you could make it. Especially with the arrival of RJ-1027 weaponry. No one survived a gut shot long enough to suffer much anymore, not when a gut shot looked like the one that had taken Randall out.

Frank gave Jesse a look over the dying boy's head, a question in his eyes. Jesse felt a rising surge of anger at his brother for even looking at him that way, as if there was any question, with the kid's leg splashed ten feet across the street and him turning the color of winter grass. He gave a jerky shake of his head and offered Gage some more water.

"Take a sip, kid, it'll make you feel better. Ease that throat o' yours." Gage opened his mouth weakly, but the water that Jesse poured into it pooled there and ran down his cheek and chin. The outlaw stopped, afraid he might drown the boy, and noticed the glazed, distant cast to his eyes. Gage was gone.

Jesse stood up in the street, offering the canteen up behind him without looking. Someone took it with a mumbled thanks and he nodded. His eyes were stuck on Gage's face. This kid had ridden into this bug nest on a brass set, full of life and his own immortality. An immortality Jesse knew he had in part instilled. Now, because of that damned metal terror, here he was, leaking his life's blood all over the parched main street of a town not worth a name.

"We still don't know what Billy's got planned, Jesse." Frank was standing beside him. He did not notice his brother rising from the corpse's side. "And the townsfolk are startin' to take notice of our little fuss out here."

Jesse looked up to see several faces watching the outlaws from different windows and doorways around town. They were pale and shocked at the devastation that had been visited upon their little town. He called out to a knot of his men standing by the shattered wall that marked the UR-30's last stand.

"You all, get some rope and truss that thing up. I want it out here faster'n a tick." He turned back to Frank. "I want you and the Youngers to round up the brains, and then take them down to the park 'n get whatever we need."

He was turning away when Frank's hand landed on his shoulder. "What do we need, Jesse? If we're rushin' off half-cocked without Billy, do we even know how far down we're gonna have to be diggin'?"

Jesse took a deep breath, focusing with some effort. He nodded. "Ok, assume we gotta dig, through dirt not rock, and assume we gotta go down pretty deep, like maybe the height of a wagon or two, stacked atop each other, but not down to China, okay?"

Frank nodded. "You got it, Jesse." He walked away, calling for Cole and his brothers. The men came running from various groups scattered along the street, disappearing deeper into town.

Jesse looked around again. "Harding, get our boys that didn't make it and line 'em up here in the street. Get me a count, an' see if anyone else is hurt. I need to know if it's just these five, or if we're gonna be down more afore our next little shindig."

Harding nodded and started pointing to the men around him. The groups started to drag the dead bodies into the center of the street. That that had worn dusters were wrapped in them, those that had not were laid bare, hats over their faces. Only Gage and Randall had their Iron Horses, and so, their kit bags. Gage was wrapped up in his duster, while two white-faced boys did their level best to gather up what was left of Randall on a blanket, rolling it up into a sodden, misshapen tube of coarse wool.

Jesse scanned the townsfolk watching from the windows and singled out an older looking gent with iron-grey hair and spectacles. He started walking towards the man, who began to fade back into the shadows of the building.

"No, no, hey!" A hyper-velocity pistol leapt into Jesse's hand, pointing steadily at the retreating man. "You ain't goin' nowhere, son! You get your flannel-mouth out here on the pronto'r I end you and find someone more punctual to talk to!"

The man's arms flew up , head shaking from side to side in denial, as he walked towards the window. "We don' want no trouble!" The man began. "You just—"

"Case you ain't been payin' attention, grandpa, what you want ain't of much concern today. And what we just, is only the beginning." He gestured toward the front door of the building. Two scorched holes marked where crimson bolts had slapped into it during the gunfight. "Come on out this door here so's we can talk like civilized folks, without this wall here between us."

The door creaked open almost immediately and the man came shuffling out. He was hushing someone behind him, making gestures for them to stay back inside the building.

"'S Okay," Jesse said, lowering the gun. "The lady folk can stay inside for now. I just got some questions, and I'll ask 'em, and you'll answer 'em like a good little burger, an' my friend's and I'll be on our way in no time, and you lot not much the worse for wear." The pistol spun once around his metal finger, slapping back up to point into the old man's face. "You lead me a dance, though, husker, an' this goes down a whole different trail. Comprende?"

The man nodded, hands still in the air, eyes still wide with fear.

"Alrighty then." Jesse turned and gestured across the street to where a group of his men were dragging the remains of the UR-30 Enforcer through the shattered hole with a great deal of difficulty. "Now, that thing there you're only law 'round here?"

The man nodded again, slowly.

"Great. You seem like a man who knows what's goin' on. You a big bug here 'bouts?"

The man shook his head. "I – I just help the mayor –"

Jesse wagged the barrel of his weapon in the man's face. "No, no, no. Helpin' the mayor, that's pretty big, you ask me. So, you know stuff, 'bout what's goin' on in town?"

The man looked confused, but nodded again.

"Right as rain. Then tell me, Billy the Kid been through here lately?" Jesse's playful tone dropped away without warning, his entire body still and dangerous, his eyes boring into the man's.

"N-n-no! 'Cept for that one time with Ringo an' the Injun, we ain't seen anyone like him'r . . . 'r you . . . fer years!"

Jesse leaned closer, the barrel drifting towards the man's nose. "You sure?"

The nodding was so vigorous this time Jesse was afraid the man's head was going to drop off. He raised the pistol away from the frightened townsman and rested what he meant to be a reassuring hand on his shoulder. Whether it was the touch itself or the nature of the limb that made it, the man squeaked and jumped sideways slightly to escape the hand. Jesse shrugged.

"Okay, I believe ya. So, no Billy, no more law." The outlaw chief turned back in the direction of the distant canyon cliff. "My brother and his friends r' lookin' fer some engineers. They gonna find any?"

The man nodded again. "Most of those folks who still know anythin' stay near the park. There's a couple saloons and a hotel still over that way."

Jesse nodded again and rested the pistol casually against his shoulder, giving the shaken man a grin. "Well, that oughta cover it, old son. Go ahead back inside with the ladies."

Jesse holstered his gun and stepped lightly back out into the street. Five pathetic bundles lay there in a row, boots to the sky. Except for Randall's of course. God alone knew which direction his boots were pointing, inside the dark-stained blanket.

"Who'd we lose?" He lit a quirley with one hand and flicked the match behind him into the street.

Harding stood over the bodies with his hat in his hands, his gruff face troubled. "Well, Randall and Gage, 'o course." Then he nodded to the three men at the end, two thin men with hats over their faces and one much larger body wrapped in its duster. "An' Boyd, Clay, an' Sisco Pete."

Jesse spat the end of the quirley down by his boot and shook his head. "Damn, Sisco Pete, eh? That boy never could dodge worth a tinker's promise."

Harding put his hat back on, nodding in reply. "No sir, Jesse."

Jesse took a long drag on a fresh quirley and moved towards the group of men standing nervously around the battered wreckage of the robot. The thing was wrapped in coil after coil of rope, as if the men were still afraid it might spring back to life despite its having been reduced to so many tangled pieces. Jesse rolled what looked like a forearm back and forth beneath his boot as he looked down thoughtfully.

"What you boys say to seein' how well our friend here flies down by the canyon rim?"

Several of the outlaws nearby chuckled nervously or muttered theirr approval, and Jesse nodded. "Okay, then, let's see what we shall see, eh?" The men hoisted the bundle of metal parts over their heads and began to walk down the street. He looked over to Harding.

"You mind watchin' the store while I take out the trash?" He grinned around the smoldering hand-rolled cigarillo.

"No, you go right ahead, boss. I don't feel no need to get any closer to that thing or a cliff than I have to." Harding jerked his chin in the direction of the retreating mob.

"Okay, then. You just watch the locals, you got that? I don't want any of'em gettin' funny ideas while I'm gone." He started to follow the mob but then turned."An' keep an eye out for Billy. I still don' know what his game is, but he's gonna pull somethin' fer sure. When he does, we ain't gonna have a lot of time to adjust." Jesse began to walk and then turned around. "Have the men start relaying the 'Horses down here to the recharge pads in town, we should get enough of a charge to make a clean getaway. 'N bury Gage an' the rest out in the flats a bit. Hurry, though, we won't be gone long."

Harding nodded and Jesse followed the rest of his men. As they left the devastated center of town behind, he paid more attention to the buildings, noting again how well-maintained they were. Back when he was riding out of Diablo Canyon, the place was a pit; half the buildings in no condition to house a dog, and the folks sporting a strange mix of squirrelly fear and wild aggression. Now, even after the big fight downtown, the folks who started coming to their doors and windows looked afraid, yes, but they were also clearly angry and outraged.

Jesse made a big show of tipping his hat to the ladies with a wide grin and nodding to the men who stood staring back with steely eyes. There was no way any of these folks could mistake what his boys were carrying down the street, or what it meant. Getting out of town before the realities started to settle on these folks was going to be important. Jesse hoped Frank was having some luck with the brains across town.

The rim of Diablo Canyon was crumbling rock and twisted scrub brush. The canyon wall fell away in a series of abrupt steps that continued, jutting out farther and farther, until it gave away to a small stream glittering in the distance. Jesse frowned. Throwing the metal man off this cliff was not going to be as dramatic as he had thought.

As Jesse looked to either side, he saw the struts of the aborted bridge sticking out into thin air a ways off to his left, and smiled. "C'mon, boys. We're gonna go make use of the local facilities."

They walked along the lip of the canyon, the weathered back walls of the town on their left. Hauling the metal body was starting to take a toll on many of the boys' spirits, and the talk had died down. But there were still wolfish smiles, especially as they stared at the metal rails springing out from the buildings ahead.

The tracks that came down the center of Diablo Canyon and continued for ten or twenty feet out into midair cut through the impromptu equipment yard that had developed over the years. Jesse paused to admire the piles of material and machines, most covered with shrouds of stained, flapping canvas. In the center of the yard Frank was talking with Cole Younger, gesturing towards a truly impressive vehicle whose canvas covering was now piled loosely up on the ground.

The thing looked like an enormous scorpion or ant, standing tall on six metal legs that arced up and then back down in wide, splayed metal feet. The body was a boxy shape that looked a lot like most wagons did in the post-RJ-1027 age, but the nose of the beast was truly awe-inspiring. An array of drills, each articulated on its own extended arm, thrust out from the cab of the wagon. Jesse could see how they were built to be able to direct their attention in a wide arc in front of the crawler, for digging large, deep holes in almost any terrain. His smile widened around his smoke.

"Well don't that just beat all, eh?" He nodded to Frank and Cole as they turned at his voice. "We got anybody hereabouts that'll be able to drive the thing?"

Frank nodded. "We found a few guys in the saloon over yonder, eager enough for a fresh perspective they were willin' to sign on." Jesse looked over his brother's shoulder at a small group of five men standing beside the drilling machine. Frank gave him a meaningful look. "I told 'em they'd be gettin' equal shares o' the treasure."

Jesse smiled even wider and raised his voice so the men could hear clearly. "Well ain't that grand! Ain't nothin' goin' on here ain't everybody gonna take home some nice coin on!" He looked back at his brother. "They got anythin' else that could help us? I'm thinkin' you didn't sign on five galoots to be drivin' this one rig, eh?"

Frank frowned. "No, I didn't. There's a bunch of equipment we're loadin' in the driller. Stuff you wouldn't believe, Jesse. They got a thing that can see through rock! An' another that can listen to the ground and tell you what you'd be lookin' at if you dug down there! You find us where to dig, we'll find this thing for you." His look grew more sober. "It'll be easier once we know what we're lookin' for, o'course."

Jesse took the cigarillo out of his mouth and spit a bit of tobacco away to the side. "Easy, Frank. Now that we got the equipment, Billy'll have to be square with us, if we can't get the info out of one of his boys. Ideal situation, we hide this stuff away a bit down south, then come findin' Billy. We either snatch one of his boys and get the name o' this canyon the Kid's been holdin' so close to his vest out of 'im, or we just talk to Billy directly, but this time with a much stronger hand, as we got the tools he's gonna need!"

Jesse looked over to where his men were waiting impatiently to toss the UR-30 into the canyon. "Ain't like we didn't pay the full ante, now was it."

Frank nodded. "We did that, Jesse. You want comp'ny? 'R you want me to get this stuff up onto the main road?

Jesse looked back towards the center of town, clearly identifiable from the columns of dark smoke rising into the air in that direction. "Yeah, get this back, and get the boys ready to go. We'll just leave the two 'Horses. Randall had one o' the slowest anyway, and Gage's ain't fit fer parts no more. I'll be done here in a jiff, 'n be followin' you directly."

Frank nodded and turned back to the giant drilling machine. "Let's get her up'n runnin' boys!"

Jesse returned to the men carrying the dismantled Enforcer. "Okay, lads, what're you thinkin'? We dump the whole thing over at once, or one piece at a time?"

*****

After disposing of the robot, Jesse and his gang gathered back in the center of town. The enormous drilling machine was snorting softly, its fuel tanks and engine core glowing red from many ports and dials. The thing had left a trail of deep divots in the street, and Jesse knew sneaking it out of town was going to cause some problems.

The bodies of his men had been buried by a detail of the younger gang members, and the two Iron Horses they would no longer need were dumped back in the equipment yard, covered in the tarp that had once shrouded the driller.

Frank and the Coles stood in the center of the street, ignoring the growing group of townsfolk that gathered along the boardwalks.

"Well, boys, think we're about ready to move out?" Jesse took the stump of the quirley out of his mouth and flicked it towards the smoldering building where the UR-30 had come to rest. "I'm thinkin' we take all this stuff south a few hours, find a nice little niche to stow it, an' wait for Billy to show himself." He tapped on the metal legs of the crawler with one metal forearm. "Think this thing can go overland, Frank? I'd rather not bump into anybody on the trail."

Frank nodded. "What it was built for, Jesse. Or so they tell me."

"Alright then, let's move out." He moved to his big Blackjack and swung his leg up and over, settling into the saddle. He raised his voice to be heard over the cacophony of sixteen RJ-1027 engines roaring to life. "Now, you folks done yourself proud, keepin' to yourselves. But I swear, I hear you disturbed my boys so's you could lynch their bodies, I'mma gonna come back, and I ain't gonna be happy ."

The only response was a universally sullen, flat glare, and Jesse smiled at their cowardice. "Alrighty then. See ya'll!"

The column of Iron Horses moved out, the Blackjack in the lead, and the lumbering drilling machine sliding along in a strange, swinging gait behind. It had been surprising, how quickly the thing could move with a full burst of power behind it. They had had to steal batteries from half the machines in the lot to top off the thing's power cells, but two of the men Frank had found were old hands at that sort of thing, and it had not taken long. They had also been able to hot-charge the 'Horses and the Blackjack, so everything was heading out fully charged. The driller was never going to keep up with an Iron Horse at full throttle, but they were making excellent time out into the brittle grasses of the badlands, and Jesse could feel everything coming together for him.

He could not quite see what Billy's plan had been, but he knew the younger man would be coming this way eventually, and when they ran into each other again, the world was going to see that Jesse was still the curly wolf in the wild west.

He was leaning back in his saddle, smiling at these heart-warming thoughts as they ran through his head, when a shattering detonation erupted just in front of him. The entire plain seemed to lift into the sky as a sheet of red fire flashed out from underneath. Dirt, dust, and clumps of grass began to rain down all around, covering the gang in a layer of grit and coating the 'Horses and the drilling rig in fine reddish dust.

Men behind Jesse were yelling and screaming, demanding to know what was happening. Jesse thought he knew. When that familiar old voice, high pitched like a young boy's, shouted at him from out of the curtain of dust, he was not surprised in the slightest.

"Howdy do, Jesse!" Billy the Kid sauntered out of the floating smoke and grit, a titanic grin across his face. "You made it!"

Chapter 13

Jesse James was plenty familiar with the feeling of a smug, self-satisfied smile. He did not, however, enjoy being on the receiving end of one.

Billy spit a stream of tobacco juice off to the side, his thumbs hooked nonchalantly behind his pistol belt. "'Course, you're not quite where I thought you'd be. Took a bit o' scramblin' to get ahead of ya, once you decided to head out across the flats." The grin grew even wider. "But wasn't much trouble, was it boys?"

A series of hoots and laughs sounded from out in the stunted clumps of yellowed grass. The great plume of dust had begun to settle, but there was still an acrid-tasting gritty fog hanging over the entire area. Jesse thought he could see a glint of light here or there reflecting off a piece of equipment or a weapon lens, but he could not be sure.

"Where ya been, Billy?" Jesse's voice was calm and relaxed. "Thought we were gonna meet up in the Canyon, no?"

"Oh, c'mon Jesse! That jig is up, friend. When you decided to go in after the equipment on your own and not wait for me an' mine!" Billy spit again, his grin reddish with the tobacco. "You think I'm some sort of mooncalf, do ya?"

Jesse made a great show of thinking for a second, then shook his head. "No, I figured you more for a chiselin' coffee boiler, who'd rather let someone else do their work for 'em, is what I figured."

Billy's grin slipped, but then shone brighter than before despite the pall of smoke and dirt. "Well, there may well be somethin' to that, Jesse, there sure is." He lazily flicked a hand towards the column of 'Horses behind the older outlaw chief. "Fer instance, I'd much ruther let you run into that mill blade metal man they had shepherdin' the fine folks o' Diablo Canyon for me. An' I knew, if I set it up for ya, you'd be more than happy to oblige. How'd that work out for ya?"

Jesse felt his own smile tighten. "Lost five o' my men goin' in alone, Billy. One o' my best." He pulled his goggles down around his neck. "That ain't likely somethin' I'm gonna forget."

Billy laughed. "That's a grand yarn yer spinnin' there, but I don't think yer foolin' anyone within earshot. Ain't no one forced your hand on that one, my friend. We was supposed to go in t'gether, an' you rushed out here an' raced in on yer own. I'm right sorry fer yer boys, Jesse, but that ain't on me, an' it ain't on none o' my boys."

Jesse ground his teeth, working his jaw in frustration. He shifted to the side and spit bitterly into the dirt. "Well, one thing'r another, we're all here now. What'aya wanna do?"

Billy's smile cranked a little bit wider. "Well, I figured, we'd take that fine contraption an' all the gear off of ya, an' yer fuel, an' you all can ride shank's mare back to Diablo Canyon, 'r Kansas City, 'r wherever, where the dice might start rollin' a bit better for ya!" Another stream of tobacco spit spattered into the dirt.

Jesse adjusted himself slightly in his saddle, his features shifting angrily. "The hell you say, Billy. I ain't gonna—"

Billy raised one hand casually into the air and a loud detonation sounded from out of the dust. A blaster shot streaked through the gritty haze and impacted into the grass by Jesse's foot. The little clump of yellow vegetation exploded in a geyser of dirt, smoke, and burning strands.

"Now, Jesse, I don't wanna gloat, but what we got here is a great example of a dry gulch. I got you pinned to the counter, Jesse, and there ain't no way yer gettin' out. I ain't got as many men as you, but I got plenty, and all mine got rifles, an' they got all you in their sights already." He called over his shoulder. "Kid, you ready?" There was a gruff bark from back in the shifting shadows of the dust cloud, and Billy nodded. "Why don't you let slide, then?"

A blue bolt streaked out of the shadows, flashing through the dust like heat lightning, and came down on the nose of an Iron Horse in the middle of the formation. The bolt sank right through the metal without a pause, and with a wheezing crack the vehicle collapsed to the dirt, throwing the rider into the grass and dust.

"Now, you see? I even got the Apache Kid back there, summonin' the spirit mumbo jumbo of his people down on yer head." The grin now threatened to split Billy's face in two. "What say you all just turn off your machines, dismount, and mosey on back the way you come? You can leave the Canyon-folks in that fine contraption. They'll be stayin' with me."

Jesse stared at the younger outlaw for moments that stretched on into minutes. Every man in the column gripped his controls tightly, wondering how it was going to go down. Far off in the distance, Jesse thought he heard a familiar sound, and he cocked his head to try to catch it better. Iit seemed to fade in and out, the surrounding cloud of thick dust playing games with his hearing.

As he thought about the cloud, his head snapped upright. He looked up to where the vast column that had been thrown into the air by the explosives was still reaching for the clouds. He turned in his saddle to look back the way they had come. The smoke rising from the center of town was dying down now, but there were still faint lines of white in the sky, fading downward towards the earth. He turned back to Billy and this time his own face wore a grin far more genuine than it had been.

"Billy, you think a'tall about your little plan when you decided to launch half the badlands up into the sky like that?" His tone was light and casual, but there was iron beneath it.

Billy's smile faltered slightly. "I'm not gettin' yer meanin', Jesse."

"Bumped into Bennett Vaughn back down in Sacred Lake." Behind Billy the pulsing sounds rose a notch, bolstering Jesse's confidence. "He had a right interestin' tale to tell. 'Bout you havin' a bit of a run in on yer way north?"

Billy's eyes widened slightly, and he looked to the left and right. He muttered something over his shoulder and one of the shadows in the shifting dust moved and disappeared deeper into the cloud.

"I'm surprised, you already knowin' you weren't alone out here, that you'd send up a smoke signal quite this big." He nodded his head up at the column towering above them. "Apache!" Jesse shouted, a smile growing wider and wider on his face. "You din't tell Billy sendin' smoke signals that high was a bad idea?"

Billy's eyes were less certain. He began to walk slowly backwards into the settling dust cloud. "If this ain't a trick, Jesse, it's gonna go poorly fer both of us, y'know."

Jesse's grin was back in full force. "Well, that's a sight better than it just goin' inta the johnny fer me an' mine, Billy!"

A series of sharp blasts diffused through the dust cloud. One large blast flashed up on his right. Incoherent screams echoed through the grit, and Jesse settled back on his saddle with a laugh as the first clear word rang out of the chaos.

"Union!"

"Okay, boys, you c'n hear it with yer own ears," Jesse called over his shoulder to his men. "Billy's done dropped it in the crapper, but he knows he ain't gettin' out of this without our help, so we face down these blue-belly mudsills side by side!" He gunned the Blackjack into motion, crouching down behind the control console. One of his fingers flicked out for the weapons toggle, setting the little light winking red. He looked back over his shoulder with a smirk and called out, "If you get a clean shot at one of his bastards, though, you go ahead and take it."

Inside the spreading haze, it was absolute madness. The grit was dispersing, and visibility was better than it had been. Still, though, everything beyond a stone's throw was shadowy and indistinct. The crimson bolts of blaster weapons streaking back and forth ignited the floating particles, leaving streaks of sparkling red stars swirling in their wakes.

Jesse could make out shapes running away to the left and right. He knew those must be Billy's men, fleeing from their ambush positions and running for their 'Horses. Farther ahead he could see the low sleek shapes of light vehicles, the source of most of the incoming fire.

Jesse hugged the controls, hunched low over his seat, and gunned the throttle of the Blackjack straight down the throat of the incoming shapes. The vehicle bounced and staggered over the uneven ground and thick clumps of desert grass, but the heavy wheels dug deep, throwing plumes of dusty earth behind him. He squeezed the firing handles with both hands and ruby darts spat out into the eddying dust ahead. Behind him, he could hear the roaring of the Iron Horses as they rushed to follow, and streaks of crimson gunfire flashed past him on both sides, slapping into distant targets.

Jesse's charge carried him through the dust cloud, amid the rushing enemy, and out the other side. He had seen one hulking shadow in there, nearly as fast as the others. That brute had gave him pause, but he was too caught up in the moment to give it another thought. He knew he had scored at least two direct hits as he watched the bulky shapes of Iron Horses caught by his blasts flip up into the air. The dust got immediately thicker around them, and a familiar, satisfied surge kicked in his gut as he heard them come crashing heavily back to earth. He smiled, feeling the caked dust and dirt crack on his face, and brought the Blackjack whipping around to face the confrontation again.

Most of his men tore out of the dust cloud behind him. The Youngers were all grinning and hollering, except for Johnny, but he was always a sour one. Frank looked grim, hunkered behind his own controls, and Jesse knew that he was wishing he could head for higher ground with Sophie to offer more direct protection to his brother.

"Okay," Jesse shouted to be heard over the grumbling engines. "We gotta get back in there and clean up right quick! Billy's gang'll be on either side of 'em, if they can rally, we'll get 'em between us all, take 'em down, an' then we can have our words with Billy in a much more pleasant setting. Anybody seen the driller?"

"They were backin' up as we rushed in, Jesse." Frank hawked up some dust-laden spit and launched it into the grass. "It ain't that fast, though. We gotta get in there if we're gonna have a chance o' savin' it."

Jesse shook his head. "They ain't gonna touch the driller. They might have sharp words for those that were drivin' it, but these blue-belly bastards'll see it as their duty to get the driller back under its tarp where they fancy it belongs." He pulled one of his pistols out and checked its charge. "But yeah, we gotta get back in there anyway. Afore Billy's gone and done all the killin' without us!"

Ahead of them, the cloud had continued to dissipate. However, many smaller clouds were now rising into the sky and expanding across the desert where the battle was raging the hottest, marking the death sites of vehicles or men. There were shapes staggering through the fading haze as well, so more than a few fighters had been knocked from their mounts. Jesse squinted into the settling dust, trying to judge from the flashing lines of blaster fire and the red-cored detonations of impacts where the best insertion point would be for his gang.

Jesse once again gunned the engine and raced back into the battle, heading for a point where one of Billy's groups seemed to have gotten itself organized into a coherent attack on the Union right flank. Jesse hunkered down, squinting behind his red-tinted goggles into the rushing wind and the harsh dust, and aimed himself at that contact point.

The battle seemed to narrow itself down to two indistinct shapes leaping closer as he accelerated, and three of Billy's Iron Horses rushed in from the right. Jesse knew that the Blackjack lacked the heavier weaponry of some of the 'Horses, but he also knew what four blasters firing in unison could do, even to an armored transport, especially from behind. He lined up on the left-most target and pressed down on the firing handles. Streams of crimson fire lashed out, his Blackjack shuddering with the blasts. He watched the four streams crash into the rear of a Union Iron Horse. It exploded, the bolts coring the engine and detonated the fuel. Burning wreckage, roiling black smoke, and swirling dust flew in all directions as the driver was thrown roughly out into the desert, trailing a streamer of dust, arms and legs flapping without control. He hit the sand and rolled loosely to a stop, unmoving.

Jesse swung his head towards the other target, but it slewed away from its spectacularly deceased compatriot. Unfortunately for the luckless soldier, he veered right into the sights of Billy's gang, who shattered it with two blasts from their mini cannons. The vehicle came apart, scattering its parts and the parts of its rider across a long streak of devastation carved into the desert surface. Jesse nodded to the two outlaws and swept around towards the center of the battle, looking for more targets.

There were wrecked Iron Horses scattered across the desert, smoke and dust rising into the sky on all sides. Jesse could tell the Union boys were getting pounded. He could not see more than ten of them still fighting. There were plenty of outlaws to finish this easily, between the two gangs.

Jesse looked around him, trying to find Billy to coordinate the last attack, when he realized that the men around him now were his own. He could see the Youngers, and Frank. He thought he saw a knot of men, most dismounted, fighting from behind disabled 'Horses. Harding was there for sure, and Chase crouching beside him. Two men were prone, firing around the corners of their machines on their bellies, and he thought it was Bryce and Ty. A few others were still driving, either with the Youngers or on their own.

A quick count revealed that they were nearly evenly-matched with the Union, even now regrouping atop a low hill nearby. Jesse scanned the desert for Billy's gang and found them exactly where his gut told him he should look: they were high tailing it back towards Diablo Canyon, pursuing the driller as it scuttled towards safety.

"You yellow dog!" Jesse screamed at the top of his lungs, feeling his dry throat tear with the strain. "You bastard, come back here!" Over the sounds of the battle and the roaring vehicles there was no way Billy could have heard him. Jesse knew it would not have mattered if he could. He watched the 'Horses disappear towards the distant town, trailing rising plumes of dust into the sky as they chased the tiny scrambling shape of the driller.

"Damn." Jesse shook his head and looked back to the battle. The Union had regrouped and were swinging wide of the main battle zone with its columns of smoke and dust, its litter of shattered transports and human bodies. One of the Union riders suddenly toppled over from his saddle, his 'Horse dropping out of formation and gliding to a halt. Looking over his shoulder Jesse felt a sudden surge of excitement and energy at the sight of Frank once again wielding Sophie. His brother gave him a quick nod and then aimed for his next victim.

"Okay, boys, this'll be tough, but nothin' we ain't done afore!" Jesse gunned his machine towards the clump of dismounted men, gesturing for the Youngers and their group to join him. "They're gonna come in on you all, cuz you ain't got any way to skedaddle. We'll swing back, like we're runnin' away, then we'll hit 'em in the side. Make sense?"

Harding looked up at the boss with a frown. "What keeps you from runnin', leavin' us to pay the bill?"

Jesse looked down at him. "I ain't gonna leave no one behind. I'm gonna need all of ya'll when we catch back up with that chiseling rat bastard, Bonney, ain't I?"

Harding nodded and turned back towards the regrouping Union force. "Just our luck, eh? To run into a Forward Patrol like this?" Chase muttered.

"I ain't sure this was luck, boys." Jesse watched as the Union troops gunned their engines and began to accelerate towards the outlaws. "But we'll have plenty of time to look into that later." He turned his head to the other mounted men. "Let's go!"

The 'Horses and the Blackjack slewed around, throwing up dirt and rocks as they spun. They made a great showing of their sudden retreat, flying off towards the far off town. The men now on foot began to fire at the approaching soldiers, shouting defiant insults and obscene suggestions at the advancing men.

Coming around wide, Jesse saw the larger, bulkier shape that he had caught a glimpse of in the dust. It was coming up behind the Iron Horses leading the charge. It looked like an Iron Horse, but instead of an open saddle there was a massive armored box. Instead of a single linked weapon system riding high on the forward body, the thing seemed to sprout a terrifying number of barrels from out of its armored bulk, thrusting out from its iron flanks.

The Union formation spread out, leaving the beast in the center with a free line of fire to the men Jesse had left behind as bait. Crimson bolts began to crisscross the air between the outlaws and their charging attackers. Most of the outlaws' fire was being absorbed the armored fairings of the Union 'Horses, or glancing harmlessly off the daunting shape of the thing holding the center of their line. The Union fire was slapping into the downed 'Horses, keeping the men cowering behind them, rendering their fire less effective.

Jesse saw the inevitable result before the first man at the impromptu barricade even went down. A series of images flashed before his mind. He saw the burning wreckage of Missouri City. He saw Billy the Kid standing tall and proud in the Arcadia. He saw a line of ragged Union cavalry with outdated equipment blocking the path of a small, wounded boy. Lastly, he saw the tiny garret above the Arcadia, a light spray of ruby droplets on the wall.

"No!" Jesse viciously wrenched at the accelerators, sending the Blackjack hurtling towards the impending disaster even though he knew he would be too late. He saw an errant Union bolt strike Chase in the leg. The poor kid, suffering pain beyond reason from the wound, leapt into the air in an effort to escape. Several bolts struck him in the chest and thigh, spinning him over and spraying blood into the sand. Bryce rose, fear getting the better of him in the last moments, and tried to run. A rocket caught him in the back, lifting him off his feet, and then detonated, spreading thin strips of the poor boy out over the sand. Harding pushed away from the burning wreckage of his 'Horse, taking potshots over its saddle, shouting defiance right up to the moment a glancing bolt struck him in the temple. His head spun around, his neck clearly snapping, as blood and grey matter foamed out of the wound, steaming as it hit the burning metal of his 'Horse.

The last survivor of the little band rose up to face his death. But Ty was not looking at the onrushing horde, nor was his expression the least concerned. He turned to look directly at Jesse and his lips stretched into a wide, friendly smile. He waved once, gave a jaunty salute, and winked. Jesse knew it must have been a trick of the light that made the kid's eye gleam that unnatural color, or it might have been the crimson bolt that was even then blasting through his head. The body took several more hits as it danced and staggered away from its cover, finally sinking slowly into the grass.

Jesse shook his head in disbelief. He desperately scanned the area for survivors. He could hear the Youngers and the last remaining mounted members of the gang behind him. Off in the distance behind the burning wrecks that marked his men's last stand, however, he found who he was looking for. Frank was crouched down behind his 'Horse taking careful, measured shots at the incoming Union forces. Every time he fired, a vehicle would fall out of formation, either damaged or abandoned by its dead driver. Jesse was not the only person on the field to notice Frank's effectiveness, and the giant monster 'Horse slewed towards him, all of its weapons roaring back into life.

The heavy weaponry chewed the ground up ahead of Frank's position and then tore, like invisible buzz saws, into the 'Horse. Dust, grass, and metal, RJ-1027 fuel and fabric scattered up into the air. Jesse saw his brother, arms thrown wide, sail back away from the detonating vehicle, a look of vague dismay on his face before he disappeared down into the growing explosion.

Jesse's eyes went wide for a moment, and then a furious, tight, pressure filled his mind, pushing at his eyes and roaring in his ears. Without conscious thought, the Blackjack swerved around and headed straight for the heavy, armored shape that had blasted his brother. The lighter weaponry of his new vehicle rained down upon the beast, but the shots glanced off like a burning fan in all directions. He was doing no damage that he could see. The pressure built even greater and Jesse pulled one of his hyper-velocity pistols, firing bolt after hopeless bolt as the range closed. Then the monster opened up with its weapons again.

Jesse did not know where the enemy shots caught up with him. He felt himself launched into the air, flying through the dust and the grit. He knew he had been thrown from his vehicle in a violent rush of fire, smoke, and swirling sand. He heard a terrific crash behind him, the wrenching of metal and the screams of components bent past their best tolerances, all overpowered by the hammering thunder of the Union weapons and their ceaseless detonations.

Jesse hit the ground hard, rolling several times before coming to a stop against a hard clump of desert grass. He could not breath, he could not hear a thing, and his mind was lost in a buzzing daze of blurred images and dull, distant pain. A curtain of red washed over his vision and then everything went black. The bright world snapped back into focus again for a moment, but when he tried to raise his head, the red leaked back in, the black followed, and his head fell back into the gritty sand.

When light leaked back into his world, the roar of RJ-1027 engines was still heavy in the air, bolts of crimson force still crashed back and forth in the distance. His vision faded in and out, and each time he tried to move, there was a crushing moment of intense pain and then nothingness.

Words, screamed over engine-noise, seemed to echo in his ears from a far way off. He thought he heard a deep, voice screaming "Grab one!" There were detonations, screams, more shouting, this time in words that would not make sense in his shaken mind.

As even these noises faded into the far distance, Jesse could think of nothing but the look on his brother's face and he fell back into the flames.

Chapter 14

The rasping sensation of sand blown across his face recalled Jesse to the waking world. It was a slow journey, with pain a constant companion and confusion hovering overhead. He felt the sand, and the scratch of the grit, first on his face, hot and stretched by the beating sun. Then he felt it in his throat, as each attempt to swallow drove jagged shards of glass across the sensitive flesh. Each of his legs made the same slow progression as his body: dull, distant ache to furious, vague itching, to pulsing, shocking pain. As the pain retreated to a manageable, steady throbbing, he felt his legs move, slowly drawing up, the heels of his boots digging furrows into the sand.

He knew a short jolt of terror when he realized he could not sense his arms. However, ,he soon began to register the odd self/alien impulses that more than a decade of familiarization had taught him to expect from the artificial limbs. He focused on one hand and then the other, clenching them into tight fists. Feedback pads dragged across dirt and grass as fingers flexed with growing strength. Finally, his gummed, sensitive eyes peeled open, the sunlight stabbing right though to his brain. He muttered in pain, bringing further agony to his torn throat. With the combination of pain and surprise, he lurched over onto his hands and knees, gasping for breath. Each one scratched further at his tormented gullet.

Coherent thought came back much more slowly. He could make no sense of his situation. He could see, through squinted eyes shaded by one mechanical hand that he was in the high desert. He was surrounded by desiccated soil and clumped up scrub grass. There were shattered wrecks all around, some still leaking black smoke up into the sky. Bodies lay amongst the wreckage, men in the mismatched clothing of the outlaws mixed with the forever-damned blue uniform of the Union Army. He stumbled over to a couple of the bodies. As was true in most modern gunfights, there was not much left to help with identification.

He found several bodies lying amidst what looked like a hasty defensive position made out of battered Iron Horses. He could not tell who the men had been, their features blasted or burnt. He recognized Harding's 'Horse among the machines, though, and knew that one of the bodies must have belonged to that tough old dog.

The thought brought his head sharply up. As last moments of the battle came flashing back, his neck wrenched around to look for his brother's final position. He saw the wreckage, far more devastated than any of the others, on a low rise. With a rising groan he stumbled towards the smoking ruin. That big monster of a Union 'Horse had unleashed an avalanche of fire on this vehicle, and there was almost nothing left but its twisted frame. The blasted remains of its bodywork, the equipment, and his brother's belongings were scattered all around, covered in a liberal coating of dust, ash, and ragged grass.

Jesse staggered up the slight slope, stumbling to his hands and knees more than once. Each time he slipped and fell his entire body was wracked with agony, but still he drove himself upwards. The wreckage was still smoking, sending several different trails of black soot spiraling up into the sky. The grass all around was charred and churned, a devastation for yards in all directions. Jesse dragged himself around the ruins of the 'Horse, collapsing to his knees on the other side. There were tattered strips of his brother's duster and the crumpled remains of his hat, but that was all. There were two deep trenches, parallel, through the blackened sand, marking where a person had been dragged from the area of burnt waste. Of his actual brother, however, there was no sign.

Jesse swayed to his feet once again, looking all around. Nothing moved on the battlefield, aside from the smoke, as far as he could see. A quick check of the remaining bodies assured him that none of the Youngers had fallen, but that was all he could tell. Maybe they had dragged Frank to safety? Or maybe the Union had gotten him . . . or maybe Frank was dead, and whoever it was had just taken the body. Jesse lowered himself to the ground again, weeping in enraged impotence.

When the moment had passed, Jesse stood up unsteadily and retraced his path through the ruin to the overturned wreckage of the Blackjack. The vehicle had definitely seen better days. Most of the protruding details and equipment had been blasted away. The shiny paint had all been blasted off, and many of the intricatespokes within each wheel were torn, twisted, or simply gone. But clearly the barrage that had descended upon him had not struck directly, but rather torn up the desert all around, tossing his vehicle and himself into the dust like toys.

With grunting, heaving effort, Jesse pushed the heavy beast upright once more. It rocked unsteadily, shedding dust in dry, whispering showers that spread out as they hit the ground. Jesse checked the telltales, looking to see if there was any way the engine could be brought back to life. Most of the power cells had ruptured, but the actual engine itself seemed to be in good enough shape to operate. He looked around again at the wreckage. If he could not find spare parts on this prairie, he would be in big trouble.

He sighed, pushed himself back up to his feet, and stumbled towards the most intact wreck.

*****

As the Blackjack stuttered its way back into town, Jesse tried to ignore the looks of the townsfolk of Diablo Canyon who had come out onto the street to watch him drive past. He kept his back as straight as he could despite the pain. He had found some un-ruptured canteens among the dead, enough that he was not dying of thirst, and he had found a little jerky, but he had been in no danger of developing a hunger for the tough meat, surrounded by the dead and the inevitable vultures who had circled down to feast.

There had been no sign of the Youngers or any of his other survivors. There had been nothing to show if Billy had returned, or if the battle had ended with everyone running in a different direction. He had looked at his reflection in one of the 'Horses' side mirrors, and knew that if he had seen that blood- and dust-stained visage tumbled into the dirt, he would have assumed the person was a goner as well. So he had been left, by friend and foe alike, for dead.

Jesse drove slowly, the only speed the damaged Blackjack would allow, and only stopped when he pulled up in front of a saloon that abutted the equipment lot on the cliff edge of town. He looked up at the sign, a simple, white painted marquee with the word "Saloon" painted on it in black. He shook his head. Whether at the sign or his own sorry lot in life, he would have been hard-pressed to say.

He was alone. Not just without Frank or the Coles, but his whole gang, dead or scattered to the dusty winds in one afternoon. He could not remember the last time he was this isolated, this lost. Never mind turning the tables on Billy. Never mind proving, once and for all, his own prominence in the hierarchy of western legends. He could very well fade into obscurity right here in this dingy little burg at the arse end of nowhere.

Jesse shook his head and dismounted. He pushed the Blackjack up onto a recharging pad and jury-rigged a connection between the built-in generator and his battered ride. He then pulled the two saddle bags from their armored compartment, and pushed his way into the darkening interior of the saloon.

Inside, the place looked much like any other frontier watering hole. With a few words to the leery bartender he was able to discover that Billy had, indeed, intercepted the driller during the battle and had made off with it back south, the way Jesse himself had intended to go. The remnants of the Union Advanced Patrol had fled back east. He felt bitter amusement at the thought that Billy must have driven right past him.

Did the Kid think he was dead? Did he even care? Jesse was troubled by the fact that the Youngers had not returned for him. Most upsetting of all, though, was the lack of any sign concerning his brother. Had Billy dragged him out of the wreckage? Had the Youngers? Had the damned Union? Jesse was shocked by how much he did not know.

The outlaw found a table in a darkened corner and carried a small bottle and glass from the bar into the shadows. The RJ-1027 lighting here was spotty, it seemed to waver gently, brighter and then softer, brighter and then softer. It was nearly enough to make him sick.

Jesse stared into the liquid in his glass. Part of him wanted that drink very badly, but another part of him was absolutely sure the pain it would cause his tortured throat would knock him out for sure. He straightened his shoulders, steeled himself, schooled his face to stillness, and tossed the shot back. He needed the alcohol more than he needed to avoid a little more pain.

He nearly screamed as the drink hit his gullet. After a moment, though, he shook himself and settled back. He could feel his body starting to relax, and knew he was going to be okay.

As he had entered, most of the folks inside had looked at him with hooded, resentful eyes. They knew who he was and what he had done, but their fear kept them cowed. He felt a slight grin twist one side of his face as he thought about how much harder his life would be if people were not such gutless sheep.

Jesse poured himself another shot and was preparing himself to toss it back when a lithe shape glided up beside him and immediately drifted down into the seat opposite without asking for permission.

"Look, kid, I don't wanna—" His voice cut short as he looked up into the eyes of Lucinda Loveless.

She looked concerned, but also angry, and a little frightened. "Fancy meeting you here, stranger." She gave him the full force of her smile, and his heart nearly stopped.

"Hey, Lucy." He pummeled his mind desperately for a witty remark. "You followin' me?" It was the best his mind could provide, and he cringed as he heard his own voice.

Her smile widened. "Sort of, yeah." She took the drink from him and tossed it back, gasping slightly as the heat hit her stomach. She seemed to be struggling with something herself, and Jesse wondered what it could be. He could not look at her without seeing that cringing form in the garret back in Kansas City, though, even though he knew Misty had never been any kind of a match for Lucy in any way. The guilt and the anger and the confusion were still very much there, and conjured every time he looked into Lucy's eyes.

So why, then, was it so hard to look away?

"You look like death warmed over, Jesse." Her words were playful, but there was real concern in her eyes. "Did you get in a fight with a mountain lion or something?"

He shrugged, putting a brave face on his injuries and his appearance. "You know what they say, Lucy: if yer bleedin', yer still breathin'." He grinned as much as his tight, torn face would allow.

She nodded, clearly not convinced that he was alright, but shrugged in return. "So," she continued, ignoring the conflict in his eyes. "I would love to hear the tale that ends with you sitting alone in a saloon in Diablo Canyon, a wrecked battlefield nearly within walking distance to the south, and a heap of machinery reported stolen from the equipment yard just yonder . . . all with a UR-30 Enforcer stalking the premises."

He stared at her for a moment, confusion and the brutal force of recent memory driving the phantoms away. Again his brain failed him. "What?"

She smiled, but generously toned it down to a more manageable radiance. "I'm just saying, the last time I saw you, you were holding court in that little dive on the back end of Kansas City, surrounded by the knights and jesters of your merry band." She gave him a brief inspection, her beautiful dark eyes running quickly up and down. "Now, I would hardly recognize you."

He shook his head and then realized that the image of the two of them sitting in a saloon in Diablo Canyon was strange on more than one level. He peered at her, taking his glass back. "Mind telling me how you ended up here? I'm sure there's an exciting tale to tell there as well.

She leaned back, one elbow thrown casually over the chair back. "Not really. Got a hankerin' for a different vantage, so came on over this way."

Jesse nodded and then made a show of looking around. "And your partner? Hank, was it?"

She laughed. "Henry. Business called him in a different direction."

Jesse shook his head. "So now you're wanderin' around the territories on your own, brazen as you please, and just happened to turn up in Diablo Canyon?"

It was her turn to shake her head. "Not just turn up, no. And not wandering, either." Her smile turned sly. "As for brazen, well, you'll have to make your own judgment on that call. You were going to tell me about the robot?"

His old grin began to return, and he settled back against his own chair, ignoring the pangs of torn muscles and bruises. "Well, why d'you assume I'd know anythin' about that?"

Lucy looked around the room. "I'm not seeing anyone else that could have handled one."

He perked up a bit, wincing at the pain but ignoring it. "So, you admit you think I could handle one."

"I'm not saying you could either." She smirked and jerked her chin towards the rest of the room. "But the rest of these boys? No, there's no way they could have handled it."

Jesse's grin was wider as he made a great show of relaxing. "Well, to tell you the truth, the way I heard it, the thing went for a walk across the bridge."

Her smile slipped a little. "The bridge that isn't finished?"

His grin grew wider still. "Isn't it? Then yeah, I guess that one."

She stared at him, either impressed or angry, he could not tell. "You destroyed a UR-30 Enforcer."

Jesse shrugged. "Don't much matter to me, now." He poured himself another drink and tossed it back without thinking. Frank's face kept rising into his mind, followed by Harding, and Gage, and Chase. Lastly the ghostly image of the kid, Ty's, face rose up in his mind, the eyes glowing a hellish red.

"You destroyed the most advanced tool of law enforcement in the world, and it doesn't matter?" It was definitely anger in her eyes now.

Jesse leaned over the table towards the woman, his mechanical hands folding together before him. "Listen, lady. You obviously know about the battle, you mentioned it. Any thought to what I might have lost out there? My brother's gone. My friends are gone, either dead or fled. I'm alone, and the last thing I'm gonna worry about is that damned metal man. Did we blast 'em? Yeah, we blasted him to hell! And yeah, we tossed the bits down into the canyon. So what?"

"Your brother is dead?" Every other emotion or thought had drained from her eyes as he'd said Frank's name, and now she reached out to lay one delicate hand over his mechanical claw. For the firsts time in his life he wished there were feedback pads on the backs of his hands, but he could not have said why.

He shook his head, not wanting to meet her gaze. "Don't know. His body ain't back there, but that don't mean much. His 'Horse got blown to kingdom come, 'n I would 'o sworn I saw him burnin' up. When I came to, he was gone, dragged away, maybe. But whether he was alive or dead? That I couldn't say."

She said nothing for several minutes, and then took his metal hands in both of hers, and he could tell from the feedback mechanisms that she was squeezing hard. "Maybe it's time to put all this behind you."

He barked a cruel laugh and moved to pull his hands away, but she held them tighter with surprising strength. "No, listen to me. Maybe now is the time to turn your back on all of this. Break the cycle and make a new choice? You don't have to chase the blood forever, Jesse. You could walk away."

He snorted and shook his head, but the dire urgency in her eyes trapped him and he could not look away.

He stared into her eyes and muttered, "You goin' to walk with me?"

Lucy pulled back abruptly, releasing his hands and looking at him as if she were shocked at the suggestion. There was a blush there too, however, and a confusion that she could not completely hide. "Me? No! I mean, why would I . . . what do I have to walk away from?"

He laughed at her discomfort and relaxed back into his chair. "Life? Eh, you know what they say, you can't cash in your chips till yer done, an' even then, no one knows what they'll be good fer. The Gospel sharpes, they'd like us to all 'walk away', eh?" He shrugged. "There's only one life I know, an' only one thing I'm good at, but I'm the best. I ain't gonna walk away 'till I can't play no more."

She watched him, then said. "Do you know what you and your gang have done, destroying the UR-30? What's going to happen now to Diablo Canyon?"

He shrugged. "Be a bit more like home?" His grin was bitter.

"This town will tear itself apart, Jesse, it will be a pit of vipers again in a matter of weeks at most. All of the people here who have spent years trying to build something of their lives will once again be at the mercy of men and women who don't care about such effort, and don't think past their next swill of whiskey, or their next bed."

"Folks like me, you mean." He shrugged again, clearly not finding the idea troublesome.

He watched her react to his words, and would have put money on her leaving right then and there. He could tell what he had said troubled her more than he would have expected. Could she really care about the sheep mewing around Diablo Canyon or any of these other two bit towns? He shook his head, the anger returning, and spit on the floor beside him.

"Don't matter one way or t'other." He put his hands on the table, but he could feel the red-tinged darkness rising behind his eyes. His brother, Billy, all the dead men who had followed him out here, every fear that had driven him, and every mistake he had made along the way, built up inside him. Now this belle wanted to know how he felt about the cattle?

Jesse's hand snapped closed, shattering the bottle and sending the rest of the whiskey washing over the dry wood of the table. He forced his hand to slowly open and looked at his palm. Several splinters of glass were embedded in the rubber pads. He quirked an eyebrow as the pain registered, then carefully pulled the long shards out. He watched as the black liquid inside spurted out into the pool of whiskey, quickly clouding it up. The fluid stopped almost immediately. He looked back up into Lucy's face. She was staring at him in a mix of concern and frustration.

"There's more you don't understand than you do, Lucy." Jesse shook his head and looked back down at his hands. All signs of damage had smoothed away. "William Bonney is convinced there's something out there in the dust and the grass that'll be worth an awful lot to the right people. Whoever gets it, though? They'll be writing their own ticket, and when everything shakes out, there name'll be written so big in the history of the territories, ain't no one ever gonna be able to erase it."

She shook her head in response. "I don't care. Whatever this thing is, how many lives have you destroyed already, just following its trail? You're better than that, Jesse. You've got real power, you've got real strength. You could be a force out here in the territories. You could help make them safe for these people, as everyone tries to build a better tomorrow than the sad today they were born into."

He snorted again. "The sheep? Who gives a tinker's fart what the sheep want? Not that it matters. I don't even know where to go next. My brother –"

"Is out there somewhere, Jesse, and finding him would make perfect sense. I could help you with that. I want to help you with that. Frank's smart, I know. He might even agree with me." One of her hands was on his again, and it was as if neither of them even thought twice about it.

He looked at her, stunned. "You want to help me?"

She nodded. "I do."

He swallowed, looked away, then forced his eyes to return to her face. "Why?"

It was her turn to look away. "Jesse, that's about enough heavy thinking today, without quite enough heavy drinking." She stood up. "I'm going to secure myself a room upstairs. It's almost dark, anyway."

Lucy turned away, but quickly turned back. "You can join me upstairs. Plenty of time to think tomorrow."

He could see she was not completely comfortable with the advance, but of all the offers he had ever received, this one was the only one to hit him this hard. His mind, once again, failed him. "What?"

She looked exasperated, shaking her head and almost walking away. With a careful breath she calmed herself enough to look down, putting her hands carefully back on the table as she leaned over. "I'm getting a room. You may come up and join me if you wish." Their eyes were locked on each other, and he felt an unfamiliar, warm burn rising in his chest. She stood abruptly and turned away, leaving him to fall back into his own mind.

"But I don't want you to make the right decision for the wrong reason, Jesse. I want you to have all the information in front of you before you make a call. Billy took the drilling machine south, wide of the battle, following the railroad a bit first to hide its tracks. And although I doubt Billy knew it, there's enough old RJ-1027 residue on the rail bed that it should mask them from anyone using tracking tech as well. You should be able to pick up their trail just south of the battle site."

His face twisted in confusion. "How could you—"

She saw a myriad of questions in his eyes, and chose to answer one. "I saw the tracks from . . . my transportation. You'll have to trust me, that's where they went." She did not look down at him again but moved towards the front of the saloon. "I'm going to get that room now. I'll see you when I see you."

*****

Lucinda made her way up to the small room and put her things in a corner. She sat on the bed, a torrent of thoughts running through her mind. What had she done? She had never been so hopelessly entangled before. She looked down at the small pistol in her hand. The barrel was not the bleak hole of a normal gun's snout, but a fork-like two-pronged affair. Tesla promised it would discharge a bolt of RJ-1027 into a target from a few feet away and knock them painlessly into a deep, instant sleep.

Did she have the nerve to shoot Jesse when he came through the door? For a woman disused to ever questioning herself, she had already shown quite a bit of nerve already that day, so who knew? She had made sure he knew what room she was in, so there was really no question he would come. But would she shoot him, or . . . ?

The agent paced up and down along the wall of the small room, the pistol in her hand. Her nerves kept her moving around the room, and soon she put the weapon on a small side table and continued to pace. Her hand writhed nervously against each other. What was keeping him?

Soon she was too tired to pace. The energy and emotion of the past few days caught up with her. She sat on the edge of the bed and meditated for a while, bringing her heart and her mind into cold alignment. The sudden exhaustion hit by surprise, and she lay back on the bed to stop her head from spinning.

Lucinda awoke to warm light streaming through the chinks in her window's slats. Warm morning light.

She sat bolt upright and reached for the weapon. A quick survey of the room showed that none of her things had been tampered with. No one had entered the room.

"Son of a . . . " She rushed to the window and threw it open, thrusting her body out into open air, hanging by one hand and her knees on the sill.

Below the window was the reason she had chosen this room; she could see the recharging platforms in front of the saloon. Most of them were occupied. All but one, in fact.

A single recharging station was empty, its pad stained with puddles of oil and other liquid, as if the vehicle that had rested most recently there had been in very poor repair.

Or severely damaged.

Lucinda Loveless slumped back against the window frame, unable to untangle her own complex emotions."Damn."

Chapter 15

The machine struggled through the rutted, reddish dust of the desert. It had bulled its way through gullies and across vast stretches of open, rocky ground for hours. Its rider, slumped in the saddle and barely conscious, watched the land drift by through slit eyes, focused on the regular pattern of massive divots and impact craters that lined his path. He had learned early on in the chase that his goggles made spotting the tracks difficult in the shifting sands. The glare and grit were small prices to pay for staying latched to his prey.

Jesse's mind kept slipping back to the previous night. He had almost taken those stairs. In fact, he had stood with every intention of following Lucy right up to the room before she had even disappeared up to the next level. As he turned, however, he had a sudden flash back to Kansas City. A flickering image of Misty crashed into his mind with force enough to drive him back into his seat. A ghostly figure of his brother loomed up before him as well, and he knew his path lay elsewhere.

Had it really only been a few short days since Kansas City? Not time enough for the memory to fade. He had struck her, or his arm had struck her, and he had left her alone; bleeding and sobbing, in that tiny little furnace of a room. And now, his brother, lost or dead or taken, disappeared into wastes while he lay unconscious. He knew, no matter how alluring he found this strange woman who had followed him into the desert, His path that night led him in a different direction.

There had been a little whiskey left in his glass, and he had downed it with a single tip. He looked back to the stairs with a mixture of regret, frustration, and determination. He had stalked out of the saloon and towards the battered shape of the Blackjack, taking the first steps towards Billy the Kid, vengeance, and, he hoped, finding his brother.

And so for hours he had nursed the damaged vehicle across the desert. He had left the scrub grass and the pine forests far behind and was now deep in the wastes, surrounded by nothing but rock, sand, and the occasional stubborn bush or tree. He had stopped at the battle scene to pick over the remaining vehicles for canteens and RJ-1027 cells, and strapped it all to the back of the

Blackjack. He had driven along the railroad tracks at an agonizing pace, watching for the telltale marks of the driller. When he found them, he turned without pause and followed them into the wastes.

He drove the first day until nightfall, having been in the saddle all night and day. He was parched despite the water he had salvaged, and his stomach was a distant rumbling insistence that he found it all too easy to ignore. As the miles reeled out beneath him, his mind leapt from image to image, replaying everything he had lost since that morning he had decided to hit the bank in Missouri City without his brother. The two images that constantly churned to the surface were his brother's face and a face he knew was Misty's, although it seemed to melt from the beautiful, smooth, young face of the dancing girl to the twisted, angry, torn face of the victim he had cruelly left on the floor of the tiny room.

Where was Frank? Was he even alive? Jesse's mind was tormented with fear and worry, but he knew he could never have tracked down the survivors of the Union Advanced Patrol. Even if he could have, what could he have done then? Billy's gang was almost completely intact, and they had to have been nearby, in Diablo Canyon, when the Union must have fled. Maybe they had seen something? It was Jesse's best hope that the Youngers had taken his brother away after the battle. The fact that they had left him but taken his brother, he thought, was a good argument that his brother still lived, while they had been convinced that he had died. Cole had always been Frank's friend and war buddy first, and Jesse's friend and loyal follower a distant second. The rest of the Youngers followed their oldest brother's lead without question. The scenario was not so far-fetched that it failed to offer at least slight comfort.

Still, if Cole and his brothers had managed to spirit Frank away, where would they have taken him? Not back to Kansas City, not after run in against the Union. So Billy's the only trail he had to follow, he chose to see this as a gift of fate. Following this path he might learn more about his brother. At the very least, he should be able to learn where to start looking. He would definitely be able to seize this moment from Billy and make sure he could not enjoy the benefits of his backstabbing scheme. If anyone was going to emerge from this whole mess as an outlaw of the first water, it was going to be Jesse.

As the sun set on his first full day in the desert, he felt the first hints of despair. There was every possibility that his damaged Blackjack would not be able to outpace the driller. He would be no match for Billy's 'Horses, he knew. He figured he could at least catch the driller, but there was no way to tell how old the tracks were as he raced along the desert. There was plenty of room for his mind to torment him, amidst all the other torturous images, with fears that he would never catch his rival.

When the flaring reds and oranges of the glorious desert sunset finally faded from the sky ahead; he triggered the Blackjack's running lamps. The frantically jumping shadows made it nearly impossible to see the driller tracks unless he slowed his movement to a crawl, however. He continued for a time, but he felt his vision blurring, his attention wavering from one moment to the next. The second time he lost the trail completely, jerking awake to realize he was staring at smooth, featureless sand, he circled back, found the trail once more, and then stopped for the night.

He took a strip of the jerky from his saddlebags, a sip of water from his last canteen, and then huddled up against the warmth of his machine, wrapped in a duster, and succumbed to an uncomfortable, fitful sleep.

His dreams were a blurred moving picture array of faces. Frank was there, then Cole, smiling his cruel, open smile. He saw Billy, forever trapped between boy and man, and he saw Lucy, looking over one smooth shoulder as she moved through a crowded room towards a steep set of stairs. Each time the faces melted into the next, however, there was a flash of Misty's face, twisted in hatred or soft in sleep, smooth as the day he met her or torn as the day he had left. The only thing that never changed were green her eyes, always boring into his, never letting him go.

Jesse came awake slowly, eyes blinking in the harsh glare of sunrise, mouth working to generate any moisture it could. He threw off the duster, took another quick swig of water, and mounted up once more. Hanging over the saddle to get a better view of the tracks, he continued on his way.

The Blackjack had sputtered along well past midday before Jesse saw, in one of his quick glances ahead, a confused jumble a little ways off from the driller's track. He found a narrow trail intersecting with Billy's path. The remains of a wrecked wagon were piled up in the sand and rock a couple hundred feet away from the driller tracks. Jesse looked up the digger trail. It took a sharp left turn and then continued on into the distance. Off the trail the tumble of wood, canvas, and metal gleamed dully in the rising sun, a silent pivot point for Billy's change of direction.

He nursed the Blackjack down into silence and then swung off, pulling a hyper-velocity pistol as he moved towards the wreckage, weapon down and to the side.

"Hey, anybody there?" Jesse shouted more to make himself feel better than in the honest thought that there might be people nearby. The wreckage looked total. Anyone left alive probably would have retreated long ago. He was not surprised when there was no answer.

"Hey, you okay?" He repeated, not knowing what else to do.

As Jesse came up on the wreckage he noted the charred blast marks of RJ-1027 weaponry across the sideboards of the wagon, and the blasted wheels, spokes scattered across the sand. The small generator that had been jury-rigged beneath the body of the wagon to drive the rear wheels was dead, none of its vents or telltale lights winking at all in the shadow of the dead cart.

Jesse moved around the wagon, his gun still held level. The canvas cover of the main compartment was collapsed, more blackened holes blown through it. Much of it had burned away. The wagon was canted to one side, resting on the remains of one shattered wheel. Pots, pans, and clothing were scattered across the desert all around, mixed in with a muddle of booted prints. He had nearly completed his circuit around the devastation when he saw the bodies.

There were two of them, slumped to the side and tied back to back. They both looked like half-Injun outcasts judging from their skin, hair, and clothing. Middle-aged, they looked similar enough to have been brothers. There were flint knives and a bow nearby, a quiver of arrows half emptied into the sand. Both of the men had had their throat's slashed. Their faces had been further brutalized with a sharp knife.

"Smiley." Jesse muttered under his breath as he crouched down beside them.

Their clothing, mostly leathers, were decorated with the bone and feather fetishes he had seen many folks of mixed heritage wear in an attempt to identify with a culture that had denied them as surely as White society. Jesse wondered if the Apache Kid was traveling with Billy, and if so, what he must have thought of this work. He shook his head again.

Jesse reached out with one hand, laying the feedback pads against one corpse's arm. Information compelled its way into his mind. The body was cold. The newly-risen sun had not had time to warm it again. They had been dead for some time.

Jesse stood up and stretched his back. Whatever had happened here, Billy had learned something that had changed his course. Could these two outcasts have known something about the artifact Bonney had been hunting? Or at least, knew of this mysterious valley the dead medicine man had mentioned?

Something about the torture, about the way the bodies had been left, filled Jesse with a new sense of urgency. He ran back to the Blackjack. He muttered a quick prayer to a God he barely thought of anymore as he turned the key and closed his eyes with a quick nod of thanks as it stuttered back to life. He leaned down to quickly check the indicator lights along the charge cells. Not strong, but no need to replace them yet. He opened the throttle on his machine and roared off after the tracks turning south, deeper into the wastes.

The new trail moved straight as Warrior Nation arrow for the rest of the day. When the light faded off to his right again, he did not even try to push himself; he simply slowed to a stop in the middle of the track and huddling down for the night.

The newfound sense of urgency woke Jesse before the sun and he resumed his travel, going as slow as necessary to keep the tracks clear in the murky dark of pre-dawn. He did not mark the rising of the sun except to slowly bring up the speed of the Black jack as the divots became clearer.

Jesse sipped down the last of his water on the morning of the fourth day. He had eaten the last of his jerky the night before. Voices of defeat and a sad, pathetic death alone in the middle of the desert had been whispering in his ear all night. His sleep had been restless and broken. He was too far gone now, though. He would never make it back to civilization now, not without water or food. If he could not catch up to Billy in the next couple of days, the voices would be proven correct. He would die, alone, in the desert.

As he rode along, Jesse thought of all the people who would be affected by his death. Most folks would think he really had died in the shootout with the Advanced Patrol. Lucy would know better, but maybe she should think he had just lit out. She would think he cared nothing for her proposal, and forgotten about her. For some reason, that thought bothered him more than he felt it should. The most driving fear he felt at the idea of dying, however, was that Frank, if he still lived, would never know he had survived the battle.

Thoughts of his brother distracted his mind so that he did not know how long he had been staring at the tall streaks of smoke in the sky. He slowed to a crawl over the sand and then stopped. Somewhere, not too far ahead, someone had lit several fires. The smoke rose up into the clear blue sky overhead. Jesse squinted up at the smoke, trying to judge how far away it was. He did not hear machinery or engines of any type, but if it was Billy, he did not want to give away his position until he was good and ready to face the puling chiseler on his terms.

Jesse killed the Blackjack's engine and slipped off the saddle. He opened up the cargo compartments and dug through the plunder there. He pulled out an ammo belt of RJ-1027 cartridges and slung that over his shoulder, pulled a holdout pistol and shoved that into the back of his belt, and was about to close the hatch when he saw the sleek shape of Carpathian's new weapons lying in the bottom of the hold. He reached in and looked again at the mysterious ion pistol. With a shrug he shoved one into a pocket, closed the hatch, and began the hike towards the distant smoke.

He heard the machinery long before he reached the lip of the shallow canyon. He heard a vicious, grinding whine, strangely muffled, beneath the dragon-roar of an RJ-1027 engine running at full power. A column of white dust or smoke rose into the sky over the canyon. He slowly lowered himself to his belly and began to crawl to the edge, moving towards a gnarled, spidery tree that might offer a little cover. He moved up behind the tree and peeked over, his heart suddenly thundering in his chest as he realized that he had actually made it.

The valley was not deep, possibly the bed of a long-dead river tangled up with countless others forming a maze in the middle of the lifeless land. Billy's men had parked their Iron Horses all along the bottom and were lounging around, taking their ease. They obviously trusted to the remote location in the middle of nowhere to provide their security. Jesse could see Billy standing near a large hole that had been blasted into the side of the canyon. The driller was backing out, accompanied by the plume of dust and grit. The men of Diablo Canyon were standing nearby, directing the drill or holding a mixture of strange equipment. Off to one side was a framework of metal struts that had been built to support another machine that seemed to be pointed at the wall.

Two of the Canyon men were arguing, one pointing to the shadowy hole, the other back at the framework with its machine. Billy walked to them, bringing them together, and listened carefully to what they said. He nodded once, patted one man on the back, and then pointed to the hole. Both of the men shrugged, and one yelled something to the driver of the drilling machine. The thing reversed course and crawled slowly back into the hole, the many drills reaching out in front of it spinning back up, creating the terrible, echoing roar that had led him to the canyon.

Jesse scanned the crowd of men below. He saw Smiley resting against the canyon wall a bit away, taking advantage of what shade there was. He saw Johnny Ringo and the Apache Kid standing together off to one side. They did not look amused, and cast constant looks along the rim of the canyon. Several times Jesse had to duck back behind his scrubby little tree to avoid their notice.

A man walked from behind a small pinnacle of rock towards Ringo and the Kid, and for a moment Jesse would have sworn it was Bob Cole. A surge of anger and hatred filled his mind. It was everything he could do to stop himself from leaping down into the canyon, both guns blazing. The anger caught him by surprise even as he realized the man was not Cole's youngest brother. Could he be harboring so much animosity towards Cole and his brothers? Jesse shook his head and forced himself back into the moment. His time had come, and his opportunity to stick Billy in the neck and grab the brass ring for himself had arrived. All he needed was a plan.

Below, the drill continued its grinding work. Choking dust blasted back out of the hole and swirled through the canyon, up into the sky. The men stopped their talking whenever the drill began to work, continuing their conversations only after the hellish noise trailed off. Most of the men turned to the Billy and the cave during these lulls. The few remaining watched the sky, or the lip of the canyon, or the dirt at their feet as their own individual impulse dictated. He saw that Ringo and the Kid usually watched the cave mouth whenever the machine was working, their expressions unreadable from this distance.

The driller stopped and backed out of the shadows again, and again the Diablo Canyon men argued about what was happening inside. Most likely the driller would head back into the darkness again, and Jesse knew he should be ready when it did. The drill's noise would present him with the best opportunity to make it into the canyon unopposed. Get the drop on Billy, bring him under the weight of the hyper-velocity guns, and the jig would be up; Jesse would be back on top. Most of the men in the canyon were men he had ridden with in the past, and they would take their share of whatever the driller found from his hand just as readily as from Billy's. Ringo would be tough, and the Kid. Smiley was a monster, but he did not much care who he was killing for, as long as he had the opportunity to kill.

No, the entire thing came down to Billy. It was always going to be between Jesse and Billy when the penny finally dropped. And here it was, tumbling towards the sand.

Frank's face floated up into Jesse's mind again. Frank was always the one he could bounce an idea off of. Frank would know which parts of his plans were good and solid, and which ones were harebrained notions that could not possibly survive the light of day. Without Frank there to listen, it almost felt as if any plan could not hope to succeed. He did not even want to think about jumping into that canyon without Frank's Sophie to watch his back.

For a moment he thought about going in brazenly calling for his brother's support, pretending he was up in the hills waiting to slap down any mudsill yahoo that got ornery. Then he remembered that there was every chance Billy and his gang knew more about Frank's whereabouts than he did. He could almost hear his brother's voice mocking him for the very thought. A chill ran down his back as he thought about what else he might have missed as he made his simple little plan.

Without Frank, this was going to be even harder than he wanted to admit. He told himself it was his best chance to learn more about his brother's fate.

And besides, Billy really needed a good spoke in his wheel. And Jesse James was just the man to do it. For the first time in days, the old familiar grin came easing back.

*****

Hanging from the flank of his wagon, Wyatt looked out at the center of Diablo Canyon and shook his head at the devastation. It had looked bad through the vision slits of the Judgment wagon, but without the solid iron frame limiting his view, he could fully appreciate the impact. Two buildings seemed to have completely burned down, and many others showed the unmistakable blast damage of countless RJ-1027 shots. Something monumental had occurred in the center of town, dwarfed only by the scatter of wreckage and bodies marking the sight of the battle a stone's throw to the south.

"Wyatt, you gonna keep movin', 'r you gonna trap the rest of us in here for the rest of the day?" Virgil's voice muttered from behind him. The Over-marshal nodded an apology and leapt down onto the street.

The marshals and deputies riding their Hogs had spread out through the center of town at the first sign of trouble. As they had ridden in, several suspicious figures fled before them. They had seen at least three bodies lying at various points along their journey that had been left to rot in the sun. Smoke was also rising from a couple points farther back in town. Wyatt had set his men to create a perimeter and move no further until they learned what had happened, but a dark thought moved in the back of his mind . . . he was afraid he already knew.

The UR-30 units with the Over-marshal had been unable to establish contact with the unit assigned to Diablo Canyon, and that could mean nothing good. An Enforcer unit, even after it was rendered non-operational through damage or malfunction, should still be able to relate its position to another unit unless catastrophic damage to its reporter beacons had occurred. They were getting absolutely nothing from the Diablo Canyon unit.

The people of the town slowly came out from hiding as they realized who the lawmen were. They seemed shy, as if expecting violence to erupt around them at any time. Wyatt tried to reassure them, but they were unable or unwilling to believe him when he said that the worst was over. He had his men interview as many folks as he could track down and it quickly became clear what had happened.

Wyatt called Virgil, Doc, and Morgan to him while he left the judge to push the cordon of lawmen wider into the city to look for some of the local perpetrators.

"Well, this ain't good." Wyatt spat into the dust of the street. "Looks like we got road agents ridin' into town, blowin' the center of the burg down to get at the UR-30, and then clearin' out with some equipment. They then run into some Army boys down south, kick up a terrible ruckus, and then . . . no one seems to know." He shook his head. "You boys get anything better than that?"

"No one's talkin', Wyatt." Virgil gave a sour look at a knot of townsfolk standing in the shade of an overhang across the street. "Since the Enforcer got taken down, things have gone to hell in a hand basket here. Folks that'd been clingin' to grudges for over a decade came out'o the woodwork. There's been a lot of dyin' ever since."

Morgan's eyes moved from face to face from within the iron framework of his support suit. It was clear he would have nodded if he could. "Someone took out the robot, then fought a major battle with the Army. They ain't here anymore, and neither is the Army. None of that makes any sense."

"Why take out the robot if they weren't plannin' on stayin'?" Doc was staring at a massive hole that had been blown in a building down the street. "It's not like it's an easy trick."

"An' our own units haven't had any luck trackin' anyone leavin'." Wyatt nodded. "A lot of trails out to the battle sight, from a bunch of different directions, and then runnin' away. But nothin' clear. An' with the ol' railroad messin' with their head lamps, there ain't no way we're gonna be able to track 'em out o' town this time."

"I don't see what else we can do, Wyatt." Virgil's face was long, his slow voice full of anger and regret. "He'll turn up again soon, his kind always does. That is, if he didn't get beefed by the Army boys over there so bad we couldn't even recognize the body." He shrugged. "Might be Jesse James is dead, Wyatt."

The Over-marshal barked a sharp laugh. "I ain't never been that lucky, Virg, and I ain't likely gonna start bein' now." He looked back at the heavy wagon. "No, someone come in here a day 'r so ago and did all this, and there ain't no way we're gonna pin it on anyone without some of these local yokels bein' willin' to talk more than they are."

"Maybe if you leave them a UR-30 unit?" Morgan's buzzing voice was nearly devoid of all human emotion, but it managed to convey a sense of dismay at his brother's resignation.

"'Course we will, Morg. We ain't gonna leave these folks high and dry." Wyatt forced himself to pat the hulking form of his brother on one broad shoulder, trying not to wonder if he could feel it. "Problem's more long range than that, though. We nearly had Jesse James, boys. We were closin' in on him, and it looked like we might even hook William Bonney into the bargain. Now . . . this?" He gestured at the shattered town.

"You reckon we move back to Tombstone, then, Wyatt?" Virgil's voice was bitter.

Wyatt shook his head. "I don't know what else we can do, Virg."

"Unless we suddenly run into an old friend that might be willing to help . . . " Doc's muffled voice was amused, and everyone turned to look at him. Without moving his eyes, Holliday nodded the brim of his hat in that direction. They all turned to stare at the distant telegraph office and the woman who had just emerged, blinking, into the sunshine.

"Well I'll be damned." Wyatt whispered.

"Most assuredly." Doc muttered, casting him a sidelong glance. "But hopefully not for awhile yet. You reckon she might know somethin' about all this?"

"I ain't got a better idea. Boys, you stay with the wagon. Keep an eye out for that yahoo partner of hers. Morgan, why don't you come on over with me. Let's go have a chat with the lovely agent, shall we?"

Wyatt crossed the street at a brisk pace, his brother's heavy footsteps thundering along behind him. He saw the woman turn towards the edge of town and called out in a sharp voice, "A word, agent Loveless, if you don't mind?"

Lucinda Loveless turned quickly, her hand flashing down and back to her bustle. She stopped as she recognized the Over-marshal. A professional smile pursed her full lips as he jogged up beside her. She nodded politely, then without missing a beat nodded to Morgan as well. "Gentlemen.Fancy meeting you all the way out here."

"Miss, if you don't mind me askin', how in the Sam Hill did you manage to beat us out here?" Wyatt's hands were on his hips as if berating a schoolgirl.

"Well, let's just say the kindness of new friends in . . . high places . . . and leave it at that, shall we?" Her smile turned slightly mischievous.

"Friends?" The word was so flat as it left the Over-marshal's mouth it could have been his brother who had spoken.

"Well, perhaps friends is a strong word." She shrugged. "Let's say happy acquaintances. Or at least, our sudden acquaintance was happy for me, anyway." Again she flashed them the perfect smile.

Wyatt waved the smile and the non-explanation off. "Never mind, then. Do you have any idea what happened here? Where is everyone?"

Lucinda looked surprised. "Why, whomever do you mean, Over-marshal? Are there stalwart townsfolk missing?"

"There's a field of corpses just outside of town, miss." Morgan's voice caught her off-guard, Wyatt could tell. "And innocent civilians are dyin' in Diablo Canyon itself. Your jokes ain't proper at a time like this. You work fer the president, you might wanna start helpin' his people, 'stead of laughin' at their expense."

That seemed to trouble her, and the smile faded. "I'm sorry. It's been terrible since . . . since the whole thing began."

Wyatt smiled with the flat eyes of a serpent. "Well, why don't we start there, then. What is the whole thing that began?"

Loveless looked into Wyatt's eyes for a moment and he could tell she was weighing something in her mind. When her smile returned, he knew whatever she said next was going to be suspect.

"Well, it was Billy the Kid and his gang, Over-marshal. Came in here, shooting up the town, and took out the UR-30 Enforcer." Her gaze was steady, her smile firm, and her tone even. He sighed, knowing the truth would be permanently locked behind that professional façade.

"That what you just reported to the president?" Wyatt nodded towards the telegraph office behind her.

Loveless nodded. "Yes, as a matter of fact it is." She injected some iron into her tone with the artful skill of a professional actress. "I'm not in the habit of including anything beyond the truth in my reports, Over-marshal."

Wyatt shook his head. "Well of course not, miss. I'd expect nothing less from Washington's finest." He made no attempt to hide the frustration in his tone. "You wouldn't happen to know what . . . Billy . . . did to the robot, would you?"

She smiled again. "Well, Over-marshal, some of the boys in the saloon were saying as how they watched Billy and his gang bring it to where the tracks lift off into the canyon and toss it down. I didn't go over to see for myself, not having a head for heights, you know. I don't see why they would have lied." Her smile grew coy. "It's not like it's a very interesting story, anyway, is it?"

Wyatt shook his head again. "Of course not. I'll have some of my men check it out, see if the remains are retrievable." He looked back at the wagon where the lawmen were gathering, coming back from combing the town. He started to walk back but then stopped and turned.

"You didn't happen to see Billy, or anyone else suspicious, leavin' town, did you?"

Again her gaze was steady, looking him right in the eye. "I'm sorry, Over-marshal. I arrived after the whole uproar was long over. I did not see anyone leave town at all. When I got here, all the major characters had already fled."

He nodded, not breaking eye contact for a moment. “So, there is no way you can assist my men and me in following these animals and stopping their violent attacks on decent folks.” His voice, again, was flat.

She looked into his eyes and he could tell there was something more churning just beneath the surface. There were choices being made, and he would not be privy to them or their consequences. She blinked once, the only concession to an expression she made, and then her beautiful face pivoted on her perfect neck in the most graceful negation he had ever seen.

“No, Over-marshal. I’m afraid I can’t think of any way I could help.”

Chapter 16

From the northern edge of the canyon, Jesse had a perfect view of the cave and the men standing around nearby. Most of Billy's gang were scattered towards the eastern end to avoid the worst of the dust and noise. Johnny Ringo and the Apache Kid, however, had not moved. They were almost directly below Jesse, with no way to avoid them. Still, they were probably the greatest threats in the entire canyon, after Billy himself, so it only made sense that he take care of them first.

The problem, as Jesse saw it, was that he did not want to kill Johnny Ringo. He knew Ringo was some kind of distant cousin to the Youngers. No matter what happened out in no-man's land, no matter where Frank was, Jesse would need to put together a new gang if he was going to take Lucy's advice and brace a more meaningful challenge. That would be a lot easier with the Youngers riding with him.

There was a pyramid of blaster rifles standing against each other about ten feet past Ringo and the Kid, and Jesse knew that if he could get there, he would be able to lay down enough fire to keep the rest of the gang at bay until he could get to Billy. He had to figure the engineers from Diablo Canyon would not a threat. As soon as he could take care of Billy, he would not have to worry about the rest of the gang.

Across the canyon, the driller stalked back into the shadows, and Jesse knew that at any moment, the horrific noise and billowing dust would begin again. They would find what they were looking for soon, and after that, there would be no chance for him to take anyone by surprise. He was going to have to strike soon or lose his chance forever.

Jesse shuffled around the lip of the canyon, shifting his weight beneath him as he prepared to leap. He had a moment's doubt. What if his arms acted up again? He was about to jump into the middle of a hostile gang. If his arms were not at their absolute best, he was going to buy a nice six foot stretch of sand for sure. But there was nothing else he could do. Alone, without food or water or enough fuel to get out of the desert, his back was well and truly against the wall.

The thought of water sent a sharp pang through his throat, which set the rest of his injuries to throbbing as well. Rather than frighten him, however, it only made him smile. He was worried about his arms being at their best? There was not a single part of his body that was currently working in tip top shape. His arms, very probably, were the least of his concerns. At the same time he reached this conclusion, the howling roar of the driller machine echoed out of the cavern. Without another thought, Jesse dropped.

He landed on Ringo's back, planting the heels of his boots on the other man's shoulder blades and pushing down with all his strength. Ringo was launched down onto his face into the sharp rocks on the valley floor. Without pausing to regain his balance, Jesse used his momentum off Ringo's back to fly up and over the Injun outcast they called the Apache Kid. He flipped his orientation over the other man's back, landing on his feet behind him.

The Kid spun in place, his hands flashing to the knives at his waist. As the ebony blades left their sheathes, they blazed an intense bluish white, spirit fire igniting up their entire lengths. The light guttered and failed as Jesse brought first one pistol butt and then the other down on the Kid's head. The man staggered backwards into the sun, legs unsteady and face slack behind the war paint. Jesse jumped back up into the air, planted one boot on the man's chest, and shoved him backwards into the pile of rifles. Following up mercilessly, one final blow to the back of the head sent the renegade warrior slumping into the rock and sand.

Jesse looked up quickly, but the other men in the canyon had noticed nothing. They were either absorbed in the raucous drilling, or looking down or away, trying to ignore the sound. Jesse moved towards the scattered rifles, picking one up and moving towards a pile of broken rock for cover. He felt a near-constant itching between his shoulder blades as his mind constantly reminded him that he was alone. Frank was not above, watching through Sophie's scope to take out any threat Jesse had missed. Cole was not nearby, ready to lend the weight of his guns to the battle. Jesse was completely alone.

He was surrounded by enemies that had once been his friends. Nearly everyone in this canyon had ridden at his side at one time or another. He had trusted most of him with his life, and they had trusted him. Even if he had been planning on euchering Billy over this latest find, Jesse would have made sure he got his cut! He was not going to cut him off completely, let alone leave him in the middle of a battle to die!

Whether Jesse believed his own thoughts would be something for a deeper man to contemplate, but in that instant, grasping the butt of a stolen blaster rifle to his chest and preparing to brace an entire gang on his own, he believed it wholeheartedly. The righteous indignation fueled his anger to new, boiling heights.

Jesse was so tense, so wrapped up with his own thoughts, that he did not at first register when the drilling machine suddenly stopped. A shout from deep within the tunnel snapped him back into the moment at the same time that most of the men he was aiming towards all turned to look into the shadows as well. A strange smell tainted the air, but Jesse was so aggravated he could not be bothered to notice. In front of him, the men began to move towards the cave. He could tell, although they were not visible from his current position, that Billy must have disappeared inside.

He was too late. They had found what they were looking for, they would take it out, and he had lost his only chance to strike from surprise. His anger, towering a moment ago, reached even new, impressive heights. There were no more distracting thoughts of Lucy or Misty, no more worrying about Frank or the Coles. He had had everything taken from him. He was alone in the middle of the desert. He had followed what he felt was his destiny laid clearly before him. And now he had nothing.

Without a thought, Jesse stood up with the blaster and started to fire into the small group of Billy's remaining men as they moved towards the cave. The first blasts caught them completely unawares. Two outlaws were struck in the chest, their bodies shuddering with the impact as dust flashed off them in a halo, knocked clear with the impact. They flew backwards into the rest, the light fading from their eyes before they even knew they were in danger. The rest of the men stopped walking, cringing backwards in surprise and reaching for their own guns.

Jesse screamed again, his wounded throat opening blood frothing from his mouth as he charged forward. He fired the rifle over and over again, bracing it against his hip as he ran. There was no way the hyper-velocity pistols would have had range to reach his targets, so it was a good thing he had grabbed the rifle. There was no room in his frantic mind for rational thought now, and he would have fired with any weapon he had to hand. More of his shots blasted into the tightly packed enemy, knocking two more men down. Blood sprayed into the dust-covered canyon.

By the time Jesse had crossed half the distance between himself and Billy's gang, the survivors had begun to return fire. They blasted bolts of crimson light back at the figure running towards them as if it were a vengeful ghost roaring up out of hell. Jesse's extensive injuries, the dust covering him from head to toe, and the hoarse, hollow cry that was escaping his wide, cracked lips all combined to reinforce the image. Fear had a terrible effect on the men's aim.

Jesse rushed through the oncoming wave of blaster fire with no thought at all to his own safety or survival. He had lost everything. Now, he would take everything. Suddenly the blaster rifle was ran dry, its charge light dull. He tossed the weapon aside and his custom pistol leapt into his hands. The sheer number of shots he poured downrange was staggering. The three survivors, faced with that hurricane of ruby light, dropped their own pistols and fled down the canyon in their efforts to escape.

Jesse had just enough presence of mind to stop himself from rushing into the desert after the fleeing shapes. He paused for a moment, breath heaving in tortured lungs, and searched around for something else to destroy. The madness of the moment clouded his eyes, but eventually his fevered gaze fell upon the cavern entrance. He pivoted on the spot to rush headlong into the darkness.

Inside the new smell was far more intense, but he was even less inclined to stop and consider it now. The floor of the cavern was irregular, and the bulk of the driller loomed up ahead, lighting the cavern with red-tinged beams slung from the thing's flanks and belly. The engine was on but idling low, giving out a constant, low-grade buzzing sound to reverberate in the darkness.

Jesse was gasping like an angry animal as he hunted through the tunnel for his next victims. There had been a world full of promise, and now there was nothing. The only thing his fevered mind could grasp upon, as a talisman against the emptiness, was this strange thing Billy had tracked across the length and breadth of the territories. Something with the power to pull Jesse so far, to make him go through so much, would have the strength and power to rise him up again. He would bring it to the Rebellion himself. Wielding that much power, he could begin to pursue the only vengeance that would satisfy him now.

And so, towards that end, no one in the tunnel could be allowed to stand in his way.

Jesse readied his hyper-velocity pistols, one held high, one held low. No matter where a threat emerged, it would be met with brutal force. But no attacks came. Instead he heard, echoing from ahead in the thick, reeking air, voices arguing petulantly. He growled under his heaving breath and inched his way forward. He had taken down Ringo and the Apache Kid, but he knew there were several more men with Billy still, and he had not seen Smiley since that first survey of the canyon.

Jesse's mind was slowly returning, but none of the anger, despair, or determination was draining away with the madness. Somewhere up ahead was Billy. If Billy had been honest from the beginning, Jesse would never have been forced into this situation. Whatever else was about to happen, Billy would answer for his part in Jesse's troubles.

Jesse eased his way along the flank of the driller, gingerly picking his way past each insectile leg. The voices echoing from up ahead became clearer with each step, and he paused to listen, in case any tactical advantage could be gained.

"I told you I heard something!" The voice was high pitched and peevish. No one Jesse recognized.

"You never said anything like this! Digging? You didn't hear digging?" It was another voice that he did not know. "How about gagging? Do you hear me gagging now?"

Jesse shook his head. It had to be the Diablo Canyon men. Something had gone wrong, and under Billy's cold eyes they were arguing over whose fault it was. Jesse smiled at the thought. Usually it took Frank to come up with conclusions like that, while Jesse was far more the man of action in the family. The thought of Frank swept the smile from his face, and the rage threatened once again to boil up. It did not matter what was going on ahead of him. It was time for someone to answer for Jesse's current predicament.

He moved forward again and came around the front of the driller, looking past the enormous array of blades and bits mounted on the armatures at the front. They were hot, releasing wisps of smoke or steam up into the fetid air. The rough, churned walls and uneven floor ended abruptly in a concave area. A soft, reddish light was pouring through a hole in the stone, about waist-high, just wide enough for a man to crawl through. The voices, still grumbling and muttering, were coming from that hole. Jesse moved towards the gap, pistols at the ready.

"I tol' 'em you'd be comin'." The thick, heavy voice emerged from the shadows. "Billy, he said nope, said you were out'a the pichure. But I said yup. An' here you are." Deeper in the darkness something stirred, moving towards him, and Jesse cursed under his breath as Jake Williamson sauntered forward, the weak light glinting off his greasy, bald head.

"Smiley." Jesse nodded to him. "This ain't between you an' me. I'm just after Billy. You can walk away."

Smiley's grin widened beneath its thick mustache. "You an' Billy, always thinkin' everythin' came down ta you two." The grin disappeared, collapsing into a vicious glower. "You an' Billy ain't no more special than anyone else, Jesse James. An' I'll be proud ta prove it to ya. Cuz today, you're story's gonna end. Time to make room for some new stories now."

Jesse tried not to react. He knew the worst thing he could do at that moment was to provoke Smiley even further. Unfortunately, he could not keep the grin from sweeping across his face. It had been too much, and Smiley was just another laugh line in a dancehall show.

Jesse snickered. "You couldn't lead a pack o' cowboys fresh off the trail to a whorehouse on nickel night, Smiley. You just ain't got the smarts." Jesse moved to turn away. "Also, you don't smell so good."

Smiley charged at Jesse, as the outlaw boss knew he would. The bigger man could not get up much speed in the confining spaces of the cave. Jesse had no trouble stepping back behind the drill to avoid his ungainly rush. The hyper-velocity pistols in Jesse's hands spun around, barrels slapping into his palms. Before Smiley could turn around, Jesse brought both weapons down, like clubs, on the back of his broad bald head. Two heavy cracking sounds echoed through the tight space, and the giant man collapsed without a sound.

Jesse watched the body for a moment. Aside from the rapid rise and fall of labored breathing, however, there was no other sign of life. With a wide grin, Jesse moved to the small, broken hole and dove through.

Jesse figured that, warned by the sound of the tussle in the tunnel, the men on the other side would be waiting for him, weapons raised. Not only were they not waiting for him, they were not even looking at him as he rolled up out of his lunge with both pistols raised and ready to fire. As Jesse took in a breath to shout an order, he fell back against smooth stonework, gasping at the smell. The scene in front of him disappeared behind a curtain of blurring tears.

Jesse quickly holstered one of his guns and pulled out a handkerchief with the freed hand, wiping at his eyes with the rough fabric.

"What in the hell is that stench!" Jesse barked, pushing himself back up to his feet and looking around owlishly as he tried to clear his eyes.

The room slowly swam back into focus. Billy stood across a large stone chamber from him, two RJ-1027 lanterns resting at his feet. Four men were standing nearby, their argument cut short by Jesse's sudden appearance. All of them were holding handkerchiefs over their mouths. None of them looked like they had any intention of drawing a weapon. Even Billy, eyes haunted and empty, was only staring at him in mild surprise.

Seeing that he was not in immediate danger, Jesse took a moment to look at the room. It was dressed stone, with designs or sculptures that looked eerily familiar carved into every wall. Angular, unnatural animals walked among strange, abstract, curlicue designs. Everything in the room seemed to focus in on a central plinth that rose out of the mosaic floor. A plinth that was completely empty, although the patterns of dust atop it suggested that, until very recently, something about the size of a small beer keg had rested there.

There were no doors in the chamber, as if it had been built to hold the plinth, and its occupant, and nothing else. The hole Jesse had leapt through had been knocked in by the driller, but it was not the only hole. In about the same place on the opposite wall was another hole, a black, empty eye staring at them from across the room. And it was from this hole that the stench came pouring.

With another quick look at Billy and the engineers, Jesse moved slowly towards this second hole, his kerchief still held to his face. It was not doing any good, however, as the reek just kept building with each step he took. Looking sideways through the hole, avoiding approaching it from the front, Jesse could not see anything but the fitful shadows thrown by Billy's lanterns.

"Get me a damned light." Jesse snapped, holding out the hand with the useless cloth. One of the engineers looked at Billy, who nodded, and then scuttled to get Jesse one of the lanterns. Jesse took it carefully, turned back towards the hole, and eased his mechanical arm through it and into the darkness.

The smell was like a wall pushing back at him as he moved his head in after the lantern. He was almost certain now what he would see, but he needed to check for himself. Sure enough, the rough cavern on the other side was strewn with desiccated, ravaged bodies. They were encased in metal and wire frameworks, built specifically to hold up dead bodies incapable of providing their own balance and support.

Some of the bodies had had mining tools surgically implanted where their hands had been, but most of them had arms ending in nothing but shattered stubs of bone sheathed in tatters of rancid flesh. They had been worked quite literally until their tools and hands were worn away, and then they had been discarded. Jesse could see the cranial battery sockets, where the cylinders would be inserted to animate the ghoulish creations. Each body completely dead, the RJ-1027 machinery dark and silent, and each socket empty, their batteries removed.

Jesse tried to get a quick count of the bodies in the tunnel, but his eyes were tearing up again and he could not keep his head through the hole any longer. He withdrew, pulling the lantern with him, and the shadows of the caves swallowed the sad remnants of the abandoned animations.

"Damned foreign bastard." Jesse spit on the mosaic floor over and over again, ignoring Billy and his three companions as they stared at him in dull confusion.

"You damned daffy European bastard. " He spat again. He knew exactly what had happened. He remembered Carpathian's welcome back in Payson with a bitter laugh. Offering to help Jesse take on another Heavy Rail. The blatant attempt to distract him seemed clear now, looking back. But at the time, Jesse had been so sure of his own superiority. And the old man had been a step ahead the whole time.

Jesse shook his head, the anger now aimed inwardly as much as at the rest of the world. He glared at Billy for a moment. The hyper-velocity pistol wavered in his hand and slowly rose. The other outlaw's eyes went round as his hands rose up in a warding gesture. Jesse shook his head again, muttered a dismissive curse under his breath and moved towards the hole in the chamber wall.

"Hey, wait!" Billy snapped out of his fugue. "You're alive!"

Jesse stopped, and spat an answer over his shoulder. "Guess it wasn't my day to die, Billy."

The younger man's hand drifted towards his pistol. "Where you think you're goin'?"

Jesse spun around so quick the three Diablo Canyon men flinched away, their empty hands raised in placating gestures. The older outlaw boss rushed across the dusty old chamber, his sleek custom pistol leading the way. The barrel jammed up beneath Billy's jaw and slammed him up against the crumbling wall. Billy's face contorted in pain as the sculptures in the wall behind him dug into his back.

"Whoa!" Billy's hands were raised high, his voice contorted by the barrel pressing into the soft flesh under his jaw. "Jesse, ease up!"

Jesse's face pressed in close to Billy's, his brows drawn down in barely-contained rage, his eyes wild. "I got a couple quick questions for ya, Billy, before I light out'a here on my way."

Billy tried to nod, but choked as the barrel pressed harder against his skin. "Ya," he gasped, minimizing the movement of his head.

Jesse nodded once, his face a mask half way between confused and furious. "Okay. First, where's Frank?"

Billy looked down at the barrel with an exaggerated roll of his eyes, and Jesse relaxed the tension in his metal arm, drawing the weapon down slightly.

Billy rubbed at the spot left behind by the muzzle, an exaggerated look of hurt innocence in his eyes. "Jeez, Jesse, you feel alright? You din't have to bury the damned muzzle in my craw, you know!"

Jesse's flat eyes grew harder and his pistol rose slightly. "Frank."

Billy's hands rose quickly again. "Whoa, Jesse! Pull in yer horns, fer Pete's sake!" He swallowed, and it looked painful enough to spark a pang of sympathetic pain in Jesse's own torn throat. "Honest, Jesse, before I talk, you gotta put the shootin' iron down, okay? I'll be straight, I promise, but it's a might hard to think with that fancy blaster warmin' my jaw."

Jesse blinked, then lowered the weapon further. "Where's my brother?"

Billy lowered his own hands a bit, sure to keep them wide, far from the butts of his own pistols. "Well, see, an' this here's the Gospel truth, Jesse." He swallowed again. "I don't know."

The hyper-velocity pistol jammed back up under Billy's jaw as Jesse's eyes burned with frustrated anger. The younger man scrambled against the wall to avoid the gun. "I swear! I swear! We lit out of there as soon as the blue-bellies showed up! You all were tearin' it up like the Kilkenny cats out there, an' we just ran! I din't see nothin'!"

Jesse lowered the gun, his shoulders sagging. "You din't come back fer 'im?"

Billy's head shook back and forth with furious, nervous energy. "No, we din't. We grabbed the driller machine with these galoots, looped through town up onto the tracks, and headed back down after the dust had settled. Wasn't none of you movin', an' we figured you'd all either run with the others 'r you was all up the flume." Billy's eyes were clear, his voice as even as he could make it. "Honest, Jesse. I thought you was dead or fled. I was hopin' you'd run oft."

Jesse turned away, his unseeing eyes scanning across the ancient carvings on the walls. "You really ain't got 'im."

Billy shook his head furiously. "If I'd'a grabbed 'im, Jesse, I'd tell ya."

Jesse started walking towards the shattered hole in the wall again, but his steps were hesitant, his eyes seeing nothing, his mind a swirling darkness circling a black, empty hole. "Then they got 'im. Alive 'r dead, they got 'im."

Billy started to cautiously follow Jesse as he crossed the room. "Who got 'im, Jesse? Those Union bastards? You think they grabbed 'im." Billy hesitated before continuing in a softer voice. "You sure he ain't beefed, Jesse? I saw that thing ridin' up on 'im. That thing was a beast, packin' more hardware than I seen on anythin' short of those wagons that're poppin' up all over."

The older outlaw's head shook in vague negation. "Naw, I picked over the bodies but good. He weren't there."

"But maybe he's okay, then!" Billy tried to sound hopeful. "If he's alive, maybe we can go get 'im!"

A light flickered deep in Jesse's eyes for the first time since he had drawn on Billy. He turned back to look at the younger man, and Billy shied away from the growing heat there. "Go get 'im from the Union?"

Billy shrugged. "Sure! We put a nice gang together, like that first train job, an' there ain't no place they can stash 'im that we can't get 'im out!" More and more energy seemed to bubble into Billy's voice. "An' you know, there ain't no outlaw in the territories, wouldn't come if you put out the call!"

Jesse tilted his head as if processing Billy's words, then shook it again. "Naw. If they took 'im, they'd mean to keep 'im. An' if they mean to keep 'im, they'll stash 'im someplace, you'd need an army to get 'im out."

A glum silence settled over the ancient room again. Jesse's eyes snapped up after a moment, looking back at the second hole breaking into the room. "An' I know some folks that got an' army they ain't doin' much with."

"Jesse," Billy inched his way around into the other man's line of vision. "You got an idea on how to make this right?" He jerked a thumb at the empty plinth.

The older outlaw was not paying attention, but he muttered aloud as he thought, and Billy nodded with the words. "Carpathian can't be far away, those animations ain't been dead again long. Should be able to catch up with 'em without too much trouble."

Billy nodded vigorously. "Yeah, Jesse, that's it! We'll catch up with the old bastard, an' take back what's ours!"

Jesse turned to take notice of the younger man again. Looking at him as if he had forgotten he was not alone in the chamber. He spoke as if he had not understood the words. "We?"

Billy gave Jesse a hard look. "Yeah, we, Jesse. This plunder's mine by rights. I found the Injuns, I got the info, I tracked it down an' dug it up. It's mine more'n it's anyone else's. So yeah, if anyone's ridin' out after it, it ain't you, it's we."

A smile tugged at Jesse's lips, the first since he had leapt into the stench-filled room. "We."

Billy nodded. "Yeah, we! Jesse, you can't take him on alone, an' you know it! He sure as Hades ain't gonna be alone, you know that! You need me!"

For a moment Jesse stood completely still, staring at the younger outlaw boss with a blank expression. Then he started to laugh, and Billy's expression snapped from eager to angry without a pause. "What's so all-fired funny, Jesse? I got out here without you, din't I? I got into this here buried room without you, din't I? You don't think you'll need me when you catch up to the old man?"

The laughter continued, bouncing off the surrounding yellow stone, absurd in the foul atmosphere. Billy's face hardened further, his right hand floating towards his gun belt.

"We made a deal, Jesse!" The hand slid over the butt of the modified six-shooter. "We were gonna ride together on this!"

The laughter cranked up another notch, but rather than fanning Billy's anger, the young outlaw backed up a pace. A manic edge had entered Jesse's mirth, a frantic energy that had not been there before. The fire was back in his eyes.

"We made a deal, Billy, you're right." Jesse nodded and took a step towards the retreating boss. "We were gonna ride this trail together, right as rain." He took another step.

Billy nodded, but there was a hesitant doubt in his eyes. "We were, Jesse. We were gonna work together, like the old days."

Jesse stopped advancing and looked down at his clenched fists, the metalwork of his arms gleaming redly in the RJ-1027 lantern light. He forced the fingers to relax, watching as the mechanisms beneath the armor moved smoothly and flawlessly. When he looked back up at Billy, the grin was back, but it was feral, and Billy tried to back up again only to find himself up against the rough wall once more.

"We were gonna ride together, Billy, 'till you let my boys die takin' down the damned robot for your gear." The broad shoulders flexed, the arms wide, and Billy's eyes flicked down to the hands and back up to Jesse's frenetic eyes.

"That was business, Jesse!" He forced himself to speak in an even tone. "That was just the way we all been workin' since long before you or me picked up a slingshot fer the first time!"

Jesse nodded, lowering his hands a bit and turning away slightly. "That's true, Billy. That's true. We ain't always been straight, an' that's business."

Billy relaxed slightly, a smile starting to cross his lips.

Jesse's right arm swung up faster than a rattler striking from the shadows. Power moved through rubber conduits, clockwork gears ran their teeth smoothly through each other and pistons pulled and released with tiny puffs of smoke. The armored back of Jesse's mechanical hand caught Billy squarely on the cheekbone with all the power of the steel and rubber machinery backed up by the hulking human muscles of his shoulder and back, and the younger man, stepping forward when the blow struck, was hurled back up against the wall with a muffled snap.

A pained gasp escaped Billy's torn lips before he hit the uneven wall with a grunt. He bounced away from the ancient carvings and fell forward as his legs collapsed beneath him. He slumped down to the dirty floor where he rolled half over, his shoulder resting against the wall and his face, twisted in pain and torn from the blow, rocked back and forth in the dust.

"You – you --- you killed him!" One of the engineers screeched, staring down at Billy in horror.

Another man pointed at Jesse. "Now who's gonna pay us!"

Jesse watched Billy for a second then shook his head. "He ain't dead. He's bleedin'. If yer bleedin', yer breathin'." He smiled slightly as he looked at the second engineer. "An' in case you missed it, flannel mouth, there ain't nothin' here. You was gonna get a cut o' what we all dug up." He pointed to the empty plinth. "Yer welcome to one hunnerd percent o' what you dug up."

"But, what about us?" The third man whined, following Jesse as the older outlaw stalked back towards the hole.

Jesse shook his head. "Ain't my problem, boys. Head on back to the Canyon, would be my best advice. Ain't nothin' out here for ya, or fer anyone, when you get right down to it."

"But they won't let us back to town! Not after we came out with you! You killed the metal marshal! The place is gonna be a mad house now, and everyone will blame us, because we rode out with you!" The second engineer was near tears.

Jesse turned at the hole and gave the three men a grin. In the vague red light and the swirling fetor he looked like a demon peering out of hell. "Sounds to me like you boys've made some bad choices, then, don't it?"

As Jesse eased backwards through the hole he looked back at the three men standing lost and alone in the foul-smelling semi-dark. "Good luck, boys. I got an old man to catch."

Even after the outlaw chief had gone, the three men from Diablo Canyon stood uncertain, their eyes flickering from the still form of Billy the Kid, to one blasted hole, to the other, to the empty plinth, and back to Billy.

After a moment the first engineer muttered, "You reckon the driller'd be any good at fishin'?"

Chapter 17

Jesse rushed across the desert on the half-wrecked Blackjack. He had almost taken an Iron Horse from the canyon, but they were all too low on fuel. None of them would be good for a long chase. The new vehicle was running rough, but with the salvaged batteries he knew he would be okay. He grumbled in annoyance as he ran back to the Blackjack. Trust Billy to let his boys lounge about while their transports sat around dry.

Frank never would have let Jesse's boys do that. The thought was true enough, but it hurt as soon as it occurred to him. Knowing the Union had Frank was eating at his mind even when he forced himself to focus on his immediate concerns. There was no telling what the blue-bellied bastards were doing to his brother while he was dancing around in the desert. Despite Billy's bravado, there was no way a band of shabby outlaws was going to assault an armed Union camp without help.

Jesse was convinced that the only prayer he had of helping his brother was at the head of an army, and the only army he could hope to win over to his cause was languishing in the swamps far to the south. He would need to have something special to convince the Confederate Rebellion to join him. Something big enough, for instance, to bring Carpathian out of his brick castle and into the desert wastes.

The Blackjack bounced and leaped over the rough terrain as Jesse nursed more speed out of the tortured engine. He had been chasing a fading plume of dust and grit for over an hour, and was finally able to make out a dot at the bottom of the plume: a large vehicle, racing away to the south. Out here in the middle of nowhere, there was no one else it could be but Carpathian. The doctor was rushing back to Payson, prize in hand.

Jesse hunched low over the control console of the vehicle, muscles straining as he willed the machine to go faster. With each violent bump over dry ridges or clumps of desert grass, he would leap into the air before slamming back down into the saddle. Aside from an occasional grimace of discomfort, he continued on without pause.

Jesse's crimson goggles were caked with dust and grime, but he could not take the time to clean them. The dark shadow ahead grew moment by moment, and with his quarry in sight, his fear, anger, and instincts all argued against any further delay. In that vehicle was the object that would bring the Rebellion back from the dead. In that vehicle was a man he had not viewed as an enemy in many years, but who had betrayed him in his moment of greatest need. In that vehicle was an old man that needed to be reminded of his place in the western territories.

The shadow ahead resolved itself into a boxy shape that could only be some kind of RJ-1027-powered wagon. There was a door high up on the rear panel and a ladder of sorts sweeping down towards the ground. The whole thing looked more decorative than utilitarian, just Carpathian's style. Atop the tall machine was a low wall or parapet, and he hoped whoever might be up there was not keeping a close lookout.

The thought had barely formed in Jesse's mind before a ragged shape, locks of thin hair waving in the wind, rose up over the parapet. The Blackjack was too far away to make out much detail. The rough, unfinished look about the face, with hollow, shadowed sockets and a flashing rictus-wide grin, however, were enough to show him it was an animation. The thing brought an arm up and pointed it at him. Its hand had been replaced with a jury-rigged blaster rifle: a red-lined muzzle-flash lashed out, the recoil pushing the thing's shoulder backward and away.

Jesse ducked as low as he could and gunned the engine. The howling of the vehicle rose another octave, but it was running with a dirty cough now. He knew he would not be able to nurse much more speed out of the tortured machine.

The animation on the wagon fired again and again. The blasts were disconcerting, but none of the shots landed anywhere nearby. Jesse thanked his stars, figuring that a stinking corpse firing from a rattling platform high atop a moving vehicle backwards at a moving target . . . the chances of a hit were probably slim enough he could afford to ignore the—

A bolt struck the forward fairing of the Blackjack with a hollow ring. The blast deflected off into the desert, but it drove Jesse even further back into his saddle. A grim snarl twisted his features below the red goggles. He wrenched the hand controls of the vehicle and dragged them backwards. The four blaster muzzles in the sloping armor ratcheted up into the sky.

Jesse stabbed his thumbs down on the firing mechanisms and grunted in satisfaction as the guns began to blaze away, the red-tinged fire lipping off their muzzles and back along the Blackjack's flanks. He marched the blaster impacts up the wagon's rear armor, unsurprised that the shots were ricocheting off into the distance without visible effect, but as he brought the stream into line with the animation up top, the blasts had a most satisfactory effect. Several bolts slapped the ungainly shape upright as they impacted across its chest.

Rotted fabric and dried, dead flesh blasted away in tatters that fluttered into the wind as the bolts battered their way through the body and flew out the other side and into the sky. The energy stood the animation up and knocked it over. The creature disappeared as it flew off the front of the wagon, then reappeared a moment later from beneath. The ruins of the corpse tumbled out from under the wide, thick-treaded rear wheels.

Jesse's grin was short-lived, however, as two strange shapes swept off to either side from in front of the wagon. Strange, ungainly vehicles, they seemed almost like mechanical pillars, each seated upon a small, furiously spinning wheel. Atop each was the desiccated body of an animation, permanently fixed to their strange, top-heavy mounts with bolts and straps. Heads lashed from side to side looking for their prey and the outlaw boss was shocked to see that they were completely encased in iron helmets and masks. What looked like weapon barrels thrust out from beneath the swaying bodies, and Jesse knew he could not let them get behind him.

He took out the left-hand abomination with a sharp burst of his lowered blasters. Mechanical parts scattered across the desert, sand thrown up into the air as the single wheel spun away as if eager to escape. He brought the Blackjack in line with the other vehicle, and his shots struck the pilot in the back and head, spraying rotting flesh and the twisted wreckage of its helmet into the sand. The machine, now without guidance, bounced over the uneven terrain and went down, cartwheeling in a furious explosion of sand and grit.

Jesse grinned before two more of the things swept into view. He looked back at the wagon to see that it was pulling ahead again. The primary weaponry on the Blackjack made short work of these new threats, but they forced him to follow an irregular course as he had to aim with the body of the vehicle, allowing the wagon to pull away. He shook his head and drew one of his hyper-velocity pistols, knowing that it would be less than ideal against an armored target at this range.

The Blackjack surged ahead again, pulling to within an easy stone's throw of the sloped ladder.

As Jesse tried to maneuver up behind the wagon, two more animations rose to take the place of the original shooter on the roof. Soon he was weaving back and forth in the wake of the wagon, doing his best to close the gap while avoiding the stuttering shots from above. Another bolt spanged off his front armor and the tone of his engine changed again. Something inside the body of the Blackjack must have been damaged from the hit. As the vehicle started to shake madly, Jesse knew his mount was living on borrowed time.

The Blackjack leapt forward in response to Jesse's desperate urgings. He sent streams of crimson bolts up at the animations above to keep their heads down, and then to one side and the other, aiming at the drivers of the top-heavy vehicles rather than the armored transports themselves. One stream of shots stitched across the torso of the creature on the left and the tall vehicle canted over, caught a high clump of red rock, and rolled away into the desert shedding mechanical parts and tatters of ragged meat as it went. Jesse's other shots, however, glanced off armored components, leaving the remaining outrider unharmed. Out of the corner of his eye he saw two more sweeping out from the left.

Jesse cursed, looking at the ladder as it bounced along ahead of him, then at the riders closing in. A sudden thought struck him and he holstered the pistol and made a desperate grab for the small shape pressing against his back. Carpathian's ion pistol felt strange against his feedback pads, but if there was ever a time to test a weapon that might shut down RJ-1027 technology, it seemed like now.

The pistol gave off a strange vibration as he fired it at the closest rider, and a snapping reddish flash zapped out and wrapped around the outlandish vehicle. Instantly, all the telltales winked out, the ruby glow of the vents and power sources faded. The entire thing slowed down, toppled over, and rolled to a gentle stop in the sand.

Jesse grinned as he watched over his shoulder as its journey ended. He turned back to point his mechanical arm rigidly at the next animation. Again the flash and buzz, and another animation tumbled into an awkward heap. But when he tried to shoot the last target as it flashed past, the small pistol made a plaintive beep and died.

Shaking the pistol had no effect, and Jesse growled as he shoved it into a side pocket. He pulled his own pistol again and fired backwards under his steering arm. A sleet of shots slapped into the animation's armored vehicle as two simultaneous bolts from above struck the Blackjack, knocking more of the vehicle's internal parts out of line.

Jesse's wild, desperate shots managed to hit something vital within the creature blasting away behind him. The tall thing began to sway back and forth as it fell away. He continued shooting, striking the body of the animation several times. When it detonated in a furious ball of red-tinged fire he spent no time celebrating. He spun around as fast as possible, eyes fixed on the ladder swaying back and forth nearby, and holstered his pistol. He took the extra moment necessary to snap the strap securely over the butt. He reached across his stomach to secure the other pistol and then rose up out of his saddle. His eyes never wavered from the iron ladder.

His eyes flicked from the heavy ladder to the wide front tires of the Blackjack, to the ornate cowcatcher between his two wheels. Each time he tried to imagined the leap across, he could see that the bulk of the Blackjack would keep him from closing the distance enough to give a jump even the slimmest chance of success.

He brought his mount over and craned his neck over, trying to get a glimpse along the side of the wagon. Two enormous wheels churned away, but between them he could just make out an access ladder leading up to an armored side door. With one more glance up at the firing animations and over at the wide rear ladder, Jesse shrugged and crouched down again, urging the Blackjack into one last burst of speed.

The two gargantuan wheels ground along beside him as he inched up on the wagon, dust and smoke and strings of dry, crushed desert grass swirling all around him. Between his own front tires and the wide wheels of the wagon, he could not get as close as he would have liked to the access ladder. However, he thought he could make a jump with a little luck. His eyes moved from the ladder to the heavy rear wheel that would crush the life from him, leaving his flattened and torn body crushed into the desert for the buzzards. He was due for a little luck.

Jesse swallowed and looked up for the annoying animations that had been clumsily from above. They seemed to have lost him for the moment. Silently, he promised them their time would come. He crouched low in the saddle, making ready for the leap.

Jesse's legs uncoiled beneath him as he launched himself into the gritty air. The enormous wheels roared up on either side as he sailed between them, hitting the armored flank of the wagon with more force than he had intended. He scrambled desperately, his metal arms clanging loudly on the armored wall. He clawed for the rungs of the access ladder as he stared at the blurring pattern of metal treads spinning past less than a foot away. He felt the feedback pads press against a textured iron crossbar and gripped with all the strength of his unnatural arms. He swung back and forth for an alarming moment until he could bring his legs up out of the torrent of dust and onto the ladder beneath him.

The Blackjack, direction, began to drift away to the left. As he climbed, it fell farther and farther behind. It hit a rocky lip that abruptly ended its journey, however, sending it flipping high into the air, trailed by a plume of dust and sand. It tumbled across the desert behind him, exploding as the jury-rigged power cells finally ruptured, scattering the remains in a wide, burning circle in the sand.

Jesse climbed up the ladder to the access door, hugging the metal for what little cover he could find from the animations still searching for him from above. He was hardly surprised when the hatch was locked, but a quick glance showed him that there were plenty of handholds above leading up to the firing platform on the roof. He began to make his way past the hatch, eyes fixed on the parapet, waiting for the animations above to realize his location.

Just as the outlaw boss came up to the low wall, the dull, empty face of an animation rose before him. The thing brought up its blaster arm with a clumsy jerk. Jesse held onto a bolted cargo ring and reached up, grabbing hold of the rifle with one mechanical hand. His metal fingers closed over the barrel and pulled with all his strength. A human would have released the rifle and lived to fight on. The animation, however, did not have that option. It followed the weapon up and over the edge, tumbling down into the swirling sand of the wagon's wake.

Jesse surged up onto the roof before the other animation could take its partner's place. He snaked a leg over the railing and swung onto the platform, not allowing himself to hesitate as he saw that there were two rotting corpse-shapes awaiting him instead of one. He brought one heel up and planted it on the closer animation's chest, pushing with a quick thrust that sent the unsteady creature up and over the far side of the parapet. It disappeared down between the two growling wheels on that side.

Before his foot even came down on the metal grating, his hands flashed down to his holsters. His metal fists came up with both pistols, clapping them together for their conjoined heat blast. He was angry, he was tired and sore, and he had had enough of these stinking abominations. He flicked the switches with his thumbs, pulled the triggers, and grinned wildly as the animation was blasted into splinters and shreds that flew off into the wind, nothing left larger than a whiskey bottle.

Jesse holstered one pistol and stripped off his begrimed goggles. He reached down for the locking wheel in the middle of the hatch at the center of the firing platform. Beneath him the wagon churned along, and the outlaw felt a moment's flush of triumph as he realized he was only steps away from confronting Carpathian. Soon, he would seize the ancient artifact that would unlock his future.

Before Jesse could pull open the hatch, it came open on its own, pushed by the bulging muscles of a misshapen animation much larger than the others he had already taken care of. With a disgusted grunt, Jesse dropped his pistol and clapped his hands to either side of the malformed head. Within their armored casings his arms' mechanisms whirred, driving his hands together, crushing the slack-jawed visage. There was a moment's hesitation as the reinforced skull resisted, and then with a wet crunching sound the face deformed and his hands met in the middle of the thing's gelid brain. A quick snap and spark marked the shorting of the RJ-1027 battery cylinder. The light faded from the thing's empty eyes.

Jesse screamed in annoyance. He grasped the loose body by the shoulders and pulled it up through the hatch, heaving it off the roof. His hands were covered in gore, further fueling his rage as he recovered his pistol.

"Hey, Doc!" Jesse grinned as he spat out the title he knew Carpathian hated. "Don't get your back up, but I think you're out'a hired hands!" He jumped down into the darkened interior of the wagon.

Jesse bent his legs to take his weight as he plummeted to the iron deck of the compartment beneath. There was a loud, surprised shout as someone fell away, but a dry hiss clearly announced the presence of another animation. Jesse brought the pistol up and fired into the corpse's face, splashing the entire head against the bulkhead beyond. The body slumped back onto the floor and Jesse brought the pistol around towards the muffled shout.

The muzzle of the hyper-velocity pistol came to rest pointing at its creator as he lay on his back on the iron floor, legs bunched up before him. Before Jesse could say anything, however, Carpathian's augmented legs came pistonning up, catching the outlaw in the arm and chest. The pistol went spinning away and Jesse was driven against the forward wall. His arms flailed wildly to keep his balance as he stumbled over the headless corpse.

Jesse brought his fists up before him, nose wrinkling once again at the familiar smell. He pushed off the wall with his elbows. Carpathian had risen and had assumed a fighting stance of his own, fists floating back and forth before him in a practiced formal boxer's form. Jesse was annoyed to see the old man was smiling.

"I'll never be out of hired hands, Mr. James. Something you might want to consider as you move forward in this brave new phase of independence you've embarked upon." One fist lashed out and wove past Jesse's defenses to strike the outlaw in the jaw. His head snapped back and then came down quickly as he moved around trying to put some space between his adversary and himself.

"As you can see, Mr. James, I may not be the helpless old man you expected when you dropped in unannounced." He moved forward, sending a rapid series of jabs flashing out to test Jesse's reactions. "Another rudeness I intend to take up with you, I might add." Another jab snapped out, followed quickly by a flashing hook that caught Jesse's mechanical arm on the elbow, knocking it aside. Feedback buzzed in Jesse's mind as internal damage was reported.

The outlaw came around again, still trying to keep his distance. His own jabs were repeatedly beaten aside with a negligence that would have been frightening if it was not for Carpathian's goading smile. Jesse reminded himself that Carpathian's arms and legs were at least as advanced as his own augmented arms. Probably more so, given it was the doctor who had invented the technology.

Jesse watched his opponent's fists warily, their speed and strength distracting him from the basic rules of fighting. And so, when the doctor shifted back and brought his foot up again, mechanisms whining and hissing, Jesse was out of position to block or avoid the kick. The heavy boot caught him in the side and battered him against the wall where he staggered, his hands tangling up with equipment hanging there, a knee fetching up painfully against a metal bench.

"I do apologize for the confining space, of course." Carpathian remarked calmly as he lashed out with two jabs and a cross that sent Jesse reeling back onto the bench as he tried to rise. "But then, mendicants must not be discriminating, as they say." His weighted foot came crashing cruelly down onto Jesse's instep.

Blood was dribbling from Jesse's mouth as he looked up at the doctor standing over him, a youthful smile out of place amidst the wrinkles and white whiskers. Jesse knew, with an infuriating twist in his gut, that Carpathian was letting him catch his breath before going at him again. It was that condescension, more than the pain or the fear or the frustration, which drove Jesse back to his feet. He roared at the doctor as his arms lashed in one after the other, landing body blow after body blow as the doctor tried to bring his elbows down to defend himself.

Jesse was beyond words, and so merely grunted as he lashed out, his arms moving with cold strength and mechanical precision. Carpathian staggered back into the equipment on the other side of the compartment, his arms pulled close as he tried to protect himself from the enraged attacks. Finally, Carpathian managed to get a foot up, planted on Jesse's thigh, and pushed him back for just a moment. In that temporary reprieve, the doctor reached down for a small dark box that was lying abandoned on the floor.

A fist lashed out and caught the doctor on the chin, sending him back against the wall. If Carpathian wanted the box, Jesse did not want him to have it. He brought a metal elbow down on the back of the old man's head and stepped aside to avoid the falling body. The mechanical hands reached down and pulled both hyper-velocity pistols from their holsters. As he lifted them up to brandish in the doctor's face, however, his eyes went round to realize that Carpathian was smiling gleefully, one hand wrapped around the little box.

"Drop the box, Doc, and I might leave you with your head." Jesse flicked the switches on his pistols with his thumbs and the power chambers burst into crimson life, glowing with a bloody illumination as a lacework of energy arced between them.

"Oh, Mr. James, I do find you so amusing. I hope we can continue to do business together in the future." And Carpathian's thumb came down on a small button in the middle of the box.

Jesse was about to open his arms and bring the pistol butts down on either side of Carpathian's head. Instead, his arms gave a sharp, painful jerk. A sudden snap of agony scorched down the feedback pathways to his brain. He gasped despite himself. A brutal, excruciating weight began to pull his shoulders down and he realized he could no longer feel anything from the feedback pads. The arms dropped like iron weights and he staggered back. His eyes rose in horror to Carpathian's vicious grin.

"Oh, Mr. James. As I said, you amuse me so." He slowly and methodically placed one boot on Jesse's chest and pushed him backward onto the bench. "Have a seat, do?"

Jesse tried to rise but could do nothing against the weight of the old man's boot. Tears of frustrated rage streaked his dirty cheeks.

"I can only assume you are coming after that little artifact your youthful compatriot stumbled upon in the wastelands?" The doctor shook his head. "Amusing as it might be to allow you primitives to run around the world for a time with such power, it does not, unfortunately, coincide with my long term plans. I would let you see it, however, I would hate for you to have gone through such exertions for nothing." He pursed his lips in a sad, disappointed frown. "Except I have already had my minions secure it for travel." He nodded to a niche in one armored wall where a wooden strongbox was secured to the bulkhead.

Jesse shook his head, barely able to form words around the storm of anger and frustration raging in his mind. "My friends—"

Carpathian threw back his head with a genuine laugh. "Your friends, Mr. James! Was it not trust in your friends that led you here? Was it not you friend William Bonney that left you for dead on that battlefield in the north, lying amongst your vilest enemies? Was it not your friends the Youngers that abandoned you in the very midst of that self-same battle? You have singularly bad luck with friends, Mr. James. But then, what might one expect, when one entrusts themselves to the honor of outlaws?" He leaned in close to Jesse, a look of pity in his eyes. "Among you who disparage the very concept of honor, what honor can there truly be?"

"You – won't – I will come for you." Jesse's voice sounded plaintive, even to himself, but his pride demanded he speak in the face of those words.

"Oh, please, Mr. James. Don't you realize yet that we're all puppets, dancing to a tune we can't even begin to understand? Well. . . at least, that is what our fiery-eyed friends would like to think." He pulled a small pistol from his belt and casually pointed it at Jesse as he sat back against the far wall. "But only one man can ever be the smartest man in the room, is that not right, Mr. James?" He gestured with the pistol, smiling at Jesse's impotent rage. "And what, please tell me, are the chances that that man is you?"

Carpathian reached back and rapped twice against the forward bulkhead. Jesse could feel the rumbling movement of the wagon slow down and then subside as they came to a stop.

"Unfortunately, Mr. James, I have pressing business elsewhere, and I will have to now cut our pleasant discourse short." Carpathian stood and stepped aside as a large hatch swung open. Jesse could not keep his eyes from widening at the appearance of the animation that came crouching into the chamber. The thing was enormous, dead muscles bulging, rough stitching marking where large pieces had been added, bulking the creature up even further. Its face was nearly blank, as most animations, but a strange, hungry light illuminated its foggy eyes. A slight snarl twisted its slack features.

"Please see our guest out the back door, could you?" Carpathian gestured with his pistol towards the hatch in the rear bulkhead.

The animation lumbered ahead, crouching in the confines of the compartment, and grabbed Jesse by the shoulders.

"Carpathian, you best kill me if you don't mean for me to come back and end you!" Jesse's voice was shrill as he felt himself lifted off the seat and dragged backward. "If you leave me alive, I swear, you'll never survive my return!"

"Mr. James, I fully expect you to return." The doctor looked kindly as he peered around the shoulder of the giant animated corpse. "And I trust that your time in the desert will provide ample opportunity to reflect upon your place in the world, and your attitude towards your betters."

With a final nod from Carpathian, the monsters unlatched the rear hatch, swung it wide, and heaved the outlaw into the heat of the open desert.

Jesse grunted with the impact as he landed on his back in the burning sand, rocks digging through his jacket.

"Oh, have some water, my boy, in case you ventured out here unprepared!" Something struck the sand by Jesse's head and the metallic slosh of water in a canteen was audible over the growl of the great wagon.

"I trust we will meet again, Mr. James, in the not so distant future." Carpathian was resting an arm against the combing of the hatch as if chatting with a neighbor through a kitchen window. He waved the little black box in a gesture of farewell. "Good luck with the vultures!"

The old man's cruel laughter echoed from within the chamber as the hatch clanged shut. The wagon rumbled into motion once again. It began to crawl away, picking up speed with each passing moment.

Jesse rolled onto his stomach and struggled to rise to his knees. All coherent thought had fled from the rage rising within the hollow of his chest. A mad hatred surged through his burning throat and flared behind his burning eyes. Words failed him as he screamed formless curses at the retreating wagon, tilting his head farther and farther back until he was howling his fury up into the empty sky.

*****

Jesse would never be able to say how much time had passed as he lay on his back in the desert. His mind wandered along sharp and jagged paths of isolation and despair as his body succumbed to exhaustion, dehydration, and the loss of hope. Slumped into the dust and sand of the deep desert, Jesse James lapsed into unconsciousness, his pain the last tangible connection to the world around him as everything faded from a flashing bright heat into blackness.

Jesse's eyes fluttered open at the sound of a raucous barking sound not far away. He could see nothing.

He knew he must have fallen off his horse. The wound must have opened while he was riding. God alone knew how much blood he must have lost, slumped in his saddle, before losing his seat. He could not hear the horse nearby, and his sightless eyes rolled at the realization that he had to add a lost mount to his list of current difficulties.

Images rose up out of the darkness to swim before his twitching eyes, then went sinking once more from sight. He could make no sense of them. He saw his brother Frank, but as an old man, face wrinkled and eyes cold. He saw a woman he did not recognize in a dancehall costume, honey-brown hair flaring out around a sweet face as she flashed through the moves of a kick line dance, green eyes smiling at him the whole time. He saw a mysterious beauty, another woman, dark eyes flashing in a smile that threatened to stop his heart. He could feel, as if far away, a smile tugging at the flesh of his face.

Jesse tried to push himself upright in the darkness, but his body refused to respond. A dull, throbbing ache pulsated through his being. It was a pain that was not isolated to one part of his body, but rather radiated out through ever limb and nerve. His breath shortened, coming in shallow gasps, but everything still seemed terribly distant and vague. He felt himself easing back against the cool ground.

Another image rose before him, an old man, strange ironmongery attached to his face in some sort of nightmare combination of man and machine. He had long white cheek whiskers and one eye was covered in a block of metal, a wide red lens flashing in the socket. Jesse's distant body tingled with cold sweat, but he could not have said why. He did not remember the strange old man.

The hoarse call sounded again, a hissing noise moving closer, but still Jesse's mind refused to focus upon it. He was lost in the swirl of images that raced around him. Cole Younger's face rose up, and a dull, brooding anger and vague sense of betrayal accompanied the image. Younger, too, seemed to have aged more than he should have, and an unpleasant pressure began to build within Jesse's mind.

With the anger, the images began to flash faster. A strangers face swam up before him, distorted as if staring blankly at him from shallow water. The face blurred and was gone. He saw Frank, fear widening his eyes; the pretty dancehall girl, tears and blood mingling on her pale cheeks; the old man, laughing a silent laugh; a strange young man whose eyes flashed with an unnatural crimson glow. As this last face disappeared, disintegrating into the darkness with a cruel, savage smile, Jesse felt his eyes snap open again, but still only blackness met his gaze.

A face emerged then from the darkness that he did not know, although he felt he should. Another young man, about his own age, with a mischievous gleam in his laughing eyes. Despite his confusion, Jesse felt another surge of anger bubble up within him. His tortured mind refused to sit idly for further blows, and he heaved up, reaching for the unseen sky . . . with arms that did not move.

Jesse collapsed back to the gritty earth with a hoarse groan of pain that was answered by an indignant hissing grunt. What was wrong with him? Had he hurt himself further when he fell off the horse? He had a sudden image of a line of Union cavalrymen watching him fall. The blue-belly bastards! Had they done something to him? Tied him up, or worse, shot him again?

The young man's head jerked from side to side, fearing now that he had been blindfolded and hogtied by the hated traitors that had stood between him and his home. The parade of faces behind his eyes was forgotten as he wrenched at his body, trying to free himself from bonds he could not feel.

Finally, Jesse stopped struggling, his breath continuing to shake his body with its short, convulsive heaves. The angry hissing grunt sounded farther away, but his mind was completely submerged in a surge of fear and confusion that threatened to drown his distant body.

With a desperate heave, Jesse sat up, his arms awkward, useless weight. The first vague hint of movement came into focus nearby, and soon a sky full of stars swam into clarity above him. It was night, the cool of the nocturnal desert caressing his heated flesh. An outraged flutter nearby caught his attention and he whipped his head around to find an enormous black vulture sidling closer. It's head bobbed as it stalked towards him, staring at him from the corner of its vicious little eye.

With a cry, Jesse tried to scuttle away, only to fall abruptly onto his side as his arms refused to move. He hit the cold sand hard, squinting against the abrasive spray. He opened his eyes wide to stare at the inert hand lying before him, as unfeeling as if it belonged to another man. It was strange, that hand so close to his face. It was as if he could see through the flesh to the bones beneath, except there was no flesh, only the hard lines of dull iron, and the bones beneath seemed to be made of the same material. Where veins, tendons, and muscles should have been were strange dark tubes, wires, small, sleek barrels holding gleaming silver rods that slid in and out, and countless tiny wheels whose teeth fit together, spinning each other in a tiny, coordinated dance as the hand rocked slightly from his fall.

A cold spike of certainty and despair plunged into Jesse's mind. The wounded boy on that far away road in the distant past was instantly replaced by the seasoned, lawless rebel whose name had risen to dark prominence throughout the Wild West. In that moment, the memory of his traitorous arms came slashing back as well. His face twisted into a snarl of maddened rage as his sanity tottered once more on the brink.

Jesse grunted and growled like an animal as he tried to rise. His throat was raw, a pink foam flecking his lips as the memory of Carpathian's laughter squeezed the breath from his lungs.

Jesse struggled back to his knees, warning the vulture away with a savage bark. He stared down at his motionless arms. He laughed with a bitter, twisted croaking. He was the big bug of the Wild West; the curly wolf every man envied and ever woman wanted. And he was reduced to a helpless, disfigured, pathetic wretch left to die alone in the middle of the desert wastes.

A long line of victims and dead companions rose up around him. Mute, haunted eyes stared down accusingly, mocking his helplessness with their cold, lifeless glares. He could not meet their illusory faces and bowed his head in defeat. When he looked up, the images were gone. He was truly alone, with the single, strange bird crouching nearby. All the visions and apparitions vanished in the cool desert night.

He remembered his confidence and ability with an empty, desolate chuckle. Everything he had done, everything he had accomplished, all the lives he had touched for good and for ill, and it all came to this, a lonely death in the middle of nowhere. The end of a line of betrayals any mooncalf idjit should have seen coming a mile away. He tried to think of the last time he had made a move on his own instead of reacting to others. Of working on his own initiative instead of racing to beat Billy to the next big caper, or taking Carpathian's advice on a job or score, or rushing off to prove himself to Frank, or Cole, or anyone else.

Jesse shook his lowered head. Carpathian was a foreign rat and a chiseler, but he had gotten one thing right: Jesse had spent too long dancing to someone else's tune. Without his arms, there was nothing he could do about it. He would die out here, and everyone in the wider world would know he had been a fraud all along. Worst of all, he was helpless to change that now.

He sat in the cold darkness, the wary vulture waddling back and forth nearby. Jesse was at first unaware of the twitching that sent the bird flapping back with a quick squawk. He looked dully puzzled down at the trailing fingers of his foreign hands only to see the metal digits twitch spasmodically. Each finger flexed much faster than a flesh and bone finger could have ever moved. Then the digits closed into two iron-hard fists.

When a violent pulse of pain ran up the metal arms and into his shoulders he gasped again, falling backwards. He reached back out of a lifetime of reflex. To his surprise, the arms flashed back to catch him. A torment of rippling sensations roared up and down the limbs, but they responded when he pushed himself back onto his knees, and then steadied himself. Slowly he rose to his feet. The prickling feeling quickly faded, leaving Jesse standing tall on the sands, his arms crooked slightly at his sides, hands hovering over his gunbelt. He turned his head slightly to glare at the vulture who had retreated further away as he stood.

"Looks like it's not my day to die, croaker." He gave the bird a twisted, bitter grin that faded quickly as it laughed a very human laugh, its eyes flashing with a crimson gleam. The ugly bird heaved itself heavily upward, wide wings pounding at the cold air. It sailed over his head and off into the dark sky, trailing the eerie laugh into the distance.

Jesse watched the bird fade into the darkness. A nearly overwhelming urge to draw and blast the filthy creature out of the sky set him to shaking, but somehow he knew it would not have done any good. He was half-sure it only existed in his mind.

Jesse looked back north to where clusters of wreckage still smoldered in the dry scrub grass, scattered over a mile behind him in the wake of Carpathian's giant wagon. Back that way he would find Billy's camp, he knew. Thinking of the camp reminded him that the doctor had heaved a canteen out into the sand with him, and a quick search nearby turned it up. Jesse dove for it and had to use all of his power of will not to guzzle the cool liquid, letting it wash down his chest. He took a quick sip, sloshed around his dry and scratchy mouth, and the spit it out to the side. Next he took a small sip and eased it down his tortured throat, wincing slightly as the water slid over the damaged flesh. He shook his head at the sweet pain and then tossed a little more back. Shaking the container, he knew he would just have enough to make it back to Billy's encampment.

The massive wagon's grinding wheels had left wide tracks across the desert and Jesse knew he could follow those as well. He looked down at one hand and tightened it into a metal fist. He could not face Carpathian now, knowing the old man could rob him of his arms at a whim. He looked back up at the stars overhead and sneered. Somewhere, he would find a way to deny Carpathian that ability. When that day came, he would come back for the old man and there would be a reckoning. No one would be playing a tune for Jesse James again.

But for now, he was still alone. Jesse's face sagged into a hopeless mask once more. Frank was gone. Without Carpathian's artifact, how could he persuade the Rebellion to stir itself from the swampy camps that had protected them for over a decade?

Jesse sank back to the sand, the canteen grasped in his mechanical arms, and stared down at his treasonous metal hands. The emptiness within rose up to devour him. It was more than Frank's absence, more than Billy's betrayal, beyond even whatever had happened with Misty. He was alone. Even the furious anger that had ridden beside him since he was a small boy had betrayed him. That rage, fixated upon the tyrannous north, had eaten away at his spirit and left a gaping hole behind. A hole that mocked the losses he had suffered since.

Lucy was right. Without a purpose, his life was a pointless dance of violence and petty revenge, not enough to justify an existence that threatened to go on forever.

He looked back at the wagon's trail, stretching down out of the north and into the distant south. The emptiness within called to him, and he rose once again to his feet, grinning as he decided at last to embrace it. He would carve his name across the flesh of the western territories in his quest for vengeance. He would exact the blood price from every opponent that had wronged him.

His mechanical hands flexed angrily, metal components sliding smoothly against each other, leather feedback pads creaking with the pressure.

He grabbed the straps of the canteen that had dropped at his feet. With a single look to the south he turned around and began the long trek down his back trail. Somewhere over the rolling, dusty hills ahead, William Bonney and his hired hands were waiting. His face twisted into a death's head grin at the thought.

About the Author

Craig Gallant spends his hours teaching, gaming, podasting, being a family man and father. In his spare time he writes outlandish fiction to entertain and amaze people .

In addition to his position as co-host of the internationally not too shabby podcast – The D6 Generation, he has written for several gaming companies including Fantasy Flight, Spartan Games and of course Outlaw Minatures.

You can follow Craig's writing experience and other fun things at:

www.Mcnerdiganspub.com

Zmok Books - Action, Adventure and Imagination

Zmok Books offers science fiction and fantasy books in the classic tradition as well as the new and different takes on the genre.

Winged Hussar Publishing, LLC is the parent company of Zmok Publishing, focused on military history from ancient times to the modern day.

Follow all the latest news on Winged Hussar and Zmok Books at

www.wingedhussarpublishing.com

Look for the other books in this series

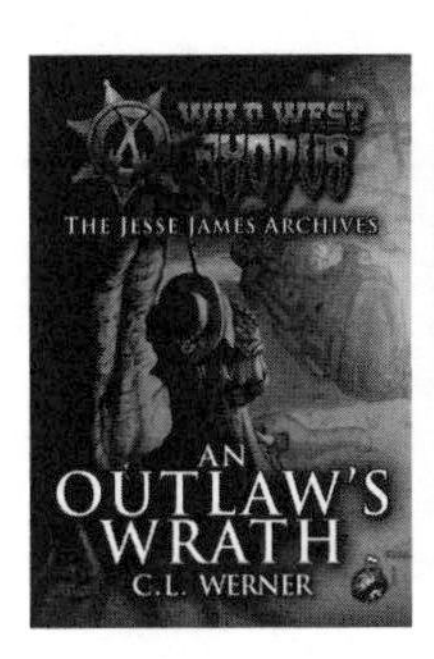

Nov 13

Dec 13